JERUSALEM

The City of God

Ellen Gunderson Traylor

ELM HILL BOOKS
A Division of Thomas Nelson Publishers
Since 1798

www.thomasnelson.com

To my husband
—Richard Schultz—
who has the heart
of an archaeologist

CONTENTS

Part

I.	*The Days of Melchizedek*	13
II.	*Adonizedek*	55
III.	*Abdi-Khipa*	91
IV.	*The Son of Jesse*	123
V.	*The City of David*	193
VI.	*David and the Ark*	243
VII.	*David and Bathsheba*	260

Introduction

Jerusalem—The City of God was originally published in 1996, in honor of the 3000th anniversary of Jerusalem. Although the Holy City is much older than 3000 years, its earliest remnants dating to about 8,000 years before the time of Jesus, the Jewish people have traditionally considered King David's capture of the city as the beginning of its designation as their cultural, political and historical capital.

1996 was a year of celebration throughout Jewish Israel, in remembrance of this feat. But the anniversary events had a mixed reception among world leaders. When invited to participate in the opening ceremony, many declined, including the U.S. ambassador at the time, avoiding the "politically sensitive" support of Israel's claim to the city.

Confusion and ambivalence regarding claims to Jerusalem are nothing new. Bitterness, jealousy, revenge and hatred have forever been manifested in tumultuous and bloody rivalry over this tiny tract of land at the "center of the earth."

Throughout her long history, quiet times in Jerusalem have been but brief respites between periods of dominance on the world stage. Like mountain peaks on an otherwise flat landscape, Jerusalem's times of glory or stress intrude her into the world consciousness. Moribund for centuries, she may arise at any time to control the moods and movements of nations around her.

Much has happened regarding the coveted city, in the few years since 1996. The cauldron of Middle Eastern politics steams and boils with ever-increasing heat, and the prophecy of Zechariah is being fulfilled as Jerusalem becomes a "cup of trembling" to all nations round about her. (Zechariah 12:2, 3, 6).

Many believe that the contest for Jerusalem is the ultimate symptom of the ancient rivalry between the sons of Abraham: the Jews and the Arabs. Even the holocaust of 9/11, they say…even the destruction of the World Trade Center in New York City, has its roots in this animosity.

No matter our views on these issues, no one can deny that Jerusalem is increasingly the focus of international concern. And only a fool would predict that she will fade in importance. Jerusalem's welfare is more critical today than it ever has been. She will continue to captivate us, and, I believe, all lives will one day depend on what becomes of her.

But, we ask, "Why Jerusalem?" What is it about this stony, desert place that people cross oceans for a glimpse of her? Why do kings go to war for her, and why do people die to possess her?

Jerusalem—The City of God is my attempt to tell her story. She is the central character of this book, though countless people, great and small, have written their own stories on her soil.

Jerusalem—The City of God is also my attempt to answer "Why Jerusalem?" It is my hope that, once you have read this book, you will have more appreciation for this timeless, holy place. And it is my prayer that, once you have seen how much depends on her, you will fulfill King David's commandment to "Pray for the Peace of Jerusalem." (Psalm 122:6)

Shalom!

Ellen Gunderson Traylor

Pray for the peace of Jerusalem:
They shall prosper that love thee.

—Psalm 122:6 KJV

Prologue

The Center of the Earth
12,000-10,000 B. C. E.

There were still times of shaking in the yellow earth. But the times were fewer and further apart than they had been before the sun rose and set through five generations.

The ground was harder now than it had been when the great waters were receding. The ooze and the magma that once had bubbled and frothed with the sucking mud were now solid, and the dreadful heavings and crushings that had reared ridges and hewn gorges across the flood-plains had created stone strata from the cooling soup, compressing it and squeezing all moisture from it. The moisture, in turn, had risen in vaporous clouds across the land or rushed into crevices, where it formed brooks and subterranean streams. And the clouds broke and watered the earth until the mountains were full of rivulets joined together until they formed one tumbling ribbon.

In those days, there were no human eyes to behold these develop-ments. There were people on earth, but they inhabited a land far distant from this one, and they survived the settling of the planet in their own part of the world.

All the earth had just endured the greatest cataclysm in history, the breaking up of the sky canopy that once sheltered the globe and the erup-tion of the underground waters upon which the earth's single continent once floated. This enormous upheaval, unparalleled before or since, would become known as The Great Deluge. But, just now, there were only a few people who had lived through it, and their concept of it would never take in the enormity, though they spoke of it in the grandest terms they knew.

As for the land of the yellow earth and the shining water ribbon, there were much more magnificent landscapes. In the part of the world where people had survived, there were much higher mountains and vaster plains. And the mighty river that split their valley was far wider and joined yet another, even longer and more splendid stream.

Still, there were no human beings to witness the formation of this parcel, the wind that passed over it at early morning and late evening resembled breathing. The creatures who migrated here over the years, the rock burrowers and the wolves, the bears and the hyenas, sensed the wind soul. In the morning, they did not emerge from their holes until the breeze tapered, and at night they disappeared before the breath commenced.

Perhaps they sensed also, as they peeked out from their caves and burrows, that the land itself was alive, yawning and stretching under the cloud-kissed sky. There was still movement in the earth, but it was more than movement they sensed. It was something like a heartbeat deep beneath the ground that raised their hair on end and kept them quiet when otherwise they would have been active.

This they could not put into words. But it governed them, calling them across hundreds of miles to take up homes in this place, in caves and hollows in the huge, virgin forest burgeoning across the hills. The caves were wonderful, so numerous that a world of animals found shelter in them. Trees flourished: oak, cypress, myrtle and pine. Shrubs covered the ground, and every few feet a spring or waterhole shone in the sun. A veritable garden hid the rubble of white and yellow rock which the flood had left just below the ground's surface, a garden that spread miles from the river to west and south.

Though the creatures had no words for their feelings, they were often drawn to the edges of their burrows, their caves, and their forests when the sun was setting. For the great light of heaven touched the hills and the forests with a radiant halo as it dipped beyond the horizon each evening.

One high point of land, situated along the ridge that ran straight up and down the length of the country, was a special strangeness. Upon this point was a large, flat rock, wide and long enough for a dozen wild horses to climb atop. Each year, at the summer solstice, this rock, unlike any other on earth, was shadowless. The sun kept it company all day and the moon all night, so that no darkness approached it. Thus the animals sensed a sacredness about the place, which no human being need ordain.

In time, of course, humans did discover the place, and when they did it impressed them profoundly. It was always difficult for those coming upon the area to explain just what it was about it that moved them. The fact that the great rock seemed to have some special celestial reference was not immediately apparent. But as humans began to drift into the region, they were compelled to call this place holy, and in time to designate it "the center of the earth."

PART I

THE DAYS OF MELCHIZEDEK

8000-1900 B.C.E.

1

The first wanderers to enter the land passed through it but did not occupy it. Coming from the distant east, they were looking for the sea. While they may have lingered over the beauty of the place, they followed its garden-strewn decline toward the coast and in time founded the cities of Tyre and Sidon and the country of Phoenicia.

But the allure of the yellow land and the rock topped mountain was not forgotten, and word of the place was sent eastward until kin of the sea peoples who had remained in the old country followed the call toward the coast and entered the garden vale. As they had been told, they found forest-crowned, cave riddled hills above a chalky wilderness east of the watershed. Twenty-five hundred feet above the land's tumbling river, primitive trails had already been carved into the limestone hills, first by the feet of animals following the scent of streams and ponds, and then by the wayfarers who had sidetracked from the coastward route.

It was the son of the Phoenician patriarch who first claimed the land as his own. Melchizedek was his name, and his father was Sidon, founder of the coast city. Melchizedek's grandfather was the humble and holy Canaan, and Canaan's grandfather was Noah, the famed survivor of The Great Deluge.

How Melchizedek came to "the center of the earth" was an epic in itself, a tale he held close to his heart but which dwindled from the racial memory after the first few generations of his followers had died away. As for Melchizedek himself, he so far outlived the contemporaries who had come with him to this land that a legend grew up about him to the effect that he had no father and no mother, but had sprung from the earth itself.

However, it was a very human Melchizedek who, as a young man, caught his first glimpse of the holy land from atop the primitive highway of the central ridge.

Wearied by years of war in the distant land of his birth, the land of Ararat, he yearned for peace, and for a place to establish a world apart. He was a shepherd at heart, but when he was quite young the mantle of leadership had fallen upon him unbidden. His very name, bestowed upon him by great-great-grandfather Noah, was an unwelcome burden. "Melchi-zedek—King of Righteousness," he had announced. And when his cousin, Nimrod, King of the South, rose up against him, years of bloodshed ensued between the cities of the northern Ararat plain, where the Ark of Noah rested, and the lusting southern confederacy. Torn by strife, the mountain of the Ark found some relief when Nimrod departed further south to found the kingdom of Shinar, one day to be called Sumer or Sumeria. But it was a sad day for Noah's people when their young king proclaimed that he, also, was being called to found a new nation in the fabled yellow land that neighbored Sidon.

Out from Ararat he went, several kin behind him, descendants of Noah's three sons: Shem, Ham and Japheth. The children of Ham were children of Canaan, from whom Melchizedek came forth. Across nearly 800 miles of uncharted land they traveled, guided only by stories they had heard of landmarks along the way, stories brought back by previous travelers to the west. The first 500 miles were treacherous, taking them through the mountainous terrain of what is today eastern Turkey and leading them down into the future Syria. But so great was the people's faith in the young king, that there was no rebellion.

It was a unique people that came with Melchizedek out from Ararat. Only those who believed in his vision and were committed to it left the now-peaceful slopes and plain of the fathering mountain. The time of war had passed; blood had cooled in the ground at the foot of the Ark, Why leave now for unknown places, unless in the conviction that some great destiny called?

So, when the company passed at last within sight of the great mountain bordering Syria, one day to be called Mt. Hermon, and when they stood with their king atop the heights east of Sidon, in the land one day to be called Lebanon, it was with awe that they cast their gazes south upon the vast, cave-riddled garden and its silver river. Venturing along the pre-

cipitous border of a large lake, one day to be called Galilee, they followed
the limestone ridge of the rainfall belt until the river was far below them.
Then, after passing through miles of forbidding, canyon-riven desert, they
at last spied the green plateau over which the sacred rock kept watch.

They did not immediately venture onto the site, but surveyed it for a
while from a sloping hill just to the east. Resting in the shade of the hill's
countless wild olive trees, the women took their ease while the children
scrambled about, plucking ripe, fallen olives from the ground. Calling his
men apart, the king led them down the rise.

Melchizedek, his dark hair and beard and his simple royal robes blowing back in the wind, stretched his arm westward across the gorge that
separated the olive mount from the plateau. "See," he said, "how easily
defended this place would be! The high flatland is bounded by the deep
valleys on three sides!"

Having just survived years of warfare in Ararat, the natural defenses of a
potential site were uppermost in the king's mind. As he observed, the plateau
was bounded not only by an eastern gorge at the foot of the olive mount, but
by another that wrapped around the western and southern edges.

"Only the north would need securing," he noted, "but it appears there
is a narrower valley cutting through the middle of the rise where we could
house our troops... should the time come."

These last were spoken with a sigh, for indeed, the king hoped the
time would never come.

Instead, in his mind's eye, as he stood upon the slope he envisioned a
peaceable community, full of commerce and industry like the Noahic
hamlets of Ararat. Speaking in hope-filled tones, he enthused, "The path
that brought us through the wilderness will one day be a highway, and
people will come and go, north, south, and toward the coast, buying and
selling and trading. Even our brothers in the east will venture here, and
we will have much contact with them!"

As the men stood with their young king, gazing upon the empty,
forested hills, it was difficult to envision things as clearly as he did. But

they believed in him, and nodded agreement, huddling together, starry-eyed pilgrims.

One of them, a lad named Tala, who was no longer young enough to be called a boy but barely old enough to fraternize, leaned out from the company, cocking one ear down the slope. "Sir!" he exclaimed, addressing the king. "Listen! Is that water I hear?"

From the southeast edge of the plateau a fingerlike spur of land projected. As the men stood breathless upon the slope, it did seem they could hear water bubbling somewhere in that vicinity. It was a good distance to the site, but the lay of the land with its narrow valleys, and the quiet emptiness of the plateau funneled the sound toward them like a megaphone.

"Come!" Melchizedek commanded, beckoning his men to run with him down the hill. Like a herd of thirsty deer they followed, chasing the king as he laughed and leapt ahead of them. Seeking the source of the water music, they found that it grew louder as they came closer to the spur of the ridge. By the time they spied a low cave in the ground, the sound was that of thunder. Skidding to a halt, they peered into the cave's dark mouth, their eyes wide with wonder.

"A fountain!" Tala shouted. "A gushing fountain!"

Melchizedek, who stood closest to the cave's edge, turned about and walked into the sunshine, lifting his eyes heavenward. It was customary to name such places, and his men sensed that he was about to do just that. When he raised his hand and called for silence, however, they did not anticipate the glorious name that he would bestow.

"Gihon!" he cried, his face radiant. "This fount shall be called Gihon, after the river that flowed through the Garden of Eden!"

Awestruck, the men considered the implication. In this one pronouncement they caught more of their master's intentions for this new land than they had ever understood before.

But the king was not finished. The spring was only a part of the land's promise. Upon the hills about, he foresaw a gleaming city.

"Salem!" he cried again. "'Peace' shall be the name of our stronghold.

For here, men shall come to learn brotherhood, and they shall lay down the tools of war!"

Riveted by the king's proclamation, Tala dared to draw near. "Salem…that is a beautiful name, Master," he concurred. "And what of the land beyond? Will there be many cities and many people?"

Scanning the region, Melchizedek surveyed the hills that ranged the three narrow valleys and considered the river, the desert, and the fields through which they had traveled. "There shall be a nation spreading far and wide," he declared, "a land fit for righteous men to call home!"

"What shall the name of that land be?" Tala queried.

Nudging the lad, the other men pulled him back into their company, fearing he imposed too much.

But Melchizedek was not offended. "My grandfather Canaan was cursed because of his own father's rebellions," he recalled, referring to the legend of Ham and his shameful treatment of Noah. "But of all the men in my family, he was the most righteous. This land," he declared, "shall be a remembrance for him." And throwing his head back, he proclaimed, "Canaan shall thy name be! And the peace of Salem shall reign within thy borders!"

2

Salem began as a hastily constructed outpost of tents and lean-tos such as the immigrants had used along the arduous journey from Ararat. Like those camps, it was temporary, but this time it would not be dismantled and loaded on camels and wagons for further travel. This time when the tents were taken down and the lean-tos rolled up, they were replaced by more solid structures of mud and yellow stone, and the people did not move on, but stayed put.

Likewise, the earliest buildings were but a shadow of things to come. Small, round huts of irregular-shaped rocks, crude as sheepfolds and roofed with thatch, were the first firm protection against autumn rains and winter winds. As the community grew and as trade with outsiders flourished, these abodes were outdone by larger, more symmetrical buildings of hewn stone and broad rooms, supported along the terrain's uneven slopes retaining walls.

The people who had come out from the land of the Ark to establish this little town had never been nomads. There were wandering tribes on the earth, folk who were not content to sit upon the slopes of Ararat, and who had wanderlust in their veins. Such people would not have been happy within stone buildings, and would have seen no need for a city. Their sort preferred the open sky, beckoning plains and valleys, and the scent of goat herds around campfires.

These were not the people of Melchizedek.

Of course, this was an irony, for Melchizedek, himself, had been a shepherd boy, and still held in his heart an intense love of freedom. But his calling had led to Salem, and his ordination from birth had been that of a king. His shepherd's staff had become a scepter, a symbol of royalty, while an ever-present reminder of his roots.

Those who established Salem were farmers who tended olive groves, vineyards, and fields of grain and lentils, exchanging their produce for meat and milk supplied by nomads who ranged the valley, managing small flocks within fenced pastures to the west of town. Likewise, many of those who had followed Melchizedek had been craftsmen and merchants in Ararat. These naturally inclined to their own callings, and in time established lucrative trade among their fellow citizens and people of far-flung places.

And not so far-flung. The reputation of the land of Canaan, which loosely designated the region from the Jordan west, and from Hermon south to Jordan's end, quickly spread, and within a few decades of Salem's settlement, people were establishing villages throughout the fertile territory. There was no "nation" of Canaan; a collection of semi-nomadic tribal confederacies was the order of the day. But there were many "kings" who, like Melchizedek, considered their city-states to be sacred trusts.

It must be understood that these changes took place over a period of tens and hundreds of years. The fact that Melchizedek lived to see it all had a condensing effect on its recorded history. But it was a time of change and growth equal to any that would come after, and the king's grasp on it all lent him a revered status unlike any other man's.

When people spoke of "the days of Melchizedek," they spoke of a very long time and a great many developments, indeed.

To the king, not all of those developments were happy ones. Years before, in the land of Ararat, the people were divided as many forsook the worship of Noah's God and turned to gods of the earth and sky. The ensuing strife had culminated in the very migration that led to Salem's founding. Now, few of the people who established new villages throughout Canaan were devoted to the One God. In fact, as a center of monotheistic worship, Salem stood alone in this virgin country.

For many years, however, despite the invasion of contrary philosophies in the region round about, Melchizedek's city remained a pocket of quiet, testimony to the awe with which the king was esteemed even by foreigners. While the various little cities up and down Canaan feuded among themselves, erecting guard towers and gated walls and practicing small-scale war, Salem maintained its reputation as the "city of peace."

Jerusalem—The City of God

And while Salem still sat open to the world, an unwalled settlement atop a high hill, with no temple and no mighty places, towns like Jericho, far down the wilderness gorge, already hid behind impenetrable fortresses and cloistered their gods within mammoth halls of stone.

Eventually, however, Melchizedek was obliged to erect defenses. It was the great, flat rock atop Salem's sacred mount, the very rock which had first attracted Melchizedek and his people to this place, that forced the issue.

It all began as a simple inter-family quarrel involving a group of farmers to the west of town. Their fields having prospered, they began to compete for more and more land until a border dispute erupted. The dispute was not over tillable land, but over one ambitious patriarch's encroachment upon a mutual threshing area. He, insisting that there were other places for the harvesters to winnow the grain and that this spot was more convenient for planting, began to plow the threshing floor and sow upon the previously compacted earth.

His outraged companions decided to take the matter to the king. But when Melchizedek, ever the peacemaker, told them to return home and to locate a floor agreeable to both parties, the malcontented farmers rebelled.

Interpreting the king's response as apathy, they decided to stir sympathies of their fellow citizens and challenge the monarch in an unprecedented show of protest. If Melchizedek would not secure their traditional site, they would thresh and winnow their harvest in the most public place possible, upon the highest mount of Salem.

Their intention was not to be blasphemous. They would not profane the sacred rock, but would do their work within its shadow. Besides, though the king made annual sacrifies upon the flat rock and had named it Moriah, meaning "Teacher of Wisdom." He had never erected a temple upon it and no shrine graced the hillside. What harm would it do for the farmers to stage their protest here, and then be gone?

It was under full moonlight that they made their move. Tala, Melchizedek's servant, was the first within the royal house to notify the king of their brazen activity. Awakened by the sound of chanting and dancing, the servant poked his head out of his window and stared up the nighttime slope. What greeted his eyes raised goose-bumps upon his skin, and like an arrow he headed for the king's chamber.

"Lord God!" he stammered as he ran through the hallway, "Lord God, the sons of Nimrod are upon us!"

Precious little ceremony attended life in Salem's modest palace. Casting even this aside, Tala pounded upon Melchizedek's door and demanded that he rise. "Your Majesty!" he cried. "Let me in!"

The king, unguarded in his room, fumbled with the latch and in an instance Tala flew past him, gesturing wildly toward his curtained window.

"See!" the servant gasped, throwing back the shades and pointing up the rise. "Sacrilege! Idolatry! The sons of Nimrod are upon us!"

As Melchizedek followed Tala's frantic gesture, he was amazed at the spectacle that greeted him from the moonlit mountain. Silhouetted against the starry sky were the haloed figures of a dozen men. At first impression they appeared to be engaged in ritual dance. Their movements and droning of their chant suggested some pagan ceremony, and their shadows, elongated against the hillside by a central fire, were eerie and unnerving.

The spectacle was reminiscent of rituals that attended pagan worship on Ararat among those who had split from Noah and his people. It was only natural to assume that some remnant of Nimrod or some cult from the nearby city-states had invaded Salem. To those who followed the God of Melchizedek, all such heresies were alike.

As the king cocked his head toward the droning chant, observing the dark dancers, other members of his household collected in the hall outside his room. Soon, people were gathering in Salem's narrow streets, muttering fearfully among themselves and turning horrified faces toward the palace in hopes the king knew what to do.

But Melchizedek had earned status as a leader through cool-headedness, not rash conclusions. Focusing upon the hilltop silhouettes, he listened closely to their song. Something about it was familiar, and soon he picked up the words. It was a slow, unhappy version of a merrier chant, a song of harvesters as they sort the sheaves. Then he saw that what appeared to be a heathen dance was only the sway of winnowers as they tossed the grain above their heads, catching it in baskets and sending the chaff into the wind.

Melchizedek pushed back the shutters that flapped against his window and motioned to the crowd in the street below. "Men and women of Salem," he called. "Do not be afraid! The people you see upon the mount are your brothers and your sons! Do not impute evil to them, for they do the work of harvest and nothing more!"

At these words, most of the people were greatly relieved and would have returned quietly to their homes. But there were others who were not so easily assured.

"They profane the holy mount!" some objected. "Moriah is not a threshing floor, like the high places of the infidels!"

They referred, of course, to the immoral practices that attended harvest activities in nearby cultures, and to the fertility rites that went hand in hand with the worship of gods and goddesses of grain, rain, and sun, practices that inevitably took place upon heathen threshing floors.

Flashing a quick look up the mount, Melchizedek raised a hand to quiet the dissenters. The harvesters on the hill also quieted, seeing that a crowd had gathered and they had the king's attention. Not realizing the controversy their actions had inspired, they hoped their fellow citizens were sympathetic to their case, and they, likewise, waited for Melchizedek's response.

"Let there be no disharmony regarding the need of a threshing floor!" the king cried. "Seeing that you have reached no agreement amongst yourselves as to where it should be located, I will assign one for you. Meet with me in the morning," he called to the harvesters. "But do not use the holy mount for such purpose, ever again!"

3

So did the building of defenses begin in Salem. Melchizedek's edict that Moriah was a holy mount and must not be profaned by mundane activities was only a legal and not a military safeguard, but for the present it was as strong a barrier to philosophical invasion as a stone wall.

Because of the awe the great rock had always inspired in the people, the mount had always been considered sacred. The king sacrificed there and, though there was not yet any temple upon the rise, the high hill was naturally associated with ideas of heaven and the dwelling place of God. All such notions were unwritten, but implicit in the nature of the site. The king and his people had never felt the need for more formal stipulation. Now the matter of the threshing floor demanded a stricter definition of the place, and so a codex was begun—a limited codex to be sure, but one which would in time be expanded upon.

When the harvesters met with Melchizedek the morning after their protest, he designated a site far to the west of town, upon the shepherd hills, as their threshing floor. Salem's borders were, thereby, enlarged, and nomads who inhabited that area were pushed farther away. No war attended this expansion. The nomads had never laid claim to the site, and there plenty of other hills for them to roam.

What did result from the move was an unspoken distancing of the farmers and the herders from the central life of the city, and especially from the high and holy mount. In fact, over ensuing years, the sanctity of the mount, and the specialized activities surrounding it, impacted the people's everyday perceptions.

Those who lived closest to the mount, whether by accident or choice, were considered privileged, and their properties more valuable than others, in time, they became the elite and governing class, and those who lived farther out were the commoners and the governed. This thinking became so instilled among the people, that over the generations it followed that nearness to the mount was a sign of special calling, and distance from the mount was distance from God.

Jerusalem—The City of God

It must be understood that such development of thought took place over a very long time. The fact that a threshing floor and its location could spark such cultural development could only be attributed to the fact that these were people of the earth, whose lives revolved around seasons and harvests, and whose economy was clearly governed by the need to survive.

It is a quirk of the human mind, however, that what is forbidden or exclusive becomes the object of the fondest desire. So it is among societies, as well. As soon as the mount became formally sanctified, it became a temptation to coveting hearts, individual and collective.

One of the harvesters who had threshed upon the mount that moonlit night was a fellow named Inri. Of sturdy Canaanite stock, he had been born and raised in Salem and revered Melchizedek from the time he was old enough to understand what a king was. As a child he had heard stories of the wars of Ararat, and how his own great-great grandfather was among those who traveled out from the old country to settle Salem.

For Inri, as for all of his people, Mt. Moriah was as sacred as Ararat, and it was surely as much the home of God as was the mountain of the Ark. Inri cradled in his heart a deep love of the Deity.

But the day Melchizedek assigned the new threshing floor, a seed of bitterness, so tiny it was not at first detected, took root within Inri's spirit.

Inri was very quiet as he returned home from the king's palace with his jolly companions. He found it difficult to share their enthusiasm for the outcome of the meeting with Melchizedek. While they were happy just to have gained the king's ear and to be given a site that expanded the borders of their tillable land, Inri struggled with other emotions. He felt put off by the king's easy relocation of their work, dispossessed, disinherited of life in the city.

When he came to his home, a small hut at the edge of a communal field, he ducked quickly inside, bidding a cursory good-day to his friends. His portly and pleasant wife asked about the meeting, but he only shrugged and said he guessed it went well enough. The rest of that day and into the evening he brooded, gazing quietly into the fire at the center of the hut and ignoring the banter of his five small children.

When the moon rose over the sleeping family, peeking through the smoke hole at the top of the hut, Inri sat up beside his snoring wife and ran calloused fingers through the stubble upon his bald head. He would need to trim his beard sometime soon, he thought, lifting it off his chest and twisting its black strands in the dim light. He was too young to let his beard grow so long.

"But too old to be treated like a child!" he grunted, recalling the king's easy dismissal of his case.

Looking about the one-room hut, he thought of Melchizedek's palace. True, Salem's royal house was modest compared to those of Jericho and other Canaanite towns. But it was far more comfortable than any farmer's hut, as were most homes in the city proper. Just because he worked the feudal land rather than owned it seemed no good reason for him to live in poverty or see his work removed from community activity as though he were a shepherd.

At the thought of the herders who ranged the nearby hills, he sneered a little. It seemed his brothers and sisters in Salem thought of him and his kind no more highly than they would a bunch of sand fleas.

Inri stood up from his bed and moved toward the door, tiptoeing so as not to wake his wife. Pulling on his cloak, he hunched outside and stood full-faced toward the moon.

It was useless to try sleeping. Glancing across the furrowed fields where he spent his working hours, he considered the distant rise that Melchizedek had designated as the new threshing floor. He might as well have a good look at it.

Though the rise was half a mile away and all uphill, he covered the distance with ease, for he was a strong physical fellow. When he reached the top, he was not even breathing heavily. The walking stick he brought with him was a comfort, for there were sometimes wild animals in this vicinity. But he did not need it just now, so he set it on the ground and turned about for a look at Salem.

There the town sat, strung along its foot-shaped terrace like the strands of a woman's neckchain, the windows of its many small buildings glistening like topaz gems. To the north, in a patch of moonlight, sat the great rock. No light of human habitation flashed from it, but in the moonglow it gleamed like the focal point of that necklace, a gem of iridescent blue.

For a moment, Inri felt a twinge of guilt as he looked upon the holy rock. It had been thoughtless of him and his friends to stage their protest in such a sacred place. But as soon as he admitted this, he bristled. Was it right for the king to shame them as he had, removing their labors so far from the city? His fellow farmers did not seem to pick up on the insult, but to Inri it was ostracism, plain and simple.

With slumping shoulders, he knelt to the ground and closed his eyes, remembering the breeze that had carried chaff from his winnowing basket upon the holy hill. Surely that breeze was like no other, refining and purifying. Surely he had not imagined its holiness.

As he relived the feel of the sacred wind, he softly chanted the harvesters' song.

Suddenly, it seemed the chant was echoed. Yes, distant voices whispered toward him, echoing and amplifying his private meditation. Opening his eyes, he cocked his head toward Salem. But the song did not arise from there. It came, instead, from behind him. Gooseprickled, he clutched his staff, leaped to his feet and wheeled about. Far away, upon another distant hill, yellow lights glistened, and it seemed the song came from them.

Like a wary buck he stood stone still, ears and eyes straining across the miles toward the mysterious lights. He had worked the fields of Salem all his life, but had never claimed beyond them. Certainly, he had never seen this coastward view in the moonlight. Was that a nomad encampment he spied? It seemed far too grand, and nomads did not sing farming songs.

It was a city! A city set on a hill like Salem!

Though Inri knew there were other cities in Canaan, the sighting of this neighboring town was like the discovery of another world. Quivering, he stood upon the ridge, his eyes fixed upon the foreign lights.

All his life he had been taught that the cities of greater Canaan, were wicked, that only Salem was good and holy. Never had he desired to visit them.

But tonight was a strange night, and Inri felt alone in the earth. Before he even wrestled with the idea, his feet decided to descend the hill, to move out across the black and vacant plain that marked the end of God's abode.

As he did so, the song of the reapers in the Canaanite town grew more distinct. It was in a tongue different from his own, but not so much different that he could not enjoy it. The tune was more sensual, accompanied by airy flutes and erotic stringed instruments.

Ascending the road that led to the gated city, he felt his heart pound. Though he was apprehensive, the pulsing rhythms lured him onward.

It was not yet midnight, and on this harvest evening the crude gates were open to celebrators. For a while, Inri hid in the shadows beyond those gates, watching with wide eyes the bright-garbed partiers who lolled and danced just inside. Then, like a moth to a flame, he entered, standing open-mouthed in a milling crowd.

He was a peculiar sight, in his bleak homespun, his hair tousled by the wind and by sleepless hours in his hut. As he stood amidst the partiers, they stared at him and snickered, but otherwise disregarded him. Inri did not notice their reaction, so overwhelmed was he by the brilliance of the street torches and gawdy costumes.

How long he wandered through the narrow lanes, gawking into brothels and disoriented by the excesses he witnessed, he would never know. He headed in the general direction of the town's high point, the hill from which the harvest song swelled. Other than this vague destination, there was no order to his fumbling trek. He asked directions of no one, and if he stumbled into people in the streets, he barely muttered to them.

The closer he came to its source, the more raucaus the harvesters' song became, and all along the winding way it was echoed by little bands of musicians and embellished by twirling dancers. Everywhere the smell of wine was strong, and so was the aroma of perfumed necks and arms.

At some point in the hike up the hill, Inri caught more than passing attention from a group of women. Painted women, they were, like all the Canaanites sisters. They were especially practiced in the art of cosmetics, as in the art of seduction.

They were having a busy evening, for it was customary for men of the town to visit prostitutes as part of their worship during harvest. Such activity, they believed, invoked the gods and goddesses of fertility and brought success to the season. Though the women had more than enough clients this evening, the sight of the dusty stranger with his rustic clothing and disheveled appearance struck them as inticing.

Bald though Inri was, and unkempt, he was a rugged fellow. Surely he was new to town, for these women, who knew all the local men, had never seen him before.

"Your turn, Reba," the group giggled, pushing an especially beautiful girl out from their midst. "Do tell us what he is like!"

Giving them a catty grin, the girl sauntered into Inri's path, nearly tripping him. Stunned, Inri took a few steps backward and gaped at the dazzling wonder. Never had he beheld such a creature. Her small but curvaceous body garbed in clinging scarlet and her ebony hair a shower of loose ringlets, she held his gaze with demanding glory and returned it with a gaze of her own. With spellbinding grace, she moved toward, and with every move a chorus of dainty bells tinkled upon her hips and ankles, entreating him to keep on looking. Not that he needed to be convinced. Inri would not have looked away had a dozen wives and children beckoned from the sidelines.

But lust was not the only emotion she provoked in him. Fear, deep and throttling, paralyzed him.

Inri had heard tales of the sons of Nimrod and the sins that had separated them from the followers of Melchizedek in the mists of antiquity. He knew also that the inhabitants of the cities throughout Canaan practiced such folly, and he knew what this woman was about.

What terrified him most, however, was the ease with which held his attention. Suddenly, Inri was two men—one who observed with caution, the other an addled fool about to fall into her trap.

Slipping up beside him, the woman reached for his hand and entwined her arm through his "You look lonely," she cooed. "You are a stranger here, no? Have you come for the festival?"

Staring bleakly at her persistent hands as they stroked his arm, he muttered, "I do not know why I have come."

Such a comment only made him more mysterious, and therefore more intriguing to the streetwalker. Most men were boringly predictable. But here was a challenge.

"It is a new moon," she said. "Harvest moon. Is there no festival in your town?"

"Throughout harvest there is dancing and singing," he replied, "but none such as this." As he looked about him at the raucous partiers, the woman sensed his disapproval. Entranced, she asked, "Where are you from? What city is yours?"

The thought of Salem and of his righteous upbringing caused Inri to cringe. Gingerly, he extricated his arm from her grasp and wiped his hands down his rumpled coat. "I shall be going now."

"Shalim!" the woman exclaimed, speaking the name of his city in her own tongue. "Home of the Evening Star!"

Stopping in his retreat, Inri looked inquisitive. "What did you say?" he asked.

"The Evening Star," she repeated. "You must be from Shalim."

"Salem," he corrected.

"Of course," she replied "One and the same. Either way, it is the name of the Evening Star. Do you worship her upon your threshing floor?"

Appalled, Inri snarled, "We worship no one but Yahweh, The One True God, and his mountain is undefiled!"

As angry as Inri was, it did not escape him that he was, at this moment, defending Melchizedek's position regarding Mt. Moriah. Only hours ago, he had struggled with resentment over this very issue; yet now, faced with this heathen and her pagan notions, he found himself protective of the holy sanctuary.

Jerusalem—The City of God

Taken aback, the woman shrugged. "I did not mean to offend," she said coyly. "I have heard that the breath of the gods passes over the mountain. It only seems right that you should celebrate there."

Inri pulled his coat tight to his chest, remembering the feel of the breeze upon Moriah as it rippled through his hair and beard the night of the protest. Surely this woman bewitched him, playing with his convictions like toys. "You speak evil!" he stammered "It is not the breath of many gods, but the breath of Yahweh that passes over Moriah. There is only one God!"

Bemused, the woman giggled. "Such a selfish god you serve," she replied, "one who does not share his power but keeps it to himself." Then, approaching him carefully, she pouted. "I hope you are not so selfish. Won't you share yourself with me?"

Once more, she reached for him, pulling him toward her. But at her touch, he recoiled.

Suddenly, the night, the dazzling lights, and the foreign tumult were too much for him. Turning away, Inri fled back through the street, dodging onlookers and heading straight for the city gate. Without stopping, without looking behind, he ran across the plain, his heart drumming. Like a gazelle escaping its hunters, he attained the ridge that stood between him and home.

Once he entered his own fields, he fell to his face, clutching the familiar dirt to his bosom. "Purge my thoughts!" he wept, lifting his face to heaven. "Restore my faith and keep me from temptation!"

4

There is a theory of history, borne out of human experience, that once a thought is generated, it finds its echo in countless other hearts. And once the thought is "in the wind," it can turn the course of events like a pilot turns the wheel of a ship. All of this can happen with little or no communication between the thinkers, as though the idea came from beyond them and had simply found its proper time.

So it was with the controversy surrounding Mt. Moriah.

Though Inri's experience in the neighboring town was enough to return him to his traditions, there was no preventing other Salemites from being influenced by such contact. And though the farmer never told anyone of his midnight trip to the foreign city, it took no time at all before other Salemites farmers were lured to the foreign lights visible from the new threshing floor.

Soon the evidence of such visits became frightfully obvious. Fellows of less moral compunction than Inri not only met the harlots of the neighboring town, but consorted with them, bragging of their illicit adventures to their friends. In some circles, it became a sign of manhood to visit a prostitute.

Such dallyings were, at first, confined to the farmers. After all they lived on the fringe of Salem and closest to temptation. The people closest to Mt. Moriah were not so easily distracted and went about their business for years largely untouched by traffic with outsiders.

These conditions served to reinforce the growing sense of separateness that Inri had resented. But, so long as Salem remained unique among all cities, its high place devoted to a God of purity and not carnal pleasure, it was inevitable that such separateness prevailed.

Over the ensuing years, the sanctity of Mt. Moriah became a thorn in the side of all who worshipped other gods. Not a few times, their resentment of Salem and its persistent claim to holiness took on warlike proportions.

One day, years after Inri's visit to the foreign city, Melchizedek, whose advanced age was only recently in touches of gray at his temples and streaks of white in his beard, stood upon his palace porch and watched a funeral procession in the street below. Throughout his long tenure as Salem's king, he had observed many such scenes, as people whose births he had witnessed grew old and passed away before him.

But today's funeral was especially saddening, for there was not just one body to be buried, but many. And the deceased had not grown old, but had died in the prime of life, young men struck down upon the field of battle.

The fallen heroes would be laid in damp caves near the retaining wall. Small pottery lamps would be placed in the niches of the caves and upon the floors, to give light to the dead upon their journey to heaven. Large stones would seal the caves' mouths, extinguishing the light from public view, just as it had been extinguished in the hearts of mothers, wives, and children of the fallen. Ghostly and dreadful, the sound of women's mourning filled the valley and swelled through the streets in all directions.

Tala, who joined Melchizedek in his vigil, drew close to the king's elbow. "They did not die in vain, Master," he insisted. "No one who defends our holy city ever dies in vain."

Melchizedek nodded vaguely and gave a deep sigh. Looking toward Moriah, he said "This is true, my friend. But it was my vision for Salem that it would always be a city of peace. It seems now that the very rock that stands sentinel over our beloved home is the minister of woe and destruction."

Had Tala not known the heart of the king as intimately as he did, he might have considered his words blasphemy. But he knew the old man spoke from sorrow. "If you really believe that," he observed, "you would not have sent your troops out in defense of Moriah. Nor would you spend the resources of the city to build the great wall and tower we see before us."

With this, he drew the king's attention to a mammoth construction project underway upon the palace hill. Bordering Moriah on the south and running along the eastern valley known as Kidron, a huge wall was in the making. The eight-foot-thick barricade would ultimately be taller than the height of four men and would be crowned at its northern end by a lofty guard tower, whose foundations were even now being laid.

Time was of the essence on this project, as evidenced by the fact that the tower and wall were being constructed of rough boulders, not hewn rock.

"You are right," Melchizedek conceded. "But how it saddens me that such steps are necessary! I had hoped to escape the need for war when I came out from Ararat."

"Perhaps by these very fortifications, we shall escape," Tala reasoned. "Perhaps we will no longer seem so vulnerable to our foes, and they will leave us in peace with our sacred mountain."

For a time, Tala's prediction held true. The fortification built by Melchizedek kept invaders at bay so effectively, it came to be called "Ophel," meaning mighty citadel. When the neighboring people of Canaan saw that Melchizedek no longer left his city open to attack, but went to the same lengths to defend it as was common throughout the region, their waning respect for the fabled king was renewed.

During this quiet time, Salem prospered as never before, devoting much energy to elaborate urban development. The marketplace was expanded and commercial buildings of two and three stories graced the winding streets.

In keeping with the mood of the day, the people prevailed upon their king to formalize the sanctuary of Moriah. "Build us a temple," they pleaded. "If the heathen honor their gods with houses of gold and silver, should we deny Yahweh a place of honor for all to behold?"

Though Melchizedek resisted the idea, preferring worship to be a matter of the heart and not of a place, Tala once again showed him another side.

On that day the king and his servant walked together upon the holy mount. As they passed beneath the shadow of the great rock, Tala noticed that Melchizedek bowed his head, obviously in prayer.

"Sir," said the servant, daring to intrude, "I know that you are a spiritual man."

The king nodded. "I hope I am," he replied.

Jerusalem—The City of God

"And you believe that God is everywhere."

"Of course," the king answered.

"Yet I more often find you at prayer upon this mount that anywhere else," Tala observed. "Why is that?"

Studying the sacred rock with great affection, Melchizedek shrugged matter-of-factly. "I feel the presence of the Lord more here than elsewhere. Don't you, Tala?"

"I have never known anyone who does not," the servant agreed. "But if you, being the most spiritual of men, are benefited by the presence of a mere rock—forgive me, Master, but it *is* a rock and not a god—would not men of lesser spirituality be benefited by the presence of a temple?"

Now Melchizedek realized the purpose of this conversation. "Tala," he objected, his voice tinged with impatience, "you know that I cannot condone the erection of any building upon this holy rock. Why do you tempt me?"

Tala's face reddened. "Forgive me, Master," he pleaded, cupping his hands and bowing from the waist. "Your servant is not so good with words as his Master. Never would I encourage you to do evil!"

Looking down upon the penitent, Melchizedek sighed, "Stand up, Tala! You shame me!" When the servant complied, still gazing sheepishly at the ground, the king muttered, "Very well. Speak your mind, and speak it clearly!"

Sometimes, sir, I fear that you are attuned to God and His ways, that you are a bit removed from the people and what is happening to them," he dared.

Melchizedek steeled himself and snapped, "Continue!" With this, however, he began to descend the mount, and Tala had to run to keep up with him.

"Have you not heard the people of the land, the people beyond our sacred city, call it by many names? 'Shalim,' 'Shalem,' 'Shalom,' and even 'Shuliman'?" the servant huffed, flapping his arms with each name.

"There are many tongues and many dialects," the king replied, exasperated. "What is your fear?"

"Surely," Tala marveled, "my Master knows that these are the names of heathen gods, deities of stars and planets whom the outsiders thank for all good things. So common is such thinking among our neighbors, that some even of your own people confuse the God of Salem with false gods!"

Melchizedek ceased his retreat and flashed pain-filled eyes upon his city. Tala, seeing that he made a mark proceeded.

"It is time, Your Majesty, to give our people a house of worship, a place they can point to in the face of their enemies, and say, 'See, here is the temple of our God, Maker of heaven and earth, a place of prayer which idolators may not profane!'"

⌘

It was a simple building, the temple raised by Melchizedek. When it was under construction, some Salemites complained that it was not as large as the temples of other gods, that the king could afford more luxurious appointments. But the majority considered it quite tasteful, and when it was completed, it defied criticism. For it was not the building alone that drew the eyes of all toward the holy mount, but the setting.

It is safe to say there was no more beautiful location for a house of worship than Moriah, and the starkest of houses would have seemed a shrine when set upon that holy mount. But Melchizedek had hired the finest artisans in Salem and even sent away to other cities for advisors, their expertise being of enough value to offset their personal beliefs. So when the temple was completed, its simplicity was sheer elegance.

No higher than two stories, its front portico was graced with two marble pillars, and its hewn rock walls were plastered over with white limewash. Edging along the gable and porch rails was of pure gold, and over the doorway was hung a thick veil, woven in layers upon gigantic looms, each layer attached side by side to another, forming various-colored stripes.

Though the temple was high enough for two floors, it boasted only one room, a chamber of prayer for the king, who was its priest.

And though he never saw God face to face, there was a sacred spirit to the room that never departed. When Melchizedek entered there, the city was silent, for the people knew it was the hour of prayer, and that the king would return with answers to any problems plaguing them.

From the first year that the people had arrived in the land of Moriah, the king had made annual sacrifices upon the mount, in atonement for their sins. These sacrifices had been the only ritual ever performed upon the rock itself. And so it continued, for when the temple was built, it was built just to the north of the rock and not directly upon it. Therefore, acts of sacrifice were still visible, in full display above the city.

With the erection of the temple, the fame of the rock and the town it overshadowed became even more profound. To citizen and foreigner alike, there was no more awesome sight than Moriah. Reports of its glory spread far and wide, so that Salem became an attraction for travelers from distant lands. Having once witnessed it, visitors were compelled to speak of it where ever they went.

"It is a gem," they would say, "the hallowed rock and its little sanctuary. And the city? It is the fairest on earth!"

This was especially true on atonement day. As the king and a small party of attendants ascended Moriah, bearing a spotless white lamb toward the altar, the citizens thought solemnly on their sins, and a holy hush filled the streets. But by evening, as the smoke from that altar curled heavenward through the blush of sunset, there was no more festive place in the world.

Music, dancing, and songs of praise filled the air, wafting out of Salem like a healing wind. All those who traveled near her borders stopped to listen, and with wondering hearts entered the town.

As the light of a crimson sun bounced off the temple and sank toward the west, even the most stubborn hearts were caught away. There was something unique in Salem's worship, something that irresistibly wooed all wandering souls and filled them with yearning they could not deny.

5

For many years, the little temple that graced Mt. Moriah kept vigil over the community unique in the land for holiness. While other cities, states, and empires came and went, grew and declined, warred and made treaties, Salem maintained peace within its borders. And the faith that was uniquely her own stood strong against onslaught. The presence of the temple, it seemed, had a preserving effect upon the city, provoking awe within all who beheld it, and instilling the town's inhabitants with a sense of privilege and responsibility.

As time went on, however, and as the outside world, with its lusts and struggles, encroached ever closer, the island of righteousness that was Salem was threatened by waves of wickedness.

It was nearing the end of the third millennium, B.C.E. as folks would later reckon time. Melchizedek had been king of Salem for so long, people had lost track of his origins and the beginnings of his administration. Tales of the Great Deluge, of Father Noah, of the Ark and Ararat, and of the legendary pioneers who had spread from there across the earth were preserved in oral tradition and scant writings. But through the telling and retelling, they had suffered many changes.

Few people any longer knew the pure rendition of those stories, and as the worship of other gods took hold, the tales were recast to accommodate them. The very names of Noah, Mt. Ararat, Nimrod, and others were replaced by the names of heathen gods or local landmarks and heroes, and the facts of history were so distorted that most of the versions bore little resemblance to truth.

The land of Canaan, likewise, underwent many changes, being overrun by a succession of conquerors with diverse ideologies. Those who currently lorded it over the Canaanites were people to the north and south, Assyrians and Egyptians. These masters of war with their brass helmets and bronze chariots competed for dominance in the region for generations, each conquering ruler styling himself similarly as "the mighty king,

king of the universe, king without rival, who shatters the might of the princes of the whole world, who has smashed all of his foes as pots."

In appearance, the two races who vied for Canaan were unlike as nay could be. The fair-skinned Egyptians with their straight hair and aquiline noses were slender build and had an air of sophisticated haughtiness, as opposed to their dark complexioned, stocky challengers. And while the people of the Nile practiced a finely honed militarism, the powerfully built Assyrians, with their wild, bushy hair and thick eyebrows, were more vicious.

Despite their highly developed civilization, which had sprung from the motherland of Babylonia, the Arryrians were barbaric warriors, but this often made up for their lack of professional training. Not that the Arryrians were less educated. While the Egyptians captured their own high thinking in hieroglyphs, the Assyrians preserved their dreams in cuneiform. And so the cities of Canaan endured a succession of monuments erected in their central squares, etched either in some pharaoh's pictorial writing or in the wedged-shaped characters of the northern empire.

All save Salem, which alone among the towns of Canaan retained its sovereignty and its original government. No foreign monument had ever competed with the temple for attention, and no blood, other than the blood of sheep and goats, had ever been spilled upon Moriah.

Was it any wonder that for centuries, throughout the land, "the time of Melchizedel" was the term applied to the period? In the long run, no matter who claimed the region, whether Egypt or Assyria, or any other jealous conqueror, Melchizedek was a symbol, to pagan and follower alike, of a higher power at work in history.

Who ruled over his neighbors was especially insignificant for Melchizedek. He had seen so many vying cultures come and go, he knew from lifelong experience the futility of men's squabbles. What mattered to Melchizedek was the growing ease with which invading philosophies seduced his own people. Despite her seeming immunity to conquest, her adherence to the old traditions and to faith in The One True God, Salem was increasingly infected by the ways of those who conquered the land and by the prevailing willfulness of her Canaanite neighbors.

More and more often, Melchizedek confronted elements of paganism creeping into worship of The One True God. The inroads made by seductive philosophies eventually went beyond mere name changes. The fact that Salem was called Shalem or Shulliman by some of the citizens, connoting the names of foreign deities, was a minor concern compared to heathen practices that were beginning to mingle with the worship of Yahweh.

The king's dear servant, Tala, had long passed away when the horrors of heathenism were played out in the most wretched fashion Salem had ever endured. Even the king himself was at last showing the millennia of his personal age in snowy hair and beard.

There were few who communed with him in his lonely status as Earth's eldest citizen. He provoked reverence and awe among those who dwelt within his palace, but he had no soulmates. Alone, he bore the memories of a simpler world and purer people. Alone, he spoke of times long past, for he alone had lived them.

His voice, ringing forth on each atonement eve from the palace parapets, crying out against apostasy rebellion, sometimes mocked. While it still served as a goad to holiness, it was less and less often a factor in the people's choices, as they questioned how it applied to their own time.

Tonight was one of those atonement eves. Melchizedek had spent all day upon Mt. Moriah, preparing the altar and the temple for his annual sacrifice. He was just returning to the palace with his servants for a season of prayer. At dawn a processional would take him again to the holy rock, and after he had slain a spotless lamb, a curl of smoke would ascend through the golden dusk, symbolic of spiritual cleansing.

Though he looked forward to the morrow, the most holy day on the Salemite calendar, his spirit was heavy as he turned for home. Sometimes he wondered what good it did to repeat the atonement ritual year after year. If the people's heart were not in it, what efficacy could it have? But the heaviness of his spirit was traded for horror when an ear-splitting shriek rent the air.

Ascending from the southernmost end of Ophel, past the fount of Gihon, the cry shuddered through the streets, quivering toward Moriah like the wail of a lost soul. Riveted in his path, Melchizedek scanned the distant gorge, and with undimmed vision it was plain to see that a gigantic fire raged in the vicinity of the cry.

Gesturing to his servants, the king ordered them to run ahead. "Go, see what dreadful thing is happening!" he commanded.

Then steadying himself with his shepherd's crook, the one which for years he used as a scepter, he hastened down the hill behind them. As he did so, he was joined along the way by terrified Salemites, all wondering about the cry, which was now joined by many others, equally eerie and spine-tingling. Down the winding path they went, the king and his bewildered citizens, until they rounded the last bend in the narrow gorge.

Only Melchizedek remembered the first time he and his people entered the adjacent vale, searching for the splashing water that would later be named "Gihon." Such an exciting day that had been—the day the land of Canaan and the city of Salem also received their names! Of course, at that point, Salem existed only in the king's imagination. But so ardently did he believe in her that his zeal was infectious, and it was long before the people made his dream reality.

But those were a different group of people, and that was a different time. The ones who accompanied him this day did not seek the source of singing water, but the cause of wrenching cries and leaping flames. Nor did they approach the vale with hearts of joy, but spirits of terror.

"O King!" a servant hailed him, returning up the gorge just as Melchizedek rounded the last rugged corner. "Do not come closer!" he warned. "Turn back, O Righteous King! Your eyes are too holy to look upon the folly of your people!"

Throwing himself upon the ground, the servant bowed repeatedly, tears coursing down his face, leaving muddy droplets in the dirt. For only an instant Melchizedek hesitated, not for fear of moving on, but out of concern for the horrified messenger.

Reaching down, he lifted him up and gazed into his fevered eyes. "What is it, Man?" the king demanded. "Is there any sin so great that the Lord cannot forgive it?"

With a stammer, the fellow replied, "I...I cannot say, Your Majesty. Only you can be the judge. But surely there are sins so great, the Righteous King, Holy Priest of Salem, should not go near to them!"

These words had no more been spoken when they were followed by more screams. But this time, the cries were joined by weaker ones, like those of a child, perhaps even of a wee babe. And this childlike wail was multiplied over and over, as though many small ones were in agony.

Not to be detained longer, the king stepped past the frantic messenger. Already he noted that each helpless wail terminated in silence, as though snuffed out, only to be echoed by more of the same.

With the agility of a young man, Melchizedek hastened down the last few yards of the path, and at last stood directly in the flashing glow of a huge bonfire.

What greeted his fatherly eyes was more awful than anything he could have imagined. He might have anticipated an orgy of grisly dimensions or a fight to the death among a horde of inebriates. But never would he have thought his people capable of the atrocities performed in this blazing light.

All about the fire stood women with tear-streaked faces, clutching at their mantles and begging for help as their young children and nursing infants were ripped from their protective arms. Some of them the king knew, women of Salem, and others appeared to be Canaanites of nearby cities. All of them bore a mark upon their foreheads, a smudge of menstrual blood dabbed there by the finger of a pagan priest, denoting them worshippers of Molech. Since their monthly cycle coincided with the festival of the god, it was their dubious honor to be selected as sacrificers to him.

This deity, whose likeness had been worshipped as far back as the days of Noah, when the people of Nimrod left The One True God, was the spirit of fire and storm, and stoked himself with the blood of human sacrifice. Insisting on the utmost devotion in his followers, his lust could only be satisfied and his threats against them quenched by the blood of their most beloved children.

Molech worship had not been imposed upon Canaanites from outside. He was not a god of the Assyrians or the Egyptians. If he had been, Melchizedek might have anticipated his influence more readily. Rather, he had been brought to the land from the distant east, from Sumer and its neighbors. Melchizedek might have hoped he was forgotten, but his worship revived from time to time.

Despite his merciless nature, or because of it, Molech was gaining a great following throughout Canaan. At the center of the gathering this evening, nearest the fire, stood his priest, receiving child after child, wriggling infant and weeping toddler, handed over by stony-faced guards. Though the mothers had come here willingly, they inevitably responded to the sight of their little ones' fate with frantic struggle and bitter skirmish. But all attempts to back out of their predicament were futile, as the husky guards pushed them aside.

"Through the fire to Molech!" the priest chanted, as he held each child aloft and then, turning toward the flames, cast it headlong to its death. "Through the fire to Molech! Through the fire to Molech!"

These words supposedly insured the child's safe passage to the halls of heaven and eternal bliss with the bloody god. But there was no comfort in them. Though the worshipful onlookers echoed their priest, elevating the children to places of glory in the courts of the fire-king, the mothers and fathers of the burning babes knew no solace. Before Melchizedek could intervene, some of the women had joined their little ones, leaping into the flames with them, rather than be left to face undying grief.

At the witness of all this, the Salemite king pushed his way to the head of the crowd and confronted the pagan priest in holy fury. "Stop, in the name of God Almighty!" he cried, stunning the unprepared heathen.

Then, despite his own frailty, he reached for the squalling babe that would have been the priest's next victim and wrenched it from his grasp.

"Whose child is this?" he demanded, turning blistering eyes upon the crowd. Trembling, a woman stepped forth, her lips quivering in speechless gratitude, though her face burned with shame. "Would you give your child to the demons?" Melchizedek shouted. "Give him instead to Yahweh!" With this, he thrust the whimpering babe into her arms.

Then, wheeling about, he climbed upon a ledge and glared down at the Molechites. "Know you not that this is the valley of our Lord?" he cried, passing his hand over the heads of the congregation. "And this is the city of our God? You people of Salem, get back to your homes! And you Canaanites, woe to you, when you shed innocent blood, when you turn your hearts from the truth! Get away from the Lord's holy mount, and do not profane my people, says the Lord! For if anyone hurts one of these my little ones, it would be better for him that a millstone were hung about his neck, and he were cast into the sea. Instead, he shall be cast into a greater fire than Molech's…a fire unquenchable, to burn forever!"

6

As much as Melchizedek hoped it would be otherwise, the confrontation with the Molechites near Gihon was only one of the many that were to follow. So seductive was the worship of the fire god that there would be countless such demonstrations over the years to come.

And always they would be staged in the same place, so that the name of the vale became a play of words. "Gehenna," it was called, a mingling of Gihon and Hinnom, meaning 'valley of the sons," or "valley of the children," commemorative of the hundreds, indeed thousands, of youngsters slain there.

For the old king, there could have been no keener pain than the witness of his people's folly, and the desecration of this second most holy place in Salem. As of yet, Moriah retained its integrity. No pagan god had ever been worshipped upon the pristine mount. As high priest of Yahweh, Melchizedek prayed that he would be taken to the abode of his fathers before such a day ever came.

As time passed, fewer and fewer of his people heeded his warnings. The ways of the neighboring Canaanites and of the marauding hordes who swept generation after generation across the land took invasive toll on Salem's spirit, until the old king believed it would not be long before Moriah was challenged. When that day came, he feared, there would be no war. Rather, the people of Salem would willingly give the holy mount to the heathens.

So far had Salem strayed from the truth that the king often thought to himself, "When they deliver Moriah into sinful hands, they shall say, 'What we do is good and not evil.'"

Though the king hoped to be spared the witness of Moriah's downfall, he alone dreamed of his own deliverance. Since the name of Melchizedek was inextricably interwoven with the history of Canaan, since the king himself was a legend of nearly super-human proportion, the eventuality of his exit from the world scene did not figure in people's thinking. To

those who lived there, and to those who had only heard of the yellow land
and its renowned river, Melchizedek was eternal. He had always been, so
far as they knew, and would always be.

Therefore, when the time actually approached that the venerable elder
would leave his vale, it was he alone who sensed it.

Melchizedek had lived a unique life for so long, and had for so long
carried a solitary view of history, that it was only fitting he should perceive
the end of his administration unaccompanied.

Of course, he was not, in truth, alone. Yahweh was with him. No
angelic visitation told him the end was nigh. Rather, the sense of God's
presence was increasingly poignant with each passing day, until the old
man hardly knew, at times, whether he trod earthly soil or had passed quietly to his reward.

Likewise, it seemed that the past was as clearly with him as the present. When he had been younger, when life had been full of activity, the
mists of Mt. Ararat had often been a distant memory—so distant, in fact,
that sometimes when he tried to recall them and the pinnacle they
shrouded, they seemed almost a myth, a phantasm that fled like a dream
upon waking. The more effort he put toward recalling the faces of Great-
Great-Grandfather Noah or Grandfather Canaan, who dwelt on that faraway mount, the more remote were the images.

But these days, as he approached the termination of his purpose here,
they often flashed across his mind like freshly painted portraits.

When they did, it was at unexpected moments, when he tended his
garden or sat at dinner in the solitude of his courtyard. Sometimes, like
this afternoon, as he stood upon the ramparts of his palace, gazing up the
terraced slope that cradled his home, he recalled the Ark that rested on
Ararat as clearly as though it sat atop the mount of sacrifice crowning his
little city.

Closing his eyes, he tilted his head back and listened for the voices of
his departed loved ones. Surely he heard them! Surely they beckoned to
him, and if he were only to spread his arms wide, like a bird spreads its

wings, he would soar upward. He would leave Salem far behind, he would pass over the fields of Ararat, over the misty peaks of the fathering range, and would join his family and the countless friends who had gone before him into the afterlife.

But something prevented him, a knowledge, still unclear, that the time was not right, that something more was requested of him on this earthly plane.

Opening his eyes, he looked toward the highway that led up the Jordan. For the first time in many, many years, he felt the heat of prophetic stirring course through his veins.

Ever since he had undertaken the journey from Ararat, leading the first pilgrims into the sacred land, it had been enough for him to be king of Salem. It had been enough for him to found a center of righteousness and stand for holiness in a world gone wrong. But today, he caught a glimpse, for the first time, of a purpose greater than all this.

What began as a warm surge in his veins became a trembling in his heart. He knew the Lord was about to speak, and he gripped the rail of his balcony with rigid fingers.

When the words came, they were familiar. He had heard them rehearsed often in his childhood and in his years on Ararat. They were words first spoken by Noah, at the prompting of God. While often used by enemies as a tool against him and all those related to Canaan, today they were not fearsome. They were a comforting confirmation of God's work in Melchizedek's life:

"Blessed be the Lord,
The God of Shem;
And let Canaan be his servant.
May God enlarge Japheth,
And let him dwell in the tents of Shem;
And let Canaan be his servant."

Like a soothing breeze, the prophecy, heralded so long ago by Noah, swept over Melchizedek's soul. What had begun as a curse on the line of Ham, devolving to Canaan and his descendants, had turned out to be a blessing. For righteous Canaan had taught his son and grandson reverence for Yahweh, and Melchizedek had become a mighty sovereign.

But today, as the king considered the words afresh, he knew they had yet to be fulfilled.

"I am separated from my kindred," he whispered, bowing his head. "How is it that I shall be a servant to the sons of Shem and Japheth, when I rule in Canaan?"

Still as a stone he stood, awaiting an answer. And, in the context of the prophecy, it tingled through his soul.

"All your life you have been their servant," Yahweh replied. "Through the line of Shem, firstborn of Noah, a savior shall arise, and he shall plant his feet upon Moriah, to rule the nations with righteousness and peace. It is you, my son, who have prepared the way for him, building for him a holy city and keeping the keys therefore, until the time appointed."

Quivering Melchizedek raised his hands to his face, as though the sunlight of the promise would blind him. "The time appointed?" he stammered. "O Lord is that time near? And how shall I know the son of Shem when I see him?"

Suddenly, it seemed the mountain shook. Melchizedek opened his fingers and peered between them, but saw no movement in the earth. The trees did not sway and the ground did not heave. But he steadied himself against the rail, and listened.

"Keep your eyes to the east," the Lord told him. "From the east shall the savior come forth. Yes, even now his footstep is heard in the land, as he prepares to judge the nations."

Prophecy is a peculiar thing. It can come in the simplest of terms and be fulfilled in short order. But more often it is multilayered and can be applied to several situations over a broad expanse of time, seeming to be fulfilled in one generation but leaving one or more aspects for completion at a later date.

So it was with the word of the Lord to Melchizedek the day he cast his gaze up the eastern highway.

Indeed, a "son of Shem," a descendant of Noah's eldest son, had recently entered Canaan, and he was making quite a name for himself throughout the region. He hailed, as the Lord had said, from the east, a wealthy merchant-prince of the Sumerian city of Ur. Abram was his name, son of Terah, and he had exchanged city life for the life of a wandering Hebrew, a shepherd who followed flocks and herds. But his wandering was not aimless. He had come to Canaan in quest of a "promise," some destiny connected with the land, of which his God had told him.

Of course, there had always been people drawn to Canaan in quest of its resources and its legends. It was the nature of this land that all who conquered it believed it held for them a place in history, a certain "destiny," In these ways, Abram was like many who had come here seeking his fulfillment.

But, unlike the others, Abram was not bent on conquest. He came with no army, other than the trained herdsmen who protected his flocks and caravan. He set up no city or kingdom, but rented a parcel at Mamre, south of Salem.

Most noteworthy, however, was his religion.

He alone, of all who coveted the land and all his kindred in Ur, worshipped a God much like Melchizedek's. In fact, he called him God Almighty, and claimed he was The Only True God, that all others were false. In a world that encouraged the worship of a thousand deities, in a multicultured setting that prided itself on religious tolerance, such monotheism was rare, indeed.

Once Melchizedek received the word of the Lord, he paid close attention to reports of Abram, for he thought it highly possible that the young immigrant might be the promised one. Just how such a non-militant fellow would come to "judge the nations," it remained to be seen. But on one level, that prophecy was fulfilled quickly.

When a Mesopotamian confederacy swept down the east side of Jordan to quell an uprising among the wealthy and wanton cities of Zoar Plain, south of the Dead Sea, Abram was compelled to fight them. Though Sodom, one of the targeted towns, was the most licentious and immoral of them all, Abram's nephew, Lot, resided there. He, along with hundreds of his fellow citizens, was taken captive and hauled off in chains by the warlords on their retreat homeward.

Lot's uncle would not sit by for this.

Though Abram had only 318 trained men at his command, he set out to rescue his kin. In an unprecedented, even miraculous foray, Abram and his little band managed to pursue the marauders as far north as the Jordan River headwaters, defeating them by night and routing the thousands all the way to Hobah, north Damascus. In the resultant victory, he managed to retrieve all the goods, save his nephew, and return the liberated slaves to their people.

When news went out of Abram's triumph, Melchizedek determined to meet the victor on his homecoming. For three days he waited, pacing his porch and straining his old eyes along the east highway. His servants waited with him, ready to do his bidding, and wondering why he attached such great importance to the man of Ur. Yes, Abram was a popular fellow, his feat broadcast far and wide. But had there not been other great warriors in the king's time?

The valets and chamberlains asked no questions. They would accompany the master to the Valley Shaveh, the "king's dale," which overlooked the highway, when the hero passed that way, for the road he traveled to Mamre would take him nigh to Salem. The gift that the king would present to Abram was peculiar, the servants thought—a tray of wine and bread.

Jerusalem—The City of God

At last the hour arrived. A messenger came scurrying over the brow of Olive Mount and hastened toward the palace. "Abram, son of Terah, approaches from Jericho! He is even now at the crest of the wilderness road!"

Arising from his cedar chair, Melchizedek grasped his crook in his hand and summoned his servants. "I will go on foot," he announced, as they offered to fetch his carriage.

Amazed at the old man's energy, the servants followed, one carrying the king's royal robe, another the tall mitre that he wore only in his priestly duties. It seemed the king intended to greet the victor not only as ambassador of Salem but as emissary of Yahweh. A third servant bore the silver tray of bread and wine, and a fourth led a donkey, in case the king should tire before reaching the vale.

Melchizedek was not in the least weary as he and his small entourage approached the grove of Shaveh. He was more energized than ever when the leading troops of Abram's little army were seen upon the rise. In their midst, upon a fine camel, rode the famed merchant-prince, handsome as the king had expected, with white turban, dark beard, and striped caftan slapping the breeze.

Behind him and about him were the soldiers, but the bulk of the great congregation that spilled over the crest of Jericho road were the people he had rescued. If anyone appreciated the man of Ur, it was these whom he had saved. And they told him so, in song and dance and chant, as they trailed after him:

"Abram, Abram of Ur!
Savior of our people!
May your god be praised,
May your children be as arrows
In your quiver!
Abram, Abram of Ur!
Savior of our people!"

Of course, they did not know the God of whom they sang. But they knew he must be a powerful one, and they would surely add him to their pantheon when they got home.

However, it was not the song of the Sodomites that thrilled Melchizedek when he first spied the man of Ur. The moment he saw him, he knew that the word of the Lord, received only days before, was of far greater extent than the rescue of these people.

Gripping his cloak to his chest, he steadied himself with his shepherd's staff. In Abram, he caught a glimpse of time yet to be, of time beyond time, immeasurable.

"Come," he whispered to his servants. "We will greet him in the name of the Lord." As for Abram, as he approached Salem, he was not a little taken aback to see the priest of Yahweh awaiting his approach. All along his victory journey, he had been greeted by masses of people and by governors of every town. Even now, the folks of Salem gathered along the highway and the city walls, eager to glimpse the returning hero, but Abram had not expected the king of this fabled place to pay him any mind.

Melchizedek, whose legend was not unknown to Abram, had a reputation for giving little regard to the wars and heroes of the land. He was elusive and aloof, people said. Why should he go out of his way to applaud a foreigner and his paltry troops?

Yet, of all the governors and kings of Canaan, Melchizedek was the one whose praise was coveted—especially by a man like Abram, who claimed to know The One True God. Legends said that the venerable and ageless monarch spoke firsthand to God Most High. If this was true, Abram longed to meet him.

⁘

It was a pivotal moment when Abram of Ur and Melchizedek, son of Canaan, met in Shaveh Vale. Only the king, the ancient founder of Salem, had any inkling just how pivotal and historic the moment was.

As Abram descended Olivet, crossing the dale to meet the high priest of Yahweh, and as Melchizedek, crowned with his mitre and robed in his royal cloak, walked across the flat to greet him, it was as if a continent were being crossed, as if all the space that separated Ararat and Sumer from "the center of the earth" were being crossed. And it was as if eons of history were being compressed, to bring the long-separated races of Shem and Ham and Japheth to a family reunion.

Only the ancient king could see it this way. Only he had witnessed enough and lived long enough to comprehend the drama being played out. When Abram rode into his presence, the man of Ur had very limited understanding. But as he made his camel kneel down, and slipped from the saddle, the victorious warrior felt terribly small.

Trembling, Abram fell before the white-haired king and feared to look upon his face, for the depths of the old man's eyes bespoke such mystery and such wisdom, they were terrifying.

This king did not greet him with trumpets. His silence was far more profound. Nor did he shower Abram with gold and gems, but the man of Ur sensed he had a wealth of wisdom to give.

Huddled against the ground, Abram dared not move, until the king bent down and raised his face in his hands. Motioning to his nearest servant, Melchizedek called for the bread and wine and personally placed it before the hero. Abram hesitated, wondering at the meaning of the gift, but at last he reached out and partook.

As he did, the two men were fixed upon one another—Abram reading volumes of inscrutable mystery in the old one's gaze, and Melchizedek sensing once again this young man's entrance upon the stage was a mere beginning, a channel of promise for all people and all races.

With tears brimming along his white lashes, the king lifted Abram to his feet. His throat was so choked with feeling, he could barely speak, but by the grace of Yahweh, he found his voice, and placing his hands upon Abram's head, he raised his crinkled face to heaven, saying,

"Blessed be Abram of God Most High,
Possessor of heaven and earth;
And blessed be God Most High,
Who delivered your enemies
Into your hand!"

Opening his eyes, the king looked fondly upon the Lord's beloved, then turned and gazed up the slope of the holy mount, to the rock that crowned it.

Fixed upon the elder's every move, Abram followed his gaze, and when he beheld the rock, awe overtook him. He did not understand the rock, nor the city whose keys he was being given.

In time he would start to understand, to know that the land he had been promised was mothered by this place, and that the sanctuary of men's hearts was the sanctuary of Moriah.

Part II

ADONIZEDEK

1410 B.C.E.

1

A small black snake slithered across the rubble of a fallen column and disappeared into a miniscule fissure at the base of Salem's flat rock. The snake's passage was silent, as was the breeze that moved sadly through the tangle of weeds and vines that had overgrown the shadowy mount.

Legend said that a temple once stood here, but the only evidence of it was the toppled column and a few angular stones peeking forth from the yellow soil, suggesting the remains of a crumbled gable. There was no gold railing or golden portico. If there ever had been, they had gone the way of looters and treasure seekers centuries ago.

Generations had come and gone since Melchizedek last offered a sacrifice here. In fact, that fabled king had long since been relegated to the realm of myth, and that which he had feared the most, the enactment of pagan rites upon his holy hill, had occurred countless times since his passing.

It was 1410 B.C.E. The only remnants of the days of Melchizedek to be found in the city were place names—Gihon, Kidron, Shaveh, Moriah, and a few others—plus the name of the current king. Adoni-zedek he was called. Like all who succeeded the first king, he retained the suffix "zedek," "the righteous." And he played a dual role as king and priest, of whatever deity the people adored.

There had been many "zedeks" since the legendary "days of Melchizedek," and many gods. All the kings boasted equally awesome given names, each a reference to the One True God, though none of them knew Him. Elelyon-zedek, Elshaddaai-zedek, Yahweh-zedek: all of the prefixes were, at one time or another, names for The Lord Most High.

But the people of the city had long forgotten who the Lord was. These days, Salem was just another Canaanite town. Its present King, Adonizedek was just a vassal of Egypt, the empire to whom all Canaan currently bowed the knee.

Although Melchizedek had never married, and therefore had no posterity, the kings who succeeded him followed a patriarchal line. At first, the men who led the city were of noble breeding, tall and handsome, like their predecessor, and keen of wit. But as time passed, and morals declined, the kings of Salem were lax in their choice of wives, intermarrying with multitudes about them, bringing pagan bloodlines as well as beliefs into their administrations.

The results sometimes manifested sadly in heirs to the throne. Intellectually, physically, and spiritually, Salem's kings were often as unlike Melchizedek as could be imagined.

Too often, the queens of Salem were painted women from the coast who taught the young princes nothing about Abram or the other mighty men who had influenced the city. And the kings were usually too preoccupied with carnal pursuits to instill much interest in the past.

As for Adonizedek, the legends and heritage of Salem meant nothing to him, apart from the fact that power had devolved to him through history. Even his own name, with its glorious prefix and suffix, had little meaning for him, apart from the power of tradition and the rights it assured him.

But then, Adonizedek's attitude was the product of many generations. Even the name Salem had been corrupted over previous administrations, until the meaning was quite open to interpretation. "Urushalim," it was now called—implying, at best, that it was not peace itself, but was founded by peace; and at worst, that it was founded by the goddess of peace, the Evening Star.

Of course, such a designation was more diplomatic than the presumptuous name "Peace." It was less offensive to the world about. "Salem" implied that the people living there had a claim on wisdom that eluded others. Or worse yet, that the king and his people were afraid of war! Either possibility made the vague title unfit.

Let no one accuse the inhabitants of exclusiveness. "Urushalim" was cosmopolitan, worldly and open-minded.

In some respects, however, Adonizedek was worthy to hold the throne once occupied by a man like Melchizedek. For one thing, his lineage was

Amorite, descended from Canaan, as were Salem's first inhabitants. And, like the king of old, his ancestry revealed itself in tall stature, dark eyes, and dignified bearing. The name Amorite, or Ammuru, itself, meant "tall one," and Adonizedek was related to the most famous Ammuru, Hammurabi the Great, of Babylon.

Like Melchizedek in his youth, Adonizedek was a great warrior. But while the shepherd-turned-king had loathed violence, and had journeyed from Ararat to found a city of peace, Adonizedel loved the taste of blood. Under his administration, Urushalim had become a powerful and contentious force in the land.

Adonizedek was the most feared and respected king among a confederacy of five Amorite cities. Next to Jericho, which was the eastern gate to Canaan, Urushalim was most coveted by would-be conquerors.

Although Adonizedek, like all his neighbors, was obliged to bow to Egypt, the mightiest empire on earth, he bowed to no one else. This day, the yearning for war boiled in his veins as it had not done in years.

Through the tangle of weeds twisting about the shattered columns of Salem's mythic temple, the king and his counselors rode this afternoon. Their horses picked their way gingerly across the rubble, their hooves carefully avoiding jagged pieces of marble.

The king did not notice the remnants of ancient times. His eyes scanned the horizon, where smoke and ash from two great cities billowed into an orange sky. "I would not have believed it!" he growled. "I would not have believed it, had my own eyes not told me!"

A wide-eyed servant boy stood behind him, ready to hold his robe or take his horse's reins. Running his sandaled toe across an unrecognizable shard of temple pavement, he sighed and looked a little abashed. "I told you sir," he replied. "Did I not bring word to the king only yesterday, that Ai had fallen?"

Were the boy not more than a servant, being son to the king by one of his many concubines, Adonizedek would have slapped him for his impudence. But he was rather fond of the curly-haired lad, who acted as a messenger as well as a close attendant, and whose royal blood was reflected in black eyes and dark winsomeness.

"Dear little Micah," the king said through gritted teeth, "had a thousand heralds brought me word, I still would not have believed it! Jericho is toppled, like a string of toy blocks! And now Ai, a city almost as great as our own! Who is the demon who invades our valley, who levels mighty fortresses as though they are haystacks?"

Of course, he knew the invader's name: Joshua. Right-hand man to Moses (the runaway prince of Egypt who had led the rebellion of three million Hebrew slaves and had brought them across the Sinai to the very borders of Canaan), Joshua had now taken over leadership of the wandering horde. The Israelites, as the Hebrews were called, had passed through the territories of the Edomites and the Moabites, south of the Dead Sea, and had worked their way up to the east side of Jordan, battling victoriously against Amorites in that vicinity.

In the last few days they had actually gone against Jericho, staging a most peculiar "attack," involving no weapons, but only perpetual marches round and round the city, accompanied by loud trumpet blasts and shouts. One entire week of this was rewarded by the complete leveling of the gargantuan walls that were the city's invulnerable hallmark. Smoke from the ruins, kindled by Joshua and his sacking conquerors, still rose in ominous clouds over Canaan, filling the horizon beyond Urushalim with warning signals.

Jericho's airborne ashes now mingled with the smoke of yet another city, the great fortress of Ai, a little to the west. For Joshua did not stop with his first success. Using the most clever trickery, he managed to lure the inhabitants of Ai away from their town, and then, with an army of thirty thousand, he invaded, burned it to the ground, and pursued those they had put to flight, destroying all twelve thousand of the uprooted citizens.

Indeed, Adonizedek knew the name of the invader. What neither he nor any of the kings who lay in Israel's path could understand was how a nation of homeless wanders, without any true king and without the fiscal support of any real economy, could produce so great an organized warforce. When he asked, "Who is this?" he really meant, "What power lies behind him? How is it that he can do these things?" Likewise, when he said that he never would have believed such feats, he was admitting to a miracle.

Climbing down from his horse, Adonizedek handed the reins to young Micah and called his counselors about him. Among these accompanying him today were two generals of his infantry, assorted princes, and seven seers, or wise men, noted for their ability to foretell the future and read the stars. He might have consulted with the generals, seeking their advice on strategy and odds. He might have asked his intelligent and capable sons how to proceed. But he sensed that dealing with Joshua required higher help.

Focusing on the seven seers, whose faces were hidden beneath black hoods, he knit his brow. "Prophets of our Lady Ashtartu," he addressed them, "is our Lady the goddess of war as well as love?"

"She is," they answered proudly.

The king took a deep breath and grilled them with his gaze. "Was she not worshipped by our brothers across Jordan, by King Og and King Bashan?"

The wise men realized the direction the king was leading and squirmed uncomfortably. "She...was," they answered.

"How is it, then," he growled, "that Og and Bashan and all our brothers across Jordan have succumbed to this demon, Joshua?"

Leaning together like black sheaves, the seers conferred in dark, quiet tones. At last, the eldest lifted the rim of his hood and struck a pedantic pose.

"The stars, Your Majesty, are not always easy to read. They sometimes align themselves in mysterious ways. But, with great effort, their intentions become clear..."

"Worthless!" the king roared, his voice carrying down the mountain like thunder. "Worthless counselors are you all!" Trudging back across the mount, he looked longingly upon his city. "Surely Ashtartu loves Urushalim," he muttered. "Will she let it fall, as well?"

Uncertain if the king only talked to the air, or required an answer, the prophets whispered among themselves. When Adonizedek turned again on them, they swallowed hard and smiled wanly.

"What can you tell me?" he quipped. "Do you know, at least, the name of Joshua's god? Is he more powerful than ours? Is he a god of Egypt?"

"We have tried to discern this, Your Highness," Dagar, priest and chief of the seers replied. It seems he is a god unknown…"

"Unknown?" the king cried. "Unknown?" Throwing his arms in the air, Adonizedek gestured helplessly toward the sky. "Worthless!" he repeated. "Must the Israelites overrun all Canaan before the prophets of Ashtartu can tell me anything?"

Cringing before the monarch, the seers pulled back within their hoods. "It is dangerous to blaspheme the goddess," Dagar said. "I should warn you…"

"Warn me?" the king interrupted. Flashing an angry face toward the slope west of Moriah, where the most recent temple stood, a temple to the Evening Star, he laughed, "It is I who warn you, Holy Man! Ashtartu is blasphemed by your ignorance! Go!" he cried, waving them away. "Go to your house of prayer and study some more! Do not come near me again until you are wise!"

Crouching beneath their cloaks, Dagar and the prophets slunk away, while the king directed his attention to the generals.

As he fried them with the same insistent stare, they shriveled before him.

"You realize that Urushalim will be Joshua's next goal?" Adonizedek began.

"It would appear so," the first general replied. "He will turn next toward our holy mountain."

"What is your plan?" the king muttered.

Little Micah was not much interested in generals or their plans. At the moment, he was fascinated by the retreating seers, who headed toward the pearly temple on the rise. Micah had always loved the goddess, and it hurt to see her prophets humiliated. But they should have known what god was more powerful than the war goddess!

Of course, there were the gods of Egypt, the mightiest empire on earth. But which of them was greater than Ashtartu? Was she not friend to the Sun himself?

Micah had learned to love the goddess at his mother's knee. One of his first memories was of her holding him up before the statue of Ashtartu that stood in the king's court. Shapely and tall, powerful of build, the goddess was robed in fine, draping linen, and stood behind a big shield, the symbol of war. The perfect blend of love and might was she. And her noble face was both loving and austere.

When the wise men disappeared behind the temple's high wall, Micah felt a tear slide down his cheeks. Lowering his damp eyes, he brushed them with his fingers, and as he did, he noticed a dark, shining object in the rubble of his feet.

Bending down, he worked it out from the yellow soil, and lifted it to the sun. Encrusted with centuries of dirt, it would not have drawn attention, except for the spindly horns protruding from it.

Micah picked away the clinging soil and blew upon it until it revealed a small head, like that of a tiny ram. It seemed the ram had many little horns, but as Micah worked at it, he found that there were only two, and they were woven about with tinier, prickly vines, all of dark metal like the ram. The animal, no larger than Micah's hand, stood on its hind legs, looking plaintively heavenward, as though it struggled to be free of the thicket.

People had often found strange objects upon this mount—vessels and implements of various kinds. Some said they were holy, though they did not know where they came from. Rarely had any idols been found here. But surly this was an object of worship, hallowed by some long-dead soul.

Micah wondered if he ought to replace it in its little grave. He wondered if it was an omen, and if so, whether it was best to leave it alone. But, being a child, with a child's curiosity, he slipped it, instead, into a pouch upon his belt, and patted it fondly.

Returning to his duties, he joined the king and his men. But he told himself he must remember to ask what the statue was, when someone had time to look at it.

2

Adonizedek stood before the long brass mirror that hung on his chamber wall, turning himself this way and that. He liked what he saw. Across his shoulders lay his most sumptuous cape, edged in red fox and studded with gems. Proudly, he joined the golden clasp upon his chest, and held the edges of the cape away from his body like wings of a soaring hawk.

He was a handsome man. When he was uncertain of himself, he often stood before the mirror, assuring himself of the fact.

Tonight, he was not uncertain. Tonight he was full of anticipation, energized by prospects of what the next days would bring.

From his banquet hall, downstairs, music and laughter spilled through the corridors, ascending to his private room and igniting his spirit. Tonight he would announce to all the warlords of Canaan, guests beneath his roof, that an alliance was required, that if Joshua and his vagabond troops were to be stopped, the kings of all the land must go forth to meet him in unified strength.

The day after he met with his counselors on Mt. Moriah, he sent forth messengers throughout the region, as far away as Lebanon and the Great Sea, asking friends and foes alike to join him in Urushalim for a war conference.

He had expected a fine turnout, but none so grand as this. Not only were all western Amorite tribes represented in his glorious hall, but nations heretofore his enemies had sent their generals: Hittites from the nearby hill country, Perizzites from the Shephelah toward the coast, Hivites from Mt. Hermon in the north, and even the Jebusites, his greatest detractors and most competitive neighbors.

The party had been in full swing for half a day. Adonizedek had given the men time to loosen up, to put old animosities aside in the glow of wine and dazzling entertainment. Momentarily, he would make his appearance, and when he entered the room, ready to call for action, the crowd would be primed.

Smoothing his thick black hair, he smiled at the mirror again and snapped his fingers. Instantly, little Micah was at his side, holding forth his ceremonial diadem. Only the best adornment would do this evening, and as he bent down, allowing the boy to place the crown upon his head, he winked at the lad.

"Ashtartu be with my king," Micah whispered, backing away and bowing.

"Is there any doubt?" the monarch quipped. With this, he turned in a ripple of gown and cape and left the room.

In the hall, the king's counselors joined him. Together they set off for the grand announcement. Micah followed, hoping to catch every word from the vantage point of a corner balcony. Dashing upstairs, he nestled into a lofty alcove.

A more colorful gathering had surely never graced the court than that which lined a dozen long tables. Dialects of the Canaanite and Semite tongues rattled from wall to wall, as men garbed in the styles of diverse cultures met on common ground. Here dark-skinned caravaneers in flowing cloaks and smelling of camels drank with seamen in short-sleeved tunics. Garlic-breathed shepherds consulted with long-bearded city dwellers and pale-faced nobles from the northern forests.

The instant Adonizedek appeared, thunderous applause and foot stomping greeted him. As the king had hoped, hours of levity and war talk had brought the men to a peak of excitement. Wine and a mutual enemy had healed old hostilities and created camaraderie between previous competitors. All were eager for retribution.

Adonizedek, basking in the reception, let it continue for some time. At last, he raised his hands.

"Gentlemen, gentlemen!" he called. "I am honored."

Again, shouts and applause broke out, and toasts were raised all around. But, business must not be postponed.

"You all know that a demon is among us!" Adonizedek cried.

"Joshua!" the generals hissed. "Joshua and Israel!"

"Who can stand against the rulers of Canaan?" the king proclaimed. "Who can go against the warlords of the coast?"

"No one!" the men declared. "There are none so great as we!"

"Who is ready to defend our homeland?" he challenged. "Men of Lebanon, are you ready?"

A small group of Lebanese generals, dressed in leather vests and short kilts, leaped to their feet, hoisting goblets in the air.

Hurrahs ascended and the king listed, one by one, tribes of the coastal strip. "Trye, Sidon, Joppa!" he cried. "Are the men of the sea ready?"

Again, little throngs jumped up, waving their cups and assuring their devotions.

"Fellow Amorites!" came next, to which a tumultuous response rang forth, for these were kin of Adonizedek himself. White-turbaned dignitaries, their striped robes signifying various clans, shook their fists in the air.

"Hittites…Perizzites…" he went on, addressing a crowd of hook-nosed sheiks.

Once more, cries of unflinching zeal.

Then, the king named his arch-rivals, the Jebusites, and without hesitation they cheered.

There was one nation left to be named. Adonizedek had purposely saved it for last, as its tribes were comparatively unwarlike, having a reputation for diplomacy and compromise, rather than militance. It was his intention that, should they have any hesitance, they would be pressured by their fellow Canaanites to comply.

He need not have worried. When he called out, "Hivite!" the patriarchs of Chephirah, Beeroth and Kirjathjearim, three great tent cities, jumped to their feet. Hamor, the eldest of these generals, raised his turbaned head. Extremely confident and impulsive, this sunburned desert-dweller was also warmhearted to a fault, and if Adonizedek had been concerned about any of his fellow governors, it was he. But instantly, Hamor put such concerns to rest. "The Hivites are with you!" he cried, circling his goblet over his head and flashing it to the crowd.

At this, the throng gave its loudest hurrah. But Adonizedek looked from one Hivite face to another, counting and recounting them.

"Thank you, brother Hamor," he replied. "I am pleased that you are among us! But, Am I mistaken? It appears that one of your cities is missing."

Hamor's face reddened, and lowering his eyes, he turned to his fellow Hivites, who were likewise shamed. Shrugging, the old sheik gave a sheepish grin. "So it would seem," he stammered. "Perhaps they were detained."

"Detained?" the king growled, showing a row of pearly teeth. "Gibeon is only a morning's journey west of Urushalim. What could detain them?"

At this very moment, from a window of his balcony, Micah glimpsed a runner approaching from the west. Being the king's personal messenger, Micah dashed downstairs and crossed the broad court that fronted the palace.

"A message for my Lord?" he greeted the sweating herald.

"For Adonizedek, in the name of Ashtartu, from the court of Jasher, King of Gibeon," the runner panted. With this, he thrust a sealed parchment into the boy's hand.

One glance at the packet convinced Micah of its timeliness. Racing past the guards, he headed straight for the king's table, and falling to his knees, he passed the paper to an astonished Adonizedek.

As the king took it, he snarled, "There had better be good reason for this disruption!"

"Pardon, Your Highness," the boy said. "It comes with the seal of Gibeon!"

An astonished crowd awaited word of the contents. But, as the king read it, his face went white. Hands trembling, he let the note slip from his fingers.

But he regained his composure and took the dauntless stance. Surveying the guests, he began to call out names, each a fellow Amorite: "Hoham, king of Hebron! Piram, king of Jarmuth! Japhia, king of Lachish! And Debir, king of Eglon! Meet with me this hour in my chamber! The rest of you, make merry until I return!"

Then wheeling about, his cape slapping angrily, he left the hall, more bent on war than ever.

3

Adonizedek paced his chamber, his eyes flaming vengeance. In his fist was the letter Micah had presented, its broken seal nearly melting in his grip.

Jabbering and anxious, the four Amorite kings filed into his room, braced for news that Joshua had overrun Gibeon. As they gathered around the ruler of Urushalim, however, they were perplexed. "Why did you summon us, and not Hamor and his fellow Hivites?" they asked. "Should they not hear the plight of their brothers in Gibeon?"

"Plight?" Adonizedek huffed. "You will be pleased to know that our friends, the Gibeonites, are more than comfortable! There is no plight other than the one they have created for us and our allies!"

Bewildered, the Amorites took seats upon cushions that lined the chamber walls. "What has happened?" Piram asked. "Was there no attack on Gibeon?"

"This letter," the king replied, holding the sweaty parchment in the air, "comes from a friend of our court in Gibeon. He informs us that only yesterday Jasher and the men of Gibeon made a treaty with Joshua at Mt. Ebal!"

"Mt. Ebal?" the Amorites marveled. "That is four days north of Gibeon! What were they doing there?"

Smirking, Adonizedek explained, "Joshua retreated to Mt. Ebal after sacking Ai. He has been stationed there ever since. While we have been planning our war conference, while our allies traveled many days to join us, the limp-wristed Gibeonites were making their own journey...to make peace with the demon, Joshua!"

Incredulous, the Amorites shook their heads and muttered angrily. Pounding his fist upon the floor, the king of Hebron shouted, "Hivites! Sons of sheep! Always they fear a fight! Should we have expected any better of them?"

"True, Hoham," Japhir agreed. "But, how did they achieve this treaty? What could they have offered Joshua to keep him at bay?"

"Ha!" Adonizedek laughed. "You will never believe it! They offered themselves! They enslaved themselves to Joshua! And, without their knowledge or consent, they also enslaved the other Hivite cities, the very ones represented by the three patriarchs downstairs!"

"By all the gods!" Debir swore. "They have invited Joshua into our very midst!"

"You said it!" Adonizedek spat.

Japhir looked bemused, as if he did not quite believe the story. "How," he wondered, "did they maneuver this? How could they even have approached Joshua's camp without his snipers picking them off?"

"Ah," Adonizedek chuckled, "that is the most intriguing part. According to this letter, their feat was achieved by the vilest trickery. Before they left Gibeon, they dressed themselves in tattered clothes and worn out sandals. They put moldy bread in their knapsacks and poured wine into patched wineskins, to look as though they had traveled many days! They told Joshua that they were from a far country, one that desired peace, and not one of the Canaanite nations which he is bent on occupying. If they could get them to sign a treaty, and to swear by his god that he would not harm them, he would have their service, forever!"

"Weasels! Sons of spitting camels!" Hoham roared. "They lack even the nerve to be themselves!"

"It is only a matter of time before Joshua discovers the truth!" Debir exclaimed. "When he finds they are our neighbors, his anger will know no bounds. They will have called the fox directly to the nest!"

"And the traitors will be spared, while all of us lie in pools of blood!" Hoham groaned.

Rolling his eyes, Adonizedek sighed, "Come, come, Hoham! You think that Joshua will keep his treaty with such tricksters, when he learns the truth? It is my only comfort that he will turn his worst revenge upon the Gibeonites!"

Hoham was a wise fellow, and a deep thinker. He had done much research on Joshua and his followers. Perhaps he knew something about him which his allies had failed to learn.

"Friend," he said, raising his bushy eyebrows, "did you not say that Joshua had sworn by his god to keep peace with Gibeon?"

"Yes," Adonizedek replied. "But what god would hold him to such a promise?"

"Have you not heard that the god of Israel is a very demanding deity?" Hoham marveled. "He requires the strictest integrity of his people! Why, Joshua could no more go back on his promise than deny his own soul!"

The king of Urushalim studied Hoham intently.

"This god," he said, "do you know his name? I have asked my own prophets and they could tell me nothing about him."

Leaning forward, Hoham ran a gnarled finger over the intricate tiles of Adonizedek's floor. "I know a little, things I have heard from east of Jordan, from the people of Og and Bashan, before they were overrun. They say that Moses worshipped a god not of Egypt, but of much older times…a god of the Hebrews, they say…worshipped by the Israelites long before they were slaves to Pharaoh."

Recalling the legends, Hoham added, "Their religion invests great power in a strange container, which they carry with them at all times. It goes before them in battle, and is rumored to have incredible magic."

"Container?" the king marveled. "They carry their god in a container?"

"A box, actually," said Hoham. "They call it the Ark of the Covenant, or some such thing."

"A box!" the men hooted, trying to imagine such an artifact. "What kind of god lives in a box?"

"I do not say their god is in the box, only that the box is powerful. And," he warned, "I would not laugh. They say that box felled the walls of Jericho!"

At this, the room grew deathly quiet, and Adonizedek felt his hands grow cold.

"But, what of a name?" he asked again. "Does their god have a name?"

"There are different reports," Hoham replied. "They mainly refer to their god by their patriarchs, men of ancient times. They call him the 'god of Abraham, Isaac and Jacob,' founders of their nation."

Something in those names, especially in the first, rang familiar to Adonizedek. But he was anxious to hear more and spurred Hoham further. "There is no name for the god, himself?" he marveled.

"Several, actually," Hoham reported. "One might wonder if they have many gods, but really, they say, he is only one. They call him variously Elohim, El Shaddai, Yahweh…though the last they consider too holy, so they alter it to 'Jehovah.'"

Then, struck by a peculiar fact, Hoham looked in amazement at Adonizedek. "Why isn't that strange? These are all names of your own city's former kings!"

A chill of wonder shot through Urushalim's king. Before he could even ask, Hoham added one more name to the list.

"Why yes, they even call him Adoni!" Hoham exclaimed. "Isn't that odd?"

Amazed, the Amorite rulers murmured together, studying Adonizedek in wonder.

But none of them could have been more amazed than the king of Urushalim, himself. For it seemed a ghost had lain a hand upon his shoulder. And his soul shivered beneath its touch.

4

The meeting in the king's chamber was not meant for philosophizing, but for action. While the war conference continued in the banquet hall, plans for another battle, not against Joshua, but against the Gibeonites, fell together in Adonizedek's room.

Since it could not be expected that the Hivite patriarchs would turn on their own brothers, Adonizedek did not even inform them of the Gibeonite treachery.

"While the allies are gathering their troops to go against Joshua," the Amorites agreed, "we shall go against Gibeon! By the time our friends are ready to proceed, we will have made an example of those who join our enemy. No one will dare abandon our cause!"

So it was two days later, when the war banquet had ended and the allies headed home to fulfill their individual assignments, the king of Urushalim prepared to confront the foolish Hivites.

With the help of Micah and his other chamberlains, he laid out his battle garb. Upon his bed lay his leather breastplate, his studded leggings and his brass helmet. "Shine the spear and sharpen the sword!" he commanded, sending his servants this way and that. "And Micah, summon Dagar. I would have a word with him!"

Thinking that the king wished to ask the priest's blessing on his venture, Micah raced eagerly from the room. The boy respected the old holy man and believed in him utterly. If he invoked the name of Ashtartu, the battle would go well.

But when the hooded priest and the young boy returned to the king, they were both in for a disappointment. Adonizedek did not want a blessing.

"Dagar," he snapped, "completely apart from your feeble help. I have learned the name of the Israelite god! Perhaps, if I tell it to you, it will ring a bell of familiarity. Then, I should hope, you will be able to tell me something about him...something to help me in the upcoming battle!"

Chagrined, the seer bowed low, his hood falling across his face. "I will do my best," he said.

The king glowered. "It seems the god is called by the very names of our glorious kings!"

Standing up, Dagar looked astounded. "Kings of Urushalim?" he marveled.

"Exactly!" Adonizedek sniped. "Elohim, El Shaddai, Yahweh! Even Adoni!"

Confounded, the priest could only shrug. "I have never heard of this," he admitted.

Fuming, the king traipsed the room, badgering the old man. Despite his burning ears, the priest was lost in thought. "I know," he offered, "that at one time our kings were named for the gods of the city—at least for one god in particular."

Intrigued the king demanded, "Yes, yes, what god was that?"

"He is an enigma," the priest sighed. "I do not know him, other than to say he was the god of Abram, who sacrificed upon our mountain."

For a long moment, the monarch pondered this. "Our first king was Melchizedek?'

"Yes. A venerable man."

"And, this Abram, would he be the same as Abraham, whom the Israelites call their father?"

Dagar took a sharp breath. "That is a new thought," he stammered.

Adonizedek was too caught up in the unraveling mystery to sneer at the priest's ignorance. Turning from him, he walked to his chamber window and gazed across the hills of Canaan. To the north, the sky was still hazy with the dying smoke of Jericho and Ai.

Dagar, wishing to redeem himself, gave a weak defense. "Of course, we know that the Supreme Being, the highest of the gods, goes by many names. It is likely that many nations called him by the Israelite names in the distant past. I would not take the matter too seriously."

Wheeling on the priest, Adonizedek glared at him with wounded eyes.

Jerusalem—The City of God

"I have called you for help! Tomorrow, I go against Gibeon, and then against the very god of whom we speak! If you, Prophet of Ashtartu, can help no more than this, of what use are you?"

Dagar, looking helplessly at the floor, bit his lower lip.

Frustrated, the king sighed. "This Abraham...you taught me about him when I was a child," he recalled. "When you schooled me in the history of Urushalim."

"Yes," Dagar replied. "The city was called Salem in his day."

"He sacrificed his own son upon Moriah, did he not?"

"Yes...well, no," Dagar faltered. "The legend says that he offered him there, in obedience to the gods. But the gods rescued the lad, staying Abram's hand as he was about to slay him."

The story was but a dim memory to the king, who had filed it away in his head with a hundred other legends about the holy mount. Today, however, it seemed it might hold a key to secret doors.

As though he was a child again, he rehearsed the tale. "And the gods brought Abram a substitute," he recalled. "A sheep...no..."

"A ram," Dagar corrected, "its horns caught in a thicket."

At this, little Micah's heart jumped, and his hand flew to the pouch upon his belt, where he kept the tiny statue found on the mount.

The king, pondering the tale, only observed, "Such stories are unprecedented. There are many tales of the gods and their tests of humankind. This tells me nothing!"

"However," Dagar noted, "we may be incorrect in one matter. The people of Abram's time would not have said it was the 'gods' who rescued the lad, but The One True God, whom both he and Melchizedek worshipped. It was *that* god, and none other, who tested Abram."

"Very well," Adonizedek sighed. "But I am no better off knowing this!"

Abashed, the old priest stood with slumped shoulders.

But Micah sensed that it was no accident he had found the little ram upon Moriah. Slipping up to the king, he tugged on his robe.

"What is it?" the monarch snapped.

"Sir," the boy faltered, "I have found something…something which I am certain is meant for you."

"Yes?" the king growled.

Reaching into his pouch, the boy wrapped his hand around the statue. "I do not know if it bodes good or evil for your campaign," he said." But surely it comes for such a time as this."

Holding it forth, Micah uncurled his fingers and revealed the tiny ram, its horns entwined in the prickly thicket. Together the king and the priest drew near and peered down at the little creature. As one, they took sharp breaths and the priest gripped his chest.

Fearfully, the king reached out and touched the statue, stroking it with his fingers.

"Where did you find this?" he gasped.

"Upon Moriah, the day you met the warlords."

Glancing at the priest, whose face was white beneath his hood, the king whispered, "The day we plotted against Joshua."

"By all the stars!" Dagar groaned. Grabbing the little statue, he pushed it back into Micah's pouch and warned the king, "Take heed, my son. Joshua is a descendant of Abraham, and his god may have many rams in the thickets!"

5

What neither Dagar nor Adonizedek knew about the story of Abraham and the offering of his son, Isaac, upon Moriah, were the purpose and the reward of the test.

According to the Israelites, who now made inroads into Canaan, their patriarch had been tested by Yahweh to see if he were worthy to father a great nation.

Before Abraham had left Mesopotamia, it was said, The One True God had called him forth, giving him the promise of a land and a multitude of descendants to populate it. Those descendants, he had been told, would "bless the whole earth."

The test that called for him to offer up his son was more than a whimsical trail, set upon him by gloating deities. It was a test of his faith: Did he believe God capable of raising up children for him, if Isaac were no more? In fact, since Yahweh had said that Isaac alone was his heir, would God restore Isaac's life?

Years before, when Abraham had only begun to discern the voice of The One True God, he had been promised that a barren wife, Sarai, would give birth. As time passed, with no sign of such fulfillment, Abraham's fledgling faith had faltered.

Taking matters into his own hands, he had decided that perhaps God meant him to hasten the process. Other men had sons by their wives' handmaids. In this there was no shame, and the offspring were even considered the children of the legitimate wives.

Reasoning thus, he took Hagar, Sari's Egyptian maid, and Ishmael was born. Strong and beautiful, Ishmael was a delight to Abram's heart. But early on, the words of Yahweh concerning the lad were borne out. "He shall be a wild man," came a warning, "his hand against every man, and every man's hand against him."

Indeed, so disruptive was young Ishmael to the peace of the tribe, that after Isaac's birth, it was necessary to dismiss him and his mother.

"Through *Isaac* shall your descendants come," God reiterated.

Therefore, the offering called for upon Moriah was a sore test, indeed.

Exiled in Egypt for four centuries, the very descendants promised to the patriarch were now reentering Canaan, the land vouchsafed to Abram, renamed Abraham, "Father of a Multitude."

Their forefathers had endured their own tests, and the Israelites, or "children of Israel," (named for the son Isaac, called Jacob or Israel, "wrestler with God") were a hardy lot, tough as leather and hardened by a generation of wandering in the deserts of Sinai and Paran.

Now, they were back, ready to take up where Jacob had left off—back to reclaim the land which Abraham had been promised, but never owned.

Joshua, son of Nun, and right-hand man to Moses, was typical of their breed. Headstrong and physically powerful, he was without rival among the millions who followed him.

Today, Joshua sat upon his black steed, at the crest above Gibeon, surveying the valley of Ajalon and the pristine stream that wound through it toward the coast.

All night he and thirty thousand warriors, along with numerous supporting legions, had traveled from Gilgal, their encampment near the Jordan River, in answer to a summons from the Gibeonites. "Come up to us quickly, save us and help us," the message said, "for all the kings of the Amorites that dwell in the mountains are gathered together against us!"

Before the tent city of Gibeon was even visible from the wilderness highway, the sound of war ascended from the valley to meet the Israelite ears. By the time Joshua had his first glimpse of the Amorite camps, spread far to the west and south, and even encompassing Gibeon on the north, the noise of horrible slaughter and the smoke of burning fields and sheepfolds filled the air.

Joshua's dark eyes flamed with zeal, and his right hand shot into the air. Urgently, he called to his troops, shouting words that he had received from the Lord during the nighttime journey. "Fear them not!" he cried. "For I have delivered them into your hand! There shall not be a man of them left standing before you!"

Jerusalem—The City of God

At this, the entire company shouted, thousands and thousands of voices ringing with foretaste of triumph: "The battle is the Lord's! The Lord's and Joshua's!"

Then, on hooves of thunder, their chargers sped downhill, following the stream of Ajalon and chasing across the open valley toward the stunned Amorites. Like the rising sun, they spread over the plain. Shafts of vengeance carried on rays of morning from out of the east, they headed straight for Gibeon, parting only as they came near the city's log walls.

Unprepared, the Amorites stumbled before them, raising their weapons in futile gestures of self-defense. They, too, parted, some fleeing northwest toward Bethhoron, and the rest toward Azekah and Makkedah in the hill country due west of Urushalim.

Behind the pursuers and the fleeing armies, from what remained of devastated Gibeon, a great cheer arose, and the rescued Hivites joined the chase, adding their strength to the fray.

But what followed was far beyond what any Gibeonite could have prayed for. Not even Joshua, close as he was to Yahweh, anticipated the coming intervention.

As if the army of Israel, with its certain victory, had not done enough to punish the foolish Amorites, the sky itself sent forth a volley of ammunition. Huge stones, the size of cannon balls and larger, hurtled through the dawn air, as though dispatched by angelic catapults.

Pursuing the trail of the Amorites toward Bethhoron and all the way south toward Akedah, the stones pummeled the plains of Ajalon and Sorek, pocking the ground where they did not crash into the enemy itself, its war machines or horses.

※

Micah, the servant boy, stood behind a parapet of Urushalim's palace ramparts, his knees trembling. The great house of Adonizedek was ominously quiet; its many servants huddled behind closed doors and most of the guards away in the king's army.

ELLEN GUNDERSON TRAYLOR

The battle at Gibeon had been too far distant for its sound to reach the walls of the Amorite capital. But as the day progressed, a noise like a gathering storm had swept down from the north, and now repeated itself like clapping thunder from across the westward plain.

No one in the palace could make out the nature of the sounds, but now and then they were joined by cries, bloodcurdling and dreadful, carried inland on the wind.

"Mighty Ashtartu," the wide-eyed boy whispered, "be with my king!"

For hours, the lad watched the western sky from his lonely post. Above Urushalim and over the fields for miles about, the sky was vivid with sunlight. But far to the west there was a dark line, as though an oppressive cloud shrouded the horizon. Yet it was not exactly a cloud. It was blacker, and streaked down from space in jagged, moving lines, as though the heavens wept black tears.

When Micah had first noted the phenomenon, it had loomed above the valley of Ajalon, to the north. Over the intervening hours it had spread out, casting its dark shafts across many, many miles. Its trumpeting flashes seemed bent on crushing the earth beneath. Mesmerized, Micah watched the spreading din, until he was jolted by an aching voice.

"Son, you would do well to come down," Dagar called.

Wheeling about, the young boy fled to the priest's waiting arms, burying himself in the folds of the holyman's dark mantle.

"Oh, Dagar!" Micah cried. "What has become of our king?"

The priest looked above to the searing sky, and then scanned the black line that cloaked the west.

"The heavens are evil this day," he sighed. "It is an evil day for Urushalim."

❧

Now and then, people of the palace took courage to creep forth from their hiding places, but when they did, they grew more bewildered.

It seemed time had stood still.

Jerusalem—The City of God

All day, the sky was bright as noon. As suppertime approached, and the women servants crossed the court to draw water at the palace well, the pavement was still hot from the overhead sun.

A few times, Micah and Dagar returned to the wall, walking along the ramparts and surveying the horizon. The weird, saw-toothed storm still smudged the western vista, and there was no sign of troops, victorious or otherwise, returning to the capital.

But, at long last, when they were about to go down for their evening meal, a little young runner could be seen passing through the western gate.

Micah immediately recognized him as the messenger who had brought word, the night of the banquet, regarding the Gibeonite treachery. "I will go greet him," he offered, turning to leave the rampart.

But Dagar reached out and grabbed Micah's arm.

"Wait," the priest said. "Look, he is about to call out his message."

Indeed, it seemed the runner had a word for the entire palace, as he pulled a parchment from his sleeve and unfurled it.

"From Jasher, King of Gibeon," the boy cried, "to all those who would come against him! The arm of the Lord has spread from our enemies in ways mightier than when he overthrew Jericho! At the voice of Joshua, the sky itself has turned upon our enemies, sending forth giant hail! And at the voice of Joshua, the sun has stood still, to give light to his weapons! Take heed, therefore, all who would go against Israel! Thus commanded Joshua: 'Sun, stand thou upon Gibeon, and thou, moon, in the valley of Ajalon!' And the sun stood still and the moon stayed, so that Israel has avenged itself upon its enemies!"

Having read the message, which he would now take to all the cities of the hill country, the boy rolled up the scroll.

Then, directly to the vacant court of Urushalim, he announced, "As for your king, Adonizedek he has fled, he and the four Amorites with him, unto the hills of Makkedah! Has there ever been a day like this? Shall there ever be again, when the Lord hearkened unto one man's voice? For the Lord has fought for Israel!"

6

The road between Urushalim and the coast was the most beautiful in all of Canaan, passing through the gently rolling hills of the Shephelah, which in the spring was emerald green. The region was farmland, dotted with orchards and sumptuous vineyards. In fact, the name of Sorek Vale, its seaward stream paralleling that of Ajalon to the north, meant "excellent vine."

Although it was spring, that lush time of year when all the earth burst forth in majesty, the terrain was forebodingly quiet. No cloudlike clusters of sheep were visible in the wadis, no farmers worked the soil. The only life for miles was an occasional abandoned donkey, or a lonely cow, left to pasture by a fleeing owner, her udder dangerously swollen. And the signs of past life were puddles and streaks of blood left upon the fields by wounded soldiers.

Villages decimated by Joshua and his sweeping troops stood like wide-eyed ghost throughout the valley, devoid of inhabitants, their charred buildings belching acrid smoke across the landscape. But more fearsome than the silence, the smoke, or even the blood, were the strange gashes that marred the ground for miles in every direction.

Like scars, they riddled the earth, imprints of the giant hail that had volleyed out of heaven. Here and there a dead animal lay, victim to the pummeling, or the corpse of a battered soldier, left behind by his terrified comrades. Chariots, their wheels broken off and their axles jackknifed, lay in heaps at the ends of swerving ruts.

Little Micah, the king's runner, tried to shut out the surroundings, to keep his eyes straight ahead, as he raced down the highway. Dominating his mind was one overwhelming desire: to find Adonizedek.

To the south, a ridge of low hills bordered the highway, pocked with countless caves, home to innumerable wild beasts and, in inclement weather, shelter to local shepherds and their flocks. According to the messenger of Gibeon, the king and his comrades had fled into those very hills, the "hills of Makkedah." Doubtless they were holed up in one of the dark and gloomy caves, fearing for their lives, for Makkedah, the city that flanked the hills, meant "the herdsman's place," suggestive of such habitats.

His sturdy young heart pounding with adrenalin, his little limbs a blur of graceful speed, Micah veered left off the highway halfway between the capital and the coast. Along one ridge could be seen Makkedah's white stone houses, which had replaced the tents of earlier, less prosperous generations of herders. These buildings, like those of other villages he had passed, were charred and battered, but he hoped that some inhabitant had stayed behind, that he might learn something of the king's whereabouts. Darting up the incline that led to the town, he reached the low gate and stopped to catch his breath.

Incredible, he thought, *that the five leaders of Canaan's mightiest people have been put to flight by one army.* The Amorite hosts had been pursued and slaughtered across a seventeen-mile stretch from Gibeon to these hills, the survivors covering the distance in a few hours as desperation fueled their escape.

Praise Ashtartu, my king was spared! Micah thought. Joshua had now withdrawn, and there was a chance that Adonizedek could return to Urushalim.

The boy would not rest until he found his master, until he knew he was safe and on his way home. Scanning the debris of the wrecked village, he knew that the Israelites had left no niche unsearched in their quest for the Amorite kings. Sword-riven bodies lay in the doorways and toddlers wandered through the burning buildings, weeping for their dead mothers.

Yes, Joshua had shown no mercy, sparing neither woman nor child, infirm nor elderly. Annihilation here, as everywhere Joshua went, was complete.

Except that Adonizedek and his four allies had escaped.

Incredible as it seemed, Joshua had apparently departed Makkedah without those five royal trophies. Word had it that he had returned to the

Jordan, to his camp at Gigal. But no one was foolish enough to think that his scouts were not still on the lookout for the Amorites.

Micah only hoped he himself might find his king and persuade him to come home before the Israelites honed in on his exact hideout.

The boy's search for an informant in this bleak village was fruitless. Weeping children could tell him nothing, and the only other souls were an ancient crone, babbling to herself beside the village fountain, and a crazed looter, searching among his dead neighbors' belongings for a little gold.

Cringing, Micah hid behind a cocked door and surveyed the hills above. When neither the old woman nor the vandal were looking, he darted across the square on silent feet and set out for the highlands.

Barely did Micah feel himself a safe distance from the city, creeping along the edge of the cave-riddled hills, than raucous voices descended from the forest line. Falling back, the boy dipped behind a rock and stilled his breathing, trying to catch their words. The tongue, however, was foreign, and the joking men sounded inebriated. A chill went up Micah's spine, as he guessed that these were Israeli scouts, and their happy condition meant they celebrated some good fortune.

"Oh, my Lady!" Micah whispered, praying hopelessly to the goddess. "Is my king their prisoner?"

Dredging up a dose of courage, the boy started up the hill. The undergrowth was good cover. Adonizedek had been smart to choose a cave in such a secluded place.

But not smart enough to outwit his enemies.

Micah's worst fears were confirmed as he came upon a small clearing at the mouth of a cavern. Seated upon large stones, which they had apparently rolled in front of the cave, were half a dozen wine-swilling Hebrews. Dark and ruddy, their visages and their physiques exemplified the strength of Israel.

Micah shuddered as he realized the behind those great stones, inside that black cave his king was hostage. Barely breathing, the boy swallowed a cry of despair. He must be perfectly still, or he would be the next victim.

Jerusalem—The City of God

Day was wearing on. Soon the sun would set, and Micah wondered what the dark would hold. He was determined to stay put. He would not retreat until he saw his king—dead or alive.

Cradling his head upon a rock, he quivered in silence, waiting for the night, listening to the increasing hilarity of the guards.

What are they waiting for? He wondered. *Why do they keep the kings trapped, rather than killing them?*

As the men made merry, one word was often repeated, the only one Micah recognized. "Joshua," they often said, speaking joyously of their general.

Then, Micah understood. They waited for their leader, for the one who had sent them into the hills. It had likely been their mission, when all others had departed, to continue the search for the Amorites. Once they found them, they had sent word to Gilgal.

Joshua would soon be coming, to see their trophies and to reward them! Once he appeared, he would determine the fate of Adonizedek…and with him, the fate of Urushalim.

7

All that night, Micah hid behind the boulder. All but two of the Israelites had fallen into deep, sonorous sleep, drugged with wine. The sober duo, apparently the designated guards, descended the hill a way to stand lookout, not realizing they passed by the little spy.

At one point during the dark hours, knowing the sleeping drunkards would not hear him, the boy crept forth from his rock and tiptoed to the mouth of the cave. Holding very still, he pressed his ear against a crack in the barricade and listened for sounds of life.

It was mixed emotions that he heard low groaning within. Perhaps one of the kings had been wounded in his flight from the Israelites, or someone was troubled by fearsome dreams. Whichever, Micah prayed that Adonizedek was all right.

Placing his small hand on the blockade, he rubbed the stone with tender strokes, as though he caressed the king's forehead. But his gesture was useless. His master did not know he was here, and it was best that way.

Turning about, the boy looked upon his sleeping enemies with contemptuous eyes. Neither did *they* know he was here, and so he silently mocked them, tweeking his nose.

But suddenly, as if in response to that childish gesture, a loud cry ascended from the guards' station. Terrified, Micah was about to flee for higher ground when the cry rang out again. This time he realized the men were shouting for joy.

"Joshua!" they sang out, again and again. Tearing for his hideout, Micah slipped down behind the boulder. And just in time, for the drowsy soldiers now awoke, stumbling to their feet, laughing and clapping one another on the backs.

Dawn was breaking, sending pale streams of golden light through the forest branches. Suddenly, the entire hill was alive with celebration, and the guards' alarm was echoed by a thousand voices in the valley.

No, ten thousand voices and then more and more swelled in chorus, alerting the region that Joshua had arrived, and with him the hosts of Israel, returned from Gilgal to finish the task they had begun.

With the trampling of thunderous hooves and the clanking of bronze shields the army ascended the hill, weaving between the trees and singing as they came. At their head rode the handsome Joshua, the hated demon of the Amorites. To the young boy hidden beside the cave, he did indeed seem evil, his black hair and beard and his ebony mount arising out of the dark forest like the death angel.

When he arrived at the scene, the two guards and their fellow wine-bibbers fell face down upon the ground.

"Where are your prisoners?" the general demanded.

"In the cave, sir," the guards announced, rising to their knees.

"Open the mouth of the cave," Joshua ordered, "and bring out the five kings!"

At this, a triumphant shout filled the hill, echoed by the thousands further down, until the valley rang with the report.

In feverish glee, the six soldiers gathered about the cave's mouth, grappling with the huge stones they had rolled there. In seconds, they had removed them, revealing the dark opening and a huddle of pathetic Amorites.

Micah's breath came in a splinter as he laid eyes upon his king. Adonizedek, the first of the hostages to be dragged forth, staggered from his knees, squinting against the dawn. Terror had drained his face of color, and his lips were trembling white. His hair, his most regal attribute, was disheveled and moss-flecked, evidence of a sleepless night on an unworthy pillow. Nor was he able to stand without help, for he was weighted down by shackles, and to his chains were attached those of his fellow captives, so that the five kings had to move together.

Micah swallowed hard, his mouth dry as flax. How he longed to run to his master! But he dare not betray his own presence.

The events that followed were such a whirlwind, the boy could barely take them in.

Summoning the captors, the general bid them bring the hostages down the hill, and when they came to a clearing, where they might be seen by the Israelites, he faced his troops and his officers, crying, "Men of Israel! And all my captains! Come near! Put your feet upon the necks of your enemies!"

At this he motioned to the five Amorites, who had been thrust to the ground before him. From the ranks of the mighty host, a thousand captains came forth, gathering on the slope and passing, one by one, the prostrate foe.

Israel's show of power was a sight never to be forgotten, and one which little Micah would carry with him to his dying day. Having followed at a safe distance, the lad had slipped from bush to rock to tree trunk down the hill, and now observed, from behind a fallen limb, the humiliation of his people.

It had been dawn when Joshua arrived. It would be nearly noon when the last of the captains had set his sandaled foot upon the kings' bleeding necks. Nearly faint with hunger, fear, and despair, Micah looked on as the Israeli general summed up the proceedings.

"Fear not!" he called to his victorious comrades. "Be strong and courageous! For this is what the Lord intends for all your enemies!"

Beneath the high noon sun, the troops of Israel gave another mighty shout. Joshua stepped down from his black steed, drew forth his own sword, and held it over his trembling captives.

Micah knew what would follow. Unable to endure another second, he threw himself to the ground behind the limb and wept, not caring if anyone heard him.

But no one would hear. The army of Israel was too caught up in victory to noticed one small boy.

As the sword of Joshua gave five powerful lunges, evoking a volley of praise from forty thousand victors, Micah buried his head in his lap and cried aloud.

His hands were gripping his belt with white knuckles, and the pouch upon his girdle pressed against his breast. Fumbling with it, he tugged it off and threw it from him.

He had not thought of its contents since the day the hailstones fell, since the messenger of Gibeon reminded him of the might of Israel's god.

Just now, he remembered, and with horror he looked at the open pouch.

From its mouth the little ram peeked forth, the ram whose horns wound through a thicket.

As Micah stared at the omen, he rocked to and fro, cradling himself for want of a parent, and weeping for the king who was his father.

INTERLUDE

Urushalim was a favored city. Among all the cities of Canaan and all its neighboring city-states, it alone endured the Israeli onslaught without a drop of blood being shed in its streets.

During a decade of warfare, Joshua's campaign took a total of thirty-one kings with their cities and villages. Following the death of the five Amorite kings above Makkedah, Joshua zigzagged across Libnah, Lachish, Eglon, Hebron, and Debir. But he never actually set foot in Urushalim.

Records of those battles attested to the scope and magnitude of Joshua's conquest. The list of his victories read like a detailed map of Canaan as city after city fell before him, as colossal armies, confederations of many nations, confronted him on the plains, in the valleys, and on the mountains, from Gaza to Hermon, from Lebanon to the Salt Sea.

In one battle alone, two dozen kings came against him, meeting in the Valley of Mera with a total of nearly half a million soldiers, to put and end to Joshua's rampage. But, in typical fashion, they all fell in a single day, and their cities came under Joshua's rule.

In fact, from Makkedah on, any king who came against Joshua brought his city under the conqueror's sword, for not only was the king and his army destroyed, but Joshua entered into each city, killing off all remaining citizens, regardless of where its specific king had done battle.

But, though Joshua had destroyed Urushalim's allies, he did not attack the capital itself.

"For," he said, "the mountain of peace belongs to the most worthy of Israelites, to the children of Jacob and Rachel, little Benjamin."

The story of Judah, one of Jacob's twelve sons, was an impressive one. Though not the firstborn, he established himself as the leader among his brothers and often distinguished himself as a generous and self-sacrificing fellow, saving his brother Joseph from his murderous kin, and even offering himself as a slave to save his youngest brother, Benjamin, when the lad was falsely accused of thievery.

It was fitting that Judah's and Benjamin's descendants should inherit Urushalim, Benjamin as the primary citizen and Judah as the protector.

But Joshua left it to fate and the future to see just how they would attain it, allotting the valley south of the town to Judah, and the city proper to Benjamin.

⚬⚬⚬

The years immediately following the death of Adonizedek and the demise of the region's Amorite alliance witnessed a muddle of political interests vying for Urushalim.

At first, it seemed Canaanites of the north might take up where their brothers had left off. At one time, the city of Hazor had lorded it over the sacred city, and it seemed reasonable that it might regain its hold. But Hazor's king was busy, himself, summoning a confederacy of all Canaanites to go against Joshua.

Between wars, there was one group of people who maintained a jealous longing for the holy mount: the Jebusites, Adonizedek's most ardent competitors. When the king of Urushalim was slain, and when no Amorite came forth to take his place, the Jebusites saw their chance to move in.

And so they did, taking the undefended city with relative ease.

As for the sacred rock and the mountain that it crowned, the Jebusites continued to worship in the temple of Ashtartu, built on the western slope. They left the rock uncovered, and paid it little mind.

When the sons of Judah and Benjamin made their foray to take the city, which they considered theirs by divine right, they found that the inhabitants were not about to give up the town they had so long coveted, and which had come so "providentially." The Jebusites, related to the ancient Hittites, were a strong lot, and, though severely crippled by repeated Israeli onslaughts, they did not fall.

They were forced, however, to let Judah and Benjamin live beside them.

Hence was struck an uneasy coexistence, which would last for cen-

89

turies, Jebusite, and Israelite dwelling together, the one renaming the city "Jebus" and the other coveting to own it all.

Especially did Judah and Benjamin desire the holy mount. While the Jebusites passed unheeding by the rock day after day, on their way to worship in the flesh-house of Ashtartu, the children of Israel plotted to build their own temple on the foundation of the sacred stone.

Part III

ABDI—KHIPA

1350 B.C.E.

1

Gershon Ben Jamin, a handsome young Israeli, stood at the gate of the pine grove above the palace of Jebus and watched as twenty black-skinned Kassites unloaded a huge horse-drawn sledge. For a fleeting moment he had the peculiar sense that he had observed such a scene before, as though he had lived long ago in Egypt or was revisiting the days of his grandfather.

But this was not Egypt, and the black men were not Ethiopian slaves, forced to serve Pharaoh by the sweat of their brows. Gershon's grandfather had worked side by side with such fellows, when he had toiled upon the monumental projects of Egypt's king as an Israelite bondman, and Gershon had grown up on tales of such bondage and on the stories of Moses and Joshua, who had led his people to freedom.

Recalling those stories as he watched the removal of a huge limestone block from off the sledge, he marveled to think what his ancestors had endured.

As the Kassites worked wedges under the block, pounding them in with hammers and then sliding thick ropes in place beneath each corner, the sledge groaned as if in pain. But real pain would begin when the men attempted to slide the block off to the ground, a project that could take many hours of back-breaking agony and would tear through several ropes before completion.

Already the task of bringing the block from the main gate of Jebus up the road past Gihon Spring, past a citadel and palace to the hilltop, had taken a full week, to say nothing of the months involved in quarrying it at Megiddo and then transporting it seventy miles to the capital.

That work had fallen to Mesopotamian slaves recently captured across Jordan. The men who worked the block off the wagon were black mercenaries enrolled in Pharaoh's army. They were among hundreds of soldiers stationed with the Egyptian garrison at Jebus, and they were a rowdy lot.

The entrance of the gigantic block within the confines of the sacred pine grove was an historical moment. This great stone would be erected here as a permanent marker for all the world to see, a colossal stele upon which would be carved the emblems of Egypt and the name of its king, so that all might know that Pharaoh Amenhotep the Fourth had set his protective seal upon the city.

Because the task of moving the block was intriguing to watch, folks gathered around, stopping on their way to market or to worship. They had witnessed such ordeals many times, as gargantuan walls and edifices had multiplied at a rapid rate over the last generation.

If the people were less than enthusiastic for the Pharaoh's stele, it was because they bore him no great affection. Jebus had been a vassal of Egypt for two centuries. As territorial wars had raged and as provincial kings had traded the throne back and forth, it was clear that Egypt was the ultimate power. The fact that a new Pharaoh had taken the imperial crown made little difference to the locals one way or another.

To Gershon, more than to others looking on, the arrival of the stone was eventful, but not because of any loyalty to Egypt. To Gershon it was important because he had been hired to carve it into the monument Pharaoh had commissioned.

Gershon Ben Jamin was a stonecutter, one of such expertise and talent that he was often engaged to design and execute various royal works. Devotion to the honored subject was not essential to his projects. Only the love of stonecutting was necessary.

Such love had always set Gershon apart and had catapulted him to the rank of artisan par excellence, so that he was in demand throughout the empire and had been responsible for some of the most beautiful steles, statues, and murals in the world.

Gershon's renown had brought him wealth and opportunities most men never dreamed of. He had seen the capitals of the world, from Sinai to Babylon, and had traveled to Egypt on several occasions. He had achieved all of this by thirty-five years of age, making him one of the most accomplished young men of his day.

Certainly one of the most accomplished Israelites!

In fact, if there was any drawback to his lifestyle, it was the conflict it posed for his heritage and the struggle it produced within his spirit. He was a Benjamite by birth and a Hebrew in his heart. Sometimes it troubled him that his talents went to glorify the gods of Gentiles.

But he was quite successful at reasoning around such difficulties. This was his work, he told himself, his way of putting bread upon his family's table. If the God of Moses wished better for him, he would be glad to comply. But, what was a man to do? There was no call for a stonecutter in Israel, no holy work for his fingers to do, no temple for him to build or stele of righteousness for him to design.

Israel was still the newcomer, the invader, the outsider come to take over. In many cities, Israelites were the ruling class, but not in Jebus. Here they had settled for coexistence. Therefore, since the Jebusites bowed the knee to Pharaoh, the Benjamites and Judahites did likewise, causing no end of soul struggle for themselves, the sons of Pharaoh's ex-slaves.

Gershon could not live without stonecutting. Rocks and carving were the love of his life from childhood. One of his earliest memories was fondling the yellow pebbles in his mother's tiny yard. Despite the Mosaic law forbidding Israelites to make graven images, he had carved upon the malleable surfaces with bronze kitchen knife, making eyes and mouths and faces. Then he made little houses, constructing them of blocks as small as thumbnails.

His first money had been made by selling some of his crafts, dolls and animals carved for the local children. And the first compromise with his soul had come when he had taken the commission of Ashtartu's priest and produced a statue for their garden, a thigh-high representation of the goddess in clinging skirt and revealing bodice.

It was only a work of art, he told him himself. He tried to believe they would not pray to it.

That had been many years ago. Much work had come his way since then, and he had become quite comfortable with his choices. Already, as he watched the unloading of the gigantic monolith, he carved upon it with his dark eyes, peeling back its rugged surface to the pictographs and raised figures sleeping within it.

A thrill of excitement surged through him, and his fingers itched to begin the unveiling.

How he wished the might be alone with the rock! The irritating crowd pressed in about him, jostling for a view of the monolith. Suddenly the sledge jolted and with a mighty crash, the stone slipped from the ropes, careening to the ground. Without thought to those about him, Gershon pushed forward, racing to the site of the unceremonious landing.

"Fools!" He shouted at the Kassites. "Would you bring the rod of Pharaoh of your heads?"

The black soldiers scuffled among themselves, blaming one another for the mishap, while Gershon knelt besides the rock, running his hands tenderly over its rugged sides.

"Enough now!" he commanded. "Return to your post! The rock is unhurt!"

Calming a little, the soldiers gathered about the stonecutter. "Master Ben Jamin, we will raise it for you," they offered, trying to appease the royal artist.

"Do you know nothing?" Gershon growled. "It must be prone for me to work upon it! I will call you to turn it day by day, and you will raise it when I am done!"

Faces burning, the Kassites backed away and bowed, as the crowd laughed and jeered.

But Gershon paid none of them any mind, neither soldiers nor citizens. Eyes and faces beckoned from within the limestone core, and the time had come to call them forth.

2

A breeze from off Mt. Moriah drifted through the pile of limestone shavings that littered the ground at Gershon's feet and played loosely with the parchment in his hands. Placing the coarse paper upon his lap, the stonecutter pushed back a tousle of his dark hair and made yet another rendering of the design he intended for the stele. Then he held it to the sunlight.

Yes—this was better than the first two. This revision allowed room for a large disk to be carved above the heads of Amenhotep and his queen. Though the two royal figures would necessarily be positioned lower down upon the stele, to make a place for the sun disk, this would not diminish them, for it was believed that the emperor was, himself, the sun deity. Also, the libation vessel that he raised heavenward would obviously connect him with the disk.

Should anyone miss this point, Gershon planned to etch an oval cartouche above the emperor's head, with the words "son of the sun" emblazoned prominently. Upon the vessel, held aloft in Pharaoh's hands, would be written "giving life to Ra, the sun," and reaching for it would be representations of Amon, the divine offspring and his goddess, Mutt, peering forth from the disk.

Subtlety was not this Pharaoh's strong point. He actually renamed the supreme deity, claiming to be the incarnation of the sun, whom he called "Aten."

Of course, the polytheism of Egypt allowed for such manipulations. In all, the people of the Nile Valley worshipped thousands of gods.

Strange as it may have seemed, however, that culture came closer to monotheism than most, for they were quite single-minded in their devotion to the sun.

Keeping such matters straight was a challenge for an Israelite, but quite necessary in Gershon's line of work. He had to be certain never to slight the god or goddess of his employer, and so was more abreast than most commoners regarding the worldwide pantheon.

Jerusalem—The City of God

Rolling up the parchment, Gershon tucked it into his belt and took up his chisel and hammer to proceed with his work. Throwing a leg across the monolith, he straddled it like a horse and bent close to the top, focusing in on the area where the sundisk would be carved.

If he had had a choice, he would have worked in the privacy of a studio and not in the public pine grove. Not only was this a noisy place, with people coming and going on the market path, but it was the last stop off before Ashtartu's temple, and thus the site of much licentious activity.

Amid pines were erected numerous "baal," small statues like the one he had carved years ago for the priest' garden. These idols, which depicted various sexual acts, were meant to inspire worship of the Canaanite goddess, and in their very shadows the acts were mimicked by her shameless devotees.

Such distractions Gershon had learned to largely shut out, or he never could have perfected his art. More often than not, he was called upon to produce in such settings and had learned to practice selective deafness and blindness.

Likewise, the general bustle of the growing city could deter him. But so accustomed was Gershon to the noise of Jebus, he never would have been happy living like his ancestors did, those wandering Hebrews of the desert. As one of the second generation of Israelites to live in Canaan, he was used to city life. While tales of the wilderness years made for thrilling history and promoted ethnic pride, they were not a part of his personal past.

Therefore, while the pounding of hammers and the shouts of construction workers down the viaducts of Jebus could be distracting, they were the background of Gershon's daily routine. He would have been lost without them.

Just now, the noise of the laborers upon the citadel addition, a few blocks from the palace, was bedlam. Though the foundations of the great fortress dated back to the earliest inhabitants of the mount, it had been expanded and glorified by countless administrations. As the military establishment in the capital had grown through the years, so had the breadth and height of the mighty castle.

The city's present king was a Jebusite, a descendant of the aristocratic Hittites who had taken control of Urushalim when the Amorites were wiped out. He was only one example of the many cultures who had come to influence the city's direction. Gershon and his fellow Israelites did not love King Abdi-Khipa, but they tolerated him, just as they tolerated a host of divergent neighbors.

For some days now, the stonecutter had expected that the Jebusite monarch would be dropping by to inspect his work. When the sound of trumpets heralded the approach of a royal conveyance, Gershon set aside his tools and smoothed his garments. Taking a deep breath, he tried to look honored by the visit.

The court of Abdi-Khipa specialized in flourishes and fanfare. Arising from his palace, the king always burst upon the street with a retinue of tambourine-waving dancers and musicians playing small harps and blowing ramshorns.

Like the sun that Pharaoh adored, this petty vassal gleamed in golden garb and helmet-like headgear, his reddish Hittite hair and beard a mass of braids and perfect curls. Also like the sun, he was borne aloft on the shoulders of husky Sudanese slaves.

As much as he liked glitter, however, Abdi-Khipa was careful never to compare himself to the sun. Such blasphemy would only bring the wrath of Egypt on his head.

Of all Pharaoh's tributaries, Abdi-Khipa considered himself the most loyal. And why should he not? He had acquired the throne of Jebus, not through a hereditary line, but by the appointment of the emperor himself.

True, his family was among the elite of the southern Hittite race, having a clannish history dating back to the time of Abraham. They had been prominent in the founding of Hebron and other Canaanite centers. But Pharaoh was not obliged to consider the status of any provincial lineage, and Abdi-Khipa owed him everything.

Jerusalem—The City of God

When the king's approach was heralded, traffic on the market path came to a standstill and all those within earshot fell to their knees. People involved in the orgies of the grove likewise ceased their play, covered themselves, and crawled into the daylight.

As for Gershon, his obeisance was strained. For his own good, he also came forward and fell to his knees, but his adoration of the monarch was pure sham. To his mind, Abdi-Khipa was a poor example of royalty. Perhaps Pharaoh had handed him the throne because of his family connections, but Gershon doubted that the emperor had ever laid eyes upon him.

Spoiled from childhood, Abdi-Khipa would have made a bad impression. While he had the strong facial features common to his race, with high cheekbones and oversized nose, and while his body had the makings for Hittite strength, he was soft and sallow. A portly fellow, he loved food as much as anything, and assiduously avoided manual labor, not even learning the equestrian arts or the ways of self-defense that were common princely fare.

As a politician, he was no less of an avoider. When he was confirmed as king of Jebus by the Egyptian governor in residence at Gaza, he cared far more to be in good graces of Pharaoh and his fellow Canaanite kings than he did for the traditions and dreams of those who had gone before him. The legends and heritage of Salem meant no more to him than they had to the Amorites.

His name designated him a worshipper of Khipa, a popular regional goddess. Khipa, like her namesake, was transcultural and inoffensive to the polytheistic Egyptians. The use of the name, while clearly provincial, was so cosmopolitan and diplomatic.

To Gershon and his fellow Israelites, Abdi-Khipa was a pompous wimp, a spineless puppet of the empire.

"Good day, Your Majesty," Gershon greeted, still bowing to the ground as the king drew near.

Barely looking upon the stonecutter, Abdi-Khipa anxiously surveyed his handiwork.

"Down, down!" the king commanded, gesturing to his cab-bearers.

Instantly, the slaves lowered the conveyance to the ground, being careful not to let their own heads come level with the king's. Only when they were nearly prostrate did they release the poles and set the cab upon the pavement.

Using the back of one of the hunched slaves as a footstool, Abdi-Khipa stepped forth from the curtained carriage and went straight to the stele.

Only then did the crowd dare to look up and watch the king's inspection in tense silence. Gershon was a likeable chap. For his sake, they hoped the work was approved.

Walking alongside the fifteen-foot monolith, Abdi-Khipa made each step a show, slapping dust from the stone with his silk handkerchief and turning the corners on golden-slippered toes, like a dancer pirouetting. Above his head, at all times, was a tasseled umbrella, held in position by a slave.

Gershon looked away, for fear of laughing. *Old Bag of Beans!* He thought to himself. *You wouldn't know the true art if it stabbed you in the eye.*

But when the king turned to focus on the stonecutter, Gershon wore a sober face.

"I trust this humble work pleases my worthy king," he said, bowing again.

"Hmm," the king sighed, his tone high and nasal. "It is not nearly finished, of course."

Shrugging, Gershon looked amazed. "Why, Your Majesty, of course it is not! I have had only one week…"

"Yes, yes," Abdi-Khipa muttered, flicking a hand in the air. "Now, about the cartouches, they will be in cuneiform as well as hieroglyphs, will they not?"

"Indeed," Gershon assured him. "My king has commanded this, and so it will be."

"And the cuneiform, it will be Babylonian as well as Hittite?"

"As you wish," Gershon agreed, not having expected this. Instantly, he began to figure how he could cram so many labels onto the monument. Perhaps Abdi-Khipa paid him enough mind that he noticed the artist's hesitancy.

"You understand that our enemies must know Pharaoh has set his seal upon Jebus!" Abdi-Khipa snapped.

"I do . . . I do," Gershon said. "But surely Abdi-Khipa has no enemy strong enough to hurt him."

At this, the king was caught in mid-breath. If he disagrees, he would be admitting weakness. "Well said," he agreed. "But it has not been many years since the Mesopotamians tried to unseat us. We will do well to remind them, in their own language, of their feelings."

"Yes, Your Majesty," Gershon consented. "The eastern enemy shall read in yours and Egypt in theirs."

"Too good," Abdi-Khipa replied, delivering a syrupy smile. "Now," he added, as he wheeled again for his cab, "you will also add a note to the bottom."

"As you wish," Gershon answered, wondering where he would fit it.

"You will say, in letters bold enough to be appreciated, but not so bold as to outshine the Pharaoh, 'Abi-Khipa, King of Jebus, Guardian of the gods of Egypt...Pharaoh's sun, his sun; Pharaoh's gods, his gods.' Do you understand?"

Swallowing hard, Gershon felt his face go white. "I shall do my best," he stammered, avoiding the king's gaze. "Surely there is room..."

"There is room!" Abdi-Khapi snarled.

With this, he climbed into his cab and snapped the curtains shut. To the sound of ramshorns and tambourines, the slaves carried him away, to his gaudy palace and ill-won glory.

3

Gershon went home that evening with a headache. Try as he might, he could not figure how to accommodate all the king's demands without doing serious disservice to his art.

To add all the words in all languages Abdi-Khipa desired would require repositioning key elements of his design and would throw off the visual balance of the stele. Perhaps an evening beside his fire with a good glass of wine, followed by a night's sleep, would do wonders for his perspective. Hopefully, he would wake with some solution to the problem.

Gershon's home was in a posh district of downtown Jebus. Though there were many old buildings above Gihon Spring, his house was erected upon a recently constructed terrace, a good ten meters above bedrock. With several rooms for the family, it also included a guesthouse perched upon the flat roof, and from the vista of that roof could be seen the entire central square as well as Moriah looming above.

Passing by the citadel, the path to his home overlooked the city's defended gate, and a short distance from the spring were rock-tombs of deceased relatives, Israelites who had been among the first to enter Canaan, and whose success in the region had afforded them the finest burial chambers.

Gershon kept his head down as he passed beneath the fortress's guard towers. As always, it was manned by Kassi, some of he same men who had delivered the monolith to the pine grove. Gershon did not care for the Kassi, nor for the scurrilous insults they were prone to hurl at bypassing Israelites.

Though they would not dare to insult the royal stonecutter, they might not recognize him as such in the twilight. The fact that he turned toward the Israelite quarter would be enough to inspire invectives.

The Kassi were Pharaoh's hirelings. Though not always loyal to the empire in their hearts, they had no use for the Israelites, whom they considered to be runaways from Egyptian slavery.

Jerusalem—The City of God

Heading straight for his front door, Gershon ducked inside, happy to be greeted by the aroma of supper on the hearth and his wife's pleasant smile.

Rushing to him, Calia took his cloak and offered to remove his sandals.

As Gershon allowed her this service, he surveyed her dark curls and lithe figure with admiration. The two had been betrothed at childhood, but Gershon could not have found a more suitable mate, had he done two lifetimes of seeking.

Calia tossed Gershon's sandals in a corner and then reached up lovingly to pat his cheek. "You look tired," she noted. "Did you have a hard day?"

"Nothing to worry about," he hedged.

"You must tell me," she insisted. "Perhaps later. We have a guest for dinner tonight."

Gesturing to the parlor, she indicated another young Israelite who sat upon the floor, playing with Gershon's two children.

"Ellasar!" the stonecutter cried. "How good to see you!"

The visitor leaped up and embraced his friend. Similar to Gershon in appearance, his handsome dark looks were Judahite rather than Benjamite. But the two had grown up side by side in Jebus and could have been brothers.

Ellasar, however, had remained loyal to their heritage. Sometimes Gershon's chosen work had tested their friendship.

"You have been away," Gershon noted. "What a week or two?"

"More," Ellasar laughed. "And I have much to tell you!"

His quick glance into the kitchen indicated that such stories should hold until after dinner. But Gershon could hardly wait. Sending his children from the room, he leaned close to his friend and whispered, "Were you with the Khabiri?"

The term Khabiri, or "Hebrews," had, in recent years, come to mean more than wandering Israelites. Since the days of Joshua, as the twelve tribes had dispersed across Canaan, taking over town after town, Khabiri connoted guerrilla contingencies of the invaders. Detested by the

Canaanites, they were folk heroes to less adventuresome Israelites, and the tales of their daring forays made great popular fare.

This was especially true in Jebus, where local Israelites had settled for coexistence with pagans. Reports of ongoing takeovers by Khabiri were conscience-pricking, but nonetheless exciting.

Ellasar's involvement with the guerrillas was particularly intriguing, for he led a double life, posing as a traveling merchant but serving as a spy and an informant to marauders.

"Yes, I was with the Khabiri," Ellasar answered. "And it is time that you lent us a hand!"

Taking a sharp breath, Gershon found it hard to meet his friend's eyes. "You know I would do all I could…" he fumbled. "You know the position I am in…"

Just then, to his relief, Calia's voice rang from the kitchen, calling the men to eat.

"The night is warm," Ellasar said with a sigh. "Shall we take a walk after supper?"

"Fine," Gershon replied. "You shall tell me of your escapades."

"Escapades" was hardly an appropriate word for Ellasar's work as a spy. It was devotion to The One True God that drove him to risk life and limb in service to Israel, not boyish daring. But he was patient with Gershon, for whom he had abundant pity.

"You are missing out," he would often quip. "You sell yourself short when you divide your soul the way you do."

As the two walked in the moonlight, heading slowly up the market path, the stonecutter hoped Ellasar would not preach.

Looking about to be sure they were not followed, he prodded, "So tell me, Ellasar, what is the news? The last I heard, the king of Megiddo capitulated. What a strike for Israel, if that is true!"

"He not only capitulated, he has become one of our friends! He sent his own troops to surround Makkedah on our behalf, to the point that the people cannot leave the gates to work in their own fields!"

"Truly?" Gershon enthused. "How can this be?"

"Such things are happening throughout Canaan, my friend!" Ellasar declared. "Kings have been known to come out to our armies, eager to surrender without a fight. After all, they are not slow to learn. Many Canaanites have more fear of Jehovah than do our own people!"

Gershon hoped this was not meant as a personal barb. But it bit into his encrusted spirit quite smoothly.

Seeming not to notice, Ellasar went on. "Now the Canaanites are so suspicious of each other that each accuses the other of treachery, writing letters to Pharaoh himself, charging neighbors with subversion!" Ellasar's twinkling eyes betrayed the delight he took in all this.

"What about Othniel?" Gershon asked, referring to the man whom Israelites throughout Canaan considered to be their military leader. "We do not hear much of him lately."

At the name of Othniel, Ellasar's expression was even livelier. There had been many mighty warriors among the Israelites, but not since the time of Joshua had been so inspirational a hero as Othniel. In fact many Israelites, who wished to consider themselves a nation separate from all others dwelling in Canaan, called Othniel their governor or "judge."

Othniel had no palace and no throne, just as Israel had no central seat of power. His lordship was more a spiritual thing than a matter of crown or title, but he wielded as much influence over the scattered Israelites as any king of a localized city-state. And for those who longed for a tangible state of Israel, he was its representative—his wars were its wars and each of his victories brought their hopes one step closer to fulfillment.

Othniel had proven himself worthy of leadership about fifteen years earlier, when he had actually led an Israeli confederacy against an invader from the east. Shortly before Abdi-Khipa ascended the throne of Jebus, a horde from Mesopotamia, under King Chushan-risha-thaim, had made great strides toward overtaking Canaan. When armies of the local city-states had retreated in defeat and thousands of the native peoples had been hauled off into slavery, it was Othniel who was able to succeed.

Not waiting for the invaders to proceed further, he went out to meet Chushan-risha-thaim with tens of thousands of troops, representing all twelve Israeli tribes. Two brief days of fighting were followed by a rollicking chase, as Othniel and the Israelites drove Mesopotamians from the land.

Of course Israel, to the minds of the Canaanites, was still an invader itself. Without any formal government and no boundaried territory, it mattered not how powerful its hosts were. When it came to giving credit for the victory, the local kings who joined forces with Israel were considered heroes.

Israel however, knew the truth of the matter and did not forget Othniel. From that time until now he was their judge and governor.

Like Ellasar, Gershon revered the great militarist. In fact, both of the young Israelites had served under Othniel in the Mesopotamian campaign.

"General Othniel is alive and well," Ellasar chuckled. "Of that you can be sure! Although he does not any longer ride into battle with us, his strategies are behind every victory Israel has achieved in the last months. He seems to feel his talents are best used now behind the scenes, and he has some dandy plans!"

At this, it was Ellasar's turn to glance behind them, wanting to be certain there were no eavesdroppers lurking.

"It is this I wanted to discuss with you tonight," he went on, gripping Gershon's arm. "We need you, my friend, Israel needs you, now more than ever. You must agree to do what you can!"

Just as Gershon had feared, this talk was turning into an exhortation. But, Ellasar was not exactly preaching. This time, he seemed to have some specific request in mind.

Nervously, the stonecutter cleared his throat. "Why me?" he objected. "I am only one among thousands…"

When Ellasar's grip tightened, Gershon winced. "Very well," he muttered, "speak your mind."

Brightening, Ellasar proceeded, trying not to let enthusiasm out weigh caution. "You could be of great help," he explained, "because you, of all Israelites, are close to Abdi-Khipa!"

"What?" Gershon gasped. "Close to Abdi-Khipa? I am no such thing!"

"You are his artisan. You work directly for him."

"True," Gershon agreed. "But that does not make me his bosom friend! I have only been face-to-face with him on a couple of occasions, and actually my face was to the ground! He is the king of Jebus, you know!"

"King by default!" Ellasar spat. "If our fathers had had more courage, Judah and Benjamin would have *owned* Jebus long ago!"

When Gershon gave an exasperated sigh, Ellasar added, "Furthermore, this holy mount would not be 'Jebus,' but 'Salem,' as it *should* be!"

"All right, all right!" Gershon growled, holding up a hand to hush him. "Watch your voice! There are Kassi on the parapets!"

"Ah," Ellasar smiled, his teeth white in the moonlight, "the Kassi! Now we come to the point of my visit!"

Bewildered, Gershon stared at his animated friend. What the Kassi could have to do with all this, he had no idea.

"Listen," Ellasar went on. "You may not be Abdi-Khipa's companion, but you do have more access to him than any other Israelite we know. Here is the point, Gershon. Take heed."

Shooting a quick glance at the citadel and at the dark figures that dotted the ramparts, figures whose spears even now gleamed in the light of the moon, Ellasar drew very close to the stonecutter. The Kassi are rebelling!" he whispered.

Gershon jerked away, about to repeat the last word, when Ellasar clapped a hand over his mouth. "Ssh!" he warned. "Just listen! Yes, the Kassi are rebelling, against Abdi-Khipa to be sure, but mainly against their master!"

For a tense moment, silence hung between the two men.

"Their master?" Gershon breathed.

Ellasar only nodded.

"You mean…Pharaoh!" Gershon marveled.

"Think about it!" Ellasar enthused.

Gershon crinkled his brow and peered mutely at the tower guards. Then, with a shrug, "So? What have the Kassi and their little rebellion to do with Israel?"

"Everything!" Ellasar sighed, his pace quickening as they approached the pine grove. "Their discontent can help our cause! We just need to use it wisely."

When Gershon only stared at the ground, plodding quietly beside him, Ellasar threw up his hands. "Do you remember the raid on the caravan that was headed for Egypt two weeks ago?"

"At Ajalon?" Gershon recalled.

"The same," Ellasar replied. "Didn't you wonder how a small band of Khabiri could rob one of Abdi-Khipa's trains when it was guarded by one hundred Kassi? Think about it!" he repeated.

"I am thinking!" Gershon said through gritted teeth. "Are you saying that the Kassi were in cahoots with the robbers?"

"You said it!" he exclaimed. "With the robbers and with Othniel!"

"Othniel was behind that?"

"All the way!" Ellasar boasted.

Now Gershon's face was aglow. "That fox!" he said with a grin. "How did he pull that off?"

Of course, he referred to the collusion with the Kassi, and not to the robbery itself. Simple highway robbery was beneath Othniel, and certainly unworthy of his talents.

"It is only the beginning," Ellasar continued. "Othniel intends to use the Kassis' discontent to far greater advantage than anyone has imagined!"

Stopping beneath the pines, Ellasar pressed close. "Can you keep a secret, my friend?" he whispered. "I know you will."

"Of course," Gershon agreed, swept up in the intrigue, though against his better judgment.

"According to our sources," Ellasar whispered. "Jebus's entire Kassi contingent will soon be revolting!"

Amazed, Gershon shook his head. "Truly?" he gasped. "But, Jebus will be undefended!"

"Exactly!" Ellasar replied, slapping his friend upon the back.

The fact that troubled Gershon was a shining door to the likes of Ellasar. Not waiting for further reaction, the merchant-spy reached again for the stonecutter's arm.

"Now," he charged, "here is where a fellow like yourself will be most valuable. You must be alert to what transpires within the palace. Israel must be appraised at Jebus's weakest moment."

"So they can move in," Gershon surmised.

Gaping, Ellasar sighed, "They? Are you one of us or not?"

The two men stood in parted tension beneath the towering trees.

Ahead, just out of sight, lay the great stele to which Gershon had devoted so many hours of energy and labor. He was glad that his friend could not see it, did not know that it was there, and did not know the words he carved upon it.

Taking a deep breath, he choked back tears, feeling the weight of the heavens close in upon him.

Barely did he hear himself as he at last found his voice. And hardly could he be certain if he spoke from the heart or out of compulsion. But at last he answered, "I am one of you, my friend. I am with you."

4

Gershon may have hoped that the meeting with Ellasar would not materialize into anything of substance. But it seemed, over the next few days, that a floodgate of opportunity to serve Israel was opened, a gushing channel that would test the stonecutter's loyalties as they had never before been tested.

A few mornings after the moonlight talk, when he arrived at the pine grove to begin a day's work, a runner from the palace came seeking him, with word from the king.

Handing him a small roll of fine parchment, the boy waited as he opened it. "His Majesty, Abdi-Khipa, requires your presence in his stateroom," the note said. It was stamped at the bottom with the seal of Jebus, but said nothing more.

Gershon nodded to the runner. "I will be there immediately," he said. "Tell the king."

With this, the boy bowed quickly and turned again for the palace. Gershon, who had just laid out his tools, replaced them in his pouch, muttering to himself about the inconvenience.

Then it occurred to him that the king might have reconsidered and realized the impossibility of the demands he had placed on the artist. Maybe he was rescinding the order to include the Babylonian cuneiform.

Gershon had been in the palace more than once. As the "royal artisan," he had overseen many works within the court, executing them himself or supervising a group of lesser craftsmen in the production of mosaic floors, stone fountains, murals and numerous statues. As for actually meeting the king, however, he had done so rarely.

He was comfortable with that fact. So little did he respect Abdi-Khipa that the less his personal involvement, the better. He must be courteous, however, and tried to wear a pleasant face as he passed beneath the towering palace wall and ascended the ramp leading past the guards.

He showed the sentinels the note he had just received, and they waved him on. But these fellows were not the usual gatekeepers. Always before, two black Kassi had guarded the entrance. Today, the guards appeared to be Hittite, like the king himself.

Gershon, sensitive to this change, glanced above to the parapets. Only last night they had been manned, likewise, by Kassi, but today the troops stationed along the ramparts were light-skinned.

Suddenly, Gershon wondered if there was more at stake in his visit than the artistic design of a stele.

The stateroom was at the center of the palace, just beyond the main courtyard. As Gershon neared the enclosed garden, he was hailed by the king's chief steward. A pleasant fellow, this elderly gentleman had served under several administrations, and despite his servant status, wielded nearly as much influence over daily palace matters as did the king himself.

"Master Ben Jamin," he greeted, "good to see you. Come this way." Leading him through the courtyard and to a small veranda adjoining the stateroom, the steward bowed.

"His Majesty will see you shortly,' he said. Then, glancing past yet other Hittite guard who stood watch at the stateroom door, he gave a nervous sigh and shook his head.

Gershon sensed more than ever that something was amiss, but figuring that the steward's perplexity was none of his concern, he pretended not to notice and studied the potted flowers arranged on the porch.

For a quick moment, the steward stepped away, conferring with the guards, and then returned, rubbing his hands together. "Wait here, won't you?" he offered, indicating a bench that fronted the porch.

When Gershon had seated himself, the steward rushed away, darting a worried glance toward the council chamber.

Today, the stateroom door was open, as often as it was closed, due to the hurried comings and goings of numerous persons. These advisors of Abdi-Khipa bore ominous expressions as they ran to and fro on commissions of apparent urgency, and seemed unaware that a mere stonecutter was thus privy to happenings within the great room.

Had this scene occurred a week ago, Gershon would have kept his eyes averted, having not much concern about what transpired. But since talking with Ellasar, he was acutely interested, and caught what he could of the proceedings.

Voices sometimes rang forth from the room, as the door swung in and out, and only a deaf man could have missed the talk. Their accents gave away the fact that Abdi-Khipa entertained Egyptians this day, though the entertainment was not merry.

On one occasion, an especially preoccupied counselor entered the room, throwing open the door so wide that Gershon could actually identify one visitor. Paura, the *rabis sharri*, or the regional governor, was fully visible, dressed in the red-and-white-striped headdress of his office. Tall and dignified, he paced before Abdi-Khipa's throne, his short, kilt-like skirt slapping angrily. Upon his brow was a bronze band, snake-shaped and terminating in the head of a python. Only the provincial governors of Egypt were allowed to wear the royal symbol and Paura bore it proudly, his bronze skin and haughty, clean-shaven features setting it off perfectly.

But Paura's face was also red with indignation. Abdi-Khipa was giving him an earful, and he did not appreciate his tone.

"You accuse me of being a rebel?" the Hittite flared, his nasal voice rising as he pounded his stubby fists upon the arms of his throne. "It was not I, nor even my father or mother who gave me my crown! It was the strong arm of Pharaoh who gave me this territory! Why, then, should I, of all people, rebel against Egypt?"

At this, Paura ceased his pacing, and silence fell across the room. Gershon, his ears burning to hear more, sat tensely upon his bench, trying to appear nonchalant.

Suddenly, the guards, remembering his presence, stepped to the door and pulled it shut.

But again, with Hittite and Egyptian counselors coming and going, the swinging door put Gershon in a spying position.

Nor could the guards remove him. He had been placed here by the king's steward, and that was as good as a royal carte blanche. Bits of information, thus received, quickly explained the palace's tense atmosphere.

"It is not I who am your enemy!" Abdi-Khipa raged. "You would do well to look at who the real enemy is!"

When, in the next breath, the word "Khabiri" was spoken, Gershon's skin prickled. "You accuse me of rebellion simply because I say you favor the Khabiri and injure the tributary princes!" the king went on. "Don't you see that the Jebusite realm and all the territory of Canaan is being ruined? Pharaoh's lands are being ruined! At one time there was an Egyptian garrison stationed here. Then they were removed by Pharaoh's deputy and replaced by these renegade Kassi! Let Pharaoh take thought and trouble for his land, or this whole territory will disappear!"

Ah, there it was, the Khabiri and the Kassi linked within one condemning statement.

From the sound of things, Abdi-Khipa had left the throne and had joined Paura. Pacing back and forth he continued to rave, until Gershon wondered if overhearing all this was putting him at personal risk.

But, determined to catch what he could, he stayed firmly planted on the veranda bench. "Are you writing this down?" the king was heard to say. Apparently a scribe had been commissioned to take notes, for the court records perhaps.

But Paura objected, "Pharaoh is aware of all that goes on here. There is no need to send him letter after letter!"

So, Abdi-Khipa intended to notify the emperor of these things. And that made Paura nervous!

"I would go to Tell el Amarna myself, to the emperor's capital, to confront him directly!" Abdi-Khipa responded. "But I dare not leave Jebus when there is no garrison stationed here! I shall indeed warn Pharaoh, by every means possible! For without royal troops, this territory will be wasted by Khabiri!"

Like a net of needles, this news descended upon Gershon. What was the king saying? Had the Kassi revolted overnight? Were there now no black troops housed in Jebus?

Folding his arms across his stomach, Gershon controlled his jitters. Indeed, he had seen no sentinels upon the ramparts this morning, or anywhere upon the palace grounds! "Do not be sure of yourself," Paura snapped. "Remember your position! The emperor was not pleased that his caravan was robbed in Ajalon—a caravan you were responsible for!"

Gershon's eyes widened. He could not help but dart a curious glance toward the door. But the guards were growing nervous, and shut it again, looking up and down the hall. Probably they hoped the steward would return, so that the stonecutter would be removed.

Abdi-Khipa was nearly shrieking now, and no door could have baffled that sound. "You blame me for that?" he cried. "I am innocent in that affair! The Kassi had to be in league with the robbers! They prove so by their insurrection! Yes, Adaya and Othniel! Strange bedfellows, to be sure! And I suppose that next you will blame me for the insurrection, as well!"

Barely could Gershon keep his seat. It was all he could do to keep from running from the palace, to find Ellasar and share all of what he heard.

Adaya was chief of the Kassi garrison. The fact that the government now linked him with General Othniel was surely important news, and not a little unnerving.

But Gershon had no time to consider escape. Suddenly, the stateroom door flew open, and Paura came storming into the hallway, followed by a flock of chattering advisors and scroll-bearing Egyptian scribes.

"I have heard enough!" he shouted over his shoulder. "You, King Abdi-Khipa, have but one responsibility. Adaya has revolted! Hold the town!"

With this, the official exited, leaving the stateroom in mayhem. There was no way the guards could undo the stonecutter's grasp on these matters. And actually, the fact of his presence was soon overshadowed, as a flood of Hittites swarmed out from the chamber, red-faced and clamoring about the squat Jebussite king.

"Do not fear, Majesty," they jabbered. "We will summon troops, more than enough troops! Jebus will be secure! Rest assured!"

Dispersing throughout the palace, the advisors went this way and that

Jerusalem—The City of God

to see to internal safety, and the king disappeared toward his private quarters in a cloud of fretting servants.

The stonecutter had been forgotten. Whatever errand he had been summoned for, it too had been forgotten.

Even the guards had disappeared, and there was no steward in sight.

Shrugging, Gershon stood up from the opportune bench, smoothed his robe, and cleared his throat. Like a cat, he slipped along the walls until he had reached the palace gate, and on quick feet he gained the street.

He must find Ellasar. Timing was everything.

5

This time Ellasar and Gershon did not talk beneath the light of the moon, or in the openness of a pine grove. This time they met behind the closed door of the stonecutter's cottage and spoke in private tones before his midday fire.

Calia kept to her own business in the kitchen and the children were at play when Gershon broached the urgent matters he had to share.

"It was as if a book of government secrets had been laid bare before my eyes!" Gershon enthused. "As though I had been brought into the inner sanctum, so much did I hear!"

"Adaya has revolted!" Ellasar marveled. "We expected this, but not so soon!"

"Yes," Gershon assured him. "And it must have been a quiet rebellion. They must have simply abandoned their posts in the middle of the night!"

"Wonderful!" the merchant exclaimed. "But where would they have gone?"

"Probably not far," Gershon reasoned. "Abdi-Khipa links them closely with the Khabiri, they must be immediate threat to Jebus!"

"So," Ellasar said, his teeth gleaming, "the king is pleading for reinforcements! Egyptian reinforcements!"

"That was his greatest concern," Gershon agreed. "But Paura was not prone to helping out."

The merchant thought a moment, his brow knit. "Still, I cannot believe Egypt will not comply. Jebus may not be Pharaoh's richest tributary, but it is the capital of Canaan. They will not leave it undefended."

Gershon nodded. "Either way," he whispered, "it is time for Israel to move!"

Ellasar sat back and gave a wondering look. "Do you hear yourself, my friend," he laughed. "Spoken like a true Khabiri!"

A tinge of apprehension moved up Gershon's spine. Indeed, he hardly knew himself these days. But he could have done without Ellasar's next directive.

"The next time you are summoned to the palace, listen for any hint that a garrison is on its way, he instructed. "With the Kassi to help us, we will waylay it."

Stunned, Gershon sat up stiffly, pulling like a fish against a net. "What makes you think I will be summoned again?' he asked. "Whatever reason they had to call me, they have much more important matters to deal with now."

Those words might have been a cue, so closely followed were they by a knock upon the cottage door.

Cringing like a fugitive, Gershon stared mutely at the entry until Ellasar tapped him on the knee. "You had better see who it is," the merchant muttered, nodding his head toward the door. "And act natural!"

Ellasar's advice was well taken. When Gershon opened the door to find the king's steward standing in the shadows, it was good that he was as poised as possible.

The steward was jumpy enough as it was.

"Master Ben Jamin!" he gasped, his eyes wide and anxious. "I am glad you are home! I fear you were badly treated today!"

"Badly treated?" Gershon marveled. "Why no, not at all." Then, sidling outside and drawing the door closed, he hoped the merchant-spy had not been seen. Ellasar's double-identity was not suspected in Jebus, but one could not be too careful.

"I did not mean to abandon you," the steward went on, rubbing his fretful hands together. "It is just...well, matters were somewhat..."

"No problem," Gershon replied. "I feared it was I who abandoned you. But when you did not return..." With this he gave an innocent shrug.

'No, no!" the steward jumped in. "You were right to go your way.

Then, in a clever attempt to learn just what Gershon might have overheard, he said, "I only hope you did not wait long."

"Not at all!" Gershon lied. "The guards seemed to think you were detained. So I planned to come again tomorrow."

"Yes!" the steward sighed, his thin face lit with relief. "That is a good idea. Abdi-Khipa does wish to see you, most urgently! Tomorrow is not too soon!"

"Very well," Gershon agreed, as the steward bowed and headed for the street. But, suddenly, he returned, fidgeting with his skinny beard. "I, uh, told the king I sent you on your way. You understand?"

Grasping the gist, Gershon chuckled. "What else?" he replied. "Would the king's steward leave a commoner within earshot of the stateroom door?"

In the past, Gershon had tiptoed around Jebus politics, serving whatever wind blew for the sake of his "art." In the past, he had served Abdi-Khipa, but now he moved in opposition to him.

Since overhearing the king's courageous diatribe against Egypt, the stonecutter had gained a little respect for the pompous Hittite. But that newfound respect was ill-timed.

Gershon now served in a different court—the court of Israel's best interest.

As he stood, today, in the king's stateroom, the same room which only yesterday sparked with foment, he wondered what the Hittite wished of him, and if it would challenge his new commitment.

Abdi-Khipa toyed with the gold fringe of his tunic and glanced out the arched window of his chamber toward Mt. Moriah. "How goes the project, Ben Jamin?" he inquired.

"The stele is progressing as well as can be expected," the stonecutter replied. "It has been a challenge, making room for the three languages without undue harm to the design. But I think it is coming along."

"The three languages," Abdi-Khipa said with a nod. "Very good. But that is what I must discuss. I have decided that it will not be necessary to use the Babylonian text, after all."

Amazed, Gershon was a mixture of responses. Part of him was, of course, relieved to hear this. He had not, in truth, found a way to include the cuneiform without straining the art, and so had progressed very slowly with that order. Another part of him, however, was frustrated by the king's vacillation.

Jerusalem—The City of God

Bowing his head, he tried to be calm, "Very well, Majesty," he said. "But, may I ask why you have changed your mind?"

Abdi-Khipa stroked his red beard, not a little agitated by the artist's presumption. "You may," he snapped. "But it should be obvious, especially to an Israelite."

His tone was biting, and Gershon wondered what his own race had to do with the change.

When the king saw that the answer was not at all obvious, he sighed. "Dear man, I had thought to include the cuneiform as a warning to our enemies, the Mesopotamians—to put our praise of Egypt in their language, that they might see where our power derives, and take heed. But, recent days have proven that we have a far more dreadful enemy than the empire to the east. Jebus's greatest enemy now moves among us and all about us. You know of whom I speak!"

Suddenly, Gershon feared that his summons to the court bore directly on his heritage, that he was being singled out as an influential Israelite, and that his loyalties were more at stake than he had imagined.

"Sire," he choked, "I am a man of Israel. Some of my brethren have, indeed, caused trouble for Canaan. But, surely, you do not think that I, a citizen of Jebus, am among them!"

The king's response came as another relief, and as a surprise. Gaping at the stonecutter, he laughed. "Relax, Ben Jamin. If I had ever suspected you of such collusion, would I have made you chief artisan of my realm?"

So easily dismissed was the notion that the answer was almost insulting. Gershon breathed easier, despite a stab of shame that past choices had so widely removed him from connection with Israel.

As the king went on, the stonecutter bit his lower lip.

"In fact," Abdi-Khipa was saying, "it is because of your race that you can be most useful to me, now."

Rising from his throne, the king walked to the archway and gazed toward the pine grove, where the stele was waiting.

"The same warnings that would have been put in Babylonian shall now be written in Hebrew," he commanded. "How providential that my royal artist knows that language and that alphabet! Don't you think, Ben Jamin?"

With this, he turned about and eyed the stonecutter, whose face was parchment white.

"Providential, indeed," Gershon croaked, his throat tight as a tourniquet.

"Good," that king enthused, sitting again on his throne. "Furthermore, regarding the words I told you to place at the bottom, 'Abdi-Khipa, King of Jebus, Guardian of the gods of Egypt…,'"

"Pharaoh's sun, his sun; Pharaoh's gods, his gods,'" Gershon joined in.

"They are to be in much larger script than before," the king ordered.

In the past, Gershon's main concern would have been that this made space upon the stele even more limited, and that his design would be even more seriously impaired than before. But today, his primary disappointment was that his love of Israel was being tested.

How could he any longer endorse the gods of Egypt, especially using the sacred tongue of his ancestors to do so?

But Abdi-Khipa was oblivious to his quandary. "How quickly can you execute this?" he asked.

Swallowing hard, Gershon inquired, "Is there a great hurry, Majesty?"

For the first time in this meeting, the king's eyes flashed anger.

"Can you ask this, when the realm is daily threatened? Of course, there is a hurry! All of Israel must know that Egypt stands behind us, and when the troops of Pharaoh arrive, they too shall know our devotion!"

Ah, there was a clue! Trying not to arouse suspicion, Gershon shrugged. "The troops of Pharaoh?" he muttered. "The Kassi know your devotion."

"Kassi! Kassi!" Abdi-Khipa snarled. "I care not for the Kassi! Make the words bold enough for the eyes of troops arriving from the south! Bold enough for them to see from the borders of Gaza and the highway of Ashkelon! And make them quickly, before they can say, 'We came upon a weak king, a king without a stele, a king without the seal of Egypt upon his holy mount!'"

6

The troops of Egypt never arrived in Jebus. As soon as the palace spy, Gershon Ben Jamin, got word to Ellasar to watch the highway from Ashkelon, convoys of Kassi and bands of Israeli guerrillas stationed themselves in the highlands along the route. These two groups constituted an army of thousands, and added to them were troops of converted kingship like Gezer, Lachish, and Ashkelon itself.

These outposts sent provisions to the mountain hideouts, and even as they awaited the arrival of the Egyptian garrison, towns not yet conquered came out to join the Khabiri, yielding their land without a fight.

In fact, so quickly did things degenerate for Abdi-Khipa, that if the Egyptians had arrived, they would have found him nearly alone in his loyalty to the empire.

In pathetic letter after letter to Pharaoh, Abdi-Khipa pleaded for help. "Let Pharaoh care for his land," he begged. "It is all hostile from Gaza to Mt. Carmel, and many of your loyal kings have been slain."

The vanquished garrison was waylayed just inside the southern border, and was actually abducted by the king of Gaza into his own territory. What became of them from that point was dreadful to speculate.

Suffice it to say that in one of his last letters to the emperor, Abdi-Khipa gave the most pitiful plea of all: "If Pharaoh cannot send troops, let him fetch away Abdi-Khipa and his clansmen, that they may die before the throne of Egypt."

Such a death would doubtless have been preferable to the one that awaited the king when the Judahites and Benjamites of Jebus took courage from their brothers and stormed the palace. Taken outside the city walls, Abdi-Khipa was thrown headlong to the floor of Gehenna Vale, and all his counselors were hung.

Few Israelites remained neutral as Jebus was torched and blood was spiked for the first time in her streets. In fact, abstainers from the cause were chased down, slain in their homes, in the gutters, and in the marketplace.

At last, Jebus was in Israeli hands. For the first time since the days of Abraham, Jehovah would be worshipped openly in the city, and the flags of Abraham's descendants waved from the ramparts.

As for Gershon, he became a legend for life-risking loyalty among the people of Israel, and the stele that had tested him became a popular anomaly. Erected upon Moriah at his instruction, after the demise of Abdi-Khipa, it was cause for admiring grins and ethnic pride for years to come. For, interspersed between the Egyptian and Hittite script, which praised the gods of Pharaoh, were strange Hebrew letters, praising the God of Abraham, Isaac, and Jacob.

And at the bottom, where Abdi-Khipa would have been remembered, were other Hebrew letters: "Design by Gershon Ben Jamin, a child of Israel—Israel's faith, his faith; Israel's God, his God."

Part IV

The Son of Jesse

1027—1020 B.C.E.

1

A velvet hush, like the whisper of a kingly robe, settled over the hills southwest of Jebus. It was the sound of a desert evening, which was the absence of sound, to which shepherds were accustomed.

On smooth, speckled wings, a hawk soared, just arising from his daytime rest to dance with the lavender sky. His eyes keen as torches, he surveyed the terrain, in wait for the wee, scurrying beasts who found their burrows too late, or for tiny lambs separated from their mothers.

Far below, a campfire lit a hollow, where a group of shepherds huddled. They did not see the hawk or discern his quiet passage overhead, but they were alert to more formidable predators, and they knew the nature of the silence.

To those unused to such quietness, the solitude and the hush could be deceiving. But the very need for shepherds meant there were dangers in the hollows and the wide spaces, dangers with which city-dwellers did not contend.

As the young men prodded the embers of their fire, they were at all times aware of their duty and that, just as the fire was their only barrier against a vacuum of darkness, so were they the only protection their docile flock had against lions and hyenas who stalked the night.

The shepherds' ears were trained to the slightest invasion of the silence. Here a bell tinkled as a dozing ewe turned in her sleep. There a rustle in nearby brush tolled the demise of some small varmint, victim to the forked tongue of a nocturnal snake. Neither sound was cause for alarm, but any noise to follow could be.

Despite the dangers of the duty, no shepherd born to the task would trade the purple dusk for a royal mantle, or the freedom of tents and open skies for the confines of streets and plastered ceilings.

Besides, shepherds in the hills of Ephrata, where these fellows spent their time, had the best of both worlds. From the vantage point of their dusty trails could be seen the highways that linked Jebus with the mighty city Hebron and, further south, Egypt. With a quick hike, they could be in touch with caravans coming and going between Babylon and Phoenicia. They could speak with merchants in shady oases if they desired news of the broader realm.

Then, just as easily, they could retreat, to the quaint simplicity of their sage-scented hills.

There were dozens of such campfires and groups of shepherds clustered across the Ephrata ridge this night. The ones who sat beneath the hawk's path were the sons of one man, Jesse Ben Obed of Bethlehem, in the province of Judah.

They were a strapping lot, these seven—rugged and windblown as the earth that had nurtured them. Each was tall and handsome, adored by the village maidens and respected by his rivals.

As was their custom when night closed in, and they sat exposed to the black unknown, they traded stories of daring feats and encounters with the predators that haunted the desert. The tales were not new. Most had been told and retold, embellished each time, to make the hero more heroic and the beast more fearsome, evoking laughs and jibes, as the brothers tried to undo one another.

The stories were more than male bragging, more than fireside entertainment. They served to alleviate unspoken apprehensions, to encourage them in darks hours that could make any man feel small.

For the people of Israel, dispersed as they were across the land of their enemies, it was easy to feel small. Especially when there were remnants of giant races sprinkled among the Canaanites—ancient races like the Rephaiim, the Anakim, and the Zamzummim, who had once predominated in the mountains.

When the children of Israel had first approached Canaan, after Moses had led them out of Egypt, they had been confronted with these titans. Joshua and his fellow spies, sent to survey the region, had returned with tales of colossal men, clothed in animal skins and bearing spears whose tips alone weighed half as much as the average Israelite. Such people dwelt

ELLEN GUNDERSON TRAYLOR

on both sides of Jordan, they discovered, and Joshua was victorious over some of them in battle.

However, the fear of them had never been dispelled.

And now, a new breed of giant had entered the land, a seafaring people from the west, known as the Philistines. Actually, they had begun to permeate Canaan from the coast about the same time that Israel had made its first inroads into the region from east of Jordan. But Joshua had not had many dealings with them.

In the past three centuries, following the time of Abdi-Khipa and the weakening of Egypt's hold over Canaan, the Philistines had become more and more powerful, vying with numerous would be conquerors, until they were the virtual rulers of the land. Mighty were they in war, merciless in government. Much of their success was due to a secret technology, the ability to make iron, and therefore unrivaled implements of battle.

Their weapons and their formidable physical size lent to them a mystique that was the substance of legends. Therefore, when young shepherds, such as the sons of Jesse, sat about their nighttime fires, tales of encounters with bears and lions were often topped by stories of the Philistines and the struggles of the Hebrews against them.

In fact, if there was anything that could entice a shepherd from his fields and his flocks long enough to switch careers, it was the desire to fight the western colossus. Many an Israelite, city-dweller or herdsman, had left home to do so.

As a matter of fact, just now there was one brother absent from the hillside gathering. Jesse had eight sons in all, and the youngest was not with the group. He had not run off to war, being only fourteen years of age. But he had departed the group an hour ago, saying that he was going to trek to the nearest mountain top to see if the lights of a Philistine battalion, rumored to be settling in the valley of Socoh, west of Bethlehem, would be visible this evening.

Concerned now that the lad had been gone too long, Eliab, the eldest, scanned the hills. "Where is that boy?" he muttered. "I swear, he is more trouble than the sheep!"

"When he isn't dreaming," Abinadab chuckled. "Although I don't know which is worse, his absent-mindedness or his recklessness!"

To this was added a round of laughter, as the men shook their heads and surveyed the slopes. "No sign of him," Shammah said. "He should have stayed home with his great-grandmother!"

Momentarily the silence of the hills was broken by a whoop and a scuttle of gravel, as the youngest came running down toward camp. "Eliab! Shammah! All of you!" he called. "Oh, you should see them! Thousands and thousands, spread out toward Azekah!"

Into the firelight he sprang, his youthful face alive with a fire of its own.

The men acknowledged him doubtfully.

"Shall we tell father of your little escapade?" Eliab scolded. "If you cannot stay with us, you shall come out again!"

"But," the boy objected, "don't you want see? They are spread across the valley like shining chains! Their chariots gleam like copper coins beneath the moon!"

"Always the poet!" Elihu growled. "You would do well to mind the sheep as much as your fantasies!"

Poking at the embers with his staff, Raddai yawned. "As for me, I will chase the Philistines in my sleep." Drawing on an extra cloak, he curled up next to the fire and closed his eyes.

But the boy would not be put off. Dancing about the flashing flames, he spun his staff in his hand like a spear and goaded his apathetic brothers. "While you sleep, amazing things are happening!" he insisted. "See for yourselves! Just beyond the ridge! Or…are you all afraid?"

He could have taunted them any number of ways, without success. But calling them cowards at least provoked attention. "Since when are you the man and we the boys?" Nethanel snapped. "Come to bed, small one, and we will see if the giants are still in the morning!"

"Small one? Small one?" the lad grumbled, tackling Nethanel like a wrestler. "Better men than you shall fight the Philistines!"

Soon, the other brothers were all over the twosome, tickling the boy and tussling together, until the youngster escaped from the klatch. Running again up the hill, he waved his staff, and they gave chase, sending a small avalanche toward their fire.

None of the elder seven anticipated the sight to which the boy at the very peak of a great ridge. There, he let them catch up, but before they could lay hands on him, he diverted their attention.

"There!" he cried, shaking his staff toward the valley. "See for yourselves! Is it not just as I said?"

Panting from the race, the brothers looked southwest, and suddenly their laughter turned to gaping silence.

Indeed, just as the lad had reported, ten thousand lights dotted the vale of western Judah. Socoh, a garden of living green, was now a hostile stronghold, the enemy of Canaan and Israel having settled there like a cloud of locusts.

For a long, awestruck moment, the seven brothers stared mutely at the far-flung lights.

At last, Ozem, next-to-the-youngest, found his voice. "Do you suppose Goliath is among them?" he whispered.

At the name of Philistia's mightest champion, the shepherds shuddered.

Ten-and-a-half feet tall, strong as the iron his kinsmen prized, Goliath had stormed his way across Canaan, cutting down his rivals like a woodsman cuts down trees. In his path, he left terror nearly as deadly.

"If he is there," Eliab answered, "he would be lodged at the head of the camp."

As one, the men looked toward the nearest lights, paralyzed by the thought that the giant might indeed be so close.

Shammah, the bravest of the bunch, swallowed hard. "Likely we will be called to fight! When we are, I shall be the first to go!'"

Aroused by the proclamation, all of them asserted their readiness.

"No, I!" one challenged.

"You?" another hooted. "Israel needs *real* men!"

"Like me!" yet another declared.

"Well," Eliab broke in, "if we cannot manage our flocks, we will be of little use on the battlefield!"

The flocks! How could they have forgotten? Recalling their duty, they laid aside their squabbles and turned toward camp.

As they descended the hill, the darkness seemed blacker than ever. Eager for the reassuring fire, they spoke little, each lost in his own imaginings and his own fears.

Nor did they notice that the boy, once again, was absent from them, having stayed behind to gaze upon the denizens.

Like a sentinel he stood, his staff firmly planted by his side, dreaming of the day he might go to war.

When Eliab at last realized his absence and shouted for him, he reluctantly returned.

But, for Jesse's youngest, the flames of the shepherd fire would inspire marvelous images that night—images of flashing swords, roaring giants, and himself—a champion for Israel, named David.

2

Five miles north of Bethlehem, another young man stood upon a mountain top, surveying the distant lights of the Philistine camp. His name was Ornan, and the mount upon which he stood was Moriah

Had this been an earlier time, he might have been a king. He was a Jebusite, as evidenced by his prominent Hittite nose, and was related to the long-gone Abdi-Khipa. But these days, there was no real king in Jebus.

Ornan was a nobleman, sharing lordship over the city with leaders of the Judahites and Benjamites, who had deposed Abdi-Khipa and for a time, been masters of the city. Eventually, the Jebusites had regained some of their power, but even so, today Jebus was a vassal of the Philistines.

Likewise, Mt. Moriah did not have the prestige it once had. As far back as the time of Adonizedek, the Amorite king who had ruled Urushalim at the time of Joshua's entrance into Canaan, the great rock, once hollowed by Melchizedek, had come to naught. A pagan shrine had been erected nearby, but no one remembered the sacredness of the site on which Salem's first king had built a temple.

Through generations of tumult and changing administrations, the esteem in which Moriah had once been held had nearly vanished, so that the exact heresy Melchizedek had ruled against had become the norm: Moriah was nothing more than a threshing floor, a windswept table upon which farmers from the fields surrounding the city brought their grain to winnow, and upon which all sorts of abominations were practiced in connection with the harvest rites.

It was Ornan's distinction to be the owner of the threshing floor. Though he was no farmer, being a counselor and lawyer who sat in the gate of Jebus dispensing legal advice and decisions of justice, he did, from time to time look in on his property.

It was Spring. There was no harvest yet. Had there been, the presence of lighted camps strung across western Judah would have been expected.

Jerusalem—The City of God

Harvesters would have been toiling into the night, and much merriment would have filled the region.

But those were not harvest lights that Ornan saw tonight. Like all who dwelled here, he had heard that the Philistines were on the warpath, and he knew Jebus might be in line for their retribution.

It was the Benjamites and their leaders who brought the threat of Philistia against Jebus.

More than a decade ago, the Israelites had begun to cry out to their judge, Samuel, for a change in government. Convinced that their unsettled status and feuding among their various tribes would increase if they had a king like other nations, they pressed their demand relentlessly.

Resistant though he was, and though he warned the people that such a change would detract from worship of Jehovah, Samuel at last capitulated.

The quest for a suitable monarch led to a young Benjamite, Saul Ben Kish, son of a wealthy and powerful chieftain. Saul, Samuel prophesied, would save Israel from the hands of the Philistines.

Since the day he was anointed king of the scattered tribes, Saul had proven himself capable and valiant in war, and he had been a stumbling block to Philistia's imperialist dreams. Establishing himself as a great general from the outset, he first engaged the Ammonites across Jordan, with and army of three hundred thousand.

In the second year of his reign his son, Jonathan, was victorious over a Philistine garrison north of Jebus. Thus signaling war with the giant race, the father and son would go on to victory after victory against the Philistines and would proceed to systematically deliver Israel from all its enemies: the Moabites and Edomites beyond Jordan, the Zobhites, Amalekites, and others.

Though Saul was a hero to Israel, his embarrassing defeats of Philistia had often brought distress to his neighbors in Canaan. Accustomed to serving as vassals to one empire or another, the native cities might have gotten on better bowing the knee to Philistia than living with the ravages of war.

The Philistines made little distinction as to who it was that fought against them. If, for instance, a battle instigated by Israel took place near Hebron, it mattered not if the Hebronites were innocent bystanders. Their city was at risk.

Jebus, in particular, was vulnerable, since Saul, King of Israel, was a Benjamite, member of one of the city's ruling tribes. Therefore, when Ornan, lord of Jebus, saw the assembled lights of the Philistine camp spread across the southern horizon, he had good reason to be apprehensive. Chances were all too good that the very mount upon which he stood tonight could, within the week, be smeared with the blood of Jebus citizens.

Ten years of living with such fears was not good for Ornan's nerves.

With a sigh, he recalled the first time he had surveyed the valley from the vantage point of Moriah's flat rock. He had been a strong buck of twenty when his father had given him the deed to the threshing floor, and he had just embarked upon his career as justice and counselor. A proud baron with no end of opportunities for advancement, he had come to the rock that evening with the title deed in his hand, and with his bride of thirty days at his side.

Since any breezy plateau or open field could make a threshing floor, every little village sprinkled across Canaan boasted such a workplace. But none was so fine as Moriah's windswept crown. Farmers came long distances to use it. Preferring it to their own, as the breeze made for quick work and actually cut production costs, despite the expense of travel.

Whoever owned the rock had a financial gold mine, for he received a royalty off all grain winnowed there and need never lift a finger to plant, sow or reap.

The first evening Ornan had stood here, he had held his head high. Entwining his arm about his wife's narrow waist, he had felt himself a king, just as surly as if he had been son to Adonizedek or Abdi-Khipa. Though the glory of Jebus was now divided, Ornan was a descendant of royalty that had once ruled here, and the night he first stood upon Moriah, he felt that keenly.

Jerusalem—The City of God

But through the warring years, anxiety had weighed him down until, at only thirty years of age, his thick black hair was flecked with gray, and his broad brow was etched with lines too deep for one so young.

Though, due to his privileged status, he had never gone to war, he had seen many of his friends march off to battle, never to return. Daily, people of Jebus came to him, seeking advice on investments under such tenuous circumstances; young war widows came asking financial aid from the city; and peasants from the war-ravaged countryside sought medical help.

It was no blessing to the people of Canaan that Israel now had a king. It would have been preferable to serve Philistia than live under constant fear of onslaught.

But such was life for the lord of Jebus. And there was little comfort, any longer, in the real estate he owned. In fact, the stress of his position played havoc with his mind. Why else would he sometimes imagine that the rock and the deed he possessed were a curse? Even now, feelings of unexplainable angst engulfed him, feelings that had come over him numerous times in the presence of the moonlit tablerock.

Nervously, Ornan wiped his brow. It was a warm night, but the sweat he felt upon his hand was cold. Stepping down from the stone, he headed home, sensing, as he often had, that someone was watching him.

Then the breeze arose—not just any breeze, but a movement of air like the passage of great wings across the landmark—a sensation he had experienced countless times.

Shivering, he thought to run, but it seemed he dare not. Instead, he tiptoed toward a tangle of vine-draped bushes just to the northwest of the rock and stood rigidly in the shadow. Gathering his coat in a bundle, he pressed it against stomach like an old woman.

A chill tingled down his spine, and for a long moment he waited, hoping there would not be other manifestations. But he was not to be so lucky. Just as he got courage to turn again for home, the breeze passed by once more, and this time the sound of it was voice-like.

"Ornan," it seemed to call, hollow, eerie and just discernable.

Gasping aloud, the Jebusite fell back against the bush, catching his skin on the prickly vines. Were those claws he felt upon his back?

Twisting in horror, he wrenched himself free from the stickers and bolted into the moonlight, where he stood shaking and feeling very foolish.

"Get a hold of yourself!" he muttered, as he picked small thorns from a dozen tears in his tunic. How would he explain his appearance to his wife?

Breeze or no breeze, voice or no voice, he would not stay another second upon the mountain. Wheeling about, he fled like a gazelle, all the way down the market path toward Gihon Spring.

Once near the city gate and the neighborhood of his home, he was more himself. He brushed off his clothes as he neared his front door and threw his cloak over his shoulders, hoping to conceal his torn shirt. The sound of his children's laughter in the inner court put to flight the fear of the breeze, and the greeting of his auburn-haired wife warmed him.

But all that night, he would wrestle in his dreams, until his wife left him to sleep by herself in the parlor.

3

To the amazement of all who stood by, to all the towns of Canaan and to the onlooking Jebusites, the war with Philistia, when it did break out, was a fitful thing. In stops and starts it proceeded, the Israelis more bent on abstaining than on full-fledged endeavor.

For more than a month the Philistines camped in the Valley of Socoh, southwest of Jebus, taunting the Israelis and threatening mayhem, before the war at last blasted in earnest across the landscape.

It was the Philistine giant, Goliath, and his colossal brother, Lahmi, who held the Israelis in check during that time. It was also those two titans who at last brought matters to a head.

The inhabitants of surrounding towns could do nothing during the weeks of tension but hide behind closed gates, wondering at the strange delay and waiting for the inevitable.

Just as strange as the Israelis' military reticence, however, was their sudden decisiveness when they did act.

Sudden and swift was the victory, which, amazingly, they won.

What finally spurred their courage and how the victory was secured was a question on the lips of all Jebusites. Ornan, being their leader, would be among the first to learn the details.

The house of the young judge bustled with excited activity. A great dinner was being prepared, in honor of warriors returning from the Israeli front: one aged and oft-decorated soldier by name of Ahitophel and his equally martial son, Eliam.

As a Jebusite, Ornan had never endorsed confrontation with Philistia, but his two Judahite friends shared his concern for Jebus's peace. Since matters had fallen out well, both for the city and for Israel, they might as well celebrate.

This banquet was not only in honor of the Judahites. Another warrior was returning this night, from another battle, far to the north, in Cilicia. Ornan's brother-in-law, Uriah, had been away for two years, and his homecoming conveniently corresponded with Israel's victory. Therefore, tonight's party would serve a dual purpose.

Lisbah, Ornan's lovely red-haired wife, worked with her servants in the kitchen of her upper-class home, preparing for the event and chatting with a young guest, Ahitophel's granddaughter.

Since their interests were not so much with the war and its outcome. The topic of their conversation inevitably turned to men and marriage. Wiping her floury hands on the towel spread across her lap, Lisbah pursued an animated discourse upon the attributes of a certain eligible bachelor.

Although most marriages among the Hittites, the original Jebusites, were prearranged early in the children's lives, there were times when the special talents of a matchmaker were necessary. Lisbah had a reputation as a matchmaker, her propensity for spotting a good union having been proven through numerous successful marriages.

Today, Lisbah had personal reasons to attempt a match, for the bachelor at issue was her brother.

"Uriah would be a fine catch," she insisted. "The woman who gets him will have a diamond in the rough."

"That is what I fear!" her companion laughed, patting a cake of dough into a flat, round pan. "Uriah is married to weapons and war. There is no place in his life for a woman."

Lisbah leaned across the rug upon which the two sat and brushed a strand of the girl's long, black locks from her pearly forehead.

"Bathsheba," she sighed, "you of all women should be used to living with such a man. Your father and grandfather are both warriors. If the tribe of Judah had a few more just like them, we Jebusites would have no power whatever!"

"There," Bathsheba rebutted, pointing a finger in her friend's face, "you make my case for me. If my mother had not died when I was small, she would have seen to it that there was a bridegroom chosen for me. My destiny would have ling ago been sealed, and we would have no need of this conversation."

At this, her eyes grew round and kittenish and her pretty face contorted into a pout. "But because my father and grandfather had no time for such matters—no time for me, Lisbah—I am left to wonder if I shall ever marry!"

It was at moments like this that Ornan's wife was reminded of Bathsheba's youth. So beautiful was her face and form, so adept was she with cosmetics, that she appeared older than her mere thirteen years.

Indeed, the girl had been forced to grow up faster than she should. Eliam and Ahitophel, though they adored her, had not been able to teach her the things of womanhood, and had left that task to as assortment of aunts and governesses who were preoccupied with families of their own.

Bathsheba's only chances for her father's company came when she tagged along with him to the homes of state officials and dignitaries. For the sake of time with Eliam, she had endured countless hours of male talk, on subjects of no interest to her feminine nature. But Eliam took pleasure in her ability to look stately and ladylike, so she capitalized on what made him proud.

"No," the girl insisted, patting the dough into the pan with vigorous swipes, "I shall never marry a warrior! Since I do have a say in the matter, that is what I say!"

Lisbah studied her determined expression. "Never say 'never'," she warned. "Besides, you must not look at your situation so negatively. As you point out, you at least have some say in the matter. Most girls, whose husbands are chosen for them before they even know or care what a husband is, have no say at all. I know it has been hard to grow to thirteen unbetrothed, not knowing what your future holds, But, look at it this way."

Here, Lisbah began to trace the stripes of the carpet upon which they sat, running her fingers along them like arrows. "See these two lines?" she observed. "They run perfectly parallel, with no curving and no variation, till they reach the end. But now," she said, her eyes twinkling, "look at these."

She indicated two other lines whose type was repeated rarely in the overall pattern. "These wind back and forth across each other in delightful spirals. They also travel together to the end, but how much happier they must be than those whose path is so predictable!"

Then Lisbah leaned toward the carpet's fringed edge. "And see, while the straight lines simply finish together, the curvy ones form a tassel, a far more blissful union!"

Bathsheba appreciated Lisbah's teaching effort, but the meaning was lost on her.

"You, my dear child, are one of the fortunate few who will marry for love, not duty," Lisbah explained. "Because your choice is not only Eliam's will, but your own, the one you marry will be one you love, not one you are obliged to."

"Ah," Bathsheba gasped, her full lips parting in a smile. "I see. And so my life and the life of my husband will be more delightful?"

"Of course," Lisbah contended.

Certain she had made her point, the redhead picked up a bowl of soft garbanzo beans and began to mash them into a paste. As she reached for her seasonings, scattered across the carpet in little wooden boxes, Bathsheba was still unimpressed.

"But, Lisbah, you and Ornan were betrothed by your parents. You seem very happy."

"Of course, of course!" Lisbah agreed. "We are among the luckier ones. I never said you could not come to love a man chosen for you. I am only saying…"

"I don't see how all of this relates to Uriah," Bathsheba interrupted. "What makes you think I will love him?"

At this, Lisbah gave a bemused shrug. "He is my brother," she replied.

4

By noon, the heat from Lisbah's beehive ovens made the kitchen a sweltering workplace. Leaving the remainder of the work to her cooks, the noblewoman and her young companion escaped to a gallery bedroom.

Since Bathsheba had no mother, Lisbah had often filled in, babysitting her when she was small and coaxing Eliam to leave her with the family when military duty called him away. She had grown to love her, almost as a daughter.

Nothing gave her more pleasure than helping the teenaged beauty choose a gown for and event. Just now Lisbah, who quickly donned her own best dress, and whose hair had been coifed in ringlets, assisted Bathsheba in selecting a veil to complement a canary-yellow chemise. Draping it over the girl's dark tresses, which were woven with flowers, she stepped back and surveyed the handiwork.

"Lovely, child! Uriah's heart will surely melt!" she declared.

Bathsheba lowered her eyes with a demure blush, and Lisbah gave a wink. "Bathsheba," she whispered, "I will tell you a secret. Every now and then, let your veil fall away, like so." Softly tugging at the corner, she drew the filmy scarf to the girl's shoulders. "Quite accidental, you see?" she giggled. "No man can resist such innocent flirtation."

Echoing her mentor's soft laugh, Bathsheba twirled before her in a spiral of golden gauze.

"You are a butterfly!" Lisbah announced. "Now, come. Let's look in on the banquet room. The guests will be arriving soon."

✑

The meal would be served beneath the stars in Ornan's sumptuous courtyard. Though the women had little interest in military matters, conversation was sure lively.

For Lisbah and her young companion, the momentous event of the evening would be the arrival of Uriah, whose stint as a mercenary was over.

Far to the north of Canaan, along the border that separated Cilicia (the future Turkey) from Aram (or Syria), another branch of the Hittite race, who were more closely related to the Amorites than the Canaanites, vied for control of the region against a loose confederation of European tribes.

Uriah, spurred by tales of those distant battles, and by wanderlust, had preferred to fight in that cause rather than join his closer kinsmen in the petty intertribal conflicts which too often typified Israel. He would doubtless have stirring stories to tell.

The women bustled about the courtyard directing Lisbah's servants, spreading colorful tarps upon the floor around a long, low table and ringing them with bevy of multipatterned pillows.

As daylight gave way to dusk and as the hot sun descended, bringing a cool breeze across the banquet room, the mood in the house was expectant. Any moment the guests would be arriving, and even Ornan had joined the preparations, greeting his wife with an excited hug and sending his steward to check the wine supply.

"See to it that the very best is brought from the cellar," he ordered, "wine from the grapes of Gilead!"

Despite Bathsheba's doubts regarding Lisbah's matchmaking, she could not help but glance frequently toward the courtyard door, wondering when she would catch her first glimpse of Uriah. More than once Lisbah caught her doing so, and as they spread fine linen towels upon the pillows, for folks to wipe their hands, she gave another wink.

"He is a handsome fellow, you can be sure," she promised. "You will not be disappointed."

Bathsheba let her dark curls fall across her face, concealing a stubborn blush.

Musicians took their places in a corner of the court and practiced an airy tune as stars began to twinkle overhead. Festive banners, in vermillion and poppy, fluttered above the court, and among them were particolored lanterns covered with green and blue parchment.

When the butler was heard greeting at the front gate, all things were ready.

Jerusalem—The City of God

Bathsheba dipped behind Lisbah and found a shadowed corner from which to catch her first look at Uriah. Although she did not want to be the first person he saw, she nervously fluffed her hair and smoothed her yellow chemise. Placing a hand upon her flushed neck, she took a deep sigh and tried to control her jitters.

To her disappointment, the first guests to arrive were her Papa and Grandpapa, Eliam and Ahitophel embraced their host and hostess as the servants took their cloaks.

"Seat yourselves, seat yourselves," Ornan offered, leading them to the head of the table.

"Brother Ornan!" Eliam expostulated. "It is a good day. A good day for Israel and Jebus!" His sun-bronzed face crinkled like his father's in the lantern light, and both men seemed full to the brim with great stories.

"Yes, brothers," Ornan agreed, gesturing toward the streets. "The sound of celebration can be heard from here, where the Israeli camp sings in the valley.

It was true. The noise of joyous soldiers as they frolicked and drank in the victorious camp below funneled through town.

For days to come, the tale of the giant Goliath and his downfall would be heralded throughout Canaan. Barely able to stand on ceremony, the two Judahites could hardly wait to share the report. But there were certain social amenities to be observed first, as the guests took their places on the soft bolsters at the table's head and received a round of steaming tea in tiny clay cups.

"Laced with my best liquor," Ornan assured them, as they lifted the cups to their hooked noses and let the steam rise through their bushy moustaches.

Ahitophel, the leader because he was the eldest, nodded appreciatively. As soon as he took a sip, his old eyes lighting with party fire, the meal was officially underway.

The musicians, taking the cue, began to pipe in the corner, and the servants flashed to and fro, loading the men's shallow bowls with tidbits from a dozen pungent dishes. Spiced partridge, warm yogurt, honey-crusted rolls, cheeses of golden and bluish hue, savory noodles and sautéed vegetables filled the court with mouth watering aromas. The delicate pink flesh of salted fish and pickled herring was served in fan-shaped layers upon beds of wilted spinach and sliced boiled eggs. And, of course, Ornan's specially selected wine flowed from cool goblets between ongoing rounds of the spiked tea.

Uriah had not yet arrived. But in the style of the culture, there was no offense in entering late, nor beginning festivities before all were present. A party was a living, growing thing, with fluid edges and easy starts and stops. Ornan's meal would last for hours.

"Where is my daughter?" Eliam asked, as servant women worried over him. The question was spoken like an afterthought, but this did not surprise Bathsheba, who knew she had never been her father's first priority.

Emerging from the shadow, where she had watched his arrival, the girl pulled her light mantle over her hair, came forward, and knelt beside him, just beyond the male circle.

"Ah, my lamb!" Eliam crooned, holding out his arms so that she cuddled against him. "The pride of the party, as always!" he boasted.

Ornan took no offense, though he had daughters of his own. Too young to be called forward, they spent the evening in a chamber off court.

"Have I a story to tell you!" the soldier exclaimed. "Greater far than the bedtime tales your blessed mother used to spin." Leaning eagerly toward Ornan, he went on. "She is welcome at our table, is she not?"

"Indeed!" Ornan assured him. Hailing his wife, who came swiftly across the room, he bade her sit as well. "It is Lisbah's fond desire that both she and Bathsheba sit in with us tonight!"

"Good, good!" Eliam enthused. "Though ladies' ears do not love tales of war, the one we have to tell will delight them!"

At this, the music in the corner tapered to a close. The host and hostess leaned their elbows on the table and grew quiet. Just as Eliam opened his mouth, however, his battle-hardened hand raised in a point of beginning, voice in the outer court interrupted.

Another guest was arriving and all eyes turned to the hall.

Like the burst of red dawn across the night sky, so was the entrance of Uriah, brother of Lisbah, upon the dinner setting.

"Master Ornan," the butler announced, as Uriah pushed past him, "your brother-in-law, Uriah...the Hittite." The last two words were spoken with a bemused shrug, as it appeared the butler had been instructed to add them.

Ornan stood as Uriah flung off his cloak like a banner, tossing it to a servant, and the two brothers-in-law embraced exuberantly.

Bathsheba, though anticipating this moment all day, was taken aback by the newcomer's flourishes, and by his flashy appearance in general. As Uriah postured about the room, bowing and greeting the Judahites, she made her initial assessment.

It could not be said that Uriah was unattractive. Had he been less flamboyant, less gaudily attired, she might never have noticed him in a crowd. But, even so, there were things about him to turn the head.

Uriah, it appeared, was a throwback, meeting descriptions of the earliest, Jebusites—with raging red hair like Abdi-Khipa's and the all-too-noteworthy proboscis, the hooded nose that was the hallmark of the southern Hittites. Unlike the ancient king, however, he was neither portly nor soft. He was tall and swarthy like the warriors depicted on ancient Jebusite monuments, and strong as a bull.

Apparently his personality was also bullish, as he could never have entered a room gracefully, but was compelled to charge upon a scene like a buck at mating season. In keeping with his personality, he chose the most vivid colors for his studded tunic and leather-edged cloak. Uriah was a red man, blood red from scarlet locks to crimson coat.

Lisbah, infatuated from childhood, rose and rushed toward her brother, smothering his thick neck with kisses and pulling him from guest to guest, as though no one knew who he was.

When she came to Bathsheba, she bent down, breathless, and drew the girl to her feet. "My dearest brother," she gasped, as though awaiting this opportunity all her life, "this is my friend Bathsheba Bath Eliam."

At the sight of Bathsheba, who had until now hid behind her father, even a charging bull like Uriah came to a standstill. His eyes melting into the vision, he was transfixed.

"Sweet thing," he sighed, lifting the girl's hand and brushing it with a kiss. As he did, his eyes did not cease their travel up and down her form, studying her every feature as though she were a map of femininity. It was obvious from his gaping expression that memories of northern wars were bowing to this new challenge. If ever a territory needed conquering, Bathsheba was it.

"My dear friend," Lisbah continued, addressing the girl, "this is Uriah, my brother."

"Uriah, the Hittite," the newcomer rephrased.

At this, Ornan drew the fellow back and guided him to a seat. Tearing his gaze from the Judahite beauty, Uriah sat down with his fellow soldiers.

"So, brother," Ornan said, slapping him on the thigh, "what is this new designation you make for yourself? No one in Jebus goes by 'Hittite' any longer. We leave that ancient name to our northern kinsmen."

"Ah," the man replied, "in that we do ourselves great misfortune! While I was away, I learned to prize that part of my heritage. The Hittites of the north are a mighty people, Ornan. Mighty and proud!"

Ornan listened respectfully. "We are eager to hear of your adventures." Gesturing to Eliam and Ahitophel, he added, "It is a grand night of stories. These two gentlemen have just returned from war with Philistines. All Jebus, as well Israel, is celebrating the defeat of a dreadful host."

"So I hear," Uriah acknowledged. "Small towns like this are probably as enthused over local battles as the empire of the Hittites over the defeat of the Europeans. We will be pleased to share your joy."

So deftly put was this comment, that its barb took a moment to be felt. Eliam and Ahitophel blanched and looked at their laps with deflated expressions.

Reaching for a plate of noodles, Uriah did not wait on amenities, but began heaping his bowl, plunging into dinner in the same manner as he had entered the room. "Never have you heard such tales as *I* have to tell!" he declared. Where shall I begin?"

5

By halfway through the meal, Bathsheba knew she wanted nothing to do with Uriah.

Braggadocios and overbearing, the soldier-returned-from-the-north made the evening one long oration on his daring exploits and on the marvels of Hittite strategy. Though her father and grandfather listened graciously, their crestfallen faces and strained smiles reflected their disappointment at not having the chance to share the feats of their own recent experience.

That Ornan and Lisbah did not try to curb the self-styled hero was an oddity. Usually they went out of their way to make every dinner guest feel important, encouraging each to speak. Besides, did Ornan not care to hear of the victory over Philistia? Jebus had just been spared what could have been virtual enslavement to the sea peoples.

When it came to Uriah, Lisbah had a blind spot, and Ornan indulged her fondness for the braggart. After all, the man had been away two years and would likely not be staying long before other conflicts wooed him away.

Bathsheba stifled a yawn. The courtyard, though open to the sky, was warm with the press of bodies about the table and waves of hot air emanated from the nearby kitchen, where servants had opened the hatches on the beehive ovens. However, it was not warmth that made the girl drowsy. She was bored to death and would have risen to excuse herself, had Eliam not found a way, at last, to turn the conversation around.

Always, in the type of gathering, when wars among neighboring nations were the subject, the topic of giants was popular fare. While it was true that remnants of colossal races roamed these parts, and while evidence of them could be seen in super-sized Philistines, encounters with true giantism were rare. The thrill of war talk, however, encouraged exaggeration, and so no evening of story swapping was complete without an account of at least one such encounter.

Uriah, inspired by wine and his own reveries, was about to fulfill the tradition. Arms wide and eyes rolled back, he declared, "I shall never forget, as my comrades and I came over the rise east of the Taunus Range, looking down a narrow valley, that we were greeted by the bellow giant Cilician—a great, mammoth hulk of a man, with fangs for teeth and yellow, I tell you, *yellow*, bushy hair. All my friends fell back, pulling on their horses' reins," he said. Plunging a thumb to his breast, he asserted, "But not I! I stood firm, then spurred my mount down the hill, straight toward the demon's spear..."

At this, Eliam interrupted. "Uriah," he pressed him, "are you sure he was a giant? Many men say they have seen giants, but they are only very big fellows, frightening to be sure, but not true giants at all."

Sputtering to silence, Uriah squinted at the Judahite. For two hours he had owned the night, rambling, unchallenged, through a dozen adventures. Why, at this juncture, should he be questioned?

"Indeed!" he insisted. "He was at least seven feet tall! And his spear was..."

Ahitophel leaned forward with a scowl and waved a hand under Uriah's nose. His long, grizzled beard quivering, he fumed, "That was no giant, my friend! Your foe was a midget, compared to the champion of the Philistines! If you wanted to fight giants, you should have been with us only this morning, in the Valley of Socoh! There, the armies of Israel met and conquered the greatest of the giants!"

"Greater than seven feet?" Uriah huffed. "Truly, I would like to see such a fellow!"

"And you shall!" Eliam boasted. "At least you shall see his head, when it is brought from the battlefield to the market of Jebus, for all the world to see!"

Uriah planted his hands upon his knees. "So", he challenged, "just how great is this man? Seven-and-a-half, eight feet tall?"

"Try ten-and-a-half!" Ahitophel announced, his voice surging through the listeners like river rapids. "Goliath of Gath was over ten feet tall, if he was a foot, and he had a gigantic brother, who camped with him at Socoh."

Now Ahitophel had the floor, his description of the giant rousing the dreary listeners. Even Ornan's children, two little girls and four young boys, who had earlier left their completed meal in the chamber and fallen asleep on their parents' laps, awoke to absorb the tale in wonder.

"Every day for forty days," the elder went on, "Goliath came out of his tent and taunted our armies from sunup to sundown, calling us dogs and daring us to send him a challenger. His brother was stationed behind him, and he too, challenged us to one-on-one combat, shaking his spear and rattling his shield."

Having forgotten Uriah's adventures, the little audience now hung on the old man's word.

"What was Israel to do?" Ahitophel shrugged, fluttering his wizened fingers. "There are no giants among our people. And since we seemed doomed to failure, we were at a loss."

Ornan leaned around a servant woman who had come to clear the table, but who knelt instead in rapt attention to the story.

"We know Israel was victorious today!" he noted. "Was there a soldier mighty enough to take him out?"

"Ah!" Ahitophel nodded his turbaned head. "That is where the tale takes a sharp turn. For the Israeli who defeated Goliath was no more than a boy, barely twice the age of the lad here." He motioned to one of Ornan's wide-eyed sons. "And the boy had no spear or sword! Only a little sling, and a handful of pebbles!"

Now not even Uriah could conceal his curiosity, his resistance softening to childlike entrancement.

Bathsheba, likewise enthralled, focused on her grandfather.

"It was a grand day for Israel!" Ahitophel went on. "A shame, I suppose to all us cowards who were hanging back in fear, but sure sign of God's favor on our nation! For the boy, no more than a stripling, emerged from our sidelines like a little phantom and walked straight across the field toward Goliath!"

The intimate gathering sat like stumps, and from the shadows of the kitchen came the rest of the servants, listening in like mice.

Jerusalem—The City of God

"Such a pair the two made, the boy traipsing across the field with a shepherd's staff, and the giant with his brass helmet, his coat of mail, his brass leggings and breastplate! Why, they say his coat alone weighs five thousand brass shekels! And his spear—why it was like a weaver's beam—the head of it weighing six hundred iron shekels! And a separate fellow carried his shield before him, which was the height of any Israeli at full stretch!"

The crowd shuddered, marveling at the inequity.

Leaning his head back, and bellowing, Ahitophel mimicked Goliath: "'Am I a dog, that you come against me with a stick? A pox on you, Judahite! By all the gods of Gath and Ashkelon, by Dagon, Baal, El and their lady Ashtartu! Come to me boy, and I will tear you limb from limb. I will give your flesh to the fowls of the air. Carrion you shall be, for the wild beasts!'"

Aghast, the listeners envisioned the scene. Ahitophel had no reason to lie, and surely, the Philistines had been defeated today. This they all knew.

"Thus did the giant boast and swagger," Ahitophel went on, swaying now on his haunches, his robe tucked up between his legs. "And then, the boy, he made reply."

Here the old man hunkered down, to show diminutive size, and his voice peeped like a bird's.

"'You come to me with sword, spear, and shield,'" he quoted. "'But I come to you in the name of the Lord of Hosts. The God of the armies of Israel, whom you defy! This day,'" he raised his hands in challenge, "'the Lord will deliver you into my hand! And I will smite you, and take your head from off your shoulders! And I will give the carcasses of all the Philistine host unto the fowls of the air and the wild beast, that all the earth may know that there is a God in Israel!'"

At this, Ahitophel took a deep breath and passed his hand over the crowd, as the boy had passed his own small hand over the valley and the mountains. "'All this assembly shall know that the Lord saves not with sword and spear. For the battle is the Lord's and He will give you, O, wretched Goliath, into our hands!'"

Utterly fixed on the speaker, the listeners waited tensely for the climax, as Ahitophel stood up from the table, running a few feet to show the boy's advance.

Reaching into his robe, he pretended to pull out a stone, place it on a phantom sling, and spin it over his head. Then with a deft flip of the wrist, he sent the invisible stone across the dining room, straight for the forehead of the imagined giant. Following the vision, the crowd gasped.

"Aha!" Ahitophel laughed, jumping up and down on his wiry legs, his tucked-up robe slipping from his thighs. "Direct hit! Buried in Goliath's brain!"

Keeping their eyes where the Philistine would have fallen, the gathering could almost hear his thunderous collapse.

"Flat on his face!" Ahitophel assured them, slapping his hands together. "Fallen like the columns of Dagon's temple! Fairly shook the whole valley, he did!"

Then, as though he were the boy himself, Ahitophel ran around the table to the site of the slain giant and, in pantomime, placed a foot upon his neck.

"The boy was just strong enough to draw Goliath's sword from its sheath," he said, bending down and imitating the move. Showing that the great weapon bent the lad's wrists painfully, he demonstrated how he managed to hoist it high enough to let it come crashing down, and with a slicing sound, how it severed Goliath's head from his shoulders, just as the lad had predicted.

With this, Ahitophel slumped to the floor, receiving the applause of the amazed onlookers.

"Even now, the Philistines are fleeting," Eliam added, taking over for his breathless father. "We slew them all the way to Ekron, and some of our people still pursue them, to the sea! We have taken all their spoil and it will be a distant day before they set foot, again, in Judah!"

At last, the story of Israel's conquest had been told, putting to shame Uriah's accounts of Hittites, Turks, and hazy northern battles.

Feeling rather small, but nonetheless awestruck, Uriah heaved a sigh. "By all gods of all people!" he blew. "How I wish I had been there! If it is as you say, the boy is a miracle worker!"

"A future general, if you ask me!" Ornan gasped. "We shall hear from him again!"

"So you shall," Eliam affirmed. "He is now Saul's favorite!"

Bathsheba, her face flushed with wonder, placed a hand on her father's knee. "Did you tell us his name?" she asked. "The name of the brave young man?"

"Oh!" Ahitophel laughed. "Could I forget such a thing? His name is David, son of a common shepherd, Jesse of Bethlehem."

6

As the guests in Ornan's house shared their stories, the sounds of celebration had grown in the streets of Jebus, swelling upward from the Israeli camp and finding its contagious echo in the revelry of the citizens. Whether they were Jebusites, Benjamites, or Judahites, the inhabitants of Canaan's capital were unanimously joyous over the defeat of their mutual oppressor, the Philistines.

Past midnight, Lisbah, her children, and the women servants of the household went to bed, leaving men folks to party through the wee hours.

But Bathsheba was not the least bit sleepy.

Resting her elbows on the ledge of her chamber window, she gazed across rooftops that ranged downhill toward the city walls and Gihon Spring where partiers danced and sang beneath the moon.

It was not the noise of the rooftops, however, that kept her awake. Certainly, it was not thoughts of Uriah that stirred her heart and charged her spirit. She had made her assessment of him within moments of his flashy arrival, and it was not a positive one. Disappointed as Lisbah would be, she must tell her tomorrow that her brother was not her type.

What filled Bathsheba's restless mind were images evoked by Ahitophel's report, the story of the courageous shepherd boy and the fallen giant.

For the first time in her life, a tale of victory on a Warfield was vastly intriguing, and not because it proclaimed one side mightier than another. Nothing wearied Bathsheba more readily than men's braggadocio. But this story contained none of that. The tale of the boy and the giant was thrilling for exactly the opposite reason: The boy claimed no power in himself.

Bathsheba was not a religious person. Her relationship with Israel was by bloodline, more than creed. Having been passed between various caretakers of diverse ethnic and ethical background, she had grown up with little sense of heritage. Even her father and grandfather, though they fought for Israel, were motivated by national allegiance more than dogma.

Jerusalem—The City of God

Bathsheba, at her tender age, was classically secular and cared little what god or goddess was worshipped in her city. Still, the words of the shepherd as he confronted the giant left a vivid impression: "You come to me with sword, spear, and shield. But I come to you in the name of the Lord of Hosts, the God of the armies of Israel!"

Bathsheba ran her hands up and down her gooseprickled arms. Something in the boy's simple assertion made her hair stand on end, and she pulled her silky mantle over her shoulders.

As much as Uriah's manner put her off, she could sympathize with one thing he had said. Like him, she fondly wished she had been in the Valley of Socoh that day. She wished she had witnessed the boy's valiant challenge and the giant's demise. Were she a man, she would have offered her life in service to the young general.

But, fortunately, she was not a man. She might suffer from loneliness, as the men in her life traipsed off to war. But she need not take up sword or shield to fight beside them.

Like other neglected women, her reward was to share the benefits of many struggles. Fear of the Philistines and their hold over her people was, for now, alleviated. And she would be certain to watch the victory march, when young David brought the spoils of war into the streets of Jebus.

It was nearing morning, the first hint of dawn tinting the crest of Olive Mount, when the girl's eyelids at last grew heavy. She had just turned in for bed when a knock at her door jolted her.

"Daughter," Eliam called softly. "Are you awake?"

Delighted, Bathsheba ran to the door and threw it open, surprised that her father would think of her after a night with his friends.

"Come in Papa!" she greeted.

"I saw your light at the threshold," he said. "I must speak with you."

His eyes danced with merriment, and Bathsheba wondered how much wine he had consumed. Entering, he embraced his daughter fondly, and expostulated, "Surely the God of our fathers has blessed us!"

Unused to hearing Eliam employ such language, Bathsheba only nodded, assuming he referred to the miracle of David and the triumph over Philistia.

"And the God of your father is with you, my dear!" he insisted.

Leading her to bed, he sat down with her and took her hands in a warm grasp. His bloodshot eyes studied her adoringly.

"Life with your Papa has not been easy, my child,' he went on. "But this night, I atone for past neglect."

Bathsheba listened in amazement, wondering what he could mean.

"Had your Mama lived," he sighed, "your future would never have been uncertain. You would have prepared to be some man's wife from your earliest years. Instead,' he said with a shrug, "your silly Papa left you to face a vacant tomorrow."

Then, standing up and slapping his thighs, he gave a hearty chuckle. "But, no more!" he announced. "My sweet Bathsheba is no longer victim of my absence! As of this night, your destiny is certain, your future bright!"

Wide-eyed, the girl observed him doubtfully.

"What is it, Papa?" she asked. "What have you done?"

"I have gotten you a husband!" he proclaimed. "A fine, dashing man!"

Bathsheba arose numbly from the bed. "You have been Ornan's guest, she stammered. "You have been here all night. When did you go looking for a husband?"

"Ah, that is the wonder of it!" he exclaimed. "I did not look! He came to me, without my looking! And so," he snapped his fingers, "it is the work of God!"

Suddenly, a grim possibility posed itself. There were no men present at the party, save the married Ornan, Grandfather Ahitophel, and . . .

Uriah! Bathsheba thought, sinking again to the bed. "No, Papa she sighed aloud. "You cannot mean…"

"The Hittite, of course!" he confirmed her imagining. "Is he not wonderful?"

The last Bathsheba had known, Eliam's feelings about Uriah were much like her own. It had been obvious, from her father's expression earlier in the evening, that he found Uriah boorish and obnoxious. What had transpired since the women had left, and the wine had flowed more freely, was apparent. The men had lulled by drink and story-swapping into an illusion of camaraderie.

Likely, they had slipped into alcohol-induced euphoria, giving away all sorts of secrets and promising all sorts of things. Bathsheba had become a pawn of their sloppy fellowship.

"But, Papa!" the girl cried. "I could never marry Uriah! He is not the man for me!"

Astonished, the besotted Judahite swayed before his daughter. "What!" he muttered "Do you say 'no' to me?"

Trembling, Bathsheba sat up straight. Desperately, she tried to recall the conversation she had with Lisbah, before the banquet.

"Papa," she said, her voice quavering, "I am of an age to choose my own husband."

Aghast, Eliam blinked his foggy eyes.

"Of an age?" he growled. "Where do you get such foolishness? So long as I live, you shall never reach such an age!"

Steadying himself, he leaned down and looked into her eyes, his vinegar breath wafting over her. "Now, get ready," he grumbled, raising her off the bed. "Morning is upon us, and Uriah wishes to greet his betrothed."

Leading her to her wash bowl, which sat beside the very window where she had watched the reveling city, he stroked her dark head. "Bathe and put on your best gown," he commanded. "Be your loveliest, and rejoice the heart of your Hittite husband."

Just as Jebus celebrated the night, so did the armies of Judah and Benjamin celebrate the demise of Goliath and the routing of the Philistines. While there were still companies of Israelis chasing the enemy as far as the coast, those who had fought in the Valley of Socoh were already enjoying the spoils of triumph.

Especially in the camp of King Saul, the victors' headquarters, merriment was the order of the evening, as the generals of Judah and Benjamin, along with all their chief captains and most heroic warriors, drank, laughed, and sang away the night.

At the center of that camp, a huge bonfire replaced the smaller fire around which the king and his counselors customarily warmed themselves. Tonight the flames suited a larger crowd, while food was prepared at a dozen littler blazes in the compound.

In the glow of the dancing light, piles of riches gleamed—bronze helmets, shields and spears, gilded chariots with iron wheels-all trophies of war secured from vanquished Philistines. Fabulous horses, bred in the deserts of Arabia or upon the plains of Egypt—warhorses bred to carry giants—stamped and snorted for their new Israeli owners. And within the tents of the conquerers, more personal treasures had been stashed—purses full of Philistine coins, neckchains and armbands worn by the troops of the wealthy nation.

Among the booty, there were no Philistine slaves to be found. Though the Israelis had no moral compunction against enslaving a conquered people, no captives had been taken in this campaign.

Saul had commanded, at the decree of the prophet Samuel, that the consequence of defeat for all Philistines was death. Not a soul among the vanquished had been spared, save those who succeeded in fleeing their pursuers.

Merciless as the chase had been, leaving, in a single day, a bloody streak across the face of Canaan, the most grisly memento of Israel's strength

stood at the center of Saul's camp. There, for all to see, was the gargantuan head of Goliath, the scarlet wound embedded in its forehead a graph-
ic proclamation of Israel's potency. Mounted upon the spear of the fallen
giant, it stood as an ensign to the faith of one boy. And though the troops
and the commandants reveled in victory, it was a humbling reminder of
the source of that victory.

Therefore, though the partying Israelis were wild and joyous, their joy
was tempered. It was not in the abandon of vain glory that they reveled,
but in praise of a greater power than their own.

David, the shepherd who had both shamed them for their cowardice
and restored their failing faith, sat this night in the tent of Saul. What neither Eliam nor Ahitophel knew, and had not told Ornan and his dinner
guests, was that young David had been invited to the king's tent several
times since the Philistines first camped at Socoh, and that the defeat of
the giant was not the first peculiar happening in his life since the night he
and his brothers first glimpsed the lights of the enemy camp from the
heights of their shepherd hills.

David's brothers had always teased him for being different, and not
only because he was the youngest of the eight sons of Jesse; such a distinction was not overly worthy of torment. What set David apart was his day-
dreaming nature coupled with a bent for adventure, as exasperating com-
bination that landed him in more trouble than most boys were prone to.

He was not a bad youngster. But too often, when he should have had
his mind on his work, he was lost in the music of a small harp that he carried everywhere with him.

It was true that he had learned to play the instrument with such
expertise and feeling his father said he could charm a poised snake before
it struck. And the songs he composed as he played were so sweet and
beautiful, people often came out from the village to sit by Jesse's fire and
listen to the poet.

The problem was that David's music, like his daydreams, often made
him a poor tender of the flocks. Wild beasts had too often crept into

camp, when, had the shepherd been more alert, they would have been forestalled. And too many times, little lambs had come close to drowning in a swollen stream, or ewes had wandered off unnoticed before his attention was jolted.

Aggravating as David's tendencies could be, however, there was something else about him that irritated his brothers even more. The boy's luck at unraveling the tangles he got into provoked jealousy and not a little anger, while winning for him a reputation as a powerful scrapper.

One such instance involved both a mountain lion and a small black bear, who had crept into camp when David tended the sheep alone. Had he been more on guard, he might have averted a confrontation, but David realized their presence only when the bleating of a lamb, snatched in the lion's powerful jaws, brought him to.

Running after the predator, David crippled him with his sling and rescued the lamb. But the lion was not dead, and when it arose, determined to have its prey, David was forced to hands-on struggle.

Limping home, with his flock in tow and the lamb slung across his back, David was cut and bruised, but the lion had had the worst of it. "I caught him by his beard!" he reported to his brothers. "I threw him to the ground, I did! And then I smote him again, with my trusty sling!"

Incredulous, the sons of Jesse and their father surrounded the boy, seeing his wounds that he had, indeed, been in a skirmish with the great beast. And they made over him, until they were put off by his boyish braggadocio.

"Yes!" he asserted. "And the bear, too! I killed it as well, when it went after the lamb! See here," he boasted, holding forth the bear's tongue, which he had severed as a souvenir.

"Very well!" his eldest brother had growled. "But tell us how it happened that both bear and lion made into your camp! Had the fire gone out? Were you asleep? Or," he grabbed David's harp from under the boy's arm, "were you lost, again, in your pretty songs?"

Wounded to the heart, the boy thrust out his lower lip, tears welling in his eyes. But Jesse came to his defense. "Don't be so hard on him," he corrected. "At least the lamb and the flock are safe. Have you never lost a sheep, Eliab?"

Such was the mixture that was David. Poet and fighter, he had already, at fourteen years of age, begun to make a name for himself throughout Ephrata. However, it was not until the prophet Samuel appeared in Bethlehem one day, seeking to bestow an unexplained anointing upon someone, that David was singled out as special.

The Philistines had entered Socoh Vale. David and his brothers had spied their camp from above their shepherd fields, and several days had passed, as Goliath taunted and tormented the troops of Israel, when Samuel came calling. Saying that he wished to make a sacrifice in the town, but giving no more reason than that, he summoned all the elders and their sons, and began to pray in earnest. Focusing on the sons of Jesse, he stood before each one, scrutinizing them as for some great commission.

When he laid eyes upon the firstborn, his old face lit up. But just as quickly, the light faded. And as Jesse nervously called the next and the next, down the line through seven brothers, sensing that the chance of a lifetime was about to be bestowed, the prophet appeared more and more disappointed.

"The Lord has chosen none of these!" Samuel declared. Are these all your sons?" he inquired, boring into the old father's soul with fiery insistence.

"There is one more…" Jesse stammered. "The youngest. He is in the hills…tending the sheep."

"Send and fetch him!" Samuel commanded, provoked by Jesse's carelessness. "We will not rest until he comes!"

That day, David was anointed in the midst of his brothers and before all the elders of the village. Taking a horn of oil from his belt, the prophet poured it upon the boy's dark curls and let trickle down his ruddy cheeks. Though no one knew for certain, just what the anointing portended, they could not look upon David from that day forward without mere respect.

While the interlude with Samuel impressed the brothers greatly, it also compounded the aggravation, for they could not understand why the day-dreamer, of all Jesse's sons, should be so honored. Nevertheless they loved him. And no one could deny that something changed for David from that day forward. The next weeks confirmed it, not only by his defeat of Goliath, but by a sudden thrusting of the lad into circles of royalty.

It was no more than a couple of days after Samuel visited Bethlehem that David was called from his flocks to receive yet another honor. A steward of King Saul came riding into the village, attired in velvet, studded with gold, and accompanied by a retinue of bodyguards. In his hand was a writ from the king himself, demanded that Jesse send his son, David the shepherd, to the field tent of Saul.

"The lad shall bring his harp," the writ cryptically ordered.

Bewildered as he had been by the prophet's little ceremony, Jesse was even more so by this unexplained summons. But, he was a commoner, and Saul was the Majesty of Israel. Who was he to question?

And so Jesse sent David forth with what meager gifts he could afford to send—a bottle of wine, his wife's finest bread, and a choice goat in tribute to the king.

Never again would life be simple for the young shepherd of the Judahite hills. Catapulted into the inner sanctum of Israeli power, he would be called upon time and again to play soothing music for Saul, a man whose manifest agony of soul did not fit with his reputation as a confident, invincible warrior.

The legendary feat against Goliath was the deciding moment in the lad's advancement. He who had been in the company of greatness, but who had never been great himself, was, in a single moment, thrust into the limelight of national attention. With the smiting of the Philistine champion, David became the instant darling of Israel and the delight of the king's heart.

Tonight the honors due a hero were being heaped upon him.

For the occasion, the tent of Saul had been opened wide, its forward flaps tied back, so that it made the backdrop of a great banquet. Saul sat at the head of a merry congregation as they feasted and drank. Besides him sat his son Jonathan, and next to him, upon a heap of pillows, sat David.

The tall, handsome king, his crowned head gleaming in the light of the nearby bonfire, even now related the story of how the lad had first come to him. Calling for the attention of the generals and all the banquet company, the king stood up from his campaign throne. "It has been over a month ago that I first laid eyes upon our brave boy," he related, gesturing to David. "You all know that I am not always a merry man." His face twitching slightly, he seemed to fumble with the confession. "The weight of my office sometimes burdens me to the ground," he explained. "I commanded my servants to seek out a musician for me, that my heart might lightened from time to time, and they brought me my sweet young psalmist."

The audience acknowledged David's renown as a singer, having heard his voice drift from Saul's tent on many occasions.

"Will he sing for us?" they requested.

"Later, later," the king replied, holding up his hands. "None of us ever imagined that the scope of the lad's talents included giant killing!"

These last words, applied to a mere boy, struck a humorous chord and the crowd chuckled.

"David has served me admirably," the king went on, "not only as my singer, but as my armor-bearer. And," he turned to his young friend, "I beg his forgiveness, for, when he came to me asking to fight Goliath, I jested with him, making him parade before me in my own coat of mail, my helmet, and my shield."

Imagining the picture, a gangly teenager in an oversized military garb, the crowd once again was tickled, but they kept silent at the king's repentance.

Then, Saul's face broke into a bright smile. "And do you know how the lad reacted to my ridicule? He said he could never wear the armor, because he had not 'tested' it!"

At this, the company broke into hilarity, commending David's good sportsmanship, as they raised a toast to the little general.

As cheer after cheer rose to the night sky, saluting the shepherd, Saul leaned down and pulled him to his feet. "Tell the men, friend David, whose son you are, and from whence do you hail?"

His throat dry, David looked out across the prestigious gathering, feeling very small. Concealing his trepidation, he answered loudly, "I am the son of your servant Jesse, of Bethlehem. And I am proud to be your warrior!"

Delighted, the crowd roared again, stamping their feet and rising as one to applaud him.

At this, Saul held the boy's hand in a fatherly grip, announcing, "From this day forward, you are my son as well, and you shall dwell in the house of the king!"

8

That night, Bathsheba Bath Eliam was not the only young person in Canaan whom sleep eluded. David Ben Jesse was likewise awake till dawn, listening to the sounds of the camp and pondering events of the day.

Across the warfield, the noise in Jebus also reached him, blending with the revelry of the Israeli troops. In fact, the whole of Canaan was alive with music and song, and all because of what transpired between himself and the giant.

As Saul's armor-bearer, David had his own tent within the headquarters compound. The king had stationed him there four weeks ago, when he appointed him guardian of his weapons. When he was not singing for Saul, he had spent many an hour, the past month, polishing and tightening the gear.

Tonight, however, it was not only the king's armor that graced his little chamber. In the center of the room, another pile had been deposited, the shield and buckler, the greaves and girdle, the helmet and mail of Goliath. Trophies of war of the finest degree, they were now the possessions of a fourteen year old boy.

Heart beating like a bird's, David rolled over on his bed and gazed upon the enormous stash.

Now that he was alone, the encounter with Goliath seemed surreal. Were it not for the flashing bonfire outside and the carousing camp, he would have thought he had just awakened in his shepherd's tent from a fabulous dream. But the fire outside cast the titanic trophies in silhouette, and there, upon the tent side, was illumined an even more haunting reminder of the day's realities.

The shadow cast by the giant's severed head, erected upon his bloody spear, made a gyrating dance in the flashing light, seeming to turn this way and that, as though seeking the young killer. At first glimpse of the phantom, David clutched the cloak he had rolled into a pillow and buried his face there.

But, he was a hero. At least that was what the songs, sung this night about Israel's campfires, said. The Lord was with him. So he had told his defiant enemy.

Taking a deep breath, he closed his eyes and recounted to himself the many times God had been with him—the time of the lion and the bear, fearsome times alone in the hills, the day Saul's emissaries had summoned him to play for the king, the day the venerable prophet had anointed him with oil…

Just as he thought on Samuel, another shadow fell across his tent. And a voice, familiar and awesome, called to him.

"David Ben Jesse," it commanded. "Arise my son. I must speak with you."

Only once before had he ever heard that voice, but it was a sound never to be forgotten, as the old prophet had intoned mysterious words while anointing him. The day Samuel prayed over him at Bethlehem, designating him "the Lord's chosen," a feeling such as the boy had never experienced surged through every fiber of his being.

He had yet to understand what "the Lord's chosen," meant. The prophet had not explained the term to any of the men gathered there, but an overpowering sense of divine presence had swept through the boy's spirit, even as the oil trickled down his forehead.

Many times during the weeks since, he had experienced that sensation. It came upon him when he played for the tormented king. It came upon him in the middle of lonely nights when he wished he were with his brothers and his flocks once again. And it had come upon him most powerfully this very day as he had confronted Goliath.

Therefore, the voice of Samuel, which had accompanied his introduction to that power, was an awesome thing, sending a chill down his back.

"Coming, sir" he replied, throwing back his covers and going to the tent door. Pulling his cloak over his tunic, he stepped into the outer light, finding Samuel just as he remembered him.

Not unusually tall, in fact somewhat stooped from old age, the man's aspect was nonetheless one of sheer authority. His white hair fell nearly to

his waist and his snowy beard likewise. His face was weathered by years
spent traveling from town to town as he oversaw the doings of his faltering people. It seemed a look of permanent disapproval, even sorrow, had
etched itself upon his brow, though the light of great joy had flashed
through his stormy eyes the day he first saw David.

Tonight, as he beheld the lad again, that ray of hope once more illumined him, and he held out a hand in greeting.

Full of holy awe, the boy bowed his head. "How am I so honored, my
lord?" he peeped.

The prophet eyed the boy who cowered beneath him. "Is this the brave
warrior?" he asked. "Is this the dreaded foe of the Philistines?"

David raised his head and tried to look fearless. "I am not always so
brave," he admitted. "I tremble under the hand of God."

Pulling back his chin, Samuel blinked his eyes, amazed at the lad's
humility. "Well spoken," he replied. Then scanning the sky, "Dawn is
nearly upon us. Walk with me."

At this, he took his staff and proceeded across the field of battle, heading north, and never once looking over his shoulder. Huffing and puffing,
David hastened to keep up with the sturdy old gentleman, astonished at
his endurance. Nor did Samuel cease his trek until they came to a rise in
the highway overlooking Bethlehem.

In a field bordering the village, a small stone building marked one of
the most historic graves in all Israel, the sepulcher of Rachel, beloved of
Jacob. All his life, whenever David had seen that tomb, it reminded him
of his heritage, the story of the patriarchs and the purpose of Israel.

His parents and even his Great-Grandmother Ruth had told him tales
of Abraham, Isaac and Jacob, Moses and Joshua, as well as the prophets
and judges who followed in their footsteps. A sense of history was his as
it was most boys' who grew up in Israeli households, and he had a keen
love not only for Jehovah, but for the oracles and the land that represented God's dealings with the people.

This predawn, as he stood with Samuel upon the highway, the very breeze that filled the valley seemed full of portent. As he gazed across the fields and hamlets scattered about the hills, it seemed as though the land was alive with promise. Lights still burned in camps and houses where people celebrated Israel's great victory, forecasting the yellow dawn that crept over the eastern ridge.

"I suppose you know every inch of these fields," Samuel said, speaking the first words since they had left the tent.

"These and others," David replied. "I have spent all my life here."

Samuel planted his walking stick in the dirt and leaned upon it, resting for a moment.

"I have learned the land well, traveling it as I must," Samuel observed. "But that is only as a grown-up. My childhood was spent in the house of the Lord, at Shiloh."

Samuel's personal reference surprised the boy, austere as he seemed. "Yes, I know," David said. "The elders say that your mother gave you to God when you were born, and that the high priest raised you."

At the mention of the priest of Shiloh (the town where the tabernacle had been before its relocation to the village of Nolo, near Jebus, Samuel's face took a curious expression, and David wondered if he had made the old man sad. When the prophet took up his staff and began the walk again, it was with a slower step, his head bent down.

"Eli," he sighed, remembering the long-dead priest. "He was a good man, and a weak man at the same time. He was like a father to me, and he raised me the best he knew how. But he had trouble with his own sons."

David recalled the stories of the two prodigals who had been such a shame to Israel and to the office their father held. Many blamed Eli, himself, for the way his sons had turned out, and rejoiced when the young men were killed in battle with the Philistines, saying that God was repaying the priest for raising them poorly.

In fact, though Eli was long gone, older folks still lamented the sorry condition to which he had supposedly lowered the priesthood, saying that he never should have been priest anyway, since he was not in the line of

Jerusalem—The City of God

Aaron's firstborn. It was divine justice against his administration and against him as a person that his sons had been killed, so they believed.

David was too young to have an opinion on the matter. Though it did not sit well with him to think of Jehovah as that retributive, he did wonder, if he thought about it, how anyone but a descendant of Aaron had taken the holiest station in Israel.

Once again, however, Samuel was speaking, his pace quickening as he drew closer to Jebus.

"I suppose no boy has ever been so honored as I," he went on. "To be raised in the house of the Lord, the very tabernacle of Jehovah…" Here his voice cracked slightly and he cleared his throat. "Every year my mother brought me a new cloak, upon my birthday, you know. But, in truth, my family were the men of the tabernacle. My chamber, where I lay down each night, was adjacent to Eli's, very close to the Holy of Holies!"

David doubted that such revelations were often shared by the old prophet, and he wondered why he was privy to these remembrances. He did not ask the reason, but listened in eager silence as images of that hallowed life etched themselves in his mind.

"Did you ever see the Ark of the Covenant?" David asked, his eyes wide with youthful wonder.

Samuel glanced at him, and then looked away again, to Jebus. "If you mean, did I ever enter the Holy of Holies where it was enshrined, of course I did not. To do so would have meant death, for no one was to enter that place but the high priest."

David remembered that the portable tabernacle which Moses designed for the wilderness years, and which was reproduced at Shiloh, contained an inner sanctum to house the Ark. He had heard descriptions of the sacred box, which was overlaid with pure gold inside and out, and which contained the tablets of Mosaic law. Upon it was the mercy seat, the very resting place of Jehovah, and on either side were winged beings, two cherubim of beaten gold, from between which the Lord communicated with Israel.

"Yes, sir," David said with a nod. "And even the high priest could enter the Holy of Holies only on the Day of Atonement."

"You have learned well," Samuel noted. "But to answer your question, yes, I saw the Ark when it was carried out from Shiloh with the Hebrew army. It went before them, always, into battle. Always, that is, until the battle at Ebenezer."

David knew the account of how the Ark was taken as booty by the Philistines in that battle, and how, when Eli heard that it was stolen, he fell off his priestly throne, breaking his neck and dying.

Reciting the phrase that has burned itself into the national consciousness the day the holy vessel was taken, David sighed, "'Ichabod! The glory of the Lord is departed.'"

"Ah!" Samuel exclaimed, raising a gnarled finger. "Well spoken! You were not even born when the treasure of treasures was taken, yet you know how poor we are for it!"

"The elders of Bethlehem always say, 'Ichabod!'" David replied. "And their hearts are sad when they speak of the Ark."

"Well they should be!" Samuel said. "Israel has not been the same since that day."

David did not know how inquisitive he might be. Still, he felt he could take courage from Samuel's openness, and ventured to ask him a question which, to his young mind, had never been sufficiently addressed.

As though he were in synagogue school, he eagerly inquired, "How is it, sir, that Israel has never been the same? Did the Philistines not return the troublesome Ark when their own idols were toppled by it?"

He alluded to reports from the coast, at the time the Philistines housed the Ark, that the image of their own god, Dagon, was found more than once toppled beside it and broken. Taking this as an omen, the enemy hastened to remove the Ark from their country, but not before their people were smitten with hemorrhoids and a variety of dreadful diseases.

It had been housed for more than two decades, in the obscure Hebrew village if Kirjath-Jearim, under the watchful care of a Levite named Abinadab and his son, Eleazer.

"Why has Israel never returned the Ark to the Holy of holies?" David asked. "Why have we never resumed our proper worship?"

At this, Samuel looked wonderingly at his young companion. "Did your Rabbis never address this?" he marveled. "What had they to say about such things?"

David's face reddened. "I was not so often in school as I would have liked," he answered. "I spent most of my days in the fields with my father's flocks. But I sometimes ask Papa these questions, and the elders in the Bethlehem gate."

Softening, Samuel nodded, urging David to proceed.

"Papa said it was a shame the Ark was neglected, and that Israel could not prosper until it was reinstated. And some said Israel is unworthy of the Ark..." Here David hesitated, for he did not wish to offend Samuel's love of Eli or his household.

"Go on," the prophet urged, listening respectfully.

David shrugged his boyish shoulders. "That is all," he said. "I do not know who is right."

Samuel stopped and studied his little student carefully. "Both are right," he replied. "Israel will not be blessed, as it could be, until it returns to the worship Moses laid out for us. Neither can the Ark dwell forever in the keeping of soiled hands."

Amazed, David stammered, "Do you speak of Eli and his successors?"

Samuel raised his chin and took off at a brisk pace, David followed anxiously behind. "Eli was the best that could be had, at the time. So far had we come from the Lord's ways, there was no proper priest to be found in Aaron's line. No, my boy, we cannot blame Eli, anymore than we can blame ourselves, for the sorry state of our nation."

Glancing across the fields where Saul's forces had just celebrated, the old man seemed deeply troubled. "I know what it is to seek for a good man, for the right man to lead our people. Such a fellow is not always easy to find."

Intuitively, David knew he spoke of the present king. But was not Saul a man of stature and glory? Had he not led Israel to great triumphs?

On this matter, David did not dare inquire further, fearful of hearing the answer. And so he kept quiet, lagging a little behind the master.

Jebus was much closer now. In the hazy dawn it emerged like a sentinel of holy secrets.

"Come," Samuel spurred him, pointing to the easterly rise. "I want to show you something."

Skirting Bethlehem, they hiked around the southern border of Jebus, across Kidron Vale, and came to the Mount of Olives. Then, without a break, they ascended the terraces of the mount, where farmers centuries before had tamed the wild trees into productive orchards. Only when they reached the top, where they could look out across the city, did they stop.

"Sit down with me," Samuel directed, patting the rock which he had chosen for a perch.

"Why are we here?" David asked when he caught his breath."

"Have you never come here?" Samuel inquired.

"Never, sir," David answered. "My father's flocks gazed in the hills of Ephrata."

"And never did Jesse bring you or your brothers here to teach you the ways of the Lord?"

Bewildered, David shook his head. "Does it matter where such things are taught?" he marveled.

Samuel placed his staff across his knees and closed his eyes. "It can matter," he replied, "especially for one such as yourself, who is meant to do great things."

As mystified by the prophet's words as he was the day he anointed him, the boy did not know how to respond. "You speak of the city across from us?" he guessed.

Pleased, Samuel opened his eyes and smiled. "You are a perceptive lad, as I knew you would be," he said with a nod.

Jerusalem—The City of God

"I know that Jebus...Salem ...is a holy city," David replied. "At least it is meant to be. And Moriah is a holy mountain."

"Indeed, Samuel said, gratified by the boy's knowledge. "Did your father teach you these things?"

"He has often said that it is a shame to Judah and Benjamin and all the tribes of Israel that the holy city is in the hands of Gentiles. He says one day it will be ours again, just as the land all about us is meant to be, and that it will be the crown of the nation."

"Your father is a good and righteous man," Samuel confirmed, sighing with pleasure. Such things are not always spoken in the houses of my people."

David placed his elbows upon his updrawn knees and rested his chin in his hands. "Sometimes when I have been alone in the fields I have gazed upon Moriah from many miles away, and I have thought..."

Silence followed as he wondered how to express himself.

"What have you thought, my boy?" Samuel spurred him.

Reflecting, David said, "I have remembered the story of Abraham and the sacrifice of Isaac,,,"

"Yes," Samuel agreed, "It took place right over there." He lifted his staff and pointed to the rock that was now the threshing floor of Ornan.

"I know," the boy said wistfully. "And Jacob's dream, where he saw heaven opened and the ladder with angels going up and down..."

"Yes," Samuel encouraged him.

"My great-grandmother Ruth taught me that the rock Jacob used for a pillow was the very rock you just pointed out."

"Praise Jehovah!" the prophet exclaimed. "It is not every Israelite to whom such insights are revealed."

"She is not an Israelite," David corrected. "She is, in fact, a Moabite."

Incredulous, Samuel looked to heaven. "Merciful God!" he whispered. "Your ways are past finding out!"

Then, turning to the lad and peering deep into his eyes, he seemed to read his soul. "Scarcely do you need a teacher," he said. But when the boy shivered under his gaze, pulling his cloak tight to his shoulders, the old man inquired. "There is more. You were telling me what you have seen when you looked upon Moriah."

"Oh," the lad sighed, "I could never put it into words. I am not certain of it, now that I speak of it."

A little disappointed, Samuel frowned. "Now my boy, you are not one to shrink from you own spirit. Tell me, what have you seen?"

Taking a deep breath, David ventured to reveal something he had kept secret for a long time.

"The first time it happened," he said, "I was just returning home from days away. My flock followed me, their bells the only sound against the quiet afternoon. I glanced to the north to see the outline of Jebus upon the sky. And..."

"Go on," Samuel prodded.

"It seemed a great hand...or a great wing...rested over Moriah."

At this confession, the boy's eyes grew wide and wondering, just as they had that long ago day, and he again fell silent. Then, taking courage, he went on. "It lasted only a few seconds. After a while I thought I had imagined it and forgot it. But then...Oh, Samuel, I have seen that hand, or that wing, more than once. And it fills me with great fear."

"Greater fear than the fear of Goliath?" the prophet asked.

"Greater than any fear I could ever know!"

Satisfied, the prophet placed his broad hands upon his knees and breathed with contentment. "Do you know that you have seen the Hand of Heaven?" he said. "Do you not understand that if the voice of God reached Abraham upon that mount and if the ladder of the angels stretched through the vault of glory from that height, that Moriah is the very door of heaven?"

Speechless, David gazed again upon the windswept table. "But sir," he ventured, "how can that be, if it is now a threshing floor? How could Jehovah permit such desecration?"

"Our God is patient," Samuel replied, "but not infinitely so. The time will come, and has come already, for the children of Israel, the offspring of the patriarchs, to reclaim their rightful priesthood, their proper worship, and…" He paused and looked directly at Moriah. "And the crown of glory!"

Shaken, David sat rigid beside the holy man, sensing that he had brought him here for just this revelation.

"You are the Lord's anointed," Samuel reiterated. "There is much you do not know. But I tell you that God has rejected Saul, for his heart is proud and not believing. Yesterday you became the prince of Israel, and today you will bear the head of the Philistine through the gates of Jebus. Do not stop at Gihon Spring. Do not erect the trophy in the marketplace. March instead to the pinnacle of Moriah and raise the memorial of God's favor upon the rock of sacrifice."

9

Bathsheba Bath Eliam stood on Ornan's rooftop, stretching her tall body for a view down the street.

Surrounding her were four men: her father, grandfather, her friend Ornan, and Uriah, the Hittite. Beside her huddle were the other members of the household: Lisbah, her servants, and children.

This should have been a happy day. Certainly, for most Jebusites it was, because today they would honor the victorious troops of Judah who had freed them from the Philistine oppression. And for the daughter of Eliam, it should have been an especially happy day, for she was now betrothed, promised to a young man as his wife-to-be.

But, as the throngs in the city grew, pressing along the main street, leaning out of windows, hanging over other rooftop ledges to view the approach of Israel's army, Bathsheba was miserable.

Cringing as Uriah leaned close to her, she tried to avoid his leering gaze. "One day, I shall fight with the Israelis," he bragged. "Surely I will be one of their generals, once they see what I can do!"

Turning from him, Bathsheba rolled her eyes. "Very good, Uriah," she muttered, fixing her interest on the boulevard. "Why don't you go out and march with them? They would be honored."

So blinded was the Hittite by his own conceit that he missed the sarcasm in her voice. "Dear lady, you flatter me. But it is not right to impose on the victors' moment of glory."

If Eliam or Ahitophel overheard this interchange, they did not let on. And Ornan, hailing fellow town leaders, was too caught up in his own affairs to pay any mind.

"We have set up a monument in the square," one of his associates shouted up to him, where the Judahites may raise their standard. And the head of the giant—may they erect it there?"

"That will do fine," Ornan called to him. "Will King Saul greet the people from the stage?"

Ornan referred to a permanent platform above the cave of Gihon Spring, where notables often addressed the citizens and the council on public matters.

"Most likely he plans to," the counselor said, "All things are ready, in any event."

Ornan sighed with relief. "That is good," he said. "It would not be wise for him to speak from the grove."

At this, Eliam and Ahitophel glanced knowingly at one another. When it came to matters of religion, they were quite circumspect in Ornan's company, speaking only in broadest terms, so as not to offend their pagan friend.

Indeed, it would be best for Saul to stop his march at Gihon Spring and not proceed farther up the hill, where the rites of Ashtartu dominated the bowers and grottos. Surely the king of Israel would attribute his success in battle to the God of Jacob, and such tribute was best relegated to the marketplace, where free speech was practiced.

After all, this was a day of celebration. Why spoil it with partisan references?

This discussion escaped Bathsheba's notice. During the night, she thought more on her Judahite heritage than ever before in her life. But today, she was encumbered with womanly frustrations and cared more for her own dilemma than for who worshipped whom, or who spoke the name of what god or goddess.

Her greatest concern, at the moment, was the fact that Uriah's breath could be felt upon her neck. Tugging at her shawl, she pulled it up to her chin and tucked her elbows close to her body. Was that his caress she felt upon her arm, or had the milling family pushed him against her?

At last, the sounds of trumpets and drums could be heard, ascending with the march of twenty thousand feet, from the vicinity of the city gate.

The troops of Israel were coming!

Suddenly, Bathsheba was swept up in anticipation. Her grandfather's vivid enactment of the scene between David and Goliath surged her again through her heart, and the hope of seeing the young hero riveted her to the sound of the approaching army.

From the vantage point of Ornan's rooftop, the flags of Judah and Benjamin could be seen passing beneath Jebus's foremost towers. A brilliant morning sun bounced off the shields of Israel's leading warriors, as a mighty blast of rams' horns heralded their triumph.

Because Saul was a Benjamite, his banner came first, flying at the very head of the mighty horde.

Made of the finest linen, it was stretched between two tall pokes, and the horsemen who bore it rode upon black stallions, their glorious standard a streak of scarlet—or princely "purple." Benjamin was the youngest son of Jacob, and hence his favorite prince. According to the words of his father, he would be a ravening wolf, courageous and devastating in battle. Therefore, the symbol of the tribe was a wolf, laid against the purple background in gleaming silver and looking as if it would leap to life at any moment.

Green was the color of Judah that followed directly behind, heralding the army of Benjamin's elder brother. Upon it, in shining gold leaf, was laid a mighty lion, the image of Judah's strength and boldness, and horsemen who held it aloft were mounted on white steeds.

Directly on the heels of the standard bearers came more musicians with shining harps and clapping cymbals, flashing horns and pounding drums. Then, between ranks and rows of stamping soldiers, rumbled wagons full of shining trophies—bronze and iron weapons of the demolished enemy, baskets of coin-filled purses, neckchains and bracelets, helmets, studded boots and leggings, mail coats and personal treasures—all torn from Philistine corpses.

As the plethora of victory passed before the bedazzled populace, excitement grew until the citizens were nearly drunk with it. Woman began to run alongside the marching Israelis, who were suddenly and acutely attractive. Whirling and dancing, the women clapped and sang beside them, throwing their arms about their necks and smearing their faces with kisses.

Of course, the troops were heady with their own joy, and with excesses of the night's revelry. They did not resist the attention heaped upon them, though they did manage to keep their forward march. By the time King Saul and his royal entourage passed under the gate, the city was wild for them.

On less military occasions, Saul would have ridden atop a camel, beneath a great parasol. Or he would have been high upon the shoulders of slaves, seated in a curtained cab upon soft pillows. But today's march was in celebration of war victory, so Saul rode in a two-wheeled chariot, driving his own horses, as he would have done upon the battlefield.

Beside his chariot was that of his son, Jonathan, his chief general.

But Jonathan was not the featured warrior of the day. In the king's own vehicle, standing directly behind him, was young David, the hero of the hour, and the one whose notoriety had filled the streets throughout the night.

Everyone had come out this morning, not only to see the Israeli army, not only to see the victorious king, but especially to catch a glimpse of the valiant giant killer.

The instant he was spotted by those nearest the gate, a great cheer arose, swelling up the boulevard and creating a sensation such as had never been experienced in Jebus, or in Urushalim, or in Salem, throughout its dramatic history.

Though the people had been prepared to greet a child, they were impressed by his boyishness upon seeing him than when they had only heard of him. Having reached bar mitzvah only a year ago, his head reached only to the breastplate of Saul's armor. The husky king, who stood head and shoulders above all the men of Israel, dwarfed him. But he was a spunky lad, his back straight as an arrow, his chin high and his eyes flashing merrily from face to face within the crowd. Now and then he waved to the people, evoking cheers and happy laughter, winning male and female hearts.

The women who graced the troops with their adoration now flocked about Saul's conveyance, tossing bouquets of wildflowers, jangling tambourines, twirling and singing in their long skirts.

David was enthralled, receiving their applause with a dazzled smile, and gesturing proudly to the prize of the parade, the head of Goliath.

Mounted upon the giant's mammoth spear and swaying, above the throng as the warriors carried it, the emblem, grotesque as it was, evoked only applause and feverish exultation, for it represented the end, at least for now, of Philistine oppression.

As for the gathering on Ornan's rooftop, there were as many reactions to the sight as there were people. Eliam and Ahitophel, of course, beamed with pride, saluting their young captain as he passed beneath their gaze. Uriah observed the boyish hero with mixture of wonder and envy, wishing fondly that he might one day serve him.

But Bathsheba's feelings were a muddle, every one of them unexpected. For when she laid eyes upon the hero of Israel, she saw not a slip of a boy, not a childish hero, nor a military conundrum. She saw him through the eyes of young, blossoming womanhood, and the instant she glimpsed him, her heart swelled with emotions new to her.

Bathsheba was a little younger than David. He, with his sun-bronzed skin and wilderness-hardened body, need not have been a grown man to stop her breath.

Suddenly, as she observed his passage beneath the shadow of Ornan's house, the world and all its battles, celebrations, and frustrations receded, dimming to a pale drone behind the spark and fire of adolescent love. She forgot Uriah. She soared above her heartless father and her distant grandfather. She cared not for the mundane joy of Jebus.

Nor did she notice Ornan's agitation when the king's entourage bypassed Gihon Spring, went directly through the marketplace, and headed uphill toward Moriah.

"By all the gods!" Ornan was cursing. "Do they mean to set up their trophy in the grove of Ashtartu?"

Pulling away from the family, his face flushed with anxiety, the Jebusite headed for the stairs and the street below, calling out for his fellow counselors.

Jerusalem—The City of God

As the rooftop gathering followed him, amazed at the gall of the Israelis, Bathsheba lingered at the balustrade.

She could not take her gaze off the chariot of Saul and its regal young passenger. Furthermore, it seemed to her enraptured heart that whatever David chose to do, he surely chose the right.

10

Ornan pressed through the crowd that lined the marketplace, trying to reach the head of the swelling congregation that was swept up in the wake of the Israeli army.

David and his followers were indeed going on. Saul would not address the citizens from the platform above the spring, nor from the steps of the public buildings that lined the market. It seemed he and his young captain intended to erect their tribal banners and the grisly head of Goliath at some higher point.

As the Jebusite trailed them, however, it occurred to him that a chase was futile. What did he expect to do? Would he challenge the victorious king to his face? Would he demand that he turn back, that he not go near the compound of the goddess? On what grounds could he do such a thing?

Slowing the pace, Ornan fell back, matching the stride to that of the crowd. Contemplating what transpired, he suddenly realized that the grove of Ashtartu might be the best place for such a show. If Saul were to invoke the name of Jehovah before the house of the goddess, it could serve to soften the lines of animosity that existed between Jebus and Israel.

Yes, he thought, *this could be an historic day in the diplomatic relations of the three factions. Judah, Jebus, and Saul's tribe of Benjamin could at last lay down the rivalry that has so long existed between us!*

Now when Ornan's step quickened, it was not out of anxiety, but out of enthusiasm, as he raced again to be at the head of the surging crowd. At last drawing near the king's chariot, he considered what he would say when Saul called on him to respond to the offer of unity. Surely the Israeli monarch would do just that!

Ornan, being the designated spokesman of Jebus, its leading judge and counselor, was the closest thing to royalty the city could boast. Without a doubt, he would be summoned to light the ceremonial fire of covenant between the two nations.

He was now side by side with the bloody stake that bore Goliath's head. Mouth agape and forehead caked with gore. It swayed above the marching troops, like some monstrous idol. Though it could not be seen, it seemed, as it dipped and jolted with the traffic, that it sometimes spied its young assassin, and that seeing him, it gaped the more in horror.

Ornan's stomach tightened. In the pagan worship to which he was accustomed, gruesome sights were not unusual, as animals, and even, in extremity, small children were sacrificed to the gluttony of Canaanite deities. But something ghastly spiritual seemed to have attached itself to the amputated head, as though demons swirled about it, and a wave of nausea threatened Ornan, so that he turned his face to the ground, slowing to a standstill and leaning against the nearest wall.

Lisbah, coming upon him, studied his wan face and shaky hands. "Husband," she fretted, "Are you ill?"

Ornan merely nodded and took her arm. Using her as a crutch, he progressed up the street, his family and guests tucked close about him.

Eliam and Ahitophel, assuming that their countrymen's daring behavior must have upset him, whispered together. "What Is Saul up to?" Eliam asked his father. "Does he mean to grace the shrine of Ashtartu with the trophy God has given us?"

"Let us hope not!" the old one answered.

But the intentions of the royal company would come as a surprise to even the most radical Israeli, for, as the grove came into view, just where Moriah sloped toward the crest, the entourage and the marching troops did not slow.

The road at this point, narrowed, becoming more of a path than a boulevard, dividing into numerous winding trails that took off there and there through the leafy grotto. Saul and his company broke off from the general march and did not head to the westerly shrine of Ashtartu, which stood on the opposite ridge. Rather, they headed directly through the grove, toward the flat space atop Moriah.

The citizens of Jebus, amazed, crowded behind the king's chariot, still singing and dancing, but their mood tempered by bewilderment.

Thousands upon thousands huddled together, bending around corners and ducking branches to keep up with the quick-moving visitors.

It had been hundreds of years since and dignitary of any tribe or nation had trekked to the great tablerock. None of those living now in the capital city had ever seen the place so honored, and the occasion was confounding.

Ornan, seeing that his property was the object of the newcomers' march, suddenly forgot his queasy stomach and raced again toward the head of the throng, pushing and elbowing his way to the fore.

"What are they doing?" commoners asked him, thinking he should know.

But he ignored his people's questions, being as much in the dark as they were.

He arrived at the head of the company in time to see young David led from the chariot by Saul's valets. The king had taken a stand atop an outcropping to the northwest of the tablerock. Next to him stood Jonathan; David, receiving the cheers and applause of his troops, joined them, taking Saul's outstretched hand and stepping up beside him.

Over and over, the praise of the troops rang from the mountaintop, filling the vales below and bouncing off the rooftops:

"David Ben Jesse, son of Israel,
David Ben Jesse, mighty giant killer!
David Ben Jesse, son of Judah,
May the God of Israel be your reward!"

Thrilling through the streets, the Israeli chant sparked an enthusiastic echo, as the citizens of Jebus picked it up and passed it on:

"Mighty giant killer...mighty giant killer...
May the God of your fathers be your reward!"

How many years, how many centuries it had been since the God of Abraham had been praised in the city of Moriah, no one thought to ask. Today, at the instigation of a boy and the command of a Benjamite king, Jehovah was, for the first time in generations, being lauded in the holy city.

The last time such a thing had happened, the city had gone by a different name. It was an ancient and almost forgotten name, predating even "Urushalim." The name meant peace, and today, peace had been waged in the streets.

The praise of Jehovah, repeated by pagan and Israelite tongue alike, was a mystical thing, gracing the mountain like a utopian banner.

Ornan, gazing upon young David, chanted the words like all those around him, but, for him, this was not a peaceful moment. For Ornan, the uninvited presence of these foreigners upon his threshing floor was desperately unsettling. What were they thinking, to be here? Why had they chosen this property, of all the sites within Jebus, to erect their emerald and scarlet banners?

As the chanting swelled, rising to the sky and spreading across Canaan, yet another emblem found its foothold upon the rocky table. Ornan cringed as Saul called to the hoisting of the Philistine's hideous head.

Several soldiers came forward, bearing the grisly exhibit, and quickly constructed a pile of stones and rubble in which to stand the bloody post.

The moment Goliath's visage could be seen staring in place above the throngs, the people went wild, stamping and calling out for David. In response, Saul placed a garland about the boy's neck and drew him close besides him, where he waved to his adoring fans.

For Ornan, owner of the site where all this transpired, it was a trancelike moment. Scarcely could he believe what he witnessed, and less could he explain it.

For years, Moriah had troubled him. Was it not a threshing floor, the place where farmers came to winnow their grain and to pay a handsome price for the privilege? But, too often, Ornan sensed a mystery about the mount, something which, even though he tried to deny its existence, had grown to near fixation.

Never had he spoken to anyone about the surreal experiences he had there. But today, the witness of a royal company and the giant's head were not surreal. Likewise, the winglike shadow that passed overhead, covering the mount, and seemingly visible only to himself, was very real.

Falling back, Ornan felt again the prickles of a sticky vine claw into his cloak, the same vine into which he had stumbled the night of his flight from the mountain. Whipping about, he tore his garment from the bush's thorny clutches and tried to steady his nerves.

There were people all about—his people, who looked up to him for leadership. Straightening his robes, he put on a calm face and strained for his dignity.

If he did not show his desperation, no one would guess it.

11

The light was dim in the tent of Saul as the king rested from the day's celebration, and the moon overhead was shadowed with fleeting summer clouds. There was quiet and peace in Israel tonight, though the sound of music and dance still rang in the people's hearts.

Jonathan sat on the tent floor, polishing his war gear to store it away and listening to the soft strumming of David's harp. A contented smile touched his lips, and a faraway look graced his sun-bronzed face as he relived the joyful events of recent hours.

It had not always been easy to be Saul's son. In the prince's younger years, he had adored his handsome and noble father, of whom he was the image. Saul had been a worthy choice as king of Israel, and the young man well remembered the day prophet Samuel had crowned him before the leaders of Benjamin and Judah.

Still, there had always been streaks of character in Saul that made life with him unpredictable, and for a boy growing up in his presence, his father's uncertain temperament made for insecurity. The king's mood had, over recent months, become more and more pronounced; hence the summoning of David Ben Jesse to be his court musician.

To Jonathan's mind, the enlistment of David for this purpose was one of the wisest things Saul had ever done. The boy's music worked magic, not only for the king, but for his family, which too often suffered in the shadow of Saul's melancholy.

Over the weeks since David had come to live with them, Jonathan had grown to love him as a brother, and hours spent listening to his sweet songs were surely the happiest the prince had ever known.

Jonathan was, himself, a military prodigy. He was now in his midtwenties, but at only fifteen years of age he had established himself as a tactical giant, victoriously taking on the Philistines early in his father's reign. Somehow, despite the instability of his homelife, he had a highly developed self-confidence and an appreciation for his heritage as an Israelite that endeared him to his countrymen.

The moment he saw David confront Goliath, his heart was knit to the lad with cords of admiration stronger than he could voice. Therefore, though the giant-killer was twelve years his junior, he was anything but jealous of him, seeing him as a savior of his father's sanity and the Godsend of Israel. Tonight, as he worked on his gear and pondered past hours, he wished he could express to David the gratitude he felt.

Perhaps Saul reflected on similar matters. Certainly, he was deep in thought, reclining upon his campaign couch, eyes closed and wrist resting on his forehead.

A curl of soft, gray smoke arose from a tiny fire at the center of the tent, and the flames cast hypnotizing shadows on the walls. Soon, Saul was humming, as he often did when David played, his baritone a soothing complement to the music.

It was all too perfect—the night, the lyrical tunes, the enchanting play of light and dark. Jonathan sighed deeply and set his weapons aside, drawing his knees up beneath his chin and closing his eyes.

How he wished the rest of the family might be here to enjoy the moment. His mother, Israel's lovely queen, and his sisters, Merab and Michal, were lodged at the royal compound at Gibaeh, four miles north of Jebus. Doubtless they had heard of the brave youth and his slaying of the giant, and how they would have heaped affection upon him!

In fact, as Jonathan thought of his sisters, he knew they would be mad for the boy, being close to his age. The prince grinned privately, imagining their girlish twitter, should they ever lay eyes upon the handsome shepherd.

He remembered how, today, as the troops of Israel had marched to Jebus, females had come out from houses and hamlets all along the way, swept up in the glory of Saul and his young captain. Then, as they returned from Jebus after marching to Moriah, the highway had been lined with dancing females who had come from all over the region of Canaan.

Their singing and their cheers, at first haphazard, had gradually become a great chorus, as they repeated certain phrases over and over.

One Chant, in particular, had caught on, and even now echoed in Jonathan's ears:

"Saul has slain his thousands,

And David ten thousands!"

Of course, David had killed only one man. At first, the giddy exaggeration evoked merry laughter. But as the women persisted, repeating it again and again, dancing and twirling and spinning their tambourines in their hands, it seemed more than the product of feminine infatuation.

It seemed prophetic.

Jonathan remembered feeling good about his father's reaction to the chant. He might have taken offense, but instead, he smiled benignly on the people and kept his royal composure. In fact, Saul had been most gracious to the lad, displaying him upon Moriah as the gift of the Lord against the Philistines, and even placing a garland of wild roses about his neck.

As Jonathan recalled the gesture, it suddenly occurred to him how he might let David know of his own admiration for him. Gleaming in the glow of the tent fire was the prince's polished armor, his most beloved possession.

Impulsively, his heart swelling with unrevealed appreciation, he lifted his shield and held it forth. "Brother David," he said, just as the lad finished a song, "you are a blessing beyond words, to my family and nation. I have thought long and hard on how I might express my gratitude. Here," he commanded, placing his shield tenderly before the musician. "I want you to have this."

As David's eyes widened, and his mouth fell open, Jonathan leapt to his feet, snatching his sword and bow from the ground and laying them atop the shield. Then, he undid his gold-studded belt from his waist and took off his royal robe, adding them to the pile.

Bowing before the boy, he placed a fist to his chest and swore, "I am you friend, forever, David Ben Jesse. And I am your servant!"

In the orange glow of the fire it was not discernible that David's face turned red. Incredulous, he did not know how to respond to the offer or the promise.

He had always admired Jonathan, having heard the stories of his daring military feats from the time Saul had taken the throne. To the son of Jesse, Jonathan was a hero—the one to receive homage, not to give it.

"My lord…" the boy stammered, "I…"

As he struggled for words, however, the king sat up on his couch, a dangerous look of agitation marring his royal countenance. For the last moments, before Jonathan had made his move, Saul had been reclining, humming to himself along with David's music, and singing very low beneath his breath. Neither David nor the prince had paid him much mind, the younger swept up in the harp's melody and the elder in grateful reveries.

But, now it became clear that the king's private lyrics revealed a troubled heart and a jealous spirit. Full-blown now, they raged forth in a torrent resentment.

"Saul has slain his thousands,
And David his ten thousands!"

"Did you hear that?" he bellowed, leaning forward. Fists clenched upon his thighs and eyes bulging from a burning face, he roared at the two young men, "They have ascribed to David ten thousands! But to me they have ascribed thousands!"

As the boys looked on, the king stood up, pacing his tent, back and forth. David, grabbing his harp to his chest, scrambled out of the way, and Jonathan reached for him protectively.

"Father," the prince broke in, "It is all right. The women love you. All the people love you! Let David have his moment of glory. You are the king of Israel!"

But there was no reasoning with Saul. He was in one of those bad humors that were all too familiar to his son. Like a caged lion, he lurched from wall to wall of his tent, his dark eyes feverish and forehead sweating.

"And now you…bone of my bone, flesh of my flesh…my own son…you honor this little urchin above your own father!"

Jonathan, aghast, sensed the threat in that accusation. Pulling back, he drew David with him into a corner, where together they huddled in terror.

Jerusalem—The City of God

Seeing this pushed the king to greater fury, and lunged as though to tear the boy from the prince's embrace. But Jonathan pleaded, "No Papa! You love him as I do! Do not harm him!"

Jerking upright, the king glared at the prince, baring his teeth in a hideous grin. "Papa?" he bellowed. "You call me Papa, and yet you protect my enemy? They have ascribed to David ten thousands, but to me only thousands! What more can he have but the kingdom?"

Out of his mind, the king swept down and grabbed Jonathan's spear from the offering pile. Lifting it to the ceiling, he hurled it with all his strength, straight toward the shepherd.

But the boy was agile and alert, and tumbling to one side, managed to avoid the lethal lance.

Jonathan, shot through with adrenalin, watched the spear impale the tent wall and jumped shakily to his feet.

"Run, David! Run for you life!" he cried.

As the giant killer did just that, the prince followed after, racing with him across the headquarters compound and into the dark fields beyond.

Never in his life had David run from a fight. Nor had Jonathan cowered in battle. David had fought a bear, lion, and a giant, and Jonathan had leveled Philistine camps.

But Saul was no Philistine, and no Goliath. It was that demon that drove Saul, a preternatural thing that Jonathan had often felt and David had now encountered.

There was no fighting a demon. It was best to run and hide.

Interlude

It would not be the last time David and Jonathan fled Saul's spear. It would not be the only time they ran into the dark of night to hide in the fields beyond Saul's camp.

Twice more, over the next several years, did Saul make direct attempt on the giant killer's life, each attempt taking place within his tent, as David played upon his harp. Nevertheless, the fame of David spread as the unpredictable king alternately threatened his safety and promoted him in the ranks of the military.

In time, David became Israel's leading general, and eventually the song sung by women the day after Goliath's death became more than prophecy. It became fact. As the king's reputation faltered and as David grew stronger, the young military genius did indeed lead armies to slay tens of thousands, to Saul's thousands.

Philistia was on the run, making a comeback now and then, only to be further humiliated. Politics of the Canaanite and Philistine area went down in the annals of local kings as an ongoing drama, matched by few other regions on earth.

Likewise, the life of David was a chronicle of personal challenges, triumphs and tragedies unparalleled, as valiant friends entered and exited his life, raised to glory on the wings of war, meeting bloody ends on fields of battle; or as he, himself, was on the run from the lunatic Saul.

When he was not fighting giants or leveling cities, he was often holed up in some cave or some monastery, even within the camp of Israel's enemies, to escape the hand of the royal assassin.

The most intimate pages if his experience were equally sensational, creating daily fodder for hungry gossips, Saul, in his mania to do away with his rival, sank to the lowest tactics, offering David his daughters in marriage if he would take the front line in battles against Philistia. Of course, David had never shrunk from the fray, but to please his king, went beyond the call of duty.

Saul, however, was never pleased. When David did as he required, the king reneged on his promise, giving his eldest, Merab, to another man. He did not follow through when it came to bestowing his younger daughter, Michal, on the son of Jesse, but only due to public pressure.

Besides his military feats and the praises of his people, Michal provided, for a time, one bright spot in David's tormented saga. He loved her dearly, even when her crazed father ripped her from David's embrace and sent her off to an adulterous marriage with another man.

On and on the stories went, piquing the interests of women and men alike. And it was easy, in the mayhem of his existence, for David to forget that God was with him.

It was not until he was thirty years old that the threat which Saul had always posed was at last removed. Meeting an ignominious end, one befitting the condition of his spirit, the king of Israel took his own life.

It happened at Gilboa, where the Philistines overtook Israel until not even Jonathan and his brothers could stand before them. The beloved friend of David was slain that day, and a badly wounded Saul fell upon his own sword, bringing death upon himself.

Not content to see their enemy's demise, the bloody Philistines beheaded Saul and hung his body, along with the bodies of Jonathan and his brothers, from the parapets of Bethshan, to the north of Jebus.

On that day, which was to that point in his life the very saddest, David played once more upon his harp. There was no threat of Saul's javelin, no conspiracy inspired by the vanquished king against him. And so he sang the agony of his heart freely:

"Your beauty, O Israel, is slain on your high places!
How have the mighty fallen
The bow of Jonathan did not turn back
And the sword of Saul did not return empty....
And in their death they were not parted;
They were swifter than eagles,

They were stronger than lions.
O daughters of Israel, weep over Saul....
How have the mighty fallen in the midst of the battle!
Jonathan is slain on your high places.
I am distressed for you, my brother Jonathan;
You have been very pleasant to me.
Your love to me was more wonderful
Than the love of women.
How have the mighty fallen,
And the weapons of war perished!"

It was a much matured and tested David, son of Jesse the Bethlehemite, who took the throne of Judah after the death of Saul. He was thirty years old and it was the year 1011 B.C.E., as people would later reckon time, when he was crowned by the leaders of Judah and established his headquarters at Hebron, south of Jebus.

During the seven years that he reigned in Hebron, he took six wives, each of which bore him a son, and in the last year of his reign at Hebron, Michal, his first and beloved wife was returned to him. Those seven years were glorious, despite the fact that David found new enemies among the family of Saul and his kinsmen, the Benjamites, many of whom resented his intrusion onto their royal position.

At every turn, David and his followers wee victorious. And while mounting court intrigue and political bloodshed might have detracted from his popularity, the young Judahite grew in favor and fame.

In the seventh year of his reign at Hebron, Benjamin and the remaining tribes of Israel came to him, imploring him to be their king, as well.

So, in 1005 B.C.E., David was crowned King of Israel and Judah.

Part V

THE CITY OF DAVID

1005-1000 B.C.E.

1

Michal, the daughter of Saul, sat in her sumptuous chamber atop the royal hill of Hebron, peering up the highway that led north to Jebus. In the light of the waning sun, the spine of hills that divided Canaan from the Jordan Valley beckoned her gaze like a purple finger, luring her thoughts even further north, to the region of her childhood, and the land which had been home for the past fourteen years of her adult life.

Through the fertile land and its twin villages, Gibeah and Gallim, she allowed her heart to wander, impressing each street, each byway and housefront upon her memory. She had been away from them just a few weeks, but she feared she might never see them again.

Only a month ago, she had been brought to Hebron, to take her place, for the second time, as the wife of David. She should have been happy. Just today, David had been crowned king over Israel and Judah, and she, his newly returned wife, was now queen of the grand alliance.

But Michal was not a young bride who, at thirteen years of age, had wed the Bethlehemite. As her brother Jonathan had guessed, she had fallen madly in love with the captain of her father's host when she had first laid eyes on him.

David had been an up-and-coming champion of her people, a hero of unmatched reputation, when Saul betrothed her to him. Never would she have dreamed that her affections for him could cool. It was difficult to remember, now, the heartache and despair she experienced when her capricious father had taken her away from David and given her to another. She had felt at the time that life was over, that she could never again be happy.

But time is a curious thing, working witchcraft upon her heart. She had been certain she could never love Phalti, the son of a Benjamite general. Not nearly so handsome or so bright as David, he had, at first, seemed boring to her, yet with patience and gentleness he wooed her until, at some uncertain moment, she realized she cared.

Jerusalem—The City of God

Of course, she had been but a child upon marriage to both men. Her heart had been a malleable thing. And, after all, she had been David's wife for only one year, compared to fourteen with Phalti.

Yes, she missed Phalti. And she missed her homeland, the region of Gibeah, Saul's royal headquarters. Her life there had been happy before she met David, and it was happy when she resided in the neighboring town of Gallim, where Phalti lived.

A royal palace in Hebron was a cold place when love was not in it.

Not that David did not love her. It seemed his ardor was as strong after all these years apart as it had been upon their first wedding night. In fact, she knew that this evening, when he came calling at her chamber door, he would be especially eager for her intimacies, for it was a time to celebrate.

But any affection she could muster toward the man who won her virginity was now strained.

With a sad sigh, Michal arose from the window, from where could be heard the revelry of thousands in the streets. Hebron had become a virtual armed camp, vast contingencies of Israelite tribes having come to make David their King, and not Judah's only. More than 20,000 Ephraimites, thousands of men of Issachar, 38,000 men of Naphtali, 40,000 Asherites, and 120,000 Transjordanians gathered together on the fields outside of town to celebrate the coronation. David and his noblemen, along with the leaders of the twelve tribes, would doubtless party until the wee hours, in honor of their new confederation. But Michal's solitude would seem all too short before her kingly husband came to press his expectations upon her.

Turning from the window, the queen crossed the room and picked up a horn-handled mirror from her dressing table. The reflection of her gaunt face was softened by the burnished glow of the mirror's bronze surface, lending an appearance of serenity that was not true to fact. Only around the eyes did the churning apprehension of her spirit shine forth, the skin pale and tight within a frame work of coal black curls.

How long she wondered, would she be able to masquerade as the king's willing partner?

Numbly, she rested the mirror in her lap. All her life she had been taught that a woman's highest duty was to serve a man. As a child, she was to unquestioningly obey her father. Once she was betrothed, she was prepared for marriage, and once married, she was to spend her life pleasing her husband in all things.

Her feelings mattered no more than the faithless image in the mirror. Regardless of inner turmoil, she was to appear serene and happy, for the man's benefit.

But what was a woman to do when two men claimed her?

David had the right, did he not, to demand her return? He had been sorely wronged by Saul when his bride had been taken from him. He was only acting properly, now that he was king, in taking her, once again, unto himself.

What right did Michal have to pine for Phalti? Shouldn't she feel guilty when she lay in David's arms and saw only Phalti's face above her? Instead, she felt she betrayed her second husband, and immeasurable guilt was hers on that account.

Hunching over, she felt a tear slide down her face, and as she bent above the mirror in her lap, it splashed onto the gleaming bronze, distorting the image.

What use were feelings anyway? Especially for a woman? There was no acting on feelings. A woman was nothing but a game piece, to be manipulated at the whims of men. It did no good to love or to hate, to feel right or wrong, if one's life was governed by others. Yet there was no eradicating the despair she felt, the longing for her husband of fourteen years, to the misery she experienced each time she must give herself to David.

For once, she was grateful that she had never borne a child to Phalti. Many times she had castigated herself for being "barren," for never fulfilling Phalti's desire for an heir. Though he had never disparaged her, she had felt keenly his disappointment and had wished above all things to offer him a son. But tonight, she was relieved that there was no child in her life, a child whose tearful face would have forever haunted her departure.

Still, there were other things to haunt her, not the least of which was the memory of Phalti's grief and panic as she was taken away. For miles, he had followed the king's deputies as they carried the daughter of Saul away from Gallim, running after them, weeping and calling out for them to reconsider.

Michal had never known such pain was possible as she has felt that day, and the remembrance of Phalti's desperation, his contorted face, his echoing pleas, always brought pain fresh upon her. Even now, as she envisioned his tormented countenance, she relived the horror of that day. Throwing herself upon her bed, she clutched her pillow to her face and smothered an agonized cry.

For a long while she lay there weeping in silence until her pillow was wet with tears.

How much time elapsed before the dreaded knock came at her door, she did not know. But when it came, she managed to stand erect, smooth her garments, and don an aspect of compliance.

Which husband was her true one, she could not say, but as she obeyed the law of man, going to the door and opening it, the law of her heart was broken.

2

David lay rigid upon Michal's bed, jaw tight and fists clenched.

He did not believe that his wife was asleep, though she lay still as a sheep prod beside him. He could not see her face, for her back was to him, as it always was once the love act was consummated. But even if her eyes were closed, he knew she was awake.

He hoped she would not cry again tonight. He had sensed her doing so on more than one occasion since her return. She did not know he was aware of her tears, as she shed them in silence. She waited until she thought he was asleep to let the sadness seep into her pillow.

But he was aware, painfully so.

It had not always been thus for David and his bride. Years ago, when they had shared the love of youth, their passion had been of the poet's kind—a fervid, glowing thing that went beyond song. So enraptured had they been, that when David took up harp to sing of her, he more often threw it down, racing to her side instead, preferring to ravish her than to deplete his energies in music.

In those days, she had never turned from him, as she did now, once their passion was spent. Together they had fallen asleep, entwined face-to-face in one another's arms.

David realized that things could change, after fourteen years apart. Michal had belonged to another man during all that time. The six other wives he had taken, though, had never fully compensated for the loss of his first love.

Confident that his embrace and his kiss could restore any dimmed affection, he had employed his royal power to get Michal back.

Never had he anticipated the degree to which her heart had shifted.

Not prone to force himself upon her, he accepted her reticence. Eventually, she capitulated, permitting him the privilege due a husband. But giving was without emotion, and for each night of the weeks since her return, David had gone to sleep with a hollow feeling in the pit of his stomach.

Jerusalem—The City of God

This night, at least, should have been different, he told himself. Staring at the ceiling, he thought on the celebration he had just shared with his friends and with the entire nation. Must he come to the end of this momentous day only to be greeted, once more, by a cold shoulder and a stony face?

Suddenly, as he heard Michal's tense breathing, longing for her acceptance was overswept by anger. She was his wife and had been his rightful possession for fifteen years! Despite the wrong done to himself and to her by the crazed Saul, she owed David the warmth of a loving spouse!

Turning his head in her direction, he gazed upon her unyielding back. Teeth gritted, he manage to whisper, "Michal…"

He could have predicted her response. There was none.

"Are you awake, Michal?" he growled.

Perhaps his tone was threatening enough. The woman stirred a little, pretending to emerge from slumber. Hesitantly, she turned over, barely opening her eyes.

As she did, her long, black hair moved over her shoulders like a fine shawl, draping the hollows of her neck and arms in a silly caress. Her breasts, like nesting birds, peeled from between the thick curls, and David felt his anger dissipate.

Steeling himself, he glanced away, remembering that her beauty concealed a callous heart. "How can it be that you utterly hate me?" He groaned, sounding more helpless than he meant to.

Before she could reply, if indeed she would reply, he swallowed hard and sat up on the bed's edge. Numbly, he threw his tunic over his naked frame and went to the window from which Michal had observed the festivities of his coronation only hours before.

With a deep sigh, he spoke again. "Do you remember the last night I came to your room? Not this room, in Hebron. But the room in Gibeah, in your father's house?"

Of course she remembered. That had been their final moment together, before they were parted. David had come to her for help, as Saul plotted to kill him once again. It was the one memory of her life with David that had never really left her, for it contained all the elements that typified their romance.

"You saved me that night, Michal," David recalled. "We shared our last kiss and you let me down through your window, by the sash of your gown. I escaped with my life, Michal, because of your love."

The woman was now sitting on the other side of the bed, drawing on her chemise and holding herself with gooseprickled arms. "I remember," she confessed.

At the sound of her voice, David wheeled about, flashing wounded eyes. "You risked your own life for mine!" he cried. "It was for that reason that your father sent you away. How can it be you no longer care?"

Michal's hand flew to her throat, as though to stifle all the unexpressed feelings she had borne since coming here—the tangle of feelings with which she had wrestled for years. Tears brimming in her eyes, she returned David's wounded look.

"Care?" she wept. "Since when does it matter what I care? I cared when I was torn away from you! I cared when I was thrust into the arms of a stranger! For months, I bore the guilt of another man's caress, until I could bear the guilt no longer. And when I began to let myself care for Phalti, I struggled with guilt of that! Since when does it matter what I care? Caring accomplishes nothing!"

By now, Michal was kneeling upon the bed, fists boring into her thighs, face twisted in helpless penitence. David, seeing her agony, stole to her side and knelt beside her, enfolding her stern body in his arms.

"Michal!" he moaned, his voice tender. "I too have suffered. You will never know my despair as I thought of you with a stranger!"

Stiffly, Michal pulled away. "I see how you have suffered!" she rasped. "Six wives and six sons—such suffering is noble, indeed!" Then lifting her chin, she asserted, "As for Phalti, to me he is no stranger. To me, Phalti was my world! He replaced you, David!"

The last words were brittle notes. Like an icy blanket, they descended upon David's heart, freezing the passion in his veins. Seeing that he had truly lost her, he had never felt so impotent.

Avoiding her sad, empty eyes, he rose from the bed and shook himself, going to the window and gazing across the hills that led toward Jebus. Like a homeless soul, he let his mind wander, wondering what glory there was for him, after all.

"You loved once," he sighed, his monologue searching for reason. "I cannot believe you will not love me again."

David did not care that she was silent. Ahead, over the spiney, northwest highway, lay the land he had often viewed as a shepherd from his childhood hills. In the distance, too far to physically see, he envisioned the rock-crowned height of the holy city, and he remembered how Samuel, the prophet, had taken him to Olivet, to show him the fabled mount.

Samuel was now gone, passed away ten years ago. But whenever David was apprehensive, he recalled the destiny to which the old man had pointed him.

"Come here, Michal," the king commanded.

Quivering, the woman crossed the room.

"You are my rightful wife!" David asserted, taking courage, as he always did, from the certainty of his calling. Still avoiding her pensive face, he slipped an arm about her waist, and drew her stiff body close. "With me you shall reign over Israel and Judah. It is meant to be!"

For an instant, Michal trembled. David did not know if the reaction bode well or not. But it was at least a response, and he was determined to build upon it.

"Across those hills, my lady, lies the greatest city on earth. It is meant to be mine...ours, my lady. I shall take Jebus, and it shall be our capital!"

Glancing her way, he found her expression inscrutable. Did she resist him out of fear? Fear of her own heart? Reaching his arms about her, he pressed her head to his broad shoulder.

"I shall give you the eternal city," he insisted. "Then you shall love me."

3

Ornan the Jebusite paced the rooftop of his aristocratic home, nervously rubbing his hands together. Beside him strode the stocky leader of Jebus's army, a practiced general whose troops had fought beside Judah and Benjamin for a generation.

"You realize that we stand alone," Remon said. "If Judah goes against us, Benjamin will join them, for David now commands all of Israel under one banner."

Ornan glanced over the balustrade with furrowed brow. "I cannot believe it. You say the hosts of David are gathering on the valley floor?"

"All the hosts, sir," Remon acknowledged, nodding his turbaned head. "The men of Judah and Benjamin departed their homes this morning, leaving Jebus for the valley floor as soon as the city gates opened." Stroking his dark moustache, he added, "Even men like your old friends…Eliam and Ahitophel."

At the sound of their names, Ornan cringed. He had hoped against hope that his worst suspicions were unfounded.

David had been king of Judah for seven years, and during that time there had been a growing unrest among the Hebrews, as certain factions had talked of Israel's "right" to Jebus.

Ornan did not understand their infatuation with the place. It had never been an Israeli stronghold; there had never been an Israeli king in the Jebus palace. Since the time of Joshua, the flags of Judah and Benjamin had waved from ramparts, alongside the ancient Hittite flag that represented the Jebusites, as the three entities coexisted here.

So long as Saul had governed the Hebrews, there had been no fear of civil strife. But ever since David had taken the throne, there had been whisperings in the streets to the effect that the "promise to Abraham" must be fulfilled.

Ornan vaguely knew who Abraham was. He knew the Israelis had some tradition to the effect that the long-gone patriarch had been vouchsafed the mountain of Jebus as a sacred possession, But Abraham had never reigned here. When he had dwelt in Canaan, he had lived in tents, northeast of Hebron. Even there, he had been only a sheik, and not a king.

The prince of Jebus had always known that his Judahite friends did not share his religion. But they had never made much of any other persuasion, and so he was troubled when they began to appear uneasy in his presence, avoiding his dinner parties and socializing increasingly with their Israeli compatriots.

It had been nearly a year since they reciprocated an invitation, requesting his family's attendance at one of their own functions. And since David had been crowned king of all Israel, they had virtually disappeared from Ornan's roster of associates.

"You think Eliam and Ahitophel would take up the sword against us?" he muttered. The question was more a statement than an inquiry.

"It is a certainty," Remon replied. "Already they have been given command of four companies of a hundred men each!"

At this revelation, Ornan's heart sank. Memories of good times shared with the Judahite commanders graveled him. Suddenly, he, who had been spared personal involvement in war all his life, found himself wishing to retaliate.

"So," he snarled, "Judah and Benjamin would bite the hand that has fed them for four hundred years!"

"It appears so," Remon agreed.

Ornan surveyed his city, its windows glowing with homey lights as the sun descended. "How many of our people know of the gathering army?" he asked.

"By morning all will know," the captain answered. "The battalions of Jebus are on alert, and the tower guards await your command."

His command? Such requirement was new to Ornan. Always before, when the forces of Jebus had gone to war, their generals had shared responsibilities with the generals of Judah and Benjamin. Now that Jebus was on its own, Ornan was thrust into a position of decision making that was foreign to him.

Vastly ill-prepared, he growled, "You address me as commander-in-chief? What are my credentials? I rely on you, Remon, to confront these issues!"

Actually, Remon had anticipated this reaction. He had deferred to Ornan only out of political courtesy. With a self-satisfied sigh, he bowed. "Very well, sir. I shall serve you to the best of my ability."

Ornan perceived his veiled condescension, and red flush tinged his cheeks. "You may go, Remon," he commanded. "Return at dawn, when you see how matters progress."

Still bowing, the captain backed away and departed for the street, leaving Ornan to face a vacuous night.

Far to the south, the moving lights of Israel's gathering forces could be seen bordering the vale where the Philistines and their champion, Goliath, had headquartered years before. Ornan's hair bristled as he considered what chance his people stood against David's formidable host.

The prince of Jebus had led a privileged life, sheltered by the three-way alliance that had once held his city in security. He had been able to enjoy power, without much price, and wealth without direct threat. Though Jebus had quaked at the approach of mighty armies, it had always had its friends to defend it, and had always emerged unscathed from the battles of neighboring tribes.

Tonight, for the first time in recent history, the city stood in imminent and immediate danger. It was the focus of a jealous horde, a people who had once been content to share its glory.

Though Ornan was no king, he claimed kinship with men who had worn the crown in times past. What, he wondered, had his predecessors done, when faced with such threat? Doubtless they had cried out to the city's overseeing goddess. Ornan, being a less-than-zealous worshiper, did not frequent the temple of Ashtartu. But perhaps it was a good time to do so.

Stepping to the head of the stairs that led to his family quarters, he cocked his head and listened to the voices of his family below.

Innocent to the threat aligning itself outside Jebus, the woman and her servants went about business as usual. Ornan slipped down the stairs and stole into the night, up the market path, without their missing him.

Bearing west, he skirted the grove where, even at this late hour, men and women tarried, savoring the carnal pleasures that faith in the goddess inspired. Oblivious to the bypasser, no one greeted him, or knew who he was, and so he made his off-hour pilgrimage in private. When he reached the marble temple of Ashtartu, its columns taking on the sheen of moonlight after absorbing a scarlet sunset, he was ready for prayer.

The trek up this incline always suggested fear to his beleaguered heart, as it forced him to come nigh his threshing floor, which lay on the opposite rise. He did not wish to encounter any strange manifestations on this night, of all nights. But as he ascended the broad steps that led to the goddess's sanctuary, he was surprised by unexpected activity, the goings and comings of priestly servants, as they carried incense to the altar.

Greeting one of them, and adolescent boy with the shaved head typical of an initiate, he inquired, "Are the priests still in the holy house? Isn't the hour of prayer long past?"

He referred to the vesper vigil that took place each evening, just before twilight. At that hour, the aroma of the daily sacrifice, offered in the form of grain and small birds upon the altar, wafted over the city, assuring the people that the overwatching spirit of the goddess had been invoked for the night.

"It is, sir," the boy answered. "But the priests are troubled. There are strange happenings, and they offer up extra petitions."

Ornan looked about, seeing nothing peculiar in the area.

"Strange happenings?" he mused.

Then realizing that the priests had a clear view of the valley from their hilltop, he figured that they had seen movement of Israel's troops in the southland and made additional prayers for safety.

"Yes," Ornan replied, "there is trouble afoot. It is this I come to pray about, myself."

Hastening toward the prayer chamber, he called over his shoulder, "Tell your master I would like to speak to him. I could use his advice."

Amazed, the boy followed after him. "Then, you have heard it, too?" he marveled. "It is audible from the streets below?

Ornan was befuddled. Perhaps the priests had noted the gathering lights on the valley floor. But there was no sound discernible from Israel's movements, certainly not from this height. "Audible?" he said. "What do you speak of, boy?"

Just as the youngster would have answered, however, he fell back, huddling in a niche of the temple wall, his hands over his ears. "There!" he cried. "Surely you hear it! We have heard it all day, and not even the priestly seers know what it portends!"

Barely was the lad's voice distinguishable above the sudden soar of a great wind overhead. Sweeping down over the temple and hovering, it moved back and forth, stirring the trees and groves with pulsating blasts, like the fanning of mighty wings. Quaking, Ornan joined the boy in the wall's stony fissure and shielded himself from the flailing tempest.

He would not confess it to this stranger, but he was familiar with this phantasm, not in such violent form as it took tonight, but surely as dreadful.

"How long has this been going on?" he shouted as the storm whipped and surged about them.

"Since early this morning," the boy replied. "About the time the gates of Jebus were opened."

Recalling his conversation with Remon, Ornan grew wide-eyed. The moment the gates had opened had been the moment of turning, when Jebus's allies had joined the cause of David.

What connection that great exodus could have with the swelling flight of Moriah's invisible specter, he did not understand. But as he pondered the mystery, the great wings thrust eastward, the sound of them fading, as though they settled over the threshing floor.

4

It was a night for looking toward the valley. Bathsheba Bath Eliam stood alone on her rooftop, just as Ornan had done upon his, gazing south and wondering over the gathering lights she saw there.

She had known since her husband's dawn departure that a war was brewing. But he did not tell her that the Israeli object would be to take the southern fastnesses of Jebus, the city that he, she, and all their family called home. He had not told her that, in serving David this time, he would be turning traitor to Ornan and Lisbah.

She had not asked him what David intended. The role of the woman-left-behind was one she had learned well, and she rarely inquired into the specifics of her husband's duties.

Twenty-two years she had been wife to Uriah "the Hittite." She had been repelled by his flamboyance and braggadocio at the beginning. But no human being, regardless of first impressions, can be forever ugly, if a tender heart shines through.

Just as Phalti had won the love of Michal, Uriah might have won his lady, had he taken more pains to do so. There had been moments during these years when Bathsheba's heart had softened, moments when Uriah took the time to speak tenderly and woo gently. But so rare had those moments been, so broken up by times of absence, that any hint of blossoming affection was clipped at the bud.

And now, repeated disappointments had built a crusty layer over her heart, so that precious little warmth emanated toward her husband.

If there was a single picture Uriah had framed of himself in the couple's household, it was a soldier making ready for war. How many times had Bathsheba seen him bent before the parlor fire, intent on polishing his weapons? Were he to die tomorrow, upon some dusty battlefield, this was the memory she would have of him, the legacy he would leave for her at the threshold of his grave.

As always, he rattled on as he worked, recounting the ways he had distinguished himself to David. Just as he had predicted when he first laid eyes on the young giant killer, he had eventually joined David's army. And he had distinguished himself for bravery, so that by the time David was king of Judah, he had caught the attention of Joab, captain of the Judahite forces.

In fact, Uriah was with Joab now.

He had departed in the early morning, the only thing unusual about his exit was that he gave Bathsheba and her maid instructions to stay home all day and go nowhere near the marketplace. This command, she would later learn, had been given to all Judahite and Benjamite families living within the city as their men departed for the valley.

If the warning seemed peculiar, Bathsheba reasoned only that some skirmish was planned for the plain outside gate, and that her husband, in and unusual attempt to spare her sensitivities, wished to prevent her exposure to unsavory sights.

Other than this, his good-bye was typically fervid and hasty. Slinging his quiver and great bow over his shoulder, sheathing his fresh-gleaming sword and grasping spear in hand, he had swept his wife up with his free arm and planted a wet kiss upon her cheek.

"Your father and grandfather wait at the gate," he said. "Pray for us."

With that, he left, not waiting to hear her unasked question. What the Hebrews planned, she was left to ponder. Even if she had managed to inquire, he surely would not have told her.

Trying to ignore the heaviness that descended over her spirit as he walked out the door, Bathsheba has steeled herself. Brushing a lock of her long, black hair back from her pale face, she had turned for a chair and taken up an unfinished needlework.

A few times during the day her portly maid had looked in on her, only to be shooed away. But it was bedtime now, and Bathsheba resisted turning for her empty room.

"Dorca," she called, summoning the rejected maid, "Bring some warm wine and sit with me on the roof."

Not surprised at this request, the maid hurried to comply. It was not the first time her mistress had called for her company on such evening. Placing a tray of wine and crackers upon a little table, she sat down across from Bathsheba and gazed with her toward the valley floor.

"Will Master be away long?" she asked, eyes wide in her oval face.

Bathsheba did not look at her as she replied, but reached forth a hand and patted her on the knee.

"You are a good friend, Dorca," she sighed. "The best a woman could have."

5

Joab, captain of the army of Judah, sat outside his tent on the shepherd field of Jebus. His sun-burnished face was tinged even more golden by the light of his dancing campfire, and as he added a small pile of branches to the flames, his eyes were lit with excitement.

A month ago, the chiefs of David's united forces, the armies of Judah and Israel, had met at Hebron. There David had announced that he would storm Jebus, and ever since Joab had lived on the edge of anticipation, his spirit alive with eager yearning.

Only this morning, Joab had met again with the king and the chief commanders, and it seemed he lived in a dream.

Indeed, it was a dream come true for any Hebrew leader to think that he might participate in the taking of the promised city, the one Jehovah had deeded to Abraham a millennium before!

Glancing toward the sound of shuffling beside his tent, he saw that Uriah had arrived and stood tentatively in the shadows. Likely he hesitated to interrupt the general's reveries, but the moment he caught Joab's eye, he snapped straight as an arrow and thrust a hearty salute toward his chest, fist clenched to denote his readiness to serve.

"Come forward," the general greeted.

Stepping into the firelight, Uriah bowed respectfully. "I received your summons, sir," the Hittite replied.

Joab could tell by the veiled surprise in Uriah's tone that he was full of suspense regarding this off-hour meeting. "Sit, sit," Joab said, patting the ground at his side. When the big redhead had taken his place, Joab explained, "I wish to speak with you, friend, regarding the assignments for tomorrow."

"Yes, sir," Uriah answered, still bewildered as to why he, one of the lesser ranking officers, should be so honored.

Seeking to put him at ease, Joab smiled. "You are a good man, Uriah," he said through gleaming teeth. Picking up a stick, he prodded the fire's flashing embers. "A good and trustworthy soldier."

Uriah, amazed at this endorsement, bowed his lion-like head.

"I am honored to serve you, my lord," he replied.

"But," Joab went on, "I doubt that you, being a…Hittite…fully appreciate the Hebrew jealousy for Jebus."

Uriah squirmed, fearing that the general harbored some doubts as to his willingness to help wrest the capital from Jebusite hands. Quickly, he responded. "The day I took the oath of service to David, I also swore allegiance to David's God. I am not a Hebrew, but I honor your belief that Jehovah has promised my city to the children of Abraham!"

Struck by Uriah's enthusiastic devotion to the Hebrew agenda, Joab gave a bemused laugh. "You have no qualms, then, about this undertaking?" the general marveled.

"I spent years of my life searching for the ultimate cause," Uriah confessed. "My quest took me to many a foreign battlefield, where I expended myself in great adventure under this king and that. The Jebusites have no king, you know. I suppose I always longed to identify with some great conqueror, having no sovereign of my own."

Uriah's expression was wistful. Joab had never heard him speak so and had not thought Uriah as a man of depth so much as the ideal, unquestioning warrior.

Leaning close to the fire, Joab studied his comrade's face, "did you ever find such a conqueror?"

"Not before David," was the simple reply.

Leaning back, Joab cupped his updrawn knees in his hands. "So, this is why you follow Jehovah?"

Uriah's eyes grew wide, like a child's. "Is it an unworthy reason?" he inquired.

Again, Joab was caught by an unexpected side to Uriah's nature. If he ever entertained doubts as to the Hittite's sincerity, they escaped him now.

"No, friend," he chuckled. "There in no unworthy reason to follow Our God."

Pulling off his turban, he laid it on the ground, wiping his brow where the leaping fire had raised a light sweat. Joab's hair, streaked with a sandy cast, reminded Uriah that the general was of mixed lineage. Though he was a step-nephew to David, ancestors on his father's side were related as much to the sea people of the west as to the darker-hair Hebrews who had come with Joshua into Canaan. The realization was a comfort to Uriah, who was a stranger to the company.

As the fair-haired Joab prodded embers again, he took a deep sigh. "This conversation pleases me," he said. "Which brings me to the reason I have called you to meet with me, Uriah."

Locking his fingers in his lap, Uriah tried to control his excitement.

"I have been making some new assignments," Joab explained. "After meeting with David and the other generals this morning, I have decided to make you one of my thirty top commanders."

When Uriah started, Joab glanced his way. "Does this suit you?" he asked.

The Hittite's head grew light. Instantly, he calculated the extent of such power.

Since the uniting of the forces of Judah and Israel, David's army numbered close to half-a-million, 300,000 on duty. With the new assignment, Uriah would head no fewer than ten thousand troops!

With a gulp, the big fellow stammered, "Why, sir, yes, sir!" he replied. Then thrusting his fist against his chest, he again saluted, this time so zealously Joab wondered that he did not break his sternum.

"I shall do you proud, General Joab!" Uriah swore.

"Very well," Joab agreed. "I expect you will. That is why you shall be one of the three generals of the thirty select."

Uriah could scarcely believe his good fortune. This was more, far more, than he had ever dreamed of. "This means that my men shall be with the hosts of Abishai, your brother, and Benaiah?" he reckoned, naming the obvious partners in the trio.

"Correct," Joab confirmed.

The Hittite already visualized where he would be in the field and how his 10,000 would arrayed.

"You shall advance from the east," Joab verified. "Abishsi will come in from the south …"

"…and Benaiah from the west!" Uriah filled in. His heart sped as he heard the sound of marching feet and pounding drums in his head.

Joab easily read the ardor in his friend's face. Surly he could trust him with more of the inner workings of the king's intentions.

Prodding the embers again, he began, "Uriah, you have satisfied me that your loyalty to David is untainted, and that you love Jehovah as much as any Hebrew. I know you believe, as we do, that the capital is meant to be ours, from the foundation of time."

Uriah got that wide-eyed look again, the one of innocent faith.

"I do," he declared.

"And do you understand why," Joab said, running his hand over his gold-tinged beard, "do you understand why David feels now is the time for the taking of Jebus? Do you know why this given moment, out of all the millions of moments since the days of Father Abraham, is the opportune one for all of Israel?"

What Joab was about to share would never lightly be shared with any Gentile. But Uriah had now been made commander of a top regiment. The general must see that he understood the agenda from a political as well as idealistic perspective.

"I had not thought of it as a question if timing," Uriah admitted, "so much as a matter of expedience. Jebus is the most defensible city on earth. Any wise king would be jealous for it!"

Joab smiled a gleaming smile. "Spoken like a true warrior!" he said, more accustomed to this side of Uriah's character.

Then, reflecting upon the Hittite's observation, he cast his eyes toward the moonlit stronghold. Nestled amongst three cradling valleys, Jebus was a strategic phenomenon. As though some titanic builder had purposely scooped fissures in the earth wherein to construct a town, and had used the scooped debris to ring fortifications all about, the pre-human earthworks upon which the town had grown were a marvel of godlike foresight.

Glistening in the night's silver light, the city was a challenge to any would-be conqueror, making her the most desirable. Yet only a few had owned her, and she had survived the wars of nations and races all around, escaping a handful of ravagers like a quick-growing field, whereon signs of fire and havoc were rapidly replaced by new dwellings and stronger fastnesses.

Indeed, Jebus, the ancient Salem and more recent Urushalim, was a worthy symbol of peace, to this point managing always to stay a little aloof from the devastations that marred less secure habitations. Not even Jericho, with its impregnable wall, had stood as long. And, as far as time was concerned, the cities of a land so great as Egypt, regardless of their surpassing grandeur, were babes by comparison.

"But," Joab went on, "you only speak the obvious, my friend. So far as Israel is concerned, there is more to the need for Jebus than mere military expedience."

Leaning close again, he scrutinized the Hittite's ponderous face. "Why," he quizzed, "does David not stay in Hebron? It has been his capital for seven years, and he has done well there. Why throw us into war, if the taking of Jebus is only a matter of possession? Is our king so proud or power-hungry as to call for war in time of peace?"

At this, Uriah snorted. Recalling the past few hours, as he had help Joab, Abishai and Benaiah organize factious groups of Israelis into fighting units, he rankled at the word.

"Peace?" he chuckled. "It is true that the people of David are presently at peace with other nations. The King has lifted you to a position of strength that holds even the Philistines at bay. But, among yourselves ...there is anything but peace.

"Especially between the Judahites and Benjamites. Right?" Joab offered.

"Exactly!" Uriah replied. "I mean no insult, sir. But never have I seen such wrangling among 'brothers' as I did this morning! If each tribe claims that your General Joshua intended Jebus for them, what will become of the city once Israel wins it?"

Now it was Joab's turn to snort. "You leap too far ahead, my friend. Let us look at the immediate results of the conquest."

Picking up the discarded stick with which he had stirred the fire, he proceeded to draw, in the dirt, a crude outline of the Israeli provinces.

"Before the unification of the tribes at the crowning of David over all Israel, the Judahites were masters of the south," he said, pointing to the region nearest his feet. Gesturing to the boundary nearest the fire, he went on. "And Benjamin controlled the area north of Jebus." With a sigh, he mused, "Joshua intended the city to be shared by the foremost and youngest sons of Jacob. Instead, it became a bone of contention between them, and, due to their divided strength, neither ever wrested it from the Jebusites."

Satisfied that Uriah was a comrade enough to take no offense, he gave a wink, and went on.

"The conquest of Jebus will serve many unifying purposes among the people of Israel." Drawing a double-tipped arrow from Benjamin to Judah and back again, he postulated, "It has surely not escaped David that in making Jebus his new capital, he will compensate the Judahites for the loss of Hebron as the chief city. At the same time, it will become common ground for the two contending tribes. "Finally," he said with a flashing smile, "the fact that all twelve tribes will be involved in the conquest will be the most unifying factor of the campaign, cementing the bonds forged by Hebron alliance!"

Shaking his head in wonder, Uriah enthused, "All of this David has shared with you? A genius he is!"

"The greatest of geniuses!" Joab agreed. "We serve no little king!"

"Why," Uriah expostulated, "with such cunning and with so many years ahead of him, he shall surely conquer the world!"

Joab had never liked Uriah so well as he did this moment. Reaching out, he clapped him on the shoulder.

"With men like you at his side, he could do no less!"

Reddening, Uriah again bowed his head.

But Joab brought him back to the moment. "Tomorrow, the future lies with us," he pronounced. "I have called you here for myself as well as for the good of David."

Tense with expectation, Uriah leaned on Joab's every syllable.

"At dawn," the general repeated, "David will give his plan for the commencement of the attack. I have sat here all evening trying to imagine his strategy," he confessed. "He has elected to save the revelation till the very hour. Nonetheless," he enthused, "I have no doubt that the king will honor the one who takes the lead in the venture, whatever the strategy!" Then, leaning forward, he proclaimed, "Until now, I have been general of Judah, only. Tomorrow, I intend to tale the *lead!* I intend, Uriah, to be made commander-in-chief of *all* the king's forces!"

Awed, the Hittite nodded enthusiastically.

"With men like you behind me, I shall succeed," Joab added. "Will you help me?"

Astonished that the general would seek his endorsement, the Hittite leaped to his feet. For him, there was no moment but this, no life before this.

"I would die," he swore, "to bring you such honor!"

6

David rode across the dewy fields north of Hebron, heading toward Jebus's dawn walls. Never in his life had he been so keenly aware of his senses, perceiving sound and smell, sight and touch as though they were amplified tenfold.

He had passed through the shepherd fields of his hometown, Bethlehem, countless times, and he knew the distant gates and hillside greenery of Jebus like his own hand, having gazed upon them in every mood and under every shade of light since childhood.

Today, as dawn played upon the white walls, it drew from them a pink luster, like that of a rare pearl. The rosy tinge blended with the haze of morning, glancing off the vapor in an aura.

The ground, too, across which David traveled, was radiant, the dew of countless grassy fronds shimmering in the twilight like diamonds on an emerald robe. Dotting the velvet slopes across the valley were ever-present, cloud-like clusters of woolly sheep and the speckled surprises that were the goat herds, their spiky horns spearing the scene wherever they raised their heads.

David was a poet. It could not be said that these subtleties of the changing horizon had never impressed him before. But today he saw them with new eyes, more keenly aware of them than ever.

Perhaps all would-be conquerors experienced such heightened perception as they approached the regions they yearned to possess. Perhaps the fact that their heads were full of strategy and risk brought an edge to their senses, rather than overpowering them.

Whatever the reason, as David turned about in his saddle to see that his ten thousands followed in rank behind him, he was as in touch with the landscape as with the imminence of war. Before the scent of battle, he smelled the dew and fields. Before the sound of ramshorn and drum, he heard the flight of crickets as his horse's hooves split the turf. And above the drama of coming conflict, he yearned to possess what was meant to be his, to render the rightful ownership of Jebus to his dispossessed people.

Since he had been a lad, watching the movement of troops upon the north-south highway that passed his haunts, the same route he now traversed, he had wondered what warriors think as they are about to attempt their greatest conquests.

Now he knew. They thought about their gods, and desired that they be with them, invoking them with each footfall, just as he now invoked the aid of Jehovah. They thought of coming dangers, but not deeply, for fear of fearing. They thought of the glory laid before them, should they succeed, just as he now thought of the kingdom he would build upon the slopes of Moriah. And they thought of the shame, should they fail. But this they did not ponder, protecting their hearts against cowardice.

To his surprise, he found himself thinking, also, of Michal. He wondered if Joshua had thought of Rahab, or Abraham of Sarah, when death taunted them. He wondered if they fought as much for the praise of their women as for the praise of fellow men.

If they did, they did not admit it, just as he would never admit it. Except to Michal herself, when the time came to bare, again, his heart.

Clenching his horse's reins, he stared toward the fabled stronghold. Jaw tight, he forced his wife from his mind and focused on upcoming maneuvers, the ones he had laid awake many a night plotting.

His charioteers, the infantry close behind, had attained the shepherd fields at the southern foot of the Jebus ascent and were now within earshot of the city's parapets and ramparts. As anticipated, the battlements were lined with armed men, spears and shields gleaming in the risen sun.

With a drumming heart, David raised a hand in the air, calling his men to halt, and like a stifled tide they did so, shifting anxiously as they studied the enemy.

At the sight of the Jebusites, David suddenly and wholeheartedly focused upon his goal. The fact that he had returned home, that he now sat astride a kingly mount in the very fields he had worked as a humble shepherd boy, did not phase him. All sentiment fled, all nostalgia departed.

Hand against hand, blood versus blood. This was all that mattered.

Jerusalem—The City of God

Scanning the hillocks that bordered the Jebus rise, David took a deep breath and gestured to his armor-bearer, a mere slip of a lad, like himself when he had first served Saul.

"Gather the chief officers. We will confer yonder," he commanded, indicating a little swale at the eastern base.

The fleet-footed lad sped off, and David proceeded toward the hollow, his pulse racing with desire for combat.

From the ramparts, as the king passed through the field, the Jebusites hurled invectives and filthy epithets, fueling Hebrew wrath.

"You think to storm the mighty citadel?" they scoffed. "Sheep ticks, all of you! Sons of mules!"

With burning eyes, David looked straight ahead, not deigning to honor them with a glance.

Behind, the sound of galloping hooves told him the generals and commanders of his united armies rushed to join him, and as they surrounded him, their stamping mounts snorted as if to protest the insults.

Though the churning mounts raised clouds of dust in the small hollow, Joab lowered the end of his head scarf from his face and announced, "Your captains are here to serve you, O king! And to silence the rabble upon the walls!"

Even as he spoke, Hebrew ears tingled at the ongoing indignities. "The blind and the lame could protect Jebus!" the city-dwellers shouted. "Your spears and arrows are worthless, you sons of donkeys! You are paralytics, amputees!"

David, pretending no offense, gathered his men close. "They're right, you know, about the city. It is the strongest on earth!"

Shrugging, the captains looked at one another. "We have always known this," they agreed.

Then, to their relief, David added, "But there is one thing they have not counted on."

Poised in their saddles, they paid rapt attention. They had expected that David had some secret in his cloak, and they knew he was about to draw it out.

"Listen," David said, leaning his head toward Jebus's eastern slope.

Thinking that he referred to the ongoing insults being hurled from the wall, the men chafed. But when he asked, "Do you hear it?" they were bewildered.

It was Uriah who dared object. "What good does it do to heed their foolishness?" he growled. "We must resist it!" he shouted, pounding the horn of his saddle with a clenched fist.

But David shook his head. "No," he corrected. "Listen carefully. What do you hear in the gully?"

Like Melchizedek of old, they cocked their heads toward Gihon Vale, until, just as that venerable founder had done, they heard the sweet song of the perennial fountain that was the city's water source.

"It is the spring," Joab replies. "But it has always been there."

"Of course," David answered. "The city's main water source. But look," he directed. "The walls are built behind it, not around it."

Again the officers were bemused. "To construct fortifications in such a low spot would have been worthless," Uriah said. "They could have been too easily stormed."

"Right," the king agreed. "But how do the people access their water without going beyond the wall?"

Uriah, being a native of Jebus, related what they all knew. "In very old times, the inhabitants of the city dug a tunnel, an underground canal. By means of it, they are able to reach the spring without being exposed."

David studied the Hittite, and for a long while, they were all silent, as the king waited for his unspoken plan to dawn upon them.

David could see by the light in their eyes, which came first to one and then another, that they did indeed suspect his secret strategy.

"The canal runs both ways," David said with a grin, "both in toward the mount, and outward, toward the spring. If the citizens can access the spring by means of the tunnel, why shouldn't outsiders be able to reach the city by the same means?"

Amazed, the men considered his plan. Was it possible that in all of the city's long history, no invader had ever thought this before?

Jerusalem—The City of God

Joab squirmed in his saddle. He had not anticipated such a method. The tunnel, he knew, must be very low. People coming and going through it did so nearly doubled over. Could he take thousands through it safely? If they were detected, they could all be caught in the shaft, the helpless target of enemies on both ends.

Nevertheless, dreams of personal glory caused his hands to itch for battle. Barely could he wait for the king to give the command.

Surveying his men with pride, David gave the challenge.

"Whoever gets up to the city through the canal and smites the Jebusites," he announced, "shall be chief commander of all my forces!"

Before another man could think to speak, Joab's hand was in the air.

"I, my Lord," he shouted. "I, Joab, your servant, shall do as you say! And I shall be the finest general Israel has ever known!"

7

Ornan's head ached, his temples throbbing with anxiety. Wiping his hands upon his robe, he paced the ramparts along which his army was arrayed.

He knew next to nothing about war, but he could not believe his city was so impregnable as his troops let on. Had it ever, in fact, been tested?

Most of its battles, in its long history, had been fought on the plains below, or its men had done duty in service to neighbors across Canaan and the armies of one foreign overlord or another. What did anyone really know of Jebus's strength?

True, she was fabled for her geography, her cradling hills and vales seemingly designed by a martial titan.

But Ornan sensed that his men put too much stock in military theory. Deep inside himself he was uneasy, filled with angst that went beyond the mere anticipation of imminent conflict.

He had felt such consuming dread before, but only in one place—the ancient threshing floor. He did not understand why it should come upon him now, when he was positioned well below that spectral place.

His troops, under the command of Remon, were stationed along the southern front of the Ophel, also called "Millo," the mighty fortress constructed by Melchizedek centuries before. Since sawn, as the armies of David had first begun to move, a dark cloud swelling across the lowlands, the fidgety Jebusites had consoled themselves by inventing insults against the enemy, outdoing one another in a contest of vile wit.

Their ribald bravado made Prince Ornan queasy, especially feeling as he did, that there was something dreadfully amiss, something that neither he in his ignorance nor his most astute counselors and strategists has taken into account.

Pacing the bulwark, he winced at the slights thrown at the advancing Israelis. Against his will, he continually glanced over his shoulder toward Moriah, as though anticipating another horde, perhaps not of this world, making its own advance.

Jerusalem—The City of God

When David and his generals were seen huddling near Gihon Spring, Ornan bristled. What they could want there, he knew not. Did they intend to cut off the city's water source? Surely not. Such a strategy would create a slow triumph, and Ornan did not imagine David planned anything slow, since he had brought tens of thousands against Jebus.

No, there was more to their gathering at Gihon than Ornan could imagine.

The sun had fully burned away the haze of morning, changing the walls from dawn-rose to glaring white, when an ominous quiet filled the valley. David's anxious troops had aligned themselves into steely ranks, like dusty statues, the kaftans and headdresses of their various tribes a crazy-quilt of unmoving color upon the desert floor.

Here and there a camel shifted from foot to foot, or a horse bobbed its armored head. But beyond such animation, the Israeli army appeared toy-like from the distance of Ophel's parapets, ready for the hand of some giant child to move them.

Far from reassuring, however, this uncanny stillness, the rigid silence of an enemy prepared, had an unnerving effect upon Ornan and his minions. For what seemed an eternity, the pall prevailed, until even the rowdiest of Jebus's troops grew somber, ceasing the catcalls and watching the plain with anxious jitters.

There was little the troops of Ornan could do as they waited for some sign of action on the part of the Hebrews. Were they to initiate the confrontation, they would be forced to do more than protect their walls. They would need to leave the citadel and invade the ranks of the enemy.

This was David's war, not Jebus's. The army of Ornan had been trained primarily for defense, not offense.

And so, as yet another hour of quiet ensued, the Jebusites grew increasingly nervous, their sweaty hands slipping on their upright spears, and their heads beaded beneath their helmets.

Then it happened. The silence was broken.

But the nature of the sound that broke the silence was nebulous, arising

223

like the cry of some lost soul from the very ground at the foot of the fortress. Chilling and dreadful, it was joined by yet other cries, swelling through subterranean caverns until they found the air, where they were amplified by their own echoes, surely the howling of demons sweeping from Hades earthward!

Then there was movement, but not among the ranks of the Hebrews who lined the valley floor. The movement and the sound, which now had traveled beneath the ground toward the center of the city, were located in the marketplace.

First detected from the rooftops of the government buildings clustered inside the Ophel, the rush of Jebusite women and the pursuit of Hebrews behind them evoked a cry of dismay from the surprised watchmen.

"The market!" The market!" they shouted. "David's men are in the market!"

How could this be? The question shot through Ornan like a lightning bolt. Spurred by terror, he ran along the ramparts until he found Remon.

"What is that I hear? David's men are inside the city?" he bellowed.

White-faced, Remon tried to answer, but found no voice. Shrugging, he turned away, gesturing wildly to his men and sending them down the narrow zigzag of the fortress ramp.

"Go! Stop the weasels!" he commanded.

Without so much as a glance back at Ornan, he joined his troops on their downward dash.

Crushed against the balustrade by passing soldiers, Ornan helplessly groaned, "How can this be? How did they get inside Jebus?"

No one heeded him. No one had an answer.

Managing to turn himself about despite the press of rushing bodies, Ornan stared wildly toward the valley. The forces of David were no longer statues. Infused with sudden life, they surged forward, surrounding the base of Ophel like a swarm of ants.

And like sand through a funnel, they slipped toward Gihon, disappearing one man at a time into the needle-eyed shaft that led from the spring to the marketplace.

Jerusalem—The City of God

By all the gods! Ornan thought. Was it possible that they had chosen to infiltrate Jebus through the unprotected channel? Was it feasible that in those hours of quiet, when the Israelis had appeared paralyzed, they had actually been dribbling, one by one, through the water course?

There was no other explanation. In an unrelenting stream they had come, crouching through the channel, popping up from the neck of the shaft, darting into the city square before anyone knew that thousands were directly behind them.

Before Remon's men could respond, rushing in their clanking armor to defend the city's interior, King David's plot was being executed.

Women who had passed earlier into the shaft to draw water from the shallow pools deposited there had been greeted by slogging Israeli troops. Now their blood mingled with water of broken pots, where they had dropped them in flight.

In death, their sightless eyes were spared witness to the horrors that followed, as David's horde, materializing from the stony maw, slashed and hacked their way across the market, easily overcoming their disoriented challengers.

The Jebusites, thus distracted, were thrown off focus, so that now the vast bulk of David's army which had waited on the hills and plain, stormed the walls, threw open the gates and overran the city, foot soldiers and cavalry alike.

The ghostly cry which had earlier issued from the shaft, the war whoop of Israel which had vibrated like the groan of the underworld across Jebus, was now replaced by the shrieks and wails of the fallen and the fleeing—and by Israel's cries of challenge and triumph.

Within an easy hour, gutters flowed crimson, and the troops of Remon, those who still stood, made for the heights of Mt. Moriah.

For some reason, which the Jebusites did not question, David did not pursue them there. He stopped short at the southern rim of the holy mount.

But he had done what needed to be done to take the city. It only remained for his men to celebrate.

This they did, rushing through the streets, thrusting their swords into vacated doorways, frolicking and embracing, as surviving Jebusites quaked in the shadows.

Had any man ever been more alone than Ornan? Stranded atop his vacated fortress, he observed the demise of his administration and his culture.

Things would never be the same in Jebus—not tomorrow, nor for the balance of time.

Jebus, Urushalim, Salem was no more. It was not Canaanite, nor Amorite, nor Hittite, nor Jebusite. It belonged to a descendant of Abraham, the patriarch whose son had been offered on Moriah, and who believed the promise for himself.

None of this was clear to Ornan. Very little of anything was clear to him. Save for bewilderment and isolation, he knew nothing. Crumpling to his knees atop the vacant ramparts, he covered his ears and wept.

He would have preferred the sound of phantom wings atop Moriah to the terrified cries of his devastated people. But tonight, nothing miraculous was his, neither omen nor salvation.

8

King David stood outside the huge goat-hair tent that had served as his home and headquarters since the taking if Jebus, now called the "City of David" or "Jerusalem." He should have been at the zenith of human joy, having attained the city for which his people had longed since the time of Abraham.

In keeping with the intent and dream of its founder, Melchizedek, David had renamed the holy site "Jerusalem," immediately after the conquest. While Salem meant "peace," Jerusalem meant "city of peace," pinning the heavenly concept to solid ground.

But David was not as happy as he should have been.

Tonight, he glowered, pacing to and fro, his ears smarting from his wife's most recent tongue-lashing.

Ever since he had taken her from Hebron to the Millo, also called "Zion" the eleven-acre town and fortification that constituted the part of Jebus he had conquered, she had become more vocal about her discontent. No longer quietly snubbing him, she was now given to outright verbal attack.

"This is no place for a queen!" she had growled tonight when he entered the veil that separated her chamber from his.

"You share the king's tent!" David objected, instantly hurt.

Not even looking his way, Michal had continued weaving at the small loom erected in her corner.

"I am not made for tents!" she snapped. "My father never made my mother dwell in tents!"

David had always thought of Michal as beautiful. But lately, she was not so beautiful as the image he held in his heart. That image was of a younger, sweeter woman. Michal was still young, but no longer sweet, and the reality of her did not match what David had once known.

Only since the taking of Jerusalem had this sad truth become undeniable. Only since he had brought her to the sacred city and the sacred city to her, a belated wedding gift, and only since she had spurned it, appreciating none of its awesomeness and none of his great risk in attaining it, had he been forced to see that Michal truly did not love him.

"We dwell inside the city walls," she snarled. "Why must we live in the tent?"

Shaking his head, David rehearsed what he had told her more than once. "I will not soil myself with the filth of the Jebusites! The king of Israel shall have a hallowed house, or none at all!"

But Michal was not impressed. Sighing, she kept up her weaving. "At least your other wives have tents of their own," she had gone on. "Give me my own tent, if I must live in one, until such time as you have real walls to give me!"

This last was a reference to the building project that had commenced shortly after David claimed Jerusalem.

Ignoring her cold back, he had stepped into her room. "Have you seen the cedars?" he barked. "Hundreds and hundreds of them, wagons of logs coming in from Tyre and Joppa, every day! In a few weeks the stone foundation will be complete, and then the palace walls will go up, the greatest of palaces for my queen!"

Slamming the loom's shuttle across the weaving, she turned about, facing him with steely eyes.

He knew what was coming. He had heard it before.

I once had a palace! It was neither goat-hair nor cedar. It was stone and simple. But it was home, and you took me from it!"

Phalti, again. Always Phalti! Lord, how he wished he had left her with that weakling! She deserved no better.

Fist tensing, David longed to strike her, but he manage to avert his eyes from her raging face. It would console him, later, that he had retained his dignity. Backing through her curtain, he sought the sanctuary of the open sky.

Even at this late hour, the sound of hammers and chisels could be heard, ricocheting from the foot of Ophel Hill to the slope of Olive

Mount, back and forth across the Kidron Valley. David had ordered that his carpenters and stone masons work round the clock, except on the Sabbath, to hasten the construction of his palace.

Among the Israelis, who came from smaller towns or dwelled in shepherd camps, there were few such artisans qualified to carry out the demands of the palatial project. Therefore, David had retained craftsmen from the coast city of Tyre, with the blessings of their Phonenician king, Hiram.

Hiram, whose island city was, itself an artistic masterpiece, was only too happy to assist the Hebrew who shared his hatred of the Philistines. Now that David was king not only of Judah, but of all Israel, and now that he had taken the capital of Canaan his own city, the people of the coast, who had lived under threat of Philistine domination for decades, felt more secure.

Many people of the greater Canaanite region felt likewise. Although David had overrun the Jebusites, his leadership and his reputation for triumph over giants mad him a popular monarch beyond his own nation.

In fact, even the Jebusites were surprised to find him a beneficent conqueror.

Following the slaughter that heralded his taking of the city, he astounded the locals by establishing a fund for surviving widows and children of the slain, not only of his own men, but of the Jebusites. Moreover, it had been learned, he had given specific instructions to spare the house of Ornan, Prince of Jebus, who had never done David harm.

That was why, this night, the sounds of construction on his mammoth project were of tools wielded by men of many nations—Phoenicians, Hebrews, Jebusites, and their neighbors. With unprecedented favor, David had won the allegiance of all who hoped for a break in the long-lived Philistine stranglehold.

Indeed, the Philistines had behaved meekly since David's meteoric rise. Their troops less frequently patrolled the Hebron-Damascus highway, and international traffic flowed more openly along the coastward arterials.

How long this tenuous peace would last, no one surmised. But for now, the reign of David seemed to herald a new era, not only for his people, but for all their neighbors.

This night, however, it was not David the mighty king, the beneficent conqueror, nor the cleaver diplomat who listened to sounds of industry ringing over his domain. It was David the wounded heart, the rebuffed husband, who surveyed the realm he had dreamed of handing his wife.

He did not dwell on the political implications of his every move, nor on consequences of this decision or that. He pondered the impossibility that Michal was lost to him. If he thought on his kingdom, it was her rejection of it that haunted him. And if he thought of his, any triumphs, of the trophies he had won, it was under the irony of the fact that he, who had everything, could nor win what he most wanted—Michal and her love.

Leaving the shadow of his tent, David followed the wall to the Millo upward toward Moriah. It was not intentional on his part to head toward the holy mountain. He simply needed to expend his anxieties in movement.

Nor was it his intention to direct his thoughts toward God.

But as he walked, memories of his old friend, Samuel, folded over him. Unbidden, unexpected, they came, seemingly incongruent with all that dominated his mind this evening.

With the memories, a dreadful sadness overtook him, a feeling of emptiness far more profound than even the loss of a wife could inspire. Shaking himself, he tried to imagine what could have brought the prophet's face before him, what could have resurrected the remembrance of his voice as though it whispered even now in his ear.

As though he were again a child, he relived the long-ago day when the prophet had taken him from Saul's tent to the brow of Olive Mount, the day he had spoken to him of the Ark, the priesthood, and the rock of Moriah, toward which he now ascended.

Lifting up his eyes to the holy mountain, it came to him that his feet had anticipated his thoughts. Each step he took, ascending the white-rock trail that led to the site of Abraham's sacrifice, impressed the image of

Samuel more persistently upon his brain, and each thought of Samuel spurred his ascent.

Was the prophet still able to speak to him, even from beyond the grave?

David was no theologian. He was a poet, and his poetry oft-times heralded truth like a prophet prophesies. But he was not given to deep philosophy. He only knew that as he claimed the ancient path, he traversed the trail of history, and the voice of Samuel haunted him.

At first it was a quiet correction, inaudibly bearing in on David's spirit like the shepherd's staff upon a sheep prone to straying. As David passed by the groves of Jebus's idols, and the flat rock of Moriah came into view, the corrective presence was more demanding.

"Son," it seemed to say, "you build yourself a palace. But where is the house of your God? You provide yourself walls of cedar, but leave me to the wind."

Stopping in the path, David cringed. Turning this way and that, he sought the source of the rebuke. "Samuel?" he groaned.

But even as he spoke the name, he knew it was not Samuel that pressed him.

Suddenly, the silver moonlight that had lit his way was interrupted. As though a great wing had passed between him and the sky, a shadow darkened his path. Ducking, David raised his arms over his head.

"Lord God!" he cried, his throat tight with fear.

Just as quickly, the shadow dissipated, moving neither away nor descending, but vanishing. And in its wake, a sad breeze passed over the trail, so that David's soul shivered.

Gazing in dread toward Moriah, he feared to move. When he at last turned for home, daring not to ascend further, his heart hammered the shadow's refrain.

"To the wind..." it reprimanded. "You leave me to the wind."

9

Once more, Bathsheba was alone. Not only was her husband, Uriah, occupying an outpost for Joab, but ever since he had sided with David in taking Jerusalem, his wife had been ostracized from the companionship of her dearest friends, Ornan and Lisbah.

When her father, Eliam, and grandfather, Ahitophel, had joined the ranks of the Israelis, separating themselves from society of their Jebusite friends, she had still been included in the gatherings of her husband's family. Lisbah, Uriah's sister, had never cooled toward her, just as she had never cooled toward her own brother. When Uriah went to fight with David in his campaigns against the Philistines, there had been no strain on family ties.

Once his allegiance convinced him to go against his own people, however, against his own brother-in-law, the Prince of Jebus, there was no way Uriah or his wife could be welcome at Ornan's hearth.

Not even the fact that, in time, many Jebusites came to appreciate David's administration, was sufficient to heal the rift.

Bathsheba, daughter of Israel, wife of an alienated Jebusite and absent warrior, felt her isolation more keenly with each passing day. Since Israeli women had entered Jebus, she found some companionship among them, but her childlessness was somewhat separating. Among the Hebrews, more than any other people of Canaan, childbearing was considered the crowning achievement of womanhood.

Bathsheba found little support in her emptiness. Pity was not support.

The only true and nonjudgmental friend left was her maid, Dorca. To this pleasant and portly female, Bathsheba increasingly turned for companionship.

As the wife of an Israeli commander, Bathsheba was financially comfortable and had never needed to work outside the home. Of late, however, she and Dorca had taken to needlecraft, designing and making clothes for the wealthy women of Jerusalem. Dorca, who was a gifted beadworker, taught Bathsheba how to embroider and decorate the gowns and veils with elaborate and colorful mosaics of Phoenician glass beads.

"My lady must allow me to purchase only the finest of beads for our work," Dorca had explained. "It is easy to think such things do not matter. But cheap beads, when laid out in a pattern, cheapen the entire piece. Besides," she said, her plump face lighting, "beading is such a demanding pastime, we should reward ourselves and customers with the finest materials possible!"

Talking to herself as much as to her mistress, she punctuated her words with little stabs of her needle as she worked on a shawl for one of their most loyal patrons. "In the long run," she insisted, "quality is its own reward!"

Finding in her maid the kindred spirit she had shared with Lisbah, Bathsheba's most cheerful hours were spent in the parlor or, on a hot evening, upon the rooftop, where the two of them marveled over recently acquired silks and velvets, and fine satin tapestries from lands as far away as India and Ethiopia.

Uriah, when he was at home, encouraged his wife's newfound interests, seeing that she was more pleasant toward him as a result, and their household coffers were a little fuller from her growing sales.

Still, there was disquietness within her spirit which, although unexpressed, did not go unperceived by her companion, Dorca. Sometimes, when the sun began to dip beyond the western hills, casting the Vale of Kidron in shadow, Bathsheba lingered near the rooftop balustrade, watching as the lights of the Millo came up on Mt. Zion.

Over the past months, the palace of David had assumed an awesome prominence within the walls of the old town. The project was near completion and stood as a symbol of Israel's wealth, power, and uncontested sovereignty over the capital.

Though Bathsheba was no longer a girl, and though it had been many years since the day she stood upon Ornan's rooftop, watching the triumphal reception of the giant-killer, David, she still thought on that scene with a prick in her heart.

She had only a few times laid eyes upon the boy, now a man and King, since that long ago day, but the mention of his name in conversation never failed to call strange emotions—feelings which she had never expressed to anyone.

Sometimes, over the years, she had tried to reason through this reaction. She had convinced herself that her initial attraction to David had been precipitated as much by her enforced betrothal to Uriah as by any real interest in the Hebrew lad. Most likely any young hero, in comparison to the distasteful Uriah, would have evoked an infatuation. Most likely, also, that girlish response had borne itself into her unhappiest moments, relieving them with fantasies that had no danger of being lived out.

Such was Bathsheba's rationale for the silly preoccupation she often indulged in.

Though she never spoke of it, however, her observant friend, Dorca, surmised the interest she bore toward the unattainable monarch.

Too many times she noted a slight reddening of her lady's face at the mention of the Hebrew's name, and the rapt attention she paid to any matter involving his activities and growing power.

Too many times Dorca had come upon her, just as she was this evening, standing at the balustrade, gazing wistfully across the housetops of Jerusalem toward Hinnom Vale, where the temporary headquarters of David was erected; and more recently, toward the palatial residence he was constructing for himself.

Dorca knew, though she let on nothing, that Bathsheba nursed a dream within her heart—once a dream of a boy, and now of an all-powerful king, whose power over her had nothing to do with nations and politics, but of the ways of a man with a woman.

Stealing across the rooftop, Dorca silently set a tray of tea and honeycakes upon a low table. Then, as though fearful of disturbing an artist's masterpiece, she studied the lovely woman who leaned against the rail.

Tall and graceful, Bathsheba tilted her head toward the softening sounds of the evening streets, and then, raising her eyes to the Millo, scanned the ramparts and the encircling walkways that linked wall with wall and courtyard with castle. Dorca knew she sought a glimpse of the king, who occasionally strolled the ramps, surveying the progress of his workmen. He especially liked to this when the day's work was ended, so he could make private notes to his steward concerning what the contractors might have overlooked.

As Bathsheba kept her vigil, however, it was not the possibility of seeing the king that captivated Dorca. It was the way the mistress's hair fell across her shoulders and tumbled down her bodice, catching the red glow of sunset, that caught her breath.

At that moment, seeing her lady's unrivaled beauty, so unrewarded by her husband, Dorca felt the bonds of loyalty and devotion upon her heart. She wished to announce that all would be well, that if she had anything to do with it, the mistress' loneliness would be ended.

But she could not promise any such thing. She could only vow to herself to do what she could to bring David's attention to the fairest of Judahites, and she decided then and there to make that her goal.

To Bathsheba, she said nothing, other than to clear her throat and announce that tea was waiting.

10

David's desire for matrimonial harmony no longer obsessed him.

Ever since his encounter with Moriah's mysterious winged phantasm, his thoughts had been lifted to a new plane, to the level they had occupied during his younger years, when as a boy he had raised his heart and his rapturous voice to the Lord of heaven.

He did not have a thorough understanding of just what God wanted, but he knew he was to put Him foremost, and he knew He demanded to be enshrined not only in David's heart, but in a physical dwelling place for all nations to see. He sensed, also, that this dwelling place was to crown Moriah, above the precinct of Jebus where his own completed palace now sat in splendor.

But circumstances did not allow him to pursue this dream just yet.

The Philistines were again on the march.

The only thing surprising about this was that it had not begun sooner, that the Philistines had permitted the flowering of David's administration in Jerusalem for as long as they had, with no attempt to squelch it.

When they advanced, it was with the suddenness of eagles on the dive, swooping over Canaan from the coast and invading the fields surrounding David's own hometown, Bethlehem. After one bloody swipe through the village, they established a garrison force there and then spread out through the Valley of Giants, just south of Jerusalem, a place that had derived its name from the many skirmishes that had transpired over the years between locals and the enormous sea people.

Just how fickle one's friends could be was demonstrated when the Philistines persuaded several of the nations who had just helped David build his palace to side with them, promising great political and fiscal rewards if they would go against the royal newcomer.

Syria on the north and Phoenicia on the west, as well as numerous smaller entities, linked arms with the giants in an unprecedented alliance to put David in his tributary place.

Jerusalem—The City of God

It was evidence of David's military savvy that he had recently completed the reorganization of his army. He had expected that the Philistines would not hold back much longer; though when they came with unanticipated allies, David was ready for them.

Under the Commander-in-Chief, Joab, were the joint chiefs of staff, noted for deeds of valor: Joshobeam, Eleazer, Shammah, one of David's own brothers. These generals, known as the "Three Mightiest Men," had specific oversight of the "Six Hundred," the elite of the military machine who had been loyal to the king during his fugitive years.

Next in the hierarchy were the "Thirty," who, under Joab's brother, Abishai, included men like Uriah the Hittite and the king's personal bodyguard, Benaiah, who was known for his David-like feats of slaying a lion in a pit on a snowy day and killing two lion-like men of Moab.

The rest of the army was split into twelve divisions of twenty-four thousand each, so that the Hebrew forces numbered more than a quarter-million. Added to this was a reserve of nearly one hundred thousand.

Despite the army's strength and numbers, however, they were not to fight the enemy on their own ground. While the men themselves were ready, Jerusalem was not. The king had completed his palace, but he was not satisfied with the fortifications of the city itself. David knew that it was not so much the city that the Philistines were interested in, but himself and his growing influence. He knew that if he headed into the outback, the Philistines would track him there, directing their attention to his army rather than his capital.

So it was that, while stationing a host within the holy city, David and finest fighting forces circled through the Wilderness of Judah, well away from the Valley of Giants, headed south and then turned west again, encamping at Adullam, some fourteen miles southeast of Jerusalem. Adullam was a site familiar to David, not only from his shepherding days, but from his days of flight from Saul.

Tonight, David sat with Joab, general of all his hosts, the Thirty, and the three captains of the Six Hundred. Down the slope was the striped campaign tent that always served as his headquarters in battle. To his back was a cave in which he had hidden from the avenging hand of the maniac king, and before him was the roaring fire, large enough to warm the war council. Sparks from the crisp flames shot heavenward, darting over the heads of the gathering like tiny torches.

David gazed on the flying embers in a distracted manner, though he assimilated every word his companions spoke. His mind was on the upcoming war while his heart was in Bethlehem, where, only days before, many of his childhood friends had been slaughtered by the invading garrison.

His father Jesse, had died years before, and the rest of his family had been safe within the palace walls when the attack ensued. But David had lost many close to him, and the knowledge that his beloved hamlet now quartered the enemy galled his spirit.

Between blazing sparks, Joab's voice reached him, punctuating the dark night with sparks of its own. "The Philistines have spread themselves out in Rephaim," he said, gesturing toward the vast open space that separated Bethlehem from this outpost. "They are exposed on all sides, and behind."

Even from this distance, the huge enemy encampment was visible, its thousand campfires casting and aurora across the northern sky.

"They will be scouting the edges of our company by morning, but if we depart first, and advance toward the rear…"

Here Joab paused, wondering if he had the king's attention. "I say, sir, if we depart first…"

"I hear you," David replied, still following the flares. "I consider what you say."

Glancing at Uriah, his favorite among the Thirty, Joab shrugged. Then, reasserting himself, he sighed, "Your Majesty, we are only on the defensive holed up here. You remember how Saul, by resting in a cave at En Gedi, put himself at your mercy, when all the time you were the fugitive?"

Waving to the steep canyon walls that shielded the king's tent, he insisted, "Should the enemy decide to move, we will be cornered. This is a fit hiding place, but not a sanctuary!"

Jerusalem—The City of God

How well David remembered the incident to which Joab referred! It seemed a lifetime ago. But it had not been so many years since he wondered if he would ever be free of Saul's pursuit.

During one of those fearsome episodes, David had hidden out in the wilds of a rocky gorge, overlooking the lowest spot on earth, the Dead Sea. A place fit for mountain goats, a lunar labyrinth of chalk and shale, it offered only brief respite. All too soon, Saul and his men entered the wadi, forcing David and his followers far up the cavernous hollow.

One night, as Saul rested within one of the rocky fastnesses, David came in upon him, bearing a knife and capable of taking him in his sleep. Thinking better of it, he realized he would only be lowering himself to the tactics of his enemy. Instead of killing the king, he spared "the Lord's anointed." He did, however, leave a sign that he had been there, proof that he could have slain Saul, but had chosen not to: He stealthily bent down and, with the same knife that could have wielded death, he slashed off a piece of the king's garment. The result, when Saul was shown he remnant, was temporary contrition on the king's part, and an end to that leg of the pursuit.

Joab's analogy was a wise one. While David might have succeeded in fending off the Philistines from the rocky walls of Adullam, he would indeed be on the defensive. If the king and his general used the advantage of surprise, striking from the enemy's backside, they might be able to rout the Philistine army from the Valley of Rephaim.

But David was in a peculiar frame of mind. He who had never held back from conflict was overswept with the spirit of homesickness. Memories of Bethlehem, now blighted by marauders, fogged his heart and spirit.

Suddenly, scanning the lights of the hated enemy standing between him and his boyhood home, he groaned, low and sad, so that his men wondered what possessed him. "Brother Shammah," he cried, getting to his feet and walking into the shadows beyond the fire, "do you remember the fountain by the gate of Bethlehem?"

His brother, one of the three chiefs of staff, gave a bewildered shrug. "Of course, David. How could I forget?" he replied.

"Oh, how I wish someone would give me a drink of water from that well!" David declared.

Joab, clenching his teeth, swallowed the rebuke he felt the king deserved. Where was David's mind, anyway? Had he forsaken his purpose?

But Uriah, displaying uncanny sensitivity, perceived David's despair. Scooting close to Joab, he whispered in the general's ear. Joab, his brow knit, studied him for a hesitant moment. At last, he nodded.

Leaping to his feet, Uriah motioned to Benaiah and Abishai, two of David's most daring warlords. Slick as panthers, they disappeared into the night, passing David without his noticing and slipping down the crags of Adullam toward the Valley of Rephaim.

11

Uriah's heart beat like a war drum. So hard did it beat, he feared it would betray his presence as he crept past the enemy camp. He had been in many wars and had fought many great men—giants, even. But his heart had pounded like this only once before, and that had not been in war. It had beaten this hard the night he had taken Bathsheba to wife, the night he made her, the fairest virgin Judahite, his own.

On no other occasion since then had he felt such tension or such importance.

Tonight, he was not going out to fight. He was seeking a cup of water for the king. It was his fond desire to make it through Bethlehem's gate with no notice, and to creep out again, unseen.

That, he thought, *is why this night is like my first with Bathsheba.* It was a night, not to make a great scene, but to go gently and tenderly toward a goal; to achieve it without arousing alarm.

Benaiah and Abishai followed his lead, dressed, like Uriah, in various Philistine garments, received as rewards for service, spoils of the Philistine town of Ziklag, and kept in their private campaign trunks of good luck trophies. Uriah had donned a long purple cape, the garb of a Philistine official; Benaiah wore a scarlet tunic and Abishai sported the bronzed leather leggings of a Philistine horseman. Before leaving David's camp, the men scurried to their tents, dressed in this camouflage, and oiled their hair and beards, parting them into slick ringlets, as was the style of the enemy.

Now their disguises would be tested.

They were nigh unto the gate of Bethlehem. Posted at each side of the entry were confident Philistine guards, rather complacent in their duty, as there was no anticipation of an invasion, and certainly the villagers, themselves, posed no threat.

Hanging back in the shadows, Uriah motioned to his companions to stay close. Should they be questioned, it was up to him, who had been in many countries, and who could most easily approximate the Philistine tongue, to do the speaking.

They each slipped from their belts empty water skins and held them so they were quite visible. Then, pulses skipping, they made for the gate. As they approached, the guards snapped to, scanning them quickly. Without a word, they let them pass. Uriah need say nothing, simply lifting his water bottle and nodding toward the fountain that splashed beyond the entry.

Is it possible this could be so easy? He marveled. Heading for the shimmering pool, he dipped his bottle and replaced the stopper, his friends doing likewise. Scarcely did they glance at one another, each equally amazed at the simplicity of the venture. Then, turning again for the gate, they bowed their heads before the guards and grunted a discreet good night.

When one of the sentinels lowered his spear, stopping Uriah in his path, the Hittite swallowed drily.

"Your name?" the guard growled.

Grapping quickly for the Philistine words Uriah floundered. "Samiath," he replied, "of the Gathite contingent. The water is for my captain, sir." At this, he held forth the bottle so the guard might inspect it.

The sentinel, glancing at his cohort, only shrugged. "Pass!" he grumbled, waving the three off.

Bowing again, Uriah and his friends turned toward the night and passed once more into shadow. As they hastened back toward the Adullam, Uriah breathed easier, and his thoughts returned to Bathsheba. Though he often boasted to her of his warring adventures, he knew she cared nothing about his stories.

But she must hear of this service to David. She would be proud.

Part VI

DAVID AND THE ARK

100 B.C.E.

1

With men like Uriah, there was no reason David should not succeed. And succeed, he did.

When the water was brought to him by the hands of the three devoted captains, he was moved beyond words. His spirit, lifted from the doldrums into which it has slumped, soared toward the God of all victory. In a show of praise for his men and for the help of heaven, he offered the water as a sacrifice, refusing to "drink the blood of these men that have put their lives in jeopardy."

The act of pouring out the water before the Lord was a fitting prelude to the battles that followed. First at Adullam and then from Gibeon to Gezer, he showed his superiority over the enemy, driving them out of Israel and back to the coast.

Tonight, after days of victory celebration in the halls of his new Jerusalem palace, David at last had a moment of quiet. Joab alone was with him, and together the Hebrews walked along the ramparts of the recently completed fortress. They had come to a high watermark in their military achievements. As they conversed, their thoughts turned to the heroes of yesteryear, the generals and patriarchs who starred in Israel's history.

The plain of Jericho and the towered city, which still had not fully recovered from Joshua's march, were not visible from the height of David's palace. Obscured by intervening hills and hidden across the wilderness that plunged from the heights of Olive Mount to Jordan Valley, the city was nonetheless very visible to the mind's eye of any Israeli.

Jericho represented one of the greatest victories in the Hebrew saga. The miracle of its demolished walls, against which no human hand made a blow, typified the work of God on behalf of the invading nation.

"Your Majesty," Joab sighed, awestruck at the thought of that triumph, "what must it have been like to win a battle without losing one man? No matter how great our victories, I mourn every drop of Hebrew blood shed upon the field."

Jerusalem—The City of God

David placed a warm hand on Joab's shoulder. "You have the heart of a great general," he replied. "It is not might, alone, that wins wars, but love of nation and of the nation's warriors."

Joab smiled vaguely. "I am honored, sir that you see me so. Still," he said wistfully, "I am no Joshua."

David would have countered that self-effacement with some glib objection, but Joab deserved more consideration. For a long moment, the king pondered the general's comments. Suddenly, as though a great light dawned in his brain, David contemplated the details of the fall of Jericho, and, as though the conversation were meant just for him, he spoke as much to himself as to Joab.

"Joshua was a giant among leaders," he agreed. "But we must not be quick to compare ourselves to men of old, for such comparison is not always fair."

"How so?" Joab asked.

"Think about it," David went on. "Joshua's victory was so miraculous because he had the visible aid of God marching with him, just as Moses did throughout the years he led the people in the wilderness. It was miraculous because, with that aid, the people need not lift a finger to bring the walls tumbling down."

"You speak of the Ark of the Covenant," Joab said, recalling the story.

"Indeed!" David exclaimed. "An assistance which Israel has not invoked since before the kingdom was established!"

It was true that the Ark had gone with the people, borne by the priests of Israel in the midst of the millions who circled Jericho. As the trumpets of the Levites blared and the people beat upon hand drums, marching about the towered walls for seven days, no weapon threatened the enemy, and without the shedding of blood or the taking of life, the walls came down. Only those who watched from the ramparts, and those in the path of their fall were killed. Once the walls were leveled, the Israelites entered the city, where they finished the annihilation of the ancient culture. And only at that point were swords drawn or shields hoisted.

Still, Joab knew the Lord had been with him as well, and wondered why he must fight in the bloodiest of manners. "Saul had the prophet, Samuel," Joab observed. "And now there is Nathan, an astute counselor. Do they not lead us in the ways of holiness? And is the Lord not with us, as he was with Joshua?"

David's throat tightened at the memory of his dear friend, Samuel. It was true that God had provided another prophet, who had been a great help to the king. But there had been no one so personal to David before or since Samuel. In fact, it must have been the thought of that holy man, combined with talk of the Ark, which, at that moment, crystallized a new impetus for David, a focus for his energies over the coming months.

"Yes," he replied. "Prophets are instruments of God, to be sure. But how often Samuel lamented the absence of the Ark from the endeavors of our nation!"

Recalling how, only weeks ago, Samuel seemed to have reached out to him beyond the grave, pointing him toward Moriah, and how that voice had then shown itself to be the voice of God, David cast a furtive glance toward the holy mount.

Again, as on that night, he was impressed with the fact that there was no temple in Israel, no holy shrine to which his people might direct their worship, and from which Jehovah might direct them. But what purpose would be served in constructing a temple if there was no Ark to place in it?

Blinking back tears, David turned to his friend. "Joab," he sighed, "we have had victories to celebrate. But in truth, we should hang our heads. There is no reason to dance and sing, so long as the Ark is kept in obscurity."

Awed by his lord's sober determination, Joab drew his fist across his chest in salute. "There is no reason, Your Majesty, why the Ark should not be brought to Jerusalem! The land is ours now, without contest, and the enemy has fled. Let us fetch the Ark and bring it hither!"

2

David, king of Israel, mighty conqueror of the Philistines, was once again in hiding.

This time, he did not hide from the menacing hand of a lunatic pursuer, as he had hidden from Saul for years. Nor did he flee the assailing sea peoples, for they had been purged from the land.

It was from himself he hid, and from God.

The dream of bringing the Ark to Jerusalem, reborn in him when he had spoken to Joab, had turned into a nightmare, and it was from this experience and from the confusion it wrought in his spirit that he hid.

Alone in his chamber, which overlooked the dawn-pink city, he tossed and turned upon his kingly bed. He had not slept for nights, ever since the disaster that had culminated his attempt to move the Ark from Kirjath-Jearim. That had been a month ago, and his counselors had sought in vain to bring him out of his depression.

Surely it was not the king's fault that someone had died in the attempted transport of the sacred box! Why must he torment himself because one of the men in the retinue was so foolish as to touch the Ark? Israel's history was full of references to the sanctity of the vessel and to the eerie powers it could manifest. David must not blame himself for the unfortunate incident.

Still, despite the pleas of his advisors, the king felt personally responsible for the mishap and had pondered, for weeks, just where he might have miscalculated. He had ordered a new cart made for the transport, and it had been hitched to two young spotless oxen, known for their steadiness and strength. He had commissioned the finest drivers in Israel, his own coachmen, to man the cart. All due players had been spoken, all proper rites fulfilled, from burning of incense to the chanting of songs by a legion of Levites all along the way from the house of Abinadab, above the Valley of Sorek.

Great pomp and circumstances accompanied the move, and great celebration, with the orchestra of Nob, where the high priest dwelled, and the orchestra of David's palace joining together: thousands of harpists, trumpeters, and twirling dancers, male and female, with bright costumes and flying hair, rattling tambourines and pounding drums.

David had ridden at the head of the congregation, regaled in crimson, azure and gold, astride a white horse whose mane and tail were ribboned and braided, and whose hooves were gilded. But when the enormous company, joined by countless citizens of all villages of Israel, came to the threshing floor of Chacon the Benjamite, just northwest of Jerusalem, something went dreadfully awry.

One of the oxen stumbled, causing the cart to teeter precariously. Uzza, who reached the status of the king's coachman by proven skill, and who had been commanded for quick thinking and flawless reflexes in other dangerous situations, reacted as his royal master would have expected: He reached back to steady the Ark.

Unfortunately, this was a fatal move, bringing instant retribution. Before anyone could think to warn him, he was smitten to the ground, thrown, as by unseen lightning, from the driver's seat. And before David even saw what had transpired, the coachman lay lifeless beside the vehicle, his neck broken by the fall.

Fear had driven David into self-imposed internment. But the fear he felt was not like any he had known before. He had faced lions and bears and giants in his life, and the spears of mortal combat. He had fled and faced the wrath of the maniac, Saul. But this time the fear was not of claw or tooth or spear. It was fear of God, who had always, hitherto, been his friend.

David knew that the God of Israel was a demanding deity. He knew that Jehovah desired perfection and obedience in his followers. David had always tried to please this Sovereign, and had, for the most part, felt His benediction. But, David did not understand this side of God, a side which seemed, to his faltering mind, altogether arbitrary and capricious.

Therefore, the emotion of fear, as David sequestered himself, was riddled with anger at the ways of the Lord, which he could not fathom.

Jerusalem—The City of God

Such anger also bred guilt, which in its course turned to rifts of depression, until there were days when the king could barely creep forth from bed and kept the blinds drawn from morning 'til night.

Today, all attempts of servants and counselors to prod him from his despair, to woo him to eat or dress or look out the window, were even futile. Even Michal, who rarely ventured near his quarters, when prevailed upon to do so was unable to rouse him. Her usually cattish voice, though purposely sweetened, had no effect but to send him deeper beneath his covers.

"Go away!" he growled. "Since when do you care whether I live or die?"

Michal steeled herself. Advancing toward him on tiptoe, she gingerly pulled back his blanket and stroked his clammy face.

Recoiling, David spat, "Away with you, woman! What do you care for my misery, being the source of it yourself!"

Face flushed, Michal swallowed dryly and controlled her temper. "What has any of this to do with you and me?" she cooed. "The king must be strong for his people. They look to you, David, for leadership."

Tugging at his tunic, she managed to coax him out a bit.

Leaning upon one elbow, he stared at her in fascination. "How can you ask what this has to do with us?" he groaned. "Do you think I have risked my life and the lives of my armies only to capture a city, or only to hold a crown?"

Michal's face reddened like a coal. "Let us not speak of such things, right now," she pleaded. "Your counselors are waiting for you. They have summoned Nathan all the way from Halhul. The prophet is willing to advise you, if you will only listen."

With a sigh, David lay down again, staring blankly at the ceiling. "Only Samuel can advise me, "he replied. "Only that wise man can tell me the mind of the inscrutable Jehovah!"

David's sarcasm sent a chill through Michal's hardened heart. "You must do what you can!" she urged. "You must try again to bring the Ark to Jerusalem!"

A smirk crossed David's wan face. "You think any mortal can tell me how to do that? We struggle against the Almighty, a God who destroys and does not reward!"

Anger sparking from his eyes, he suddenly grasped his wife to him, holding her in a painful grip so that her face was only inches from his.

"A God, my dear lady, who denies a man his heart's desire, and laughs at him thereafter!"

Michal knew he referred to her. Was it possible he could think of such things at such a time, when the nation was reeling from his negligence? Daring not to pull away, she let herself go limp in his clenched fists and rested her head upon his chest.

The unexpected feel of her long hair upon his skin, soft and silky, caused David's heart to race. As though he forgot her rebuffs, he suddenly found his hand moving down the supple curve of her back.

In her most persuasive voice, she whispered, "Nathan can help you. And I am here to help you, too."

Could it be he heard right? Was Michal really here for him?

Slowly, she drew, back gazing into his fevered eyes with dove-like tenderness. "You must bring the Ark to the city," she pleaded, brushing his lips with hers so that his whole body responded. "Do it for me, David," she whispered, kissing him again and again.

Then slipping beneath his covers, she pulled him close. "Do this one more thing for me."

3

On a wave of hope and certainty, David set about, once more, to bring the Ark to Jerusalem.

With Michal's encouragement, ulteriorly driven as it may have been, he felt again the hand of God upon him. His meeting with Nathan spurred his hopes, too, though it was corrective in nature.

"Do you not recall," the prophet quizzed him, "That Moses taught us how to carry the Ark? It was never to be moved upon a cart, but was to be borne by means of staves passed through the rings upon its sides. And these staves were to be borne upon the shoulders of holy Levites, and never taken out, but put to rest with the Ark wherever it went. No man was to touch the Ark, on penalty of death. Do you not remember these things?"

David knew Nathan was a prophet, commissioned by God, but his heart had been so entwined with Samuel, it was not until the day of this conversation that David learned to appreciate Nathan's personality.

Surrounded by earthy shepherds as a youth, and by rough men-of-arms since adulthood, David was used to dealing with forceful fellows. Samuel, especially, had been a man of strong disposition, a man who could silence skeptics or challengers with a single glance.

Nathan, on the other hand, was a quiet person, given more to allegory and instruction than to rebuke. His ways were gentle, and it was easy for David to dismiss him. But the day he called upon the king in his stateroom, his very gentleness appealed to a deeper strain in David, the part of him which had been spent in song and poetry as a youth, and which had inclined him to meditation in the hills of his homeland.

Meek and calm, Nathan stood before him, conspicuous against the backdrop of the palace grandeur. His dusty, road-worn robes and windblown hair told that he had just traveled many miles, and that he had greater things on his mind than his appearance.

He was a young man, younger than David, which somewhat detracted from his credibility. Always before, when he had addressed the king, on occasions of battle or in regards to politics, David needed to remind himself that this was indeed the spokesman of God, and that not all prophets are hoary-headed or steely-eyed.

"Do you remember these things?" the question still hung in the air.

David squirmed uneasily on his throne. "I have learned them at some time," he replied. "I had …forgotten."

Coming as close to confrontation as David had ever seen him, Nathan drew near the throne and rapped his walking stick upon the tiled floor. "Your poor memory, O Majesty, has cost a man his life!"

Red-faced, the king ran a clammy hand through his dark locks and fidgeted with his beard. "So it has," he said. Then, feeling the full weight of his guilt, he asked, "Is there hope in heaven that I may try again? Will Jehovah permit me to bring the Ark into my city?"

Nathan studied the king for a long moment, until David was forced to close his eyes. "Your heart is right," Nathan at last announced. "The Lord hears you and will give you success."

As David looked with relief upon the prophet, he found that the holy man was scanning the hand-wrought rafters and the cedar paneling of his stateroom.

"But, tell me," the prophet went on, "where will you place the Ark when it arrives? Have you given thought to this?"

Shamed by the fact that there was, as yet, no holy house for the sacred vessel, the king replied, "It is my desire to build a house for the Lord our God. But if I wait until this is achieved, we will not have the Ark within the sacred city for many, many years. I have commissioned that the tabernacle of Nob be moved to Jerusalem and erected nearby." Attempting to read the prophet's face, David found his reaction inscrutable.

When at last Nathan responded, the king felt some of his shame lift. "It will do for now," the prophet said.

Then, without further comment, Nathan left the room, passing through the palace and into the open air, where the sky was his ceiling.

Jerusalem—The City of God

The journey from Chacon to Jerusalem, in which David at last delivered the Ark to its new abode, was one that would forever live in the king's memory of Israel. The fanfare and ceremony that had attended the first attempt were repeated, but this time even more jubilantly. Nathan's correction and David's determination to follow it gave a sense of confidence to the proceedings that they had lacked before. Everyone, from the king to the youngest dancer, from the Levites to the feeblest elders, knew that God was with the move and that He smiled down from heaven upon them.

As he had done the first time, David again rode upon a colorfully decked horse, its white coat gleaming in the sun of a perfect day, and the king's own crown reflecting the light of glory. On every side and for miles behind came singers and dancers and musicians, first the Levites with their four thousand harps and then choruses of every village, echoed by impromptu song and spontaneous frolic.

Along the way, as the thousands became tens of thousands and the valley vibrated with happy tread and gleeful stomp, the celebration grew uproarious. At last, David's spirit so echoed the mood that he could no longer stay seated upon his steed. Compelled to join the people, to lead them in their frolic, he dismounted and danced beside them.

In the distance rose the noontime city, its towers fretted with sunlight. When David saw it, his heart soared so that he felt he would surely fly right off the ground. Swaying and twirling, he began to sing, his voice rising above the heads of the Levites.

Youngsters clustered about him, free to dance with the singing king, and hundreds of young women, beautiful as gazelles, hair flying and skirts whipping, recalled to him the day he had entered Jerusalem with Goliath's head. "Saul has slain his thousands and David his ten thousands," they had sung.

That chorus had caused no end of trouble for the young giant killer, rousing Saul's jealousy and calling down years of torment. But today, David remembered it joyously for it had long since proven true.

And though his heart was wild for the Ark and for all it represented, his rapture was enhanced by Michal's recent demonstration of love, by hope that he might actually have recaptured her lost esteem. She had come to him more than once in the past few weeks. He did not know what had turned her heart toward him, but he did not question that blessed cause.

Suddenly, his ecstasy was like that of his youth, when during lonely vigils in the hills above Bethlehem, when only the Lord and the sheep observed, he danced and sang about his campfire, leaping across the flames, rejoicing in the nearness of his God. On those occasions he had strummed his harp and laughed aloud, effortlessly composing songs that would later become part of a national legacy. He had sometimes torn off his cloak and his undercoat, dancing in his tunic, as the cool night air refreshed his perspiring body.

This moment was like those, his spirit so close to heaven that he forgot all about him. Indeed, he may as well been alone, so little did it matter who looked on.

In the zeal of unbridled joy, he whipped his regal robe from off his shoulders, and then his undercoat, dancing up the hill toward the holy city in nothing more than his embroidered tunic.

Eyes closed, he frolicked and laughed, while the people spun and clapped about him. If anyone took note of his "nakedness." They did not object, swept up as they were in the same fervor.

Surely, there were others, too who cast off their restraining garments. But no one castigated them.

This was no show of the flesh. This was liberty, inspired by the nearness of Jehovah and the nearness of His city, like the liberty of Eden where the original spring of Gihon sang across the ground.

4

Michal, daughter of Saul, wife of the king, leaned forth from her third story palace window and felt the blood rush to her cheeks. Was she seeing correctly? Eyes wide, she surveyed the wild scene on the highway that twisted toward the western gate and she clutched the windowsill in horror.

Ark or no Ark, she could not countenance the excesses of her husband's celebration. Stripped to his tunic, his royal cloak a banner in his hand, he gyrated toward the city, his followers twirling and clapping about him like a horde of mindless drunkards. Such behavior might have attended a Canaanite festival, but, to Michal's mind, was altogether unbecoming for Israel, and unbefitting the station of monarch.

Shamed to the quick, she glared down upon the dancers who escorted the Ark.

Israel did well enough without the ancient box, she thought. If this is the effect it had upon its worshippers, better to leave it in the hands of pagans!

Falling back from the window, she threw herself upon her bed and sobbed bitterly. Why, oh why, must David be such a fool? Phalti would never have lowered himself to such indignity.

Gritting her teeth, she felt tears sting her clamped eyes. Must she forever compare the king of Israel to a commoner? Why was it that she could not love David?

She had tried. God knew she had. When she saw that David languished in depression, his attempt to bring the Ark having failed the first time, she determined to rally his spirits, to convince him, and herself, that she could be a supportive wife. She had let him love her, and during those times, she imagined she recaptured some of the old stirrings, that her hardened heart was renewed with the affections she had known in youth.

But all too easily, she slipped again into despondency, remembering Phalti and the peace of her life with him. All too easily, little things David said, things which she had adored as a girl, left her cold and filled her with irritation.

His emotionalism toward Israel and its ancient ways, his adoration of a deity she knew only through impersonal tradition, even his way of standing when he was swept up in things—what had once been attractive confidence now seemed cockiness, what had once been wondrous zeal, now seemed braggadocio.

Oh, Michal was an enigma to herself!

She knew David was the most comely man in Israel, the most intelligent, the most courageous, the most successful—and yes, the most godly. She knew all women adored him, and that he was hers alone.

True, he had other wives. But he had taken them when she was gone, when he no longer had her. And he, himself, had told her they had never taken her place—could never take her place!

So, she owned the man most loved of her generation.

Yet, she did not love him—his wife did not love him.

Aghast at this private confession, at the certainty of her helplessness, she cringed again at the thought of him upon the highway, at the knowledge that even now he passed through the gate of the city, clad like a crazy man, unclad like a lunatic.

"For God's sake, David!" she groaned. "How can you shame me like this?"

David raced up the stairs inside his palace, taking two at a time, his heart drumming and his breath coming in excited chugs.

Passing his chamberlains, he shouted, "Where is Michal? Where is my queen?"

Not waiting for an answer, he flew toward her door, hoping to find her alone. Such a glorious day there had never been in all of the history of Israel! Surely not even the exodus from Egypt could have excited such joy as the success of this day!

The holy vessel of the law, the container of the covenant, the oracle delivered to Moses on Sinai, had been returned to its rightful place. No longer would Israel go forth into battle without the power of its presence.

Jerusalem—The City of God

No longer would the people worship at an empty shrine. For the very seat of Jehovah was secure once again within holy walls!

Now, nothing prevented David's dreams of building a house for God, a glorious temple for the worship of Yahweh!

As the processional from Chacon had entered the Jerusalem gate, David's family had been present to greet him. Arrayed in grandeur along the market road, six of his wives and their children, garbed in velvet and purple, had joined with the throng, though partitioned from the crowd by guards with velvet ropes.

They had followed along, singing and dancing like the commoners, all the way up to the boundary of the Jebusites, the area allotted to the displaced people whom David had conquered, the region of Moriah and the backdrop of Zion.

All of them, save Michal, had been there.

David looked for her the moment he entered town, his eyes darting over the crowd, piercing the congregation with each turn, in the hopes she would race out to him, flinging her arms about his sweaty neck.

But soon enough, he saw she was not present.

Not allowing this fact to impede his purpose, he had joyfully gone through the rituals and sacrifices that attended the Ark's enthronement, robed in his cloak again and bearing himself with dignity as he watched the priestly installment from the edge of the holy compound. With the setting of the sun, however, while his people still celebrated the night-long festivities, returning to their homes to sing and dance about their own fires, he dismissed himself and hastened for his palace.

Commanding his stewards as he left the scene, he told them to gather his family in the palace yard, that he would bless them there, as patriarch of his own house. Then he hurried off to find Michal.

Was she ill? Was she distressed? He could think of no reason why she would have missed the events of this miraculous day. Without ceremony, he raced through the palace halls, until he came to her door. Anxiously he knocked upon it, and receiving no reply, lifted the latch.

"Michal!" he called, stepping into the darkened room. "Are you all right? Where are you, my wife?"

His face was still flushed with the joy of the day. But the instant he entered the chamber, his bright eyes saddened. As though his spirit absorbed hers, it was suddenly downcast, and his heart gave a painful surge. In the dismal shadows, he saw the woman prone upon her bed, and he knew she slept from sorrow, that she had been crying once again. Creeping up to her, he sat upon the bed's edge and groaned, "What is it, my love? What dreadful thing happened?"

As though she could, even in her sleep, suck the life from him, he sensed that she had been weeping because of him, that she did not share his joy and that her misery was a broken heart.

At the sound of David's voice, she roused and opened her swollen eyes. Peering up at him, it was more that a broken heart she manifested in her gaze. It was hatred, absolute and pure.

As though he recoiled from a poised viper, David stood up and looked down on her in horror, backing through the door and into the hall. He did not know what had overcome her, but he could not stand for it. He would not have her demons, whatever they were, rob him once again.

"Tell her to join the family in the yard!" he ordered a passing servant.

With that, he hastened to meet his other wives and their children. They awaited him in the dusk of the courtyard, just as a pink sunset, a fitting benediction to the hallowed day, was fading over the western wall. The priest of his palace, a subordinate to the high priest of Nob, was there to ask God's blessing on the house, a censer of sweet perfume smoking in his hand.

As David entered, He raised a simple gray and white mantle over his head, one like any other Israelite might wear upon this evening. This was not a night to dwell on his royalty, but on his duty to his family.

Coming alongside his wives, he bade them kneel before the priest, and he did likewise, bowing his head as the holy man waved the censer over them, chanting the familiar invocation: "Hear O Israel, the Lord Your God is One God. You shall have no other gods before Him."

Jerusalem—The City of God

But just as the priest was about to call the traditional sacrifice, raising a small lamb to his breast and placing it upon the courtyard alter, a disturbance was heard at the top of the stairs from which David had just descended.

There was Michal, unceremoniously pushing past the surprised guards and coming resolutely down the flight. Glancing up, David felt the blood rush to his face. He sensed no good boding from this sudden appearance.

Heedless of the sacred proceedings, the queen hissed down at him, waving her hand in a mocking gesture. "How glorious was the king of Israel today," she cried, boring down upon him with hot eyes, "Who uncovered himself in the eyes of the handmaids of his servants! Just like a fool, he exposed himself!"

David, cut to the quick, managed to stand to his feet, confronting her with clenched fists. "It was before the Lord that I did this!" he replied, his voice trumpetlike. "The Lord who chose me in the face of your father and all Israel, to be ruler over His people! Because He honored me, I will play before Him, with sport and frolic!"

Gaining strength from his own assertion, he approached her on the stairs, glaring up at her with determination. "Yes," he cried, "if that was vile, let me be even more vile, and humble before the Lord! As for the maidservants, whom you disparage, they, at least, will honor me!"

Withering before his stormy gaze, the woman trembled. Seeing that she did not counter, he turned sullenly away, rejoining his wives and motioning the priest get on with the blessing. Not once, as the censer swung and the chant recommenced, did David look again toward Michal. But he knew he had intoned the death-knell upon their relationship.

And she, retreating numbly up the stairs, felt a sudden hollowness in her groin, a hollowness which smote her womb, so that she would never bear a child, nor know the joys of motherhood all the days of her life.

Part VII

DAVID AND BATHSHEBA

1000—975 B.C.E.

1

So battered and bruised had David's heart been over the years with Michal, the final break proved not to be a devastation, but liberty. Surprising himself, he found a new lightness in his chest, a spring in his steps. While the malcontented woman would live out her days in barren isolation, preferring the cloister of her room to the company of David's other wives, David turned his eyes energetically toward the future.

This was cold-heartedness on his part; only the reaction of a man who realizes, with finality, the hopelessness of winning a woman's love, the resignation and release that follows a letting go. Perhaps he would always love Michal, but he would no longer let her misery own him.

Besides, there were a multitude of reasons to be optimistic. The dreams of his administration were fulfilling themselves at a rapid pace. The Ark was safely enshrined in Jerusalem, he had overseen the organization of civil service, and he was at rest from his enemies. The king dwelled in a fabulous palace, full of cedar beams and soaring ceilings, architecturally intricate and heavily adorned. It seemed the next logical step, now that the Ark was here, to proceed with his dreams of building a temple to God, who had set him in a place of honor for all the world to see.

Summoning the council, he told them to begin the task of identifying the most gifted architects, craftsmen, and engineers inside and out side of Israel. Of course, many of those who had worked on the royal palace would be enlisted again, but the task of the temple would call for many thousands more workmen, and it was best to waste no time procuring them.

"Ah, oh yes," he said, hoping it was not an afterthought, "call Nathan. I wish to have his blessing upon this project, above all else."

In the vale of the shepherds that led toward Bethlehem, in a small hut on the outskirts of Jerusalem, the prophet Nathan sat prodding his evening fire with a stick.

His spirit was strangely heavy, though he could not imagine why.

He had been summoned to the king's palace this afternoon, and David had shared with him his desire to commence plans for a glorious temple.

Before moving to the site nearer the royal city, Nathan had dwelled in the mountain hamlet of Halhul, near Hebron. He had always preferred open skies to the confinement of walls, and a simple hut to the grandeur of palaces, but the idea of a holy sanctuary to honor and house the God of Israel thrilled him.

Like a youngster with a new toy, yet altogether reverent, David laid out before the prophet the preliminary sketches which he himself had made, rough drafts to be sure, but indicative of the grand scale and august glory he wished to bestow upon the House of God.

"Where do you intend to construct this edifice?" Nathan had inquired. "Surely within the City of David there is no room for such a building.

Of course, the prophet anticipated the answer, as would anyone astute to the spirit of Jehovah and the spirit of the holy city. Still, David was not hasty to reply, his feeling for the subject so profound that he did not speak of it lightly. "Sir." He always addressed the holy man thus, though he was younger than himself, "the site I wish for the temple is presently in Jebusite hands, though only as a concession to our treaty with them. I will need to approach the owner and offer to buy the parcel. For it is my dream to build the holy house upon the threshing floor of Ornan, the very place where Abraham offered Isaac, the place where Jacob is said to have seen the staircase to heaven and the angels coming and going."

As he said this, he left the table upon which he had spread his designs for the building and went to his window. His eyes were drawn magnetically toward the site, and Nathan stepped close behind him, looking past his shoulder toward the northern height.

"Moriah," the prophet said with a nod. "Should I have doubted?"

Turning toward his younger mentor, David saw that the prophet's eyes were misty, just as Samuel's had been when he spoke of the holy mount. In that instant, David's heart was knit to the seer's as it never had been before.

"You approve, Father?" he asked, honoring the prophet with the title that befitted his station and calling.

Jerusalem—The City of God

Placing a loving hand upon the king's shoulder and looking up into his face, Nathan's throat grew tight. "Go, my son," he said. "Do all that is in your heart. For the Lord is with you."

Having given that blessing, the prophet hastened away, eager to be with the Lord himself, his feet light as air as he ran through the city streets, passed through the southern gate, and headed for his humble abode. As he neared home, however, the strange heaviness with which he now struggled descended upon his spirit, making it impossible for him to pray with ease.

He longed to pour out his heart in thanksgiving, in the privacy of his little house, to praise Jehovah for the mighty thing that lay in store for Jerusalem and all the people. But it seemed God stopped his voice, that praise was not called for. With an ache in his chest, he wondered if he had misspoken the word of the Lord to David.

"What is it, My Sovereign?" he cried, so distressed that he threw himself upon the dirt floor. Weaving back and forth before his fire, he pleaded to know if he had run ahead of God.

The idea that he might have misspoken was fearsome indeed, not only because it implied he had not listened, but because, by the law of Moses, any prophet who lied was a "false prophet" and was worthy of death.

Beads of sweat dotted Nathan's forehead, and he fell into a mode of self-defense. "I spoke for myself, O Lord," he said, "and not for You. Forgive me," he pleaded, "for surly there is forgiveness in you!"

With this confession, there came some relief. Still, it was underlain with apprehension.

Standing, Nathan paced his room, filled with familiar sense that God was about to speak. In this knowledge was a mixed blessing, for while it implied that God had not abandoned his prophet, Nathan still felt that the words to come were not entirely happy.

He stared mutely into the fire, when the Lord's message drifted between the flames, burning into his heart:

"Tell My servant, David, that he did well to desire to build a house for

263

Me. Nevertheless, he shall not build the house, but his son, which is yet to be born, shall build the house for My name."

Astonished, Nathan bowed his face to the earth floor, "My Lord, he wept, "always You have been with your servant, David, and You have blessed him beyond all the princes of the earth. What has he done that You should withhold this greatest of privileges from him? What shall I tell him, O Lord?"

Suddenly, the breeze of God's word that had moved between the flames ceased and, with utmost compassion, the answer was given: "Tell My son, David, that because he has shed blood abundantly and has made great wars, therefore he shall not build a house for Me. Rather, a son shall be born to him who shall be a man of rest. I will give him the rest from all his enemies, for his name shall be Solomon, 'Peace,' and I will give peace and quietness unto Israel in his days. It is he who shall build a house for me…and I will establish the throne of his kingdom over Israel forever."

Now since the prophet was altogether human, the full significance of this pronouncement did not immediately dawn upon him. His focus was still upon the disappointment he must share with David.

Lest the king should feel guilt for all the wars he had conducted in God's name, the Lord rephrased the message. "Tell David," He went on, "that I took him from the sheepcote and from following the sheep, to be ruler over my people Israel. And I was with him wherever he went, and destroyed all his enemies, and made his name great, as great as any man's upon the earth. Moreover I will appoint a territory for Israel, and will establish them, that they may dwell in a place of their own, and move no more. Neither shall the children of wickedness afflict them any more."

With this there was a pause, and the prophet shook himself, absorbing the gracious words just spoken.

Was it possible that Israel would know a time of peace? Never in her history, since the time of Jacob, had Israel had a place of its own for certain, a place that would not be threatened, or a generation free from fear. Such a thing seemed too much to hope for, or even pray for.

Jerusalem—The City of God

But here was God promising just that!

As Nathan dwelled on this blessing, the Lord put an ironic twist upon David's dream. "Tell David," He said, "that *I* will build a house for *him*. His house and his kingdom and his throne will be established forever."

2

Because of the promise imbedded within the disappointment, the words of the Lord to David, delivered by an obedient Nathan, served to energize the king to greater accomplishments than ever.

He would not build the temple, but he would go on to build the nation of Israel, to expand its borders far beyond what he had ever dreamed, and to gather along the way resources for the future temple, which his yet unborn son would establish. Which of his seven wives would bear this unknown son, he did not try to guess, although, since he had ceased to be a husband to Michal, there was no way she would be the queen-mother.

The whens and hows of the birth, he decided, were in the hands and timing of God. Meanwhile, he turned himself to expansionism with an imperialistic vengeance.

Within a mere three years he managed to extend the borders of Israel to nearly cover the realm originally promised to Abraham. Defeating enemies to the north, south, east, and west, he established a dominion that spread from the Euphrates to the borders of Egypt. From Gath on the coast, homeland of his first challenger Goliath, to Moab on the east, and then to Syria on the north, he proved himself the ongoing "man of war," leveling town after town and setting himself in lordship over them.

From the Syrians he took magnificent booty to be placed in store for the future temple, and from the grateful neighbors to the Syrians he received vessels of gold, silver, and brass, which he deposited in the temple treasury.

His great captain, Abishai, went on to defeat the Edomites, who centuries previous had refused to allow Moses and his people to pass through their way to the promised land.

The region of Edom, which lay south of the Dead Sea, was now Israel's target, as they proceeded to slay eighteen thousand in the Valley of Salt, where once the decadent cities of the plain, Sodom and Gomorrah, had stood. Edom's strange capital, the red-rock fastness of Petra, now belonged to David, and for six months General Joab completed the task of subduing the Edomites, obliterating the male population and setting up garrisons in the largest cities.

There was nothing, now, to stop David from expanding further along the Fertile crescent. The power of Egypt had waned; Assyria and Babylon had made no inroads into Canaan. In one engagement, David had even taken on allies of the Syrians from across the Euphrates and had shown himself a force to be reckoned with, killing forty thousand horsemen.

There remained only the Ammonites, holdouts across Jordan, to subdue. Hebrew military power had almost reached the ultimate, and with the defeat of Ammon, it would indeed be at the pinnacle of achievement for the world of David's day.

It was the eve of that final, establishing battle, that Uriah the Hittite sat with his friend Joab in the light of the general's campfire, north of the Dead Sea. What a familiar scene this had become for the enthusiastic proselyte! How many times had he been favored with Joab's confidences, drawn into the inner circle of military decision-making on just a night as this?

Tomorrow the armies of Israel would advance across Jordan once more, to engage the men of Ammon. This time, the enemy would have no reinforcements, for since David had defeated Syria and the Euphrates contingent, no one dared ally with Ammon.

Hopes were high among the tight circle who fellowshipped about Joab's fire: Benaiahm Abishai, and Uriah. They did, however, but briefly speak of the next day's plans. They were familiar with the territory they were about to invade. They had worked together so often, they knew one another like brothers and scarcely needed briefing in what they were to do or expect.

It was easy, therefore, as the night drew on, and the hundred thousand tent lights faded in the dark, for the men's minds to turn to homier things. As they passed a small wine-skin between them, avoiding too much drink for the sake of alertness, but nonetheless allowing themselves an hour of relaxation, they spoke of their wives.

All the men knew of the exceptionally beautiful Bathsheba. The bombastic Uriah spoke of her often, far more often than the neglected woman would ever have dreamed. To her husband's mind, because she was so often the subject of his thoughts, she was anything but neglected. To his way of thinking, everything he did was for her, and it never occurred to him that she did not see it that way.

He bragged to the men of her enterprise, of the business he had "permitted" her to indulge in, and how her reputation as a needle-worker had brought gain to the family. She would be well set up, he said, should he meet an untimely end upon some battlefield, not only by his military pension, but by the craft she had perfected.

And then, there was no woman so comely. He did not say this outright, for fear of offending his fellow husbands. But they all knew it, and should they forget, he was always eager to remind them of the good fortune he had in her attentions. Likeable as Uriah was, and loyal, he was thoroughly blind to Bathsheba's feelings, indeed to the point that he thought her dutiful ministrations amounted to love.

Tonight, as he boasted of her, he believed what he said.

Stretching his legs before the fire, he leaned casually back upon one of Joab's parti-colored bolsters. "Even now, my wife most likely paces our rooftop, looking out toward Jordan and praying for my safety. Bathsheba is a good woman, comrades, the best of all!"

3

There was, as Uriah had said, a woman upon his rooftop this evening, but it was not Bathsheba. Bathsheba would be ascending to the rooftop soon, but for now it was her maid, Dorca, who occupied herself there. Nor were Dorca's eyes turned toward Jordan and the troops of Israel. Rather she was busy pouring a bath for her mistress.

Dorca's eyes did glance up now and again, as she nervously timed her actions to the stroll King David was known to take, many such pleasant evenings, upon his own rooftop.

It was spring of the year, when, as the saying went, "kings go forth to battle." Strange, Dorca thought, that just as new life was blossoming forth upon bush and tree, just when the wild goslings were hatching, when farmers in the valley looked forward to the green shoots that dispelled winter and shepherds rejoiced in the birth of new lambs, kings and governors set out to do their killing.

Of course, it was the way of men, Dorca reasoned, and the way of kings to conquer, to expand. It was their method of growing, as the earth produced growth. Still, it heralded death for the weakest, and Dorca was glad she was not a man.

Stranger still, it was, that King David had not "gone forth" with his men this year. For reasons known only to the monarch, he had chosen to remain in Jerusalem, in the comfort of his palace this season, as his men set out to risk their lives in his service. It was the first time he had ever stayed behind.

Perhaps, she mused, he had reached a point in his career where he felt it unnecessary to personally play at war. Perhaps he felt he had earned the right to the comforts he had fought so hard to achieve.

David would never be like the pampered kings of the east, or the pharaohs of Egypt, who were born to their position and who indulged in war only when it suited them. Many never tasted of battle, sending their troops across the map as heedlessly as a board player sends game pieces across a board.

David had cut his teeth on a sword, earning his reputation, and indeed his throne, on his excellence as a warrior. He was no coward and no lazy fellow. It must be, then, that he felt, in his fiftieth year, that he deserved the pleasures of his palace, that his army had matured enough to do without him.

Dorca could give him this, as could all Jerusalem. Still, it was a little unnerving to imagine the warrior king at rest as his men plotted strategy in the fields.

Be that as it may, such a circumstance quite suited Dorca. It meant that the king had never been more alone, his advisers either away with the generals or distracted by civil affairs. And, as everyone knew, David's personal life was quite empty. The queen was queen in name only. There was no great love in David's life. What better time to attempt the plot that had been brewing in the handmaid's mind for so long?

It was no light possibility she plotted. It was quite likely, given David's absolute right as king, and his lonely male vulnerability, that, should he ever lay eyes upon Bathsheba, he would not only make inquiries about her, but he would make a move to have her.

So convinced was Dorca of her mistress's irresistible attractiveness, that she set about to fulfill her scheme with unflinching confidence. It had only awaited the perfect timing of this evening for the temptation to be advanced.

And perfect, it was!

Never had there been a more sensuous or sultry evening in Jerusalem. There would be many a citizen seeking the cool breezes that blew across housetops tonight, many a young body basking in the waters of splashing baths. They would be discreetly veiled, just as Bathsheba would be. But few would be so inline with the view from the palace roof, and only one would suggest such comeliness as to merit a second glance.

Dorca had draped the bath basin in a gauzy tent, positioned so that the retreating light of the western sky would cast her lady's silhouette in perfect outline upon it.

Jerusalem—The City of God

As the devoted maid considered the likely consequences of such a display, her heart tripped excitedly. Fumbling with the stopper on a bottle of myrrh, she poured the spattering contents into the basin and fluttered the water with her plump fingers.

A warm wind blew across the roof, teasing her own veil, and, as though naked herself, she tugged it quickly over her face. It was the witching hour—not midnight, but the walking hour, when kings go forth to stroll upon their decks.

With a little tremble, she glanced again over her shoulder and stood up. David had not appeared yet, but soon enough he would.

Was her mistress ready? Running lightly to the roof door, she called downstairs. "Your bath is ready, mistress. It is a fair night for a lady!"

ℝ

Dorca's estimates of David's reasons for staying in Jerusalem were quite accurate. He was very near the pinnacle of his achievements and felt it time to let his army proceed under the able direction of Joab.

He had given such a decision due consideration. It was in keeping with what other kings did, and he saw no reason to continually put himself at risk. Indeed, he reasoned, it was not good for the country for its monarch to always be overseeing some battle. Let Joab prove of what mettle he was made, this time without David.

But, in truth, there was more to David's spirit of retreat than mere self sparing.

As often happens with the greatest of achievers, especially at those junctures when the future appears most secure and the next move will be of a completing nature, they step back. Almost as though they are afraid of the ultimate success, they step back.

Such was the case with David.

Nathan could have told him, if the king had sought his advice, that his hesitancy was rooted in depression.

After all, what realms were left to conquer, once Ammon was defeated? And who was there to share his conquered world, once he attained the summit?

Despite David's response to Michal's severance, the sense of buoyancy and freedom that had carried him from height to height, there were times when his spirit sank so low from singleness and isolation that he could barely creep forth from bed of a morning.

True, he had other wives. But he had no great love, as Dorca had surmised.

Little did his men guess the impact of such a condition upon their valiant sovereign. Constrained as David was from sharing his feelings with any comrade, the absence of a woman in his life had taken a severe toll.

Sorry was his condition when the time came, this year, for kings to "go forth to battle."

This evening, David had just completed a tasteless meal—his blunted appetite rendering the finest culinary efforts useless. He was reclining upon his couch in his lonely room as the western sky cast a fawn glow across the rampart. He was not ready for sleep, it being early yet, but he avoided socializing.

Fighting lethargy, and telling himself he must find a way to occupy his failed energies, he stood and went to the portico overlooking the Jebusite territory. David's city spread to the south, toward the Hinnom Valley, and the Jebusite reserve to the north, toward Moriah.

Blowing a soft sigh through pursed lips, David wearily surveyed the area that the treaty had designated to the children of Jebus. He did not resent the arrangement, but felt it rather ridiculous. Jebus was his as surely as was the rest of Jerusalem. It had been reserved for the Jebusites only as a political accommodation, and everyone knew who really had the power.

Of course, whenever he stood upon his private roof, his eyes always drifted toward the sacred rock, and his throat tightened at the sight. It was true that God had vouchsafed to him and to his posterity the kingdom of Israel. The worth of such a magnificent promise was incalculable, and he had never, since the day Nathan proclaimed it to him, underappreciated it.

Yet how he wished he had been permitted to build the temple!

Jerusalem—The City of God

Even now, he could envision the edifice of his dreams upon Moriah's brow, and his heart was hollow at the knowledge that he would live to see his vision fulfilled.

The best he could do was store up materials and riches with which to build and grace the House of God. This he did with each campaign, and it was standing orders that his commanders were to bring all booty to the storehouse for parting out to the temple treasury, before any other budgetary needs were offset. Thus, within the bowels of the city, in great caverns, were riches surpassing those of Pharaoh, reserved for future sanctuary.

Although his son, this enigmatic and yet unborn "Solomon," would have the pleasure of erecting the holy shrine, David had hired architects who were permanently in residence in his palace, and who spent their time designing and refining drafts for the temple. These he would pass on to the designated son, when he was ready for them.

Thoughts of the temple, therefore, served often to console the king in his loneliness. And dreams of the son-yet-to-be kept his spirit alive. Impressing the vision of the temple upon his heart, he was about to turn for bed, when, with a final survey of the northern streets, his eyes happened upon a certain rooftop.

There was life upon many a roof this evening, the balmy air having drawn out folks out from stuffy parlors and humid courtyards to seek its breeze. What caught his attention upon this particular roof was not really apparent. It may have been a flash of movement, a flutter of veils, or a graceful outline, the sort that inspires a reflex, a quickened beat of the heart, and captures a second glance before a man is even cognizant of an attraction.

Whatever it was, he found himself anchored to the rampart. His eyes fixed by a vision equally as compelling as any edifice he had imagined upon Moriah's brow.

A white bathing veil had been erected upon the rooftop, a veil like no others to be seen atop the houses of Jerusalem, a light, roofless tent within which family members might perform their daily ablutions in privacy.

It was usually reserved for the women of a house, and noblewomen could afford veils large enough to admit their handmaids, who helped them with their baths.

It was the clever positioning of this particular veil that permitted the explicit view the king was privy to. In a halo of golden sunset, a woman's silhouette was revealed against the drape—long, willowy, sumptuously curved. Above the veil only her head and her bare shoulders were visible, the dark mantle of her unfretted hair moving across her back as she stepped into the basin.

Caught in mid-breath, David gripped the balcony rail, his eyes wide with admiration. Never, to his memory, had he ever seen anything so lovely. He had seven wives, all of them beauties, and he had hundreds of concubines, captives of his wars, gifts of his tributaries, whims of his eyes whom he had procured with a snap of his royal fingers.

But he had never been so instantly smitten.

Incredibly, this reaction was to a suggestion only, a possibility of beauty that he could not be entirely sure of. For he could view the shadow only, and not the real woman. Yet such was Bathsheba's charm, that the mere hint of her was enough to glue the king to his railing.

There was obviously another woman in the tent with the bather. Little Dorca huddled at the mistress's feet, pouring scented water into the basin and running it up the lady's long legs with a soft sponge. All of this David could interpret, by the play of dark and light against the veil.

The maid stood up, her head no higher than the tent top. As she did, the lady compliantly raised her own slender arms in the air, turning this way and that as the attendant sponged her torso.

"O Lord!" David whispered, his heart thrumming. "let the veil slip," he thought without thinking. "Come wind, be my friend!"

But such was not to be. The most David was allowed was the sight of the woman as she stepped forth from the airy chamber, garbed in a skimming tunic, magnetized to her damp body.

In the light of the waning sun, she sat upon a stool, enjoying the breeze as Dorca ran a brush through her curls. Lifting her face to the pink sky, she smiled in satisfaction, her eyes closed to all about her.

Only Dorca slyly glanced toward the palace roof. Only Dorca saw that her scheme had been successful; the king was gazing, as she had hoped, upon the fair Judahite.

Dorca had her dreams for happiness of her mistress, dreams she had taken great pains to facilitate. Never would she have imagined, however, just how quickly they would be fulfilled.

It was morning of the day after she had orchestrated the bath on the roof. The plump little maid was bustling about her housework when a clatter of horses' hooves was heard outside the front gate, and then a banging upon the door.

Setting aside her dust rag, she wiped her hands upon her apron and hastened to unbolt the entry. What greeted her impressed itself forever upon her memory, not only for the fear it inspired, but for the change it portended for the household from that day forward.

Standing before her was a palace officer, regaled in the finest velvet, a gold chain about his neck and a leather helmet upon his head. To his back was the chariot in which he had arrived, drawn by two stallions, its bare-chested driver muscled like a Philistine and staring straight ahead like a sentry.

Awestruck, the diminutive woman sank back from the door, bowing meekly.

"Is this the home of Uriah the Hittite?" the officer demanded, looking past Dorca.

"It is, Your Lordship," she managed. "But the master is not at home."

"Very well," the man replied, barely gracing the maid with a glance. "It is the lady of the house that we seek. Is she home?"

Dorca gasped. Daring not to think this summons could actually be the answer to the plot she had contrived, her first assumption was that Uriah had been wounded, and this emissary was sent to tell the widow.

Drawing a blank, Dorca did not readily answer. But when the officer glared at her, she straightened.

"Yes sir'" she croaked. My Lady is at home. Shall I fetch her?"

At this, the officer reached into his cloak and drew forth a small parchment, rolled and sealed with a golden seal. "Give this to your mistress," he commanded. "Tell her it is from the king. Tell her to make herself ready, as is befitting a proper female, for she is to come before His Majesty this evening."

David paced his chamber anxiously, clenching and unclenching his hands in nervous anticipation. Scarcely did he recognize himself when he chanced upon his reflection in the long copper mirror that graced the wall.

Was he the same man who, only last night, had envisioned a holy temple upon Moriah? Was he the same man who had received the promise of an ongoing kingdom from the Lord's prophet?

How was it that his heart and soul were suddenly consumed with thoughts of a strange woman, a woman who was not his wife and never could be—the wife, in fact, of one of his most devoted captains?

How was it that he planned, quite consciously, her seduction?

She held him in her grip, as surely as a keen-eyed eagle holds a mouse in its swooping grasp. And all of this without her even trying, all of this without her even knowing he had laid eyes upon her, innocent to the seething impulses she inspired.

He tried to tell himself that he would only interview her, that he was summoning her as one of his captain's wives, to see that she had been receiving her military stipend and that she was being properly cared for by the state.

This was the reason he had given his men when he sent them for her, and it was the reason he would give her for the summons.

Of course, before he had called for her, he had inquired after her identity. This morning, he had had no idea who she was, least of all that she was the wife of Uriah. But now that he knew, rather than such knowledge being an impediment, it gave him an excuse to send for her.

He knew his reasoning was lame, that his men could see right through his motivations. But he was king, and a king could do as he pleased.

Nonetheless, it was best to give a rationale for his actions. It made everyone, all around, feel better.

As for the woman herself, she doubtless had no inkling of his real purpose. When she came, he would handle her tenderly, devoting whatever time was necessary to put her at ease. Her trust was absolutely essential, and once won, could lead to the winning of her heart.

But how he hoped she was lonely, like himself! It was very possible she was. Uriah was the consummate soldier, and such men were notorious for neglecting their wives.

If he detected any hint of such loneliness; he would seek to fill the vacuum Uriah had left. He knew how to do that. David was good with women.

The hours since he had seen Bathsheba upon her roof seemed like days, so many thoughts had passed through David's heart. All night long he had tossed and turned upon his bed, reliving the mere sight of her and helplessly imagining more.

When guilt of his carnal conjurings got the better of him, he wallowed in self-justification, declaring that she should have known better than to display herself so wantonly, that she surely knew men walked the roofs at sunset, and that she would be seen by many. Possibly, even, she knew that David himself went from time to time upon his roof, and that the king of Israel was like any man.

Then he would soften, thinking her too lovely to be capable of such crime.

Back and forth his tormenting ruminations took him, as he alternately swelled with ecstasy at the possibilities she inspired, and then agonized over how available she might be.

What if she were another man's wife? What would he do then?

At first hint of dawn, he had sent for a discreet detective to find out who she was. The forthcoming information had burned his heart, as he told himself she was beyond grasp. But then, the telling moment had come, the moment that comes to all men, when what seems an innocent fantasy has the possibility of turning to action.

David decided to do what he could to make her his.

Jerusalem—The City of God

Even now, he could barely admit to himself what he was about to do. But it was useless to deny it. Whatever he told others, whatever he told the woman, he knew full well that his goal was determined.

Lunch sat untouched upon his table that day. Eagerly he awaited the coming dusk, and the hour when she would be announced at his door.

Yes he would receive her here, in his private chamber. Would it make any difference to receive her in his stateroom?

Everyone knew. It would make no difference.

5

Bathsheba Bath Eliam, wife of Uriah the Hittite, stepped forth from the royal carriage, which had arrived at her home this evening, and approached the main gate of King David's palace. Slowly the driver, who had been sent to bring her here, pulled away, looking after her with a knit brow, though she was entering the safest place in Jerusalem.

In her hand was the parchment with the strange message, the words of the king calling for her. Though the conveyance in which she had ridden was marked with the crest of David's house, she moved as in a dream, wondering if the parchment she carried was real, or if it was forgery, and if she would be shunted away by angry guards.

But Dorca had insisted that it had been delivered by an auspicious gentleman, and that his carriage, also, had been marked with the royal crest. Surly, the parchment was legitimate.

Her hand quivering, she smoothed her velvet robe, the dark green one that Dorca.had suggested she wear. Although last evening had been very warm, tonight a fickle breeze played off Moriah, and she was glad she had put the cloak over her paler green tunic.

In the few hours since she had received the summons, she had given almost as much thought to what she would wear as to why she was being called at all. She hoped, now, that her choice had been good.

Certainly, this dress and this robe were among her most precious possessions, she having spent countless hours designing and placing intricate beadwork upon the bodice and the yoke. She had, in fact, made these pieces the first time Uriah left for war after their marriage, to console herself in her loneliness. But she had never had occasion to wear them.

Rather, she had never taken an occasion to do so. She could have worn them for her husband.

A blush rose to her cheeks as she realized this. But she suppressed the feelings that inspired it and ran hasty hand through her tumbling locks, where Dorca's handiwork of braids and curls did not confine them.

Jerusalem—The City of God

Again, here was the mysterious letter in her clammy hand. Smoothing it, as she had her cloak, she walked to the outer gate of the mammoth compound. Her head bowed, she approached an iron-jawed sentry and held out the parchment so that its broken seal was foremost.

To her great surprise, the guard only glanced at the letter, and, as though prepared for her arrival, nodded for her to pass. Before she knew it, she was inside the enormous walls of the first court, and a man, perhaps the one who delivered the summons, was there to greet her.

"This way, my lady," he said, taking her by the arm. "The king awaits."

Corridor after corridor led to the king's sanctum. As Bathsheba passed conference rooms and great halls, she wondered that the official did not lead her into one. Would the king not be meeting with her in some public place?

It seemed, as they progressed, that the official led her to more and more remote hallways.

As she followed, she had that peculiar sensation, which she had heard described by men who had survived great trauma, of her entire life passing before her eyes. Memories of her girlhood, of her first meeting with Uriah, yes—of her first sight of the giant slayer, David himself—flashed to mind. Then, the times she had beheld His Majesty in parades, at public ceremonies—even from the sanctuary of her rooftop, as she had observed his late evening walks along his own high garden...

Suddenly, her heart tripped. She had always had a good sense of direction, and even through the convoluted corridors of this palace, she felt sure the official was leading her toward the very chambers that lined the palace's northwest corner, the chamber she could see from her house, the region of the king's private rooms!

Lord God! She thought. Was she being taken to David's room?

A shocking suggestion posed itself. If David could be seen from her rooftop, was it possible she could be seen from his? She had no time to piece together the entire possibility before she was left at a great golden door. Giving a cursory knock, the official stepped inside.

Bathsheba, breathless in the hall, heard only a low murmur of introduction before the man reappeared and ushered her into the chamber.

David stood beneath his balcony arch, his back to the room. He knew the woman arrived, not only because his valet had announced her, but because he had envisioned this moment for a night and day.

Now that it was here, it paralyzed him, so that he could not turn to face the open room.

David had confronted giants in his day; he was the mightiest of warriors, and knew no fear upon a battle field. Likewise, David had many women—many wives, many concubines. He had never known fear of a woman; consternation perhaps. Anger and frustration, certainly. Even hatred—yes, he had sometime hated Michal.

But he had never known fear as he knew it now.

He knew that the trembling of his hands and tremor in his heart were prompted as much by guilt as by desire. Still, he was a king. He must not be a coward, especially not for a female! He must turn himself about, and face her!

As he did, holding onto the heavy curtain at his side, his breath came like an arrow.

Lord, there she is! He thought. *Yes—this is the one—more beautiful than I imagined!*

For along moment, he drank in the vision that was Bathsheba, unaware of the paralyzing fear which he, likewise, inspired in her. As he studied her, his eyes taking in the length of her, the wonder of her statuesque quietness, he suddenly thought of Uriah, and a smirk crossed his lips. *Fool,* he breathed to himself. *What a fool, to choose the sword over this glorious creature!*

Surely, he thought, if he ever owned Bathsheba, he could not leave her, would not hanker after the thrill of any battle or any conquest!

At last, he realized that the poor woman was pale with dread. He had promised himself that he would soothe her and had rehearsed just how he would woo her.

Clearing his tight throat, he stepped into the room and smiled at her. The instant he moved, she sank to her knees, as courtesy demanded, keeping her face to the carpet until he spoke.

"Stand," he managed to say, assuring himself with a kingly tone. "We are not so formal in this room."

Then, casually he went to his couch and sat upon it, leaning on one elbow and gesturing to a pile of pillows near his table.

"Take your ease, my lady," he offered, trying to stifle his admiration. "Your husband is a dear comrade, and so we are family."

Family? The word stunned her.

Imagining no other way to respond, she stayed standing and said, "Uriah is your devoted servant, Your Majesty."

A little irritated, David gestured again to the pillows. "Sit, sit," he commanded, "We shall speak of Uriah."

With this, he reached for a carafe upon the table and poured for her a glass of ruby wine.

Numbly, she complied, seating herself on the pillow farthest from his couch and eying the goblet dubiously.

Be gentle, David told himself.

Disregarding his own wine glass, he flashed a benign smile. "Surely you wonder why I have called for you," he began. "Uriah is one of my champions. Therefore, I and my administration are concerned for his household."

This rang hollow. Bathsheba fidgeted.

"Are you comfortable?" David inquired.

Glancing at the pillows, Bathsheba nodded. The king, amused, chuckled.

"No, no, my dear. I mean, is your household well taken care of? Are you receiving monthly payments from the army, while your husband is away?"

Blushing, Bathsheba stammered, "Oh, yes, of course, Your Highness. We are well established. We want for nothing, my maid and I."

Intrigued, David inquired further. "You have no children?" he asked.

At this, Bathsheba's countenance fell, and the king knew he had touched on a painful point. Studying her tenderly, he longed with all his heart to reach out to her, to take her in his arms and comfort her.

Instead, he observed, "You are alone, then."

Bathsheba glanced at him reflexively. Of course, she was alone! Lonely was her middle name. But no one had ever spoken of it to her. No one had ever inquired into the emptiness and isolation she had known.

She shook her head. "We are well, My Lord. Uriah sees to it that we are well provided for." At this, she reached for the wine glass, and took a tasteless sip.

Knowing she lied, David took courage, "You are fortunate," he said. "To never feel lonely must be a true gift. I, for one, know the feeling all too well."

It was now Bathsheba's turn to study the king. Confounded by this confession, she surveyed him in curiosity. "The office of a king must have its lonely moments," she observed. "There are few who could manage such responsibility."

David fingered his wine glass. Why shouldn't she think of him only as a monarch? She did not know him, did not know the vacuum of his mannish heart that compelled him tonight.

He remembered the first sight he had had of her, the picture of her upon the roof, a she had stepped forth from her bath. With a dull ache in his chest, he glanced away and pretended to analyze the weather beyond his balcony. "It is cool tonight, my dear, but warm within this room. Take off your cloak, and be at home."

Hesitant, Bathsheba drew the cloak tighter to her. But when she saw that this displeased the king, she shyly undid the clasp and let the garment fall back from her shoulders.

Emboldened by the sight of her supple arms and neck, David nodded gratefully. "Very good, my lady. You can't imagine what a pleasure it is for me to have your company. I am not lonely only because I am a king."

Now the woman perceived, without a doubt, that David had summoned her for reasons other than he suggested. She did not let herself ponder the full extent of his longings, but she knew he desired more than to speak of Uriah and her financial welfare.

"Sir," she objected, "you have wives. How can it be that you are ever lonely?"

At this, he rankled. Rolling his eyes, he rose from his couch and paced the carpet. "Is it not possible to be surrounded by people, and yet be alone?" he countered. "You surely go to market, or sit with your maid of an evening, yet long for. . ."

He stopped his pacing. Aggravation was too evident in his tone. At last, he turned to her directly. ". . . you long for a touch. . . a voice . . ."

Bathsheba's face reddened as she felt his intentions ever more strongly, and especially since they echoed the long buried dreams she had never admitted to anyone.

"You have wives . . ." she said again, but this time in a whisper.

David stood now exactly beside her, brooding over her with sad, dark eyes.

"Let us speak frankly," he said, daring to place a hand upon her bowed head. As he did a jolt passed through her from her skull to her feet.

"You know that the queen and I are man and wife in name only," he said. "All Jerusalem knows this, and all Israel."

Shaken to the core, Bathsheba lifted a trembling hand and held his where it touched her. He did not mention the rest of his harem. He did not love any of them as he needed to. That was apparent. But why was his focus upon Bathsheba—of all women in his kingdom?

Thoughts of Uriah flooded over her, and tears rose to her eyes. She knew what was about to happen, and she felt all but powerless against it.

Now, the king was kneeling at her side, slipping around in front of her and joining her upon the pillows. Ever so gently he caressed her bare arm and whispered, "What of you, my lady? When was the last time you were held? And when by a man you loved?"

Turning her face from his insistent gaze, Bathsheba felt a quake go through her, and the sting of tears upon her cheeks.

"There now," David said. "We are two of a kind, are we not? You have seen me upon my roof, and I have seen you upon yours. We have loved from afar, have we not?"

So, she had guessed rightly. He had observed her, as she had observed him!

David could see by her awestruck expression that he read her heart correctly.

Drawing her stubborn body to his breast, he enfolded her in his arms and breathed into her hair. "Take comfort, my dear, in the arms of your king," he whispered. Following the curve of her side with one hand, he grasped her closer, as though to crush her into himself, and pressed her lips to his.

"Never," he sighed, kissing her over and over, "never shall you be alone again!"

6

Uriah the Hittite spurred his horse over the crest of Jordan's west bank and headed toward a shallow ford that let to the camp of Israel. It was sunset, and the lights of the sprawling tent city already flickered like fireflies upon the distant slopes.

Beyond them, in the rolling hills of Ammon, stood Rabbah, the enemy capital to which Joab had laid siege.

How glad Uriah was to be coming home!

In truth, the army camp was more home to him that his own house in Jerusalem. Not only did he spend more time with the troops of Israel than with his wife, but he was more fulfilled when he served as warrior than as husband.

At the same time, to Uriah's way of thinking, he loved Bathsheba ardently. Everything he did was for her, in the long run. Even his refusal to pay her an overnight visit during his recent stay in Jerusalem would ultimately benefit her, being part of his loyalty to the nation.

Still, he was bewildered by the king's peculiar summons, which had taken him from this men and his mission of the field to a mystifying encounter with the monarch. Coming in the very midst of the all-out advance against Rabbah, the call to David's palace had been untimely, to say the least.

And the purpose of it was not more clear, now that it was passed, than it had been when it was delivered.

Since when did a king summon a commander from the war zone only to inquire as to his well-being and that of his troops? Since when did he drag a captain of 10,000 away from the thick of battle, away from the deployment of men and strategies, only to ask, "How goes the battle?"

Then, too, it had been most strange how the king insisted on Uriah's taking a brief respite at home. "Go down to your house, and wash your feet," the king had suggested, using the traditional euphemism that implied Uriah should indulge in the love of his wife.

As the captain had left the palace, bemused by the offer, men from the king's kitchen had met him with gifts of food for the family and dainties for Uriah's lady. But he had not been able to indulge in the luxuries of his house and his woman's arms when he remembered his men on the war front, and the risks they took hourly in service to Israel.

Joining David's sentries at the palace gate, he had slept in the guardhouse and had not even notified Bathsheba of his presence in the city.

To the captain's further consternation, David sent for him again the next morning, seemingly distraught that he had not complied with the royal suggestion that he spend the night at home.

Red-faced and fidgety, the king had met with him in a private chamber. "You came a great distance from the battlefield," David grumbled. "Why didn't you go home for a visit?"

Utterly bewildered by the king's insistence, Uriah had objected, "The Ark, and Israel and Judah abide in tents. And my Lord Joab and all his servants are encamped in the open fields. Shall I then go into my house, to eat and to drink and to lie with my wife? As the king lives, and as your soul lives, O King, I will not do this thing!"

Was that anger he had seen in the king's eyes? On the few occasions that Uriah had interacted personally with David, he had always been well received, given to feel that the might warrior considered him one of his best men.

But the day he refused David's offer, appealing instead to his sense of duty and patriotism, the king obviously bristled, flashing a bitter scowl and leaving his couch to pace the floor with anxious tread.

Uriah still pondered his inscrutable response. "Stay one more day," David had suddenly commanded. "Tomorrow I will let you return to the field."

With that, he had clapped his hands, calling for his valet and ordering a round of drinks. "Join me this afternoon," he told him, "and we shall sup together."

That day, Uriah was treated like a royal ambassador, wined and dined until the sun set, and he was fairly drunk. It seemed, looking back, that the king had gone out of his way to overwhelm Uriah with the most tantalizing beverages—liquors, rare wines, and beers. Together the two men talked and laughed and shared war stories, in the most brotherly of fashions. Uriah quite forgot that David was his king as they sang and joked together.

Then, when the captain could take no more and still walk upright, David had called for his cloak, draping him with it in a most affectionate manner.

Uriah recalled, as he rode now toward the Jordan, that the king had sent him on his way with instructions, again, to go and visit his home. "Surely your wife is a fair and lovely lady." He had said, "Why leave her lonely, when you could so easily comfort her this night."

Yes—Uriah was certain David had used those words. They came back to him now in perfect clarity. At the time, he had been too inebriated to follow through on the offer. Too inebriated, and too sentimental.

Uriah's sense of patriotism and devotion to Israel, far from being overwhelmed by intoxication, was enhanced by drink and song, and by the fellowship of his king. When he left the palace and saw the uniformed guards at the gate, the officers on the tower, and the king's soldiers along the palace ramparts, he determined to show his loyalty by sleeping again the sentry stationhouse.

Without further ado, the next morning, David's messenger had rousted him, thrusting a sealed letter into his hand and telling him that he was to deliver it to Joab. His head throbbing from the evening's excess, Uriah had stumbled into the daylight, receiving the mysterious letter with a salute.

Seeing the hard look upon the messenger's face, he thought about asking whether the king was unhappy with him. However, he could not imagine a reason why he should be, and so accepted the assignment with relief. He was going back to his troops, and this was all he cared about.

Spurring his horse through the shallow waters of the wilderness river, he headed for the tents of Joab and the companionship of his valiant men. He hoped he had not missed much action and that he would be leading his men, tomorrow, against the enemy capital.

7

Joab's troops were plotting the final maneuvers against Rabbah when the general, stationed atop the east bank, saw Uriah returning from Jerusalem. His sun-bronzed face crinkling into a grateful smile, Joab waved for his comrade to make haste.

David's mystifying summons of the captain had almost confounded the general's planned assault. Had Uriah's underlings not been so well trained, they would not have been able to proceed without the Hittite's presence. Either way, it was a great relief to see Uriah returning, and just in time for the decisive foray against the capital.

Standing up in his saddle, Joab looked over the heads of his comrades, Abishai and Benaiah, who watched with him, and hailed the Hittite, calling him to his side.

Uriah, proud as always totally himself with the generals, sped across the desert, his red hair and beard flashing in the hot wind.

With his typically hearty salute, he cast all thought of his peculiar palace adventure from his mind and galloped through the sage to a skidding halt beside his mentor.

"Greetings, friend!" Joab enthused. "How was Jerusalem?"

"The queen of cities, as when we left her," Uriah answered.

"And the king? I trust he is well," Joab inquired.

"He is well," Uriah replied, hiding his skepticism. "He sends his greetings to my general, and sends a message for you." He drew the king's sealed letter from his cloak and handed it to Joab.

Fearing that David was commissioning Uriah to serve in some administrative capacity, and that this was his reason for calling him to Jerusalem, Joab reached gingerly for the little scroll. Even before he opened it, however, he thought it unlikely that, were Uriah to be serving on the home front, David would have sent him back to the field to say so. Word would have come via some messenger, and not by the hand of Uriah, himself.

Pushing his blond hair back from his forehead, Joab fumbled with the seal and unrolled the parchment. Never would he have dreamed the contents of the baffling document!

As Uriah looked on, wondering what could be the portent of the letter, he was careful not to glimpse the writing. This was a private communication between his king and his commander, and was none of his affair, unless Joab wished to reveal it.

He could not help but notice, however, that the general's face grew deathly pale as he read the notice. When Joab rolled up the little paper again, tucking it into his sleeve, he did so with trembling hands.

"What is it, sir?" Uriah inquired. "Is there some trouble?"

Joab seemed not to hear him. For a long moment, the great general sat stunned, unspeaking, as Abishai and Benaiah looked on quizzically.

"Very well," Joab said at last, his voice thick with tension. "You have done well, Uriah. Watch with me for a space, and then you may join your men."

How David wished he had gone forth with his army to smite the Ammonites! How he wished he had not succumbed to the temptation, this one and only time, to tarry behind in his capital, while his valiant men took up swords in his service!

What had possessed him to stay home? It had had something to do with privilege, with earned luxury. He could not remember his reasoning any more. He only knew that it had been a dreadful mistake, and that he, the warrior king, had come to no good dallying with the fruits of his position.

He could not even talk to God about his error. He had tried to expunge his guilt in poetry and song, crying out his fears and his regrets to the music of his harp, but it had done no good. His soul was wracked with remorse, and shame ate at his spirit as no amount of grieving for Michal or fear of Saul had ever done.

Bathsheba was pregnant. She had notified him of the fact only weeks after their first encounter. Just how far pregnant, she was not certain. They had had more than one liaison, more than one night of passion, as she had bowed to his way with her in shameless eagerness, and as he had desired her ceaselessly since first taking her to his heart. Regret followed each rendezvous, but loneliness and lust led to yet another. And so love became a twin to sorrow, as the sin-knotted couple felt powerless over themselves.

David's foiled attempts to get Uriah to spend a night with his wife destroyed all hopes of foisting the pregnancy off on the husband. Now the king had added an even greater crime to his growing catalog of indiscretions. He had sent a letter to Joab, by the hand of Bathsheba's husband, consigning the unwary Hittite to the front ranks of the hottest part of the battle.

"When he is there," the letter said, "pull back from him all of his supporting troops, that he may be smitten, and die."

Virtually, he had called for the murder of one of his most worthy officers, all in an ill-purposed attempt to cover his own tracks.

With Uriah out of the way, David would be free to make Bathsheba legally his, and there would be no need to hide the parentage of the child she carried.

So embroiled had David been in dealing with guilt and contriving plots, that he dared not think much of the child. The fact that, nearly a decade ago, Nathan had prophesied a future heir, a son to build the illusive temple, did intrude, from time to time, upon his consciousness. But so riddled was David with fear and shame, he could not imagine Bathsheba's unborn baby to be the child of promise.

Nor could he bring himself to ask God's blessing upon the impending birth.

The knottiness of David's circumstances and the schemes to extricate himself were of far weightier importance than any dream he had once held dear. No thought of the temple or the promised heir entered his mind this evening, as he paced the eastern ramparts of his palace, studying the darkening sky and hoping for word from the front.

When he saw a runner speeding down the road that skirted Olive

Mount, his heart leaped. Surely this was Joab's messenger, the fleet-footed lad who frequented the route between the war zone and the capital.

Yes, David recognized his brilliant green headscarf, the one that bore the insignia of the Lion of Judah.

Racing down the stair, the king went to meet the boy.

~∞~

It was with trepidation that the messenger boy entered the palace this time. He had come here often with news from the front, but never before had he received such odd instructions from Joab concerning what he was to say.

The king might be angry, the general had warned, when he learned how close the Israelis had gone to the walls of Rabbah in this battle. The boy knew that messengers were often punished for bringing news that displeased a monarch, and Joab wanted to forestall any repercussions against the innocent lad.

"If it should happen that the king's wrath arises," Joab had said, "and if the king should say to you, 'Why did you approach so close to the city when you fought? Didn't you know that they would shoot from the wall? And if he should recount the time that Abimelech, son of Jerubbesheth, was slain by a woman casting a millstone from the wall at Thebez, then say to him, 'Your servant Uriah the Hittite is dead also.'"

How such a message was going to quell the king's anger, the lad could not imagine. It seemed to him it should spark it to a grater peak.

Still, the boy must do as Joab said. And so he was very apprehensive as he passed through the palace gate and sped toward the king's receiving hall.

As it was, David met him in the corridor, obviously quite eager for a report. Falling to his face, the boy bowed before him, and David snapped his fingers, summoning him into a side room.

"Tell me, boy," the king prodded. "How goes the battle?"

Quickly the boy gave a briefing, recounting all the major moves the Israelis had made and how the enemy had responded. When he came to the part about the wall, and how General Joab had sent some of his finest men beneath its very shadow, he rushed through it with well-rehearsed explanation:

"Surely the men of Rabbah prevailed against us, Majesty, and came out to us into the field. And we chased them, setting upon them all the way to the gates. And the archers shot from the wall . . .and some of the king's servants are dead."

Eyes wide, he waited for a reaction. But to his amazement, David neither grew angry over the method, nor inquired further into it. Instead, he paced nervously, glancing over his shoulder as if to catch eavesdroppers. Then he inquired, "Who was slain, my boy? Were all the captains spared?

"All, Majesty," the boy answered, "save one. Your servant, Uriah, the Hittite, was fighting in the very hottest part of the fray, and . . . he is dead, Majesty."

Again, to the lad's confounding, David reacted in a most unexpected manner. Rather than showing dismay or anger, rather than being grieved over the matter, he took a deep breath and seemed to relax a bit.

"Return to your master," he said, "and tell him. 'Do not let this thing displease you, for the sword devours one as well as another. Make your battle stronger, and overthrow the city.' Do you understand, boy?"

"Yes, sir," he replied in a croak

"You must encourage the general," David commanded. "He has done well."

With this, he gave the boy a fleeting nod, and retired to his chamber.

8

Though David may have convinced himself that his tracks were covered, nothing was hidden from the eyes of God.

Forever in his heart and memory would live the day that Nathan the prophet came to him in his guiltiness, confronting him squarely with the fact that he had not hidden his sins from God Almighty, no matter how much he may have rationalized them to himself or concealed them from the public.

Dusty as always, and windblown, the rustic messenger had arrived at court, separating the guards at the door with the butt of his staff and crossing the glossy tiles with a determined tread.

"Majesty," he had called, not bothering with formalities, "I would have a word with you!"

"Of course," the king said, wondering at his brash demeanor. Always before, Nathan had been of meek disposition, much humbler than Samuel in his approach.

"There is a case of some complexity that I would like your opinion on," the prophet explained.

"Very well," David replied. "But if it is a civil case, there are courts to handle—"

"As I say," Nathan interrupted, "this is an unusual case . . . one requiring your advice."

Now Samuel had been a judge, as well as a prophet, but that had been before the days of the kingship, when matters of justice were handled by such itinerant governors. Nathan was not a judge. Matters of law and order were consigned to district and tribal magistrates. Why, then, was Nathan stepping into a role other than that of prophet, coming to David with a legal matter?

Nevertheless, the king respected this bold seer and called for a scribe to begin taking notes.

Without a pause, the prophet proceeded: "There were two men in a city, one rich and the other poor. The rich man had a great many flocks and herds. But the poor man had nothing, save one little eve lamb, which he had bought and nourished. And it grew up together with him and his children. It ate of his own food and drank of his own cup, and even slept with him. Why, to this man, it was like a daughter!"

David leaned forward upon his throne, entranced. It crossed his mind that Nathan had not named any of the parties involved, but he did not interrupt.

"Now," said Nathan, "a traveler came to visit the rich man, and the rich man did not take a sheep from his own flock, or a calf from his own heard, to prepare a meal for his visitor. Instead he took the poor man's lamb and made a meal of it!"

The prophet's tone evinced distress as he reported this, so that it seemed he must know these people personally. Perhaps this accounted for his direct involvement in the case.

Picking up Nathan's sentiment, David felt his own ire growing. "Why, such a thing is unforgivable!" he fumed. "As the Lord lives, the man that has done this shall surely die!"

Glancing at his scribe, he directed him to write down the sentence. "He shall also make restitution to the amount of four times the lamb's value, seeing that he showed no pity!"

When he turned back to Nathan, however, he was bewildered to see a scowl of grave disapproval imprinted on the prophet's face. Before he could ask the reason, the holy man lifted a hand and pointed rigidly at him.

"You are the man!" he cried.

Stunned, David gawked at the prophet. "What?" he stammered. "I am no shepherd. I have stolen no man's sheep!"

But even as he spoke, there was a hollow ache in his heart.

Grilling him with an insightful gaze, Nathan stepped closer to the throne.

"Thus says the Lord god of Israel," he growled, "I anointed you king over Israel, and I delivered you out of the hand of Saul! And I gave you your master's house and his concubines. Indeed, I gave you the tribes of

Israel and Judah! And if that had not been enough, I would have given you more!"

By now, Nathan stood upon the very platform of the throne, toe to toe with the seated monarch, and he flashed accusatory eyes, crying, "Why, then, have you despised the commandment of the Lord, to do evil in his sight? You have killed Uriah the Hittite by the sword of the Ammonites and have taken his wife for yourself."

Cringing before the prophet, David pulled himself into a knot of shame and diverted his face.

Upon the scribal chair at his right sat his secretary, still taking notes on all Nathan said. It was now the preacher's turn to pronounce a sentence, and David grew white as death.

"Therefore," Nathan commenced, "because of these things, the sword shall never depart from your house. 'Because you have ignored me and have taken the wife of Uriah the Hittite,' says the Lord, 'behold, I will raise up evil against you out of your own house, and I will take your wives before your eyes and give them to your neighbors, and they shall lie with your wives in public! You committed this evil in secret, but I will do this before all Israel, and in front of the whole world!'"

As though he had received a physical blow, David slid form his throne, falling face down upon the floor and weeping. Though there was a grisly relief in the fact that his sins were no longer secret, that he need conceal them no longer, the assurance that he would live to pay so dread a price seemed more than he could bear. "I have sinned against the Lord!" he cried, tearing his clothes.

Nathan, observing his contrition, pronounced that God had forgiven him. But there was still more that he must endure. Approaching David, the prophet lifted him up from the floor and required him to look into his eyes.

"Because you have given great occasion to the enemies of the Lord to blaspheme, the child that Bathsheba shall bear for you shall surely die!"

Bathsheba lay in the opulent suite that was hers as the newly installed Queen of Israel. But there was no pleasure in her position or her surroundings.

A week ago she had given birth to the ill-begotten child of her illicit union. Weak and sickly from the moment he took his first breath, the baby had been a worry, rather than the joy she had hoped for. Delicate and pale, he had wriggled into the world with a whimper, rather than a lusty cry. Ever since, he had been listless.

Bathsheba had kept him close to her from the moment he was born, refusing to let him be taken over by a wet-nurse, as was the custom among aristocrats. Except for changes and baths, he had been beside his mother, nestled beneath the covers.

To Bathsheba's dismay, however, he showed no interest in eating, turning from her breast more often than not, whenever she offered it.

Though David had been with her when the child was born, not lingering like most husbands outside the birthing room, there had been a shadow in his eyes at the imminent birth, rather than the normal expectancy. That shadow had been there for months, ever since the prophet, Nathan, had made his last visit to the palace. The king had never told Bathsheba the things Nathan had said, yet ever since that day, she had sensed her husband's growing depression and knew the prophet had brought dreadful tidings.

That the tidings related, at least in part, to the anticipated birth, she had no doubt. Each time she spoke of the coming child, or placed David's hand upon her swelling abdomen, he evinced at best a hesitant pride, at worst a deep sadness. The past week, since the baby had come, his viability tenuous and fragile, David had spent most every hour at prayer in the family courtyard. Refusing, himself, to eat, it was reported that he spent each night prone upon the ground before the altar, praying and weeping.

How Bathsheba wished David would stay with her! If it was true that the baby might not survive, shouldn't his father spend as much time with him as possible? And what of Bathsheba, herself? Now, of all times, she needed David's tangible support, the feel of his arms about her, and the sound of his comforting voice.

But why should she expect anything more at this time than she had had from the beginning? Her relationship with David had been insecure from the start, founded on the unstable ground of lust, violence, and deceit.

Not even Bathsheba had suspected the truth of Uriah's death until the day Nathan paid his momentous visit.

But such information as had come forth from Nathan's denunciation could not long be kept silent. The scribe who had taken the notes, the guards at the stateroom door, various servants—several of the palace staff had been privy to the prophet's words that day.

The king, no longer attempting to hide his sin from the world, had made no effort to further conceal his murderous crime from Bathsheba. Only the prophecy of her child's imminent death did he desire to keep from her. Threatening his staff with dire punishment should the queen learn of the baby's curse, he had managed to shield her a little.

Once Bathsheba knew the facts of Uriah's death, she had been a churning cauldron of emotions. She did not utterly hate Uriah. The part of her that bore him some tenderness was filled with grief; the dark chambers that housed her guilt echoed with the tormenting knowledge that had she been a better wife, had she never been unfaithful, he would not have died as he did; and what she hated most to learn about herself was that she could take any relief at all in the fact that she was widowed, that her untimely pregnancy might not be so hard to manage after all.

Yes, she participated in the sham of traditional mourning, wearing black for weeks and tearing the neckline of her trunk to symbolize that her soul was torn. She wept and wailed on her rooftop, as was customary, while Dorca brought her ashes to sprinkle through her hair. And when she looked at herself in her long mirror, seeing that the black of her widow's dress stretched unseemly over an increasingly distended abdomen, she hoped no one else would notice.

Likewise, she hoped against hope that David would keep his promise to wed her when the time of mourning was past.

It had been a great confirmation of David's love that he did, in fact marry her. For a brief time, she had been able to hope the future might brighten, that the unstable beginnings of the relationship might at last solidify.

But then had come the shadow in David's eyes, the sadness he betrayed regarding the child to come. Now she feared she knew what that shadow portended.

Cuddling down beside the wee child, she ran a warm finger down his tiny cheek. Countless times she had done this over the past days, more and more often as the fear grew that he might not long be with her. As she traced his face's smooth contours, sallow though they were, she fixed his image upon her heart.

Never would there come a time, she was determined, that she would not be able to recall her baby's face. If he were to be taken from her in the flesh, he would not be taken in spirit. His memory would live so long as she lived.

Tomorrow would be his eighth day, the day on which, by tradition, he would be circumcised, and the day on which he would receive his name. She and David had discussed what that name would be. If he was the heir promised by the prophet years ago, he should be called Solomon.

But David had seemed hesitant about that.

Bathsheba feared she knew why. She feared David knew something he had not told her, and that this knowledge was the cause of the shadow that passed through his eyes when he spoke of the child.

"O, sweet baby," Bathsheba whispered, as she cuddled close the wee infant. "All will be well if you stay with me until morning. If you see the light of your eighth day, I know you will grow strong and inherit your father's kingdom. 'Solomon' shall be your name, for you will be a king of peace."

Was that a smile she saw upon that baby's face? It seemed he was contented, as he nestled close.

Jerusalem—The City of God

Peace, Bathsheba thought, *How I would love to have peace, after all my turmoil!*

Drifting into the warmth of a night together, the mother and child put all worry to flight.

God was good and full of forgiveness. Surely no evil would befall an innocent babe, for the sins of his parents.

9

On the morning of the eighth day, David lay face down in the dirt at the foot of the family altar. He had slept this way, when he was not praying, for the past week.

Many times his servants had come to him, to raise him up and encourage him to eat. But he refused, fasting and imploring Heaven to spare the child.

This morning, David's servants had hesitated as they came to the court-yard, lingering in the shadow of the house. They might have thought the king was too exhausted to notice the slight alteration in their behavior.

Instead, he was keenly aware of it, perceiving, before they said any-thing to him, that they whispered together, looking at him doubtfully. Sitting up, David wiped his tear-caked face and called to them, "Is the child dead?"

The servants came forward gravely, their own faces wan and strained. "He is dead," they replied.

The king, rather than vexing himself more violently, as they had feared, reacted quite unexpectedly. Slowly he arose from the ground, called for a washbowl, and proceeded to cleanse his face. Then he went to his room, changed his apparel and told his valet to summon the palace priest.

"Prepare a sacrifice," he ordered. "I will worship and then I will go to my wife."

❧

David crept into Bathsheba's dark room, his heart heavy as lead.

The silence of the chamber was broken by muffled sobs, as the griev-ing woman clutched her pillow to her chest and rocked it like a baby. David drew near the bed, softly speaking his wife's name.

"Bathsheba," he whispered, bending over her, "the worst is over, my darling."

The woman, looking at him through red-rimmed eyes, groaned, "the worst is just beginning, my king. How can I live without him?"

David sat down on the bed and tried to draw the pillow from her vice-like embrace.

"The child's suffering is over," he said.

"But mine is just starting!" she wept, clutching the pillow with amazing strength. "Oh, David, what have we done? What have we done?"

He knew she spoke of the obvious connection between their sin and this loss. Biting his lip, he fought the grief that had consumed him for months.

"You knew," Bathsheba guessed. "Nathan told you, didn't he? You knew we would lose the child!"

David sighed and lifted his eyes to the ceiling.

"I knew," he admitted. "I prayed it would be otherwise. But, now, it is over."

Bathsheba shook her head in anger as David went to her window, pulling back the heavy curtain and admitting the sun.

From the court below a curl of smoke rose gently past the window, the remnant of David's altar sacrifice.

"The worst is over, my queen," he said "Whatever else Jehovah intends for us, the greatest punishment has been endured." Then turning to her, she sighed. "It is my supreme sorrow that you have had to suffer for my sins, and not myself alone."

With that confession, the woman's heart began to soften. Seeing his torment, she held out her hand to him, and he returned to her side, "I was not innocent," she replied. "I partook of the same indiscretions, and what I did not perform, I allowed. There is no difference, my king, between the wishing and the doing."

David leaned down, burying his face in the pillow she still clutched, and let the tears flow.

"The child," she wept, stroking her husband's dark curls, "he would have been named today. Now, my lord, he will never have a name."

David drew back and gently touched Bathsheba's face.

"The Lord shall give him a name," he said. "And though he cannot come back to us, we shall one day go to him."

Interlude

If any man ever suffered the fruits of indiscretion, it was David. If any man was ever meant to learn that unwise decisions made in the heat of passion or the fear of exposure could cleave a life in twain, it was David.

Just as the last half of Abraham's life was governed largely by the error of pushing God's timing, the taking of Hagar and the creation of a son through human impatience; just as Samson was brought to a grisly end through his capitulation to the wiles of a beautiful woman; so was David forced to bear an unending stream of unhappy repercussions because of his folly with Bathsheba and his attempt to cover it up with the murder of Uriah.

David endured one tragedy after another, each involving his own household. Following the prophesied death of Bathsheba's baby, the couple was blessed by the birth of a second son. But from that point, divine justice was meted out in one unhappy incident after another, from incest between a son and daughter, to the death of that son at the hands of another, to outright revolution inspired by the murdering son and led by him.

At almost sixty years of age, David was once again on the run, a fugitive from the rebel son who was bent on taking the throne: Absalom, offspring of his fourth wife, Maacah.

The entire nation was shaken by civil strife, as twenty thousand of the prince's insurgents were slain in the dark woods of Ephraim. Absalom, himself, was killed by the loyal General Joab, and David relived the grief he had known twice before, the death of a beloved child.

As if this were not enough, rivalry again flared between the tribes of Judah and Israel, and even the Benjamites revolted.

David saw his last day upon a battle field when he collapsed in a skirmish with the Philistines, whose hostilities were a fresh threat. At sixty-one, he would never again be the mighty warrior-king, as his advisers insisted he lay aside his sword and retire from the warring life.

It cannot be said that here were no bright spots during these years of restitution. The exacting Deity permitted David to enjoy the love of his devoted Bathsheba, and the son she bore, whom the king named Solomon in accordance with God's command, proved to be a blessing in David's advancing years.

The king succeeded in expanding his empire to the fullest extent it had ever reached since Abraham had been promised the land, its boundaries extending from the Gulf of Aqabah on the south to Kadesh on the north.

He also managed to amass an incredible treasury for the upcoming temple, laying aside materials and supplies, gold and silver and precious stones, for use in the construction, décor, and funding of the mammoth project.

He delighted in planning, with Solomon, the heir to his throne, all the details of the holy house he had been constrained from building.

Despite the sorrows of his sunset years, he grew closer to the Almighty through all he suffered.

Many were the hours he spent with Solomon, speaking of the things of Israel, her law and prophets, as they sat in his chamber, visited far flung places of the empire, or walked together along the palace ramparts. A ready learner was Solomon, grasping easily the deep things of the spirit, and seeming to bear a wisdom beyond his years.

But never were the two men closer than when they looked across the housetops of their kingdom, to the slopes of Moriah and the vacant rock that crowned it.

"There, my boy," the father would always conclude, "there is the sacred mount. When the day comes for you to build God's house, build it there. This was Samuel's word to me, and this is the Lord's word to Israel."

10

For every human being there comes a time when the span of days between the present and ensuing death is shorter than that between the present and his or her birth.

For David that time was now, and had been for some years.

Israel's "sweet psalmist" had composed many songs regarding the Almighty and His ways with people. He had sung about the fleeting days allotted to the human condition, comparing people to the most transitory life forms: "As for man," he had sung, "his days are as grass; as a flower of the field, so he flourished. For the wind passes over it, and it is gone, and the place thereof shall know it no more."

These days, such words haunted him often, and the specific warnings of another psalmist, Moses, came often to mind: "We spend our years as a tale that is told. The days of our years are three-score years and ten, and if by reason of strength they be fourscore years, yet is their strength labor and sorrow. For it is soon cut off, and we fly away."

Like a voice from the great beyond, such reminders came to him, sometimes awakening him in the night as he lay alone in his room. David had nearly reached seventy, the threescore and ten alluded to by Moses. In his life he had known both the rapture of communion with God and the agony of separation from Him. Now, the consuming focus of his thoughts was what he had accomplished or left undone, and what he would be leaving to his successor.

Perhaps it was the depression of advancing age, the knowledge that the end was near; perhaps it was pride, the desire to calculate just what he was worth. Whatever the reason, in his sixty-sixth year of life, and his thirty-sixth year as monarch, he decided to establish specifics regarding the worth of his empire.

He resolved to begin with a census, a numbering of all souls from Dan to Beersheba, with a breakdown of the number of males capable of serving in the military. Such information would be handed on to Solomon when he began his reign, and updated by a reasonable formula, so that the new king would know the strength of his empire.

The taking of a census was not unusual. It was done by kings all over the world. Even Moses had numbered the Israelites when they left Egypt, and again after the forty years' wandering in the wilderness.

No, in this there was nothing wrong.

But when David summoned Joab to his rooftop garden, telling him of his plans and assigning the task of overseeing the census, no small mission in a realm as vast as this, it struck the general strangely. Observing how eager the king was to proceed with the job, the insightful commander felt something was amiss.

Now, David had his seers and his prophet. It usually fell to Nathan to prick the king's conscience. But today, Nathan was not present. Joab, however, knowing David as well as anyone had ever known him, picked up the all-too-human motivation behind the decision.

Saluting the king, the general bowed his head, asking his indulgence. "Pardon me, Your Majesty," he said, "but does Your Majesty glory in the strength of Israel?"

Caught off guard, David turned from the fountain where he had just taken a drink and wiped his damp hand upon his robe. "Such a question!" he objected. "Can you tell me that you take no pride in the forces you command?"

"I do," Joab gave a weak smile. "But. . . "

Frowning, David prodded him. "What then?"

"I just want to know . . .it seems . . ." he stammered. "Why does My Lord the King delight to do this thing? Why would you be a cause of stumbling for Israel?"

Had anyone else shown such audacity, David would have had him flogged. But, this was Joab, his right hand man, challenging him. The most he would do was show his anger.

"Of what do you accuse me, Joab?" he demanded. "Be careful of your words!"

Fully aware of his subordinate position, Joab did not forget diplomacy. Bowing his head again, he respectfully rephrased himself.

"My Lord," he said, "even if God were to multiply your people a hundred times—and praised be His Name, may He do so—even so, Majesty, they are all your servants. Why then do you require their numbering? Is it not folly to do so?"

Joab's words were a numbing blow. Somehow he had seen in David what David himself had failed to admit, that the motivation behind his order was less than noble.

Still, the king would not be humiliated by an underling. Swallowing hard, David lifted his chin in defense. "Is it wrong to glory in what Jehovah has done, in the successes He has given us, or in the way He has multiplied his people?"

He could see from Joab's expressionless face that he was unconvinced. But he was not about to debate with him.

"Go now!" he commanded. "Number Israel from Beersheba to Dan, and bring a report to me!"

⁂

It took nearly ten months for Joab and his captains to complete the census. What they found was that in the region of Israel, Transjordan, and the original twelve tribes, and not including any Israelites who resided elsewhere, there were nearly six million souls, including nearly a million-and-a-half men of military age.

Indeed, were a man to take pride in the size of his nation, David had every reason to.

But ever since Joab had challenged the motivation behind the census, the king had struggled with misgivings. He was a man all too familiar with guilt, and with the fact of his own weaknesses. He knew in his heart that his purpose in numbering the people had been for self-aggrandizement, and that reliance on human strength was a departure from faith in God.

Being altogether fallible, he did according to human nature, and did not fully regret his error until after it was accomplished. In fact, it was the very morning after Joab brought to him the results of the census that the gravity of his crime set in upon him, leaving him unable to eat his breakfast or drink his morning tea.

He did hope against hope that God did not see the thing quite so darkly, and that He would overlook an indiscretion, just this once.

He was not surprised, however, when one of his seers called upon him before noon.

Again, it was not Nathan who challenged him. But it was one of the prophet's disciples, a young Transjordanian by the name of Gad.

How quickly the consequences of David's pride were dispensed! And how readily did he admit his indiscretion!

As a matter of fact, the young seer had barley entered the room, and had just greeted the king, when David blurted out, "I have sinned greatly! I beseech the Lord to take away the iniquity of His servant! I have been very foolish!"

"Very well," said the prophet. "The Lord is willing to offer you your choice of punishments. You may choose between three things. Shall seven years of famine come upon Israel? Or will you be a fugitive again, fleeing for three months from your enemies? Or, shall there be three days' pestilence in your land?"

As the king squirmed, knowing there was no bargaining. Gad prodded him. "Tell me now, what answer shall I return to the One who sent me?"

11

Clouds gathered over the threshing floor of Ornan the Jebusite, threatening rain and an end to the night's harvest work. The elderly governor of Jerusalem's northern precinct and his four patriarchal sons hurried to cover the wooden threshing instruments with tarps and to usher the oxen who treaded the grain into the corrals at the back side of the rock.

It seemed all of nature had conspired against this harvest season, just as it had a year ago. But his year, instead of famine across the lowlands, it was sleet and hail that devastated a good part of the crops.

Coupled with the unkind weather, a strange disease had swept through Israel, in only two days decimating the population. By the third day, there was not one household throughout Ornan's community where there was not at least one person smitten by the plague.

So far Ornan's family had been spared the onslaught, but he planned, as soon as he closed up for the night, to head directly for Ashtartu's temple to offer up prayers and a sacrifice for the well-being of his household.

Had this been a normal harvest season, the rock would have been full tonight with threshers and winnowers, tossing wheat and barley in large, flat baskets, and sending the chaff to Moriah's predictable, gentle breeze. They would have been throwing their grain beneath the great stone wheel which Ornan's oxen turned round and round. They would have been working the trodden grain upon wooden racks, separating the kernels from the chaff, tasks which had been played out upon a thousand threshing floors across a thousand lands since time immemorial.

They would have worked through the night, sleeping and eating in shifts, so as to complete the work before sunset and rejoin the reapers in the fields below.

Their work would be relieved by frolic, as the threshing floor was among the liveliest scenes in the world, full of dance and song, and enlivened by drink. Most cultures allowed harvesters amazing liberty as they came to the end of their task, so that threshing floors were synonyms for fleshly excess.

Jerusalem—The City of God

But tonight was not typical of fall seasons in Jerusalem. The harvesters were leaving the mountain, hitching up their little wagons with bundles of grain still intact upon them. They would find the stony path down Moriah treacherous with rain, and they would return downcast to their masters, fearing damage to the unwinnowed grain should it remain much longer upon the stalk.

They would know no merriment, and would face a day of unrelieved toil tomorrow, hoping only that the next night would be more successful.

But after Ornan and his sons had rounded up the beasts of burden and gathered them into the pens, the old Jebusite was to find that this night was more unusual still. Bidding his sons good night and telling them he would meet them at home, he turned to make his way to the goddess's temple.

It was then that it happened, the eerie experience that was to be the culmination of many he had known upon this rock.

Almost he had relegated such occurrences to the past, thinking the wind and the shadow of wings would never disrupt his life again. For it had never come upon him since the day, thirty years ago, when the forces of David gathered to take Jebus.

The evening before that critical event, Ornan had stood within the cloisters of Ashtartu, a monkish novice at his side, covering his ears against an unearthly howl and watching as the dark Shadow passed overhead.

That evening had heralded the demise of his nation, and the advent of David's conquest of Jerusalem.

What more could the nameless power want?

Yet, here it was again, the Shadow and the cry, and the fanning of colossal, invisible wings above Moriah!

Dipping behind the bushes beside the trail, he brushed his long gray hair from his eyes and peered between the branches of the grove. In the sporadic light that shown between patches of heavy clouds, the equipment he had just covered looked like hulking monsters. And from the corrals where he had just secured his oxen, the animals lowed piteously for fear.

Rushing back up the trail, his four sons came to join him, wondering at the mysterious manifestation. "What is it, Father?" they cried. "Is there a fire?"

But it was more than lightning that suddenly throbbed in blue-white brilliance upon the site. Raising their arms against the glare, they glanced overhead.

It appeared something hung between the earth and sky, a great white column of light that seemed to turn this way and that. As they watched it, the hair bristling on the backs of their necks, the spectral pillar seemed to move with some kind of intelligence, surveying the city below.

Then, the enormous column assumed more distinct shape, another dart of light shooting forth from the front side, like a drawn sword, and the pillar itself hinting at the form of a man. In one second, all of Ornan's nightmares, the accumulated experiences associated with the rock, converged. The phantom he had witnessed as sound and shadow only took on substance.

A spidery chill crawled up his spine, his aged knees trembling so that he could barely stand. Falling back, he steadied himself against a tree on the northern edge of the surrounding grove and watched the phantasm from the shadows.

Forgotten was his intended trip to the sanctuary of Ashtartu. He did not even attempt to reason what god this might be that seemed to intend evil for his city.

It occurred to him it was related to the plague that decimated the population. Beyond this he could not reason, and slumped at last to the ground, cowering and quaking beside the rock's spiny hedge.

His sons, astonished as he was, huddled with him.

Had a sound, emanating form the market path, not roused Ornan, he might have remained paralyzed with fear. He watched in wonder as a regal entourage approached, entering the tablerock just to the south. Hidden in the shadows, he and his sons looked on as their arch-rival David stepped forth from the gathering and prostrated himself beneath the hovering column.

Though they shared the same city, David as king of the Israelis and Ornan as price of the Jebusites, it had been three decades since the two men had confronted one another. On that sad day, Ornan had been obliged to accept David's conquest, despondently signing the treaty that was more figurative of equality than real.

In the intervening years, they had seen each other only on occasions of mutual importance, when the warriors of both groups had successfully routed some challenger, or at affairs of state, such as weddings or feasts shared by both nations. Beyond this, the two had avoided interaction.

Certainly, David had never entered the Moriah precinct. The threshing floor of Ornan was private property, used only by harvesters, and the king of Israel had had no occasion to go there since he and Saul had erected Goliath's head on the mountain.

Ornan could not imagine why he was here this night, unless he had witnessed the strange light from the vicinity of his palace far below. It appeared, however, that the entourage, which included a priest and several royal attendants, had not come together on a moment's notice. They had probably met at the place, perhaps for prayer, some time before they had made this trek.

Now Ornan had as much reason to be mystified as he had to be afraid. Not only was it amazing that David should be here, but he come with a most humble aspect, clothed not in royal purple, but in sackcloth, and weeping face down upon the stony pavement.

Likewise, his priest was dressed in the rough weave of penitence, and his holy station was obvious only by the scepter he carried, a tall golden staff like the rod of Aaron.

Flinching as the specter made another sweep of its sword over the city, Ornan managed to step forth from the shadows, listening in on David's pathetic cry.

"O, My Lord," he was wailing, "truly You are a consuming fire, a jealous god!"

Ornan was only a little familiar with the Israelite religion. But he was troubled by this confession. If Jehovah considered Jerusalem to be a holy city, it was strange that he would wish to destroy it—not only strange, but terrifying.

At the sound of their king's words, all those who were with him fell, likewise, upon the ground, pleading for mercy for themselves and their people.

Then David's voice rose in contrite cry, as he took full responsibility for the plague that had beset the city. "God," he wept, "am I not the one who commanded the people to be numbered? It is I who have sinned and done this evil! As for my sheep, my people, what have they done? Let Your punishment, I pray, O Lord My God, be on me and on my father's house, but not upon Your people! Please remove this plague!"

Suddenly, as if in response to this confession, the wind, which had been howling fearfully, tapered. The dreadful tossing of the treetops quieted to a gentle sway.

David rose to his knees, his tear-streaked face glistening in the blue light.

Joining him, his priest bent over and whispered in his ear. With trepidation, David stood, bowing his head. It seemed, if possible, that he communicated with the Being above. When he lifted his eyes, he looked directly toward the spot where Ornan stood.

Holding his head upright, Ornan tried to conceal his fear as David approached him, the Being of light still hovering, as though observing what transpired.

But Ornan could not hold this pose for long. Suddenly overwhelmed with the knowledge that he was involved in a supernatural drama, he went out upon the rock to meet David and crumpled to his knees, putting his wizened face to the ground.

"Friend Ornan," David said humbly, "allow me to have this threshing floor, that I may build an altar there unto the Lord, so that the plague will be lifted. I shall pay the full price, whatever you ask."

Quaking with holy awe of a God he knew not, Ornan feared to lift his hoary head. Weaving back and forth upon his knees, he waved his hands in objection.

"No, no! Take it! Take it!" he cried. "My Lord King David, do whatever you please!"

Before David could reply, Ornan managed to stand and wheeled about, gesturing to the threshing machines and the corrals across the way. "take the oxen also, for burnt offerings! I give it all! All!"

Pacing back and forth, he waves his arms wildly. "Take the wheat left by the reapers for an offering! I give it all! All!"

David turned quizzically to his priest, who shook his head in firm rebuke.

"No," David replied, trying to soothe his old enemy. "I will pay the full price. I will not take something that is yours to give to the Lord Jehovah. What is your price?"

Ornan glanced above at the overseeing figure and shrugged his shoulders. Then, with a nervous nod, he called for his sons. After a brief consultation, he proposed a price of six hundred shekels of gold, then ducked for fear of retribution.

But David smiled and offered his hand to seal the bargain.

As the two men stood upon the wind-swept hill, gripping one another's forearms to bind the contract, the unearthly light drew back its sword and paled away, leaving only a starlit canopy above Moriah.